Praise for

'A compulsive, page-turning thri
from start to finish. Loved it'

'The innocence of children blo
hazy days of a beach summer only to be devastated by a terror
tragedy is so beautiful and deftly handled . . . It's as twisty as a sand
worm castle with a plot that sizzles with dread and suspense'

TINA ORR MUNRO

'A gripping, knotty web of secrets with a cast of complex characters.
The setting is wonderful, drawing the reader in . . . before whipping
up a storm that brings a cloudy, claustrophobic atmosphere of lies
and paranoia that leaves you turning the pages faster and faster'

NATALIE CHANDLER

'Atmosphere, intrigue and decades old secrets and lies uncovered on
the tide – this novel has it all'

SARAH LAWTON

'A tense and compelling tale of love and loss, secrets, and lies –
and their terrible consequences. Builds to a thrilling ending. I tore
through this in two days!'

M.K. MURPHY

Leah Pitt grew up on the Dorset coast and has been a barrister for ten years. She is a graduate of Curtis Brown Creative's Novel Writing Course. She now lives in Hertfordshire.

Also by Leah Pitt

The Beach Hut

The Funfair

Leah Pitt

**HODDER &
STOUGHTON**

First published in Great Britain in 2025 by Hodder & Stoughton Limited
An Hachette UK company

This paperback edition published in 2025

The authorised representative in the EEA is Hachette Ireland,
8 Castlecourt Centre, Dublin 15, D15 XTP3, Ireland (email: info@hbgi.ie)

1

A CIP catalogue record for this title is available from the British Library

Paperback ISBN 978 1 399 72657 3
ebook ISBN 978 1 399 72658 0

Typeset in Plantin light by Manipal Technologies Limited

Printed and bound in Great Britain by Clays Ltd, Elcograf S.p.A.

Hodder & Stoughton policy is to use papers that are natural, renewable
and recyclable products and made from wood grown in sustainable forests.
The logging and manufacturing processes are expected to conform
to the environmental regulations of the country of origin.

Hodder & Stoughton Limited
Carmelite House
50 Victoria Embankment
London EC4Y 0DZ

www.hodder.co.uk

To Si and Bonnie, the lights that are on when I get home.

Prologue

We all love a ride, don't we? The anticipation of rising up into the air, the ground falling away, that moment where everything teeters and your breath is held . . . then the drop, that happens faster than your stomach can go, as you plummet, screaming, to the bottom.

We all love a ride.

Because we all love to be afraid.

Chapter One

Rachel

2000

*T*he classroom was stuffy and noisy, the windows steamed up from the rain. Mr Simmons hadn't arrived yet and everyone was talking loudly across the classroom at each other. I doodled 'R 4 L' on my maths exercise book, then drew a little heart around it. I was admiring my handiwork when someone scraped the chair beside me back and I jumped.

Tom sat down next to me, his face red and his pale blonde hair wet from the rain. His school shirt strained a bit across his stomach, showing a hint of soft pink flesh.

'You okay?' I asked, taking in his dishevelled appearance.

'Football practice,' he muttered, bending over and taking his maths book and pencil case out of his bag.

'Since when do you play football?' I asked in disbelief. Tom and I had been friends since Year Four and I had never seen him go near any kind of sports equipment.

'My mum. She said I needed to start doing some exercise this term.' His face went even redder and I felt my own growing hot in embarrassment.

'Well, that's good,' I said, awkwardly. 'Maybe Year Eight will be your year.'

'When has any year been our year?' Tom asked, rolling his eyes. 'We're losers.'

'We won't always be losers,' I said, looking across the room at where Isaac Evans and Khalid Malik were sitting on Sasha Kennedy's desk, both vying for her attention. Her skirt was rolled right over, showing smooth thighs. 'We'll only be losers if we never try and change anything.'

'I see you've really changed,' Tom said, pointing at the italics and heart I had drawn on my maths book. 'Still obsessed with Liam Haughton, are you?'

I flushed and quickly picked up my pencil, rubbing the drawing out. As I did so, the classroom door opened. I expected it to be Mr Simmons, but it was Liam Haughton. My heart seemed to stop in my chest. Liam's hair was wet, like Tom's, but Liam's looked like he was on a modelling shoot: it was all spiky and cool-looking. His blazer was slung over his shoulder and his shirt sleeves casually folded up to his elbows. For one second, his eyes seemed to meet mine across the classroom and I stopped breathing. Then I blinked and he was no longer looking at me. Isaac and Khalid were calling him, making room for him on their desk whilst Sasha quickly reapplied lip gloss. Liam ignored them, however, and stayed in the doorway, pulling out a brand new Nokia 3210 from his trouser pocket.

I turned excitedly to Tom, my heart racing.

'Wait, do you play football with him, now?'

Tom narrowed his eyes at me suspiciously.

'Yeah, so?'

'Well, you can put in a good word for me, can't you? Just mention how funny I am, or something.'

'No way! I'm not doing that,' Tom said, immediately. 'I'll get booted in the head. Also, I don't have any breath left for talking, I can barely get up the pitch.'

I folded my arms and sat back in my chair with a huff.

'Listen, if you want to speak to him, go and do it. You're the one who said we should start trying to change things. Go for it.'

I bit my lip for a second, looking over at where Liam was now typing on his phone. With a sudden burst of adrenaline I got to my feet. Tom was right: I needed to change something, to make something happen. Now was the perfect opportunity.

I clumsily pushed my chair back and hurried over to where Liam was standing. My limbs felt weird and prickly, like they could just drop off.

'Hey Liam,' I said, coming to stop in front of him. For one second, he didn't register my greeting: his eyes stayed fixed on his phone. My mouth went dry. Was he seriously just going to ignore me? Leave me standing here in silence in front of him? But then he looked up, his dark eyelashes mesmerising as he blinked at me.

'Alright?'

'Yeah,' I said breathlessly, wishing I had thought to crunch a quick Polo first. There was a long pause and I could feel my hands shaking. Say something, I thought desperately. I took a deep breath.

'I just . . .' I began, but before I could say anything else, a paper spit ball came flying through the air, landing hard on the side of my head. I shrieked and immediately tried to claw the disgusting thing out of my hair, but it was wet and gooey. In the corner, Sasha and her stupid mates were howling with

5

laughter. I looked over and saw Khalid holding a straw in his hand, rolled up paper on the desk in front of him.

'Sorry Raquel,' Sasha called loudly, her face red with suppressed laughter.

'It's Rachel,' I snapped. When I turned back to Liam, instead of looking shocked, he looked like he was trying hard not to laugh. My face burning, I hurried back to my desk. Tom gave me a sympathetic look as I sat down and started scrabbling in my bag for my hairbrush and mirror.

'Maybe it's time to give it up, Rach,' he said, as I finally located my hairbrush and started trying to get the disintegrating spit ball out of my hair. 'It's been years now. I don't think Liam Haughton is ever going to notice you.'

Chapter Two

Rachel

Now

I wake suddenly, well before my alarm goes off. At first, I can't work out what has woken me. Then I hear the creak of floorboards above me and the muffled sound of vomiting. I listen for a minute, my head lifted from the pillow, until there is another creak, followed by silence. Slowly, I kick the duvet away and climb out of bed.

I creep upstairs, trying not to make too much noise. The first door on the right, Dad's study, is closed: neither Mum nor I ever go near that room, anymore. The second door along the hallway is ajar. I enter the room, which is dark, the heavy curtains blocking out the summer light. There is something unpleasant in the air: the warm, stagnating smell of body odour and unwashed sheets.

'Mum?' I whisper into the darkness. There is no answer from the bed. I walk further into the room, letting my eyes adjust to the dim light. It has been fifteen years, but it is still strange, being in my mother's bedroom like this. Uncomfortable to see parents in their softer, private states. Dad had been better at keeping her in a routine, making sure she wasn't allowed to wallow for too long in the mornings, getting her fed and the hangovers cured as quickly as possible. I am a pale imitation of his caring nature. I can't even begin to look after her the way he did. I am not sure either of us want me to.

As I approach the bed, I make out the unmoving shape of my mother. Even from this distance, she smells sharply of alcohol and stale cigarettes. I lean closer, my hands clammy, listening. Silence. I hold my own breath, waiting, unsure whether to reach out . . . and then Mum gives a low snore and rolls further onto her side. I sigh and my shoulders drop. She is fine. She is breathing. I creep back out of the room and close the door gently behind me. Tomorrow morning, no doubt, will be the same.

I leave the house an hour later, coffee thermos in one hand. Even this early in the morning, the salt-tinged air is already heating up. In the distance, the steep incline of the road provides a clear view of the sea, shimmering under the morning sunlight. Standing out against the horizon is the unmistakable shape of a Ferris wheel. Unmoving. Empty.

I begin walking down the sloping road lined on either side with grand, red-brick Victorian mansions. They were the most desirable houses in town, once. Four storeys, jutting bay windows, wrought-iron railings and intricately decorated archways over the porches. Now, a faint air of melancholy seems to hang in the air instead, the houses sad imitations of what they once were: loose slates on roofs, overgrown gardens, patches of flaking rust on the railings. Just like the rest of the town, the houses bear the hallmarks of better days gone by. The small seaside town of Hollow Bay, once a vibrant place to live, had been missed off the list of towns worthy of a commutable train link or trendy high street, like the nearby Margate or Whitstable. And so it was forgotten, like everyone who lived in it. Out of date. Irrelevant.

As I walk, the summer air lifts some of the heaviness that clings to me from being in the house I have spent thirty-four years living in. I pretend, sometimes, that the house I am leaving is my own: with a bright, modern kitchen and a fridge covered in magnets and photos, leaving behind a husband and a dog, or even a child. That I will come home to the smells of dinner and chatter, perhaps the soft pop of a wine bottle being opened. Anything but the tense silence.

I reach the bottom of the road and turn right, where the promenade is separated from the sandy beach by a low stone wall. The main row of shops lining this end of the promenade have all grown tired and sad, either shutting down completely or becoming cheap takeaways or phone shops. As I walk, my eyes are drawn to one particular shopfront at the very end. A boarded-up restaurant, where a wooden sign above the door reads '*John's Catch*' in faded ocean-blue. Beneath this, in small, peeling letters: '*Fish and Seafood Restaurant – Est. 2005.*' The paint has chipped away over the years and some letters have vanished. I can't bear to look through the one sliver of grimy window that isn't boarded up, to see reminders of Dad's coastal charm vision: whitewash walls and distressed wooden tables and chairs. A restaurant forever waiting to be opened by a man who never arrived. It is just another reminder, as if the whole town wasn't enough, that nothing turned out the way it was supposed to.

Chapter Three

Rachel

Now

Twenty minutes later, I walk into the front office of the small high-street law firm, Rowland & Associates, and put my bag down on my desk.

'Good *morning*,' Didi, the only other secretary trills, stirring her yoghurt pot. She is dressed in her usual attire: a black blazer and neon-bright dress that matches the colour of her nails. The phone rings, but she doesn't make a move to answer it.

'We don't open for another four minutes,' she informs the flashing switchboard.

'Morning,' I say, also ignoring the phone. My head is heavy from my early morning wake-up and I stifle a yawn. 'Coffee?'

'God, yes.'

I leave the secretarial area at the front of the building and head upstairs to the kitchen on the first floor. The office building is small and tired, made up of little more than a handful of rooms where the firm's lawyers work, a basement full of old paper files and broken computers, the kitchen and one bathroom. The kitchen, like the rest of the floor, is painted a sickly pale yellow that reminds me of tobacco-stains, but it is bright and, with the windows open, you can just about hear the sound of the waves. I put the kettle on and water the wilting plants on the too-hot windowsill whilst I wait for it to finish boiling.

Back downstairs, I hand Didi a fresh mug of coffee and she smiles gratefully at me.

'How was your weekend?' I ask, sitting down at my own desk.

'Oh, it was okay,' she shrugs. 'We've been trying to persuade Dad to get a new boiler before the winter, but he keeps saying no. It's so frustrating.'

'Why doesn't he want one?'

'Says he can't afford it and he doesn't want handouts. My mum's new boyfriend said he knew someone that can get a discount but he went ballistic, said he wasn't a charity case. He's so proud.'

I feel a wave of sympathy for Didi: after Dad died, Mum and I were left with very little. Once his life insurance had run out, it was up to me to keep a roof over our heads. Mum was hardly in a state to work. I know I would have hated accepting help from anyone; not that any was offered.

'Has he always been like that?' I ask. Didi opens her mouth to reply but the door bangs open and Charles, the firm's owner, walks in, his mahogany-coloured face – thanks to hours spent on the local sun-beds – screwed up in annoyance.

'Three a.m. at the police station, representing some *arse-hole* who decided his interview was the perfect time to tell his whole life story,' he says, by way of greeting. His usually pristine grey hair is slicked slightly off-centre and his eyes are red. '*Bloody* alcoholics.'

Didi meets my eye and looks away, quickly. Most people in town know about Mum. But if Charles realises that he has said something awkward, he doesn't show it. Not that he would be remotely bothered, in any event. He stops in front of my desk and pulls a blue legal pad out of his bag, dropping it onto my desk where it lands with a *slap*.

'Get those attendance notes typed up, would you?' he asks, already picking his bag up and heading towards the door.

'With pleasure,' I mutter sarcastically under my breath. Didi pulls a look of sympathy.

'And Shelly McKenzie is coming in today,' Charles says over his shoulder, 'make sure you buzz me as soon as she arrives, don't keep her waiting.'

Once Charles has gone Didi rolls her eyes.

'Unbelievable.'

'Don't you just love Mondays?'

'What did you get up to this weekend, anyway?' Didi asks.

'Oh,' I say, caught off-guard. 'Just . . . saw some friends. The usual.'

'That reminds me, don't forget about my party next Saturday,' she says, as she flicks through a pile of files on her desk, looking for a particular one. 'The weather looks a bit shit, but my friends are going to lend me a gazebo. You can bring whoever you want.'

My stomach knots. Didi and I had both grown up in the area, but she had gone to a school in another town, where her mum worked, so neither of us knew the other until she joined the firm two years ago. We had an immediate bond, but she's been increasingly inviting me to things outside of work, despite how often I find excuses. This party is the latest one, and she made sure to ask about the dates I was free before she organised it.

I haven't answered and I look up to see Didi watching me with an odd expression on her face.

'You'll have fun,' she says. 'My school friends are really excited to meet you.'

Her words feel loaded, as though she isn't going to give me an out.

'Sure,' I say, already thinking of a million excuses to use before next Saturday. 'I, uhh, I'll be there.'

'Good.'

Didi looks happy and I dismiss the small fissure of guilt that I have no intention of going: I don't want to go to a party full of Didi's friends from school.

I turn back to the post, trying not to think about the school friends I had had, once upon a time. I had also loved parties, once, too. But that had all changed, fifteen years ago. *Don't think about it.* That is the last thing I want to think about.

Chapter Four

Rachel

2004

The music pounded through the house, making conversation almost impossible unless you yelled in someone's ear. It was hot, too, all the bodies pressing against each other in the lounge, dancing to the music. It was weird to see so many people crammed into my house, carelessly bumping up against my parents' sideboards, standing on the sofa, knocking pictures on the wall so they were wonky. I would have to make sure that absolutely everything was put back tomorrow, before my parents got back from visiting Grandad in Essex. I looked around the room, hopefully, but didn't spot who I was looking for. It's still quite early, *I told myself.* There's time.

'Hey Rach,' *a girl called Chloe said as she danced near me. My eyes widened when I saw she was with some of the popular crowd who had just finished Year Thirteen. They were actually here, in my house.* 'Thanks for the invite. Tonight rocks!'

'No problem,' *I said, as cool as I could manage.*

'I heard you didn't invite Sasha Kennedy,' *Chloe said, her eyes going wide.* 'She's furious at you.'

I shrugged and gave a fake-innocent look.

'Must have slipped my mind.'

Chloe burst out laughing and went back to her friends.

'Great party!' Isaac Evans yelled in my ear, coming up to me, holding a beer bottle. His free hand drifted down the small of my back, skimming my behind in my denim skirt.

'Get lost, Isaac,' I said, wriggling away from him. 'I'm not interested.'

'You were interested last summer,' he said, his face dropping.

'I wasn't interested, I was bored. Big difference.'

I left him in the lounge and pushed my way through the crowd, out into the kitchen. People called out to me as I passed, telling me what a great party it was. I smiled, smugly. I had been desperate to host a party for ages, jumped on the opportunity as soon as it arose. It was the done thing, to solidify your place in the social rankings. Which is exactly why I made sure not to invite Sasha Kennedy.

A group of people, including my best friend Penny, were playing beer pong in the kitchen: the wooden table was covered in spilled beer and cups were all over the floor. I glanced around, but the person I was looking for was still nowhere to be seen.

'Rach, come join,' Penny said, as she raised her arm and released the ping-pong ball. It bounced once on the table, arced through the air, and then landed just shy of one of the cups. The group erupted, and the full beer cup she was expected to drink was presented to her by one of the guys in our year. Penny squealed and grabbed my hand as she threw the drink back, her eyes screwed up.

'Your turn!' Penny said when she was finished, pulling me towards the circle and wrapping an arm around me.

'I'll be back in a minute,' I said, glancing towards the back doors. 'Save some beer for me.'

Penny nodded and released me. I walked through the kitchen and out of the open back doors to where groups of people were scattered around the back garden in the warm June night. I scanned the groups smoking and messing around and felt my heart sink. Nothing.

I pulled my cigarettes out of my back pocket and lit one up, just as Tom appeared on the patio beside me. Over the past four years, he had carried on playing football and started going to the gym, too. The result was that his puppy fat was almost completely gone, though he still wore baggy shirts a lot, as though he hadn't quite realised he didn't have to hide his body anymore.

'Hey,' he said, tugging the packet out of my hand and putting a cigarette to his own lips. 'This is a serious party. Have you seen Georgina Clarke and her friends are here?'

I nodded, unable to shake the sinking feeling of disappointment, even if the rest of the party was still a success. Tom sat down on the garden bench behind us and I joined him. He held out a glass of vodka and Red Bull, which we shared back and forth for a while.

'When did this happen?' Tom asked, looking around at the people laughing and chatting in the garden. 'When did we become part of the popular crowd? No longer the weirdo and the fatso. And you, queen bee, no less.'

'Other people haven't come,' I said, the same sinking feeling creeping over me, ruining the exhilarating feeling of hosting a successful party.

'You're not seriously talking about Liam?'

I nodded, reluctantly.

'Wow, you really are hung up on him, aren't you? What's it been, like four, five years?'

'Six, but who's counting?'

'Listen, there are plenty more fish in the sea. I mean you should know, you've done a hell of a lot of swimming the last year or two,' Tom sniggered.

'Hey!' I said, hitting him on the arm. 'Shut up.'

'Speaking of fish in the sea . . .' Tom said, suddenly looking a bit awkward. 'Reckon you could put in a good word to Penny for me?'

I grinned. Penny had had her eye on Tom for ages but neither had approached the other one.

'I don't think I need to put in a good word, Tom. I think you just need to talk to her.'

He squinted at me through his cigarette smoke.

'You reckon?'

'Yes. She's inside, go find her.'

'Okay great.' Tom stood up and chucked his cigarette on the floor. Then he looked back at me.

'Are you going to be alright?'

I nodded.

'Don't worry,' Tom said. 'I'm sure he'll come.'

Chapter Five

Rachel
Now

The next few hours pass in the usual blur of phone calls, typing up statements, and dealing with clients. At eleven, the door opens and a woman steps into the foyer wearing a tight, bodycon dress, her blonde hair poker-straight and her eyes hidden behind too-large sunglasses. Expensive tennis bracelets and diamond earrings sparkle in the August sunlight. Though she is in her early thirties, something about her outfit gives the impression of a child playing dress up in their mother's clothes and jewellery.

'Mrs McKenzie,' I say, standing and buzzing her through to reception immediately. 'How are you?'

'It's Shelly,' the woman says, removing her sunglasses to reveal bloodshot blue eyes underscored by dark circles. 'And I'm a fucking mess. I keep hoping I'm going to wake up, that this is just all one big nightmare.'

She sinks into one of the faded blue armchairs in reception, rubbing her temples with her fingertips.

'Let me get you a coffee,' Didi says in her reassuring tone and slips out of the room. I glance at the clock: Charles said to bring Shelly straight up but I want to give her a moment.

'I spoke to my mum this morning,' Shelly continues, looking up at me with wide eyes. 'Do you know what she said? "I'm worried about you, dear, there's a lot of innocent people in prison." She's been watching all these true crime documentaries, she's convinced I'll be next.'

I bite my lip as Shelly buries her face in her hands. The McKenzie attempted murder trial is one of the biggest cases the firm has ever dealt with. Shelly McKenzie – a wealthy woman from the next town over – is charged with the attempted murder of her much older husband whilst he slept. Shelly insists that she is innocent, but there was no visible break-in. No witnesses. The press are having a field day with the case and Charles is more stressed than ever: it was pure luck that he was the solicitor on duty the night that Shelly was arrested, but he now needs to keep the case, which is increasingly attracting media attention.

'Everything is going to be fine, okay? You'll get through this. Just one day at a time,' I assure Shelly, echoing, I suddenly realise, the words my own dad said to me back when I was eighteen. I suppress the chill that erupts across my skin.

Didi reappears with a coffee for Shelly.

'Shall I take you up to Charles? He's ready for you,' Didi says, with a gentle smile.

Shelly sniffs and stands up. She looks at me for a moment, her jaw tense. I feel as though she wants to say something, but she doesn't know how.

'It's going to be okay,' I say. 'We'll make sure of it.'

At this, Shelly's tanned shoulders drop and a tight smile breaks through her stiff expression.

'Thank you,' she whispers.

Didi takes Shelly upstairs and I stand in the middle of the office for a moment, feeling jittery. Shelly's case is everyone's worst nightmare: something happening to the person you love, you being accused of the crime. For something to do, I pick up a cardboard box of files from next to my desk and make my way out of the room and along the hallway to a heavy wooden door at the very end. Reluctantly, I pull it open and, shifting the box to my hip, feel for the light-switch with my free hand. The lights flicker on with a soft humming sound, casting a dim orange glow across the metal spiral staircase leading to the basement. I swallow. I hate going down into the basement. It brings back claustrophobic memories of the darkness, of danger lurking in the shadows. Already I can feel pinpricks of sweat breaking out across my skin. *Don't be ridiculous. You're in the middle of an office building.* Seeing Shelly McKenzie must have stirred something within me. Swallowing my irrational fear, I carefully make my way down the spiral steps, my palms clammy against the thin cardboard.

Once I am down into the dark, musty basement, I navigate the rows and rows of shelves holding cardboard boxes of files in alphabetical order and slot the one I am holding back into the waiting gap. The decades of old client files are supposed to be transferred onto the new digital systems or destroyed, but it is slow going and hundreds remain. Hundreds of stories, of police interviews, of trials.

On my way back, I pass the rows beginning with the letter *K*. There, on the shelf, is a file with my name on it.

It is a thin file, faded over time, with only a small handful of papers in it. I have never gone looking for it in the nine years I have worked here, never taken it off the shelf. That file is the reason that I haven't spoken to my school friends in fifteen years, the reason my own mother blames me for my dad's death, the reason that it took me so long to get a job in town. It was only after Charles, who had recently moved to the town and taken over the firm, took a chance on me, despite my lack of qualifications. I doubt he even knows this file is here. I should have told them, really. So that they could move it somewhere confidential. But I have never wanted to bring it up. Goosebumps erupt across my skin and, with a shudder, I hurry back through the basement and up the stairs, emerging gratefully into the warm, bright office.

An hour later, Shelly McKenzie leaves looking just as tense as when she arrived. After he has seen her out, Charles re-enters reception.

'How did it go?' Didi asks, ever keen for information.

'It didn't,' Charles says tersely. He has always been blunt but recently his mood has been worse than ever. 'She still can't prove where she was that night. She just keeps saying she was out walking the dog in the woods behind the house, the same as she does every night, but no one saw her.' He scowls at the wall and shakes his head. 'We need some evidence, we need an alibi for her.'

Didi and I exchange a grimace and Charles seems to give himself a shake.

'I've got some files for you to deal with,' he says to me, 'can you come and get them off my desk?'

I sigh internally. I already have a huge amount of work to do: Charles has been steadily increasing my workload over the past few months, without any acknowledgement. A dark brown spider suddenly scuttles across my arm and I flinch, shaking my arm quickly to get it off.

'You need to speak to him,' Didi hisses, glancing over her shoulder to check Charles has gone back upstairs. 'He promised you a promotion and a chance to train to be a solicitor. Even without the McKenzie case you're doing half his work, with none of the reward. *And* you've been covering Justine's clients whilst he looks for a replacement. It's not on.'

'I've already asked him,' I reply, lowering my voice in case Charles suddenly re-appears.

'Rachel that was *months* ago. You've been here for almost ten years, stop selling yourself short and tell him what you want. He knows you're invaluable.'

I flush at the reminder that I have been at the firm for so long. I know Didi didn't mean anything by it but it makes me wonder, as I so often have, whether I will ever go anywhere else? Do anything else? I was so grateful when Charles gave me the job, I kept my head down and I did the best I could do so that he didn't change his mind. But now that the rest of the mortgage on Mum's house is almost paid off, shouldn't I be standing up for myself a bit? After all, Didi is right: I am doing work that is far beyond my job role, let alone my pay grade.

'You're right,' I say decisively and Didi's face lights up. 'I'll go and talk to him.'

I leave the room and climb the stairs to Charles's office. The door is open: I enter to find him at his computer, dictation machine in one hand.

'The files are there,' he says brusquely, gesturing to the end of his desk, without taking his eyes off his screen. I immediately sense this isn't the right time. I should have waited until he was in one of his chattier moods, lingering for too long near Didi's desk. Not when he's been up since the early hours at the police station and Shelly McKenzie has only just left, unable to help Charles with her alibi.

'Sorry,' I say, then mentally curse myself for apologising, 'but can we have a quick word about what we discussed at the end of last year? At my appraisal?'

Charles stops looking at his computer, then, and put downs his dictation machine. For a moment I think he is going to say no, but to my surprise he nods and gestures for me to sit down in the chair opposite him. Taking this as a good sign, I quickly sit down. Charles touches his fingertips together beneath his chin and waits. At some point this morning he re-did his hair so that his grey quiff is now perfectly straight.

'I was hoping we could talk about next steps for my development,' I say, trying to sound more confident whilst my insides squirm. 'I've almost been here ten years; we discussed a promotion so that I was taking on more of the paralegal work that needs doing. I've been looking into my exams and how the firm can sponsor them . . .' Charles raises a hand and I trail off.

'Listen, Rachel, you don't need to justify yourself to me, I know how good you are. You keep this firm afloat.' He gives me a little wink and I suppress a wave of nausea.

'Great. Thank you.'

Charles sits back in his chair, scratching his short beard.

'I'm grateful you've brought it up, it's something I've been meaning to talk to you about, actually. You know that with Justine on maternity leave,' his face betrays a small, dismissive twitch, 'we've been looking for someone to cover her work for the next twelve months. You've been doing an excellent job covering her cases so far but we really should make things more official.'

My mouth almost drops open and I have to quickly compose my face. This is *huge*.

'Charles . . .' I say, even as excitement I've rarely ever felt in my adult life courses through me, 'I'm not sure . . . I'm not even qualified.' *Don't undersell yourself, you can do it.*

But Charles raises his eyebrows and lets out a sudden bark.

'I wasn't talking about *you*, Rachel. I mean an actual lawyer. The fact is, the firm just can't afford to recruit for a new lawyer and also pay for your exams or give you a raise right now. And with the McKenzie case, we need another pair of hands. I'm meeting with a possible new lawyer next week, in fact. Lots of experience. You'll learn a lot from them, I'm sure.'

Disappointment sweeps through me. I should have known. It's been the same every year, always an excuse.

Last year it was budget cuts, now it's the McKenzie case. Dangling a carrot that never gets any closer.

'Chin up,' Charles says, his eyes already flickering back to his computer, 'let's revisit at next year's appraisal. Until then, keep up the hard work, yeah? I'm still very pleased I took a chance on you all those years ago.'

His message is a clear reminder that he gave me a job when I really needed one. I should be grateful. But I had never wanted this job. I never wanted any of this. Sometimes I wish I could scream it in his face.

Chapter Six

Rachel

Now

As soon as five thirty hits, I say goodbye to Didi and leave the office. My feet carry me automatically along the usual route, so familiar now I don't have to think about it. Along the promenade, down the steps and onto my favourite section of the beach, breathing in the warm late afternoon air, tinged with the smell of vinegary chips and barbecues. To my left, the beach is busy with lingering parents, their children on summer holidays, dogs delightedly chasing waves along the shore. When the sun is out like this, the place looks deceptively attractive: but out of shot is the tired pier with its rotting support beams and long out-of-order 2p slot machines.

I choose a section that is more pebbled, which means it is quieter, and put my bag down on the sand. In a ritual that is as automatic as breathing, I strip down to my swimming costume, already under my work clothes, leave my towel a few metres from the shoreline with my bright blue dryrobe and sandals, and walk into the water.

The water is chilly, but I am so used to it, I barely flinch anymore. I wade quickly through the shallows and, as soon as the water reaches my hips, I dive beneath the surface. The coldness is sharp, needling my skin, but I surrender to it, and as I move quickly through the water, my body and mind begin to adjust. I never wear goggles, preferring the freedom I feel without them. Beneath the waves, the depths are green and murky, dappled sunlight dancing across the rippled sand. As soon as my head is under, everything else seems to slow down, muted by the water. The sounds and people around me fade into a muffled hum and I can forget who I am, and all the things that keep me awake at night. I kick out and begin my front-crawl. My muscles are strong and I glide through the water, keeping an eye out for surfers and other swimmers, the sunlight flashing off the tips of the waves.

As I swim, my thoughts turn to the conversation in my head with Charles. I replay it, wishing, as always, that I had said something different. Stood up for myself. I am angry at him for taking advantage of me, after almost ten years working for him. I know others would have quit by now, but his is the only law firm in town. Where would I go? Yet the thought of remaining in this directionless limbo is almost as terrifying. Never moving on, always lying to Didi about seeing friends on a weekend.

Once my muscles begin aching too much to continue, I swim slowly back to the shore. I never like leaving Mum for too long, anyway. And if I am not home, she likely won't eat. I pick up my dryrobe, a rare treat to myself a few years ago, and dry myself off as best I can before slipping my sandy feet into my sandals and walking up the beach.

As I turn and start walking along the promenade, my eyes are drawn to a large, colourful poster that has been freshly attached to the beach railings. Emblazoned across it are the words: *The Funfair Returns! Retro Rides and Classic Vibes! Grand Re-opening This Summer!* There are pictures of a red and white striped big top tent, rides, food stalls, music line-ups. I come to an abrupt halt, staring at it. Then slowly, I turn my gaze back towards the pier. Right beside it, by the beach, is the old, abandoned fairground, surrounded by tall railings. The old Ferris wheel looms eerily over the landscape, its once-bright gondolas now tarnished, many now hanging precariously by a single joint. Next to it stands the skeletal, twisted remains of the roller coaster frame, its steel tracks no longer connected, weeds creeping up the structures. The blue and red paint of the prize booth has faded almost completely, its roof half caved in.

For as long as I can remember, the old fairground has been closed, its rides and amusements falling deeper into disrepair with each passing season. Now, thanks to some nostalgic private backers, it is being regenerated, complete with a diner, penny arcade, and photo booths. The perfect tourist destination for retro entertainment. A brief return to the past everyone but me is chasing. Construction workers are starting to finish for the day, their white hard-hats bobbing up and down as they leave the site. The memories of what happened there hit me, as they so often do, no matter how many years have passed.

The gates loomed before us, and an excited thrill ran through me. I was being reckless, I knew that, but I didn't care. Not tonight. I put my hand on the cold bars and began to climb.

My gaze lands on the dilapidated Funhouse, which is now covered in scaffolding. Some kids set it alight a few years ago, almost destroying it. I wish they had. I wonder if I will ever be able to walk past the old fairground gates without the cold grip of dread squeezing my chest. Open or closed, I still know what happened there. Crossing my arms tightly across my chest, I put my head down and carry on walking.

Chapter Seven

Rachel

Now

By the time I'm walking home, the light has almost completely faded from the sky. My wet hair drips down my neck, like a cold finger trailing against my skin. Once or twice I am sure I hear footsteps behind me, but whenever I turn around, the street is deserted.

When I finally reach home, I see through the soft navy twilight that all the lights in the house are on: Mum is home. My nerves, already taut, stretch further as I unlock the door.

I find her in the kitchen; her pale, shaking hand clutching a large glass, hunched over the table which is covered in photo albums. There is an empty bottle of wine on the counter, a second bottle half empty beside her. Her hair is matted and tangled at the back from a day lying in bed and her eyes are red-rimmed. I hate seeing her like this. I can't get through to her on the best of days, but when she is lucid enough to be sentimental, I can rarely reach her to bring her back again.

'Have you been out today?' I ask, trying to ignore the ominous photo albums and putting my bag down on a spare kitchen chair. She doesn't respond. Why, I think, does it have to be like this? This constant feeling that I am being smothered. By my caring duties to Mum. By the past. I walk across to the kettle and fill it up, determined to make her a chamomile tea.

'He was so handsome,' Mum slurs.

I flick the kettle on and grit my teeth. *Here we go again.* My swimming costume clings damply to my skin and I am desperate to leave the kitchen, to have a warm shower. I have found the best approach is to keep things high-level, like carers often do. Disengaged engagement. It only sort of works. *If you smile, it sends happy signals to your brain.*

'He certainly was,' I reply as cheerfully as possible, pulling two mugs off the ancient mug tree.

'He cared, too. He looked after me. After us.'

Despite my determination to remain detached from the conversation, I feel the dread rise within me in slow, sickening fashion. I could act like I can't hear her, but her words still slice through me, even after all these years. Because, like her, I haven't healed.

There is a long, painful wait for the kettle to boil. When it finally does, I start to pour the water carefully into each mug, hyper-focussed on my task as though it will drown her out.

'He was the best thing that ever happened to me, you know.' Her voice is louder now, trying to get my attention. She knows what she was doing. My hand shakes slightly as the boiling hot water pours into the mug. The teabag bobs and dips under the scalding stream. I hate the way she speaks about him, like she had adored him whilst he was alive. She might have loved him, but she had treated him cruelly, too, a lot of the time. Only I can't point this out because it is hard to tell where Mum ends and her alcoholism begins. And then *I* would be the cruel one.

I top up Mum's mug with some cold water so she doesn't burn herself and carry it over to the table. I try to place it down without looking at any of the photos, but it is impossible: they cover the entire surface of the table. I slide a collection of grainy colour photographs out of the way to make room for the tea and my gaze lands on one I haven't seen in years; one of those many photos that don't make it into a frame. I pick it up. It is of me and Dad. I must be about three years old, wearing a frilly white bonnet and striped dungarees. Dad's hair is wind-swept, standing out on the pier with me in his arms. He is smiling happily at the camera and I am smiling happily at him, chubby hands reaching towards his ears. My breath sticks in my throat. Even after all this time, I still miss him horribly. I have never got used to his absence in the house, to the Dad-shaped hole that he left behind. Sometimes I think he might have been the only person who truly cared about me.

Mum reaches out a slim hand. I think she is reaching for her tea, but she stretches towards the photo I am holding, instead. Surprised, I hand it to her. Perhaps, like me, she has forgotten it existed: forgotten that he had loved me, too.

Then she looks up at me with her red, watery eyes.

'It's your fault he's gone.'

Her voice isn't slurred, this time: it is cold and razor sharp.

'No, Mum . . . that isn't fair.'

'Yes it is. He would still be here if it wasn't for you. If you hadn't done what you did. If the police hadn't been here.'

I look at her, hurt and anger clenching my stomach. I know I am not directly responsible for Dad's death. But his final moments and what happened the night at the old fairground are forever inextricably linked, and because of that, she will always blame me.

Chapter Eight

Rachel

2005

*T*he sunlight bounced off Penny's copper hair as we walked home from school along the promenade. It was a surprisingly warm afternoon for early April and we had taken off the smart tops sixth-formers were supposed to wear, so we were just in our T-shirts.

'Tom's mum is out on a date this weekend,' Penny said enthusiastically. 'He's asked me to come over to watch a film. He's going to make dinner and get a Blockbuster in.'

I had to suppress a twinge of jealousy. Not over Penny and Tom's relationship, but over them being in a relationship, especially one that was so happy. I was tired of being single. Tired of trying and failing to get anyone to measure up to the idea of Liam Haughton.

'You know what that means, don't you?' I asked, with a meaningful look at Penny. She took a deep breath and nodded, her green eyes filled with anxiety for a moment.

'I think I'm ready. I've waited long enough. And I think it's really important to do it for the first time with the right person. Someone you love, not just anyone.' She suddenly stopped talking and looked anxiously at me. 'Sorry, I didn't mean . . . I just meant me personally. I'm a bit more . . . boring. You know?'

'It's fine,' I muttered, not wanting to think about how easily I lost my virginity, just so I could get it over and done with. I could barely remember it. 'Have you heard back from any universities, yet?'

'Not yet,' Penny said, chewing her lip. 'I'm so worried I won't get any offers.'

I laughed out loud at this and nudged her.

'Don't be daft! You're one of the smartest in our year. Sometimes I wonder why you're mates with me.'

'You're smart,' Penny said, immediately. 'You know more about the world than I do. You'll be amazing at drama school.'

'I haven't got in, yet.'

'No, but you will.'

We walked in silence for a bit. The pier loomed on the horizon and, beside it, the old, abandoned fairground with its Ferris wheel and broken-down roller coaster. It had been there for as long as I could remember. Eerily still and unmoving.

'I can't wait to get out of this place,' I said fervently. 'It's so boring.'

'You will visit me, won't you?' Penny asked, suddenly. 'You won't just get all caught up with cool actor mates and never leave London?'

'Of course I'll visit you. You're my best mate, I'm not just going to forget about you. Anyway, we've got ages left, still.'

'I guess.'

Penny and I parted at the bottom of my road and I walked up the hill to my house. When I walked through the front door, I heard Dad's voice coming from the kitchen. Dropping my keys onto the console table, I headed down *the hallway and into the kitchen. Dad was standing at the kitchen table, with his back to me. He was in his usual jumper and smart trousers.*

' . . . speak to a lawyer. But I am interested. I'm happy for you to set up a meeting to discuss it in more detail. Okay. Thanks.' He pulled the phone away from his ear and frowned at it for a second. He still wasn't used to having a mobile.

'What was that about?' I asked. Dad gave a start and turned around.

'I didn't see you there, sweetheart.'

'Who were you talking to?' I asked. 'Why do you need a lawyer?'

'Oh, no reason, just some business stuff,' Dad said. 'Nothing very interesting.'

Dad worked in the IT department at the local council: what would he need a lawyer for?

'On more interesting topics,' Dad said, sliding a piece of post across the table towards me. 'This arrived for you this morning.'

My heart stopped as I took in what I was seeing: a large cream envelope with the name and emblem of my first-choice drama school embossed across the top in gold foil. Slowly, I picked it up, feeling its weight.

'It's heavy,' I said to Dad, who was watching anxiously. 'Feels like more than one sheet of paper.'

'Don't torture yourself sweetheart. Open it.'

I tore open the envelope and pulled out the contents. The sheet of paper on the very top was posh and thick, its edges perfectly crisp. I scanned the first few lines, my heart thumping hard.

. . . are delighted to inform you that you have been offered a place on our BA (Hons) in Acting program, commencing September 2005. This is an unconditional offer and we therefore hope to welcome you in September. Details of the course and fees can be found . . .

The rest of the words blurred. I had done it: I had been accepted. My chest tightened as I handed it over to Dad without speaking. I watched his eyes scan the letter, as mine had, then his face broke into a huge grin.

'That's my girl!' He stepped forwards and wrapped me up in a tight hug. 'I am so proud of you, sweetheart. I knew you would get in.'

'I can't believe it!' I said, breaking away from Dad and dancing around the kitchen. 'I don't even have to worry about my A levels!'

'Oh yes you do. You have to have something to fall back on, young lady,' Dad said firmly. 'Look what happened to . . .' he stopped suddenly, looking guiltily up at the ceiling.

'Where is Mum?' I asked, glancing up, too.

'She's in bed. She's got a headache. Maybe . . . maybe we save your news until later. When she's feeling better?'

I nodded and Dad smiled, again, but it wasn't quite as wide this time.

'I'm so proud of you. This is the first day of the rest of your life, sweetheart.'

Chapter Nine

Rachel

Now

The rest of the week continues in the same way it always does. I get up, I check on Mum, I work, I leave at five thirty, I go home again. It is predicable, monotonous; except for the ever-present tension of the McKenzie case that hangs over the firm. My only respite is the cold feel of the sea whenever I go for a swim.

On Friday, however, I go into the toilets before I leave work and get changed out of my work clothes into jeans and a slightly nicer top. Then I brush my hair, which is getting too long, and apply some make-up. I survey myself in the mirror. I look almost identical to my mum at this age: long, dark brown hair that hangs in gentle waves, not quite straight, not quite curly. My dark eyes have faint shadows beneath them, thanks to the cruel, silent grip of insomnia. No amount of concealer can cover those.

Didi is still there when I leave, though everyone else has gone home for the evening. She looks up from her computer and does a slight double-take when she sees me.

'Where are you off to?'

'I, uhh, have a drink. A date, I guess.' The words feel foreign on my tongue. I am already regretting this, worrying about what Mum will do tonight, even though my presence in the house changes nothing in her drinking habits. Sometimes I wonder if it makes her worse.

'Not that same guy who accosted you at court?'

'Accosted is a little strong, but yes. Him.'

'Wow. I wish I could find a boyfriend that easily.'

'He's not . . . that. I don't know what he is.'

Didi switches off her computer and sighs.

'Meanwhile I get to enjoy an evening at my dad's house pretending to enjoy reruns of *Only Fools and Horses*.'

'Did you manage to persuade him about the boiler?' I ask, as we gather up our things.

'Nope. I've got half a mind to get it installed behind his back.' She keys in the alarm as I wait with the door held open for her.

'Some people are funny about money,' I say, sympathetically, thinking of the behaviour of some of the firm's probate clients.

'It's not about the money, not really. It's about his pride.'

'What do you mean?'

'He can't stand getting help. He thinks it means he's failed, at least in his eyes.' Didi sighs again and I suddenly realise she looks as tired as I do.

'I'm sorry Dee.'

She shrugs.

'Nothing I should be boring you with on a Friday night.' Her face brightens as I double-lock the office and we turn away from the building into the warm summer evening. 'Have a great time. Can't wait to hear about it on Monday.'

I wave goodbye to her and make my way along the promenade. Ten minutes later I arrive at Morley's, an old hotel that doubles as a seafront café and bar. Connor has already texted to say that he has arrived and is outside. I scan the wide terrace, which has panoramic sea views and is currently rammed with couples, groups of work colleagues, and families. I spot him in the far corner and wend my way through tables to get to him, my heartrate increasing slightly. As I cross the terrace, I am convinced people are looking over at me. Whispering. It is the same old feeling, that people are looking at me, after what happened. Judging me. *Stop it. You're just being paranoid.*

'Hey,' Connor smiles warmly as I approach him and sit down. As usual, his black hair is shaved close to his head, flecked with the odd silver strand. The top two buttons of his white shirt are undone, revealing a hint of a broad, muscular chest.

'Hi,' I reply. For some reason, my mouth has suddenly gone dry.

Connor first introduced himself to me a few weeks ago at the local magistrates' court where I was filing hearing papers for Charles, and Connor was covering whatever trial was unfolding at the time. Since then, we have been out on a couple of coffee dates and one beach walk. He has been disarmingly upfront about his interest in me, yet I still have absolutely no idea what to do with him. Or what I want to do with him. It has been so long since I have had to navigate these waters, since someone so openly showed an interest.

'How was your day?' I ask.

'Busy,' Connor says, running a hand over his short hair. 'I've got a new story to cover. I was doing interviews all afternoon, trying to figure it out.'

'What's the story?'

Connor frowns, unexpectedly.

'Not sure I should really tell you. It's quite a sensitive one.'

'Oh,' I say, feeling a ripple of unease. 'I won't say anything.'

Connor leans towards me across the table, glancing around the busy terrace.

'There's been a spate of crimes,' he says quietly.

My heart begins thumping. It is silly to think it would be linked to anything from my past . . . yet the back of my neck prickles.

'Really?' My voice comes out in a low whisper and Connor nods.

'Yes.' He is so close now his breath tickles my face. Heat rushes through me. 'Apparently . . . someone's been stealing cat collars.'

'*Cat collars?* Oh for god's sake, Connor. You really scared me.'

Connor sits back and laughs heartily.

'Yep, that's what I've been charged with. Covering a story of how half the town's cats are coming back home *sans* collars. There's been an outcry. From the owners, not the cats.'

I shake off the uneasy feeling Connor had given me and roll my eyes at him. His face settles into a more pensive expression, after a moment.

'It's not exactly high-profile journalism, is it?'

'I guess this town isn't exactly cutting-edge.'

'Apart from the McKenzie case, of course.'

'You know I can't talk about that,' I say pointedly.

'I know,' Connor says, holding up his hands. His pensive expression returns. 'I've been working on a new piece, actually. Just on my own time. Something a bit different.'

'What's it about?'

'This town. The history. The seaside town everyone forgot. Maybe a whole piece on Britain's lost pleasure beaches.'

His words linger in the air. *The seaside town everyone forgot.* It is impossible to forget what happened within it, though. Connor is waiting for a response and I quickly snap back to the present.

'Well that sounds a lot more interesting than stolen cat collars. Shall I go order?'

I head inside to the counter to order, needing to clear my head. In front of me, a tall woman with long hair is tapping her foot impatiently at the slow-moving queue, but I am glad of the chance to gather my thoughts. For some reason, Connor's words have caused an ache in the pit of my stomach. It isn't so much about the town – he is right, it is a sad place to be a lot of the time – it is the reminder that he wants more. He has ambition, he's already made it clear he wants to leave this town. It stings. *Everyone leaves, eventually.* Perhaps that's the only reason I've allowed him in, a little.

The foot-tapping woman in front of me turns around, apparently having given up waiting for the queue to go down. She makes to move past me and then stops.

'*Rachel?* Is that you?'

The night is black. I am stumbling. My hand is on the Ferris wheel frame when a voice cuts through the darkness. Penny.

'Rachel, stop!'

I ignore her. Why does she always have to be the perfect one? Her face is screwed up, angry.

'You can't be serious. This isn't funny, anymore. You're going to get us all in trouble.'

'Oh come on, Pen, it's just a bit of fun.'

'This isn't about fun, Rachel. You need to stop this,' Penny insisted. 'You're going too far.'

I ignore her.

My stomach drops: it is a voice I have not forgotten, could never forget. Slowly, I turn around and find myself looking at my old best friend for the first time in fifteen years.

Chapter Ten

Rachel

Now

It's her. It's actually her.

During the few seconds that Penny and I stare at each other, the memories come flooding back, as though it has been days, not years. The rush of painful emotions almost takes my breath away. We haven't laid eyes on each other since that summer. Since it all happened. I have no idea how to react, no idea how Penny will react, now that we aren't kids anymore. *What is she doing here?*

Penny speaks first.

'Oh my god,' she says, in disbelief. She takes my arm and steers me out of the way of a group of women and buggies trying to get to the counter. 'I can't believe it's you. It's been forever.'

It doesn't feel like forever to me. It feels like yesterday, when we were all on the cusp of leaving town and setting off on our new adventures. I have pictured this moment so many times in my head, what would happen if we ever saw each other again. I used to think about it all the time, used to look obsessively around town for a sign of her, Tom or Liam. But as the years passed and nothing happened, I stopped expecting to her see around every corner.

I stopped wondering. I just tried to shed it all, shed the memories as though they were a layer of sunburnt skin and I could find smooth, pale newness underneath. Now here she is. She looks stunning: her copper hair is still long and thick, but instead of straightening the life out of it like she used to, it is artfully wavy, one side tucked sweetly behind her ear. Gone too is the dramatic smoky-eye and bronzer: now she wears nothing but mascara and a pearly sweep of highlighter on her cheekbones. Her long floaty dress perfectly hugs her pear-shaped figure.

'Wow. Penny. You look great,' I manage, suddenly wishing I wasn't in my old, faded jeans.

Penny smiles and brushes her hair away from her shoulder.

'Thanks, I gave up the GHDs.'

As she sweeps her hair back, I notice the large diamond solitaire sitting on her left hand. Penny sees me looking but doesn't say anything. There is a moment's awkward pause. I am struggling to get my brain into gear, to work out what to say or do after all these years. To work through the pain, the anger, the regret.

'How come you're in town?' Penny asks. She seems far more comfortable finding herself in this situation than I am. 'Are you visiting your mum?'

She doesn't know I live here. She thinks I left town, like I was supposed to. And she clearly knows, from her reference to just Mum, that Dad is gone. Yet she never called. Not once. My mouth opens and closes again. I don't know what to say, how to begin. Penny's eyes flicker to my own left hand, which is bare. Without thinking, I glance at Connor out on the terrace and she follows the direction of my gaze. Connor is looking over at us politely but quizzically.

'Oh he is *gorgeous*,' she murmurs conspiratorially at me. Her perfume floats towards me, all floral sophistication. 'Well done, girl.'

I don't have the energy to tell her Connor isn't my boyfriend, or my husband. I should do, but I don't want to justify my life to someone I haven't seen in so long. Someone who left town all those years ago and never so much as looked back.

'What are you doing in town?' I ask. My tone comes out more accusatory than curious. Like I have forgotten how to speak to people.

Penny's eyes suddenly flicker to the left and her smile seems to become forced.

'I'm, uh, visiting Granny. She's not very well.'

'I'm sorry.' Penny was always extremely close to her grandmother, who lives on the other side of town in a large house that was always too warm.

'So, it's just a weekend visit?' I ask, needing to know.

'Something like that.'

Penny's smile slips and she looks distracted. *Is it me? Does she want to get away?* Then she seems to recover herself.

'And how long are you back for?' She smiles, almost embarrassed. 'I always looked for you on TV, you know. I was just waiting for you to pop up. Tom always told me I was being silly, that it takes actors forever to get on TV.'

Tom. Another name from my past. Were they still in touch? I quell the sharp sense of embarrassment that arises with the reminder that I didn't make it to drama school, let alone onto TV. How could I, after everything that happened? Thankfully, before I can answer, Penny checks her phone.

'Listen, I have to get going, I was just grabbing a quick coffee . . .'

'No problem,' I say quickly, keen to get the moment over with. I push my trembling hands into my pockets. Penny looks up again.

'Well, it was lovely to see you again, Rach,' she says. For a moment, we just look at one another. It is as though we are both remembering how it had been, once. How used to each other's company we were, almost as though no time has passed at all. As though things hadn't gone wrong.

'You too,' I say. 'Bye, Pen.'

Penny gives me a sad sort of smile as I step around her and make my way back out towards the terrace where Connor sits. Just before I reach him, however, I hear Penny calling my name. I turn around, confused, as she hurries over to me. Her face is flushed.

'Are you free this weekend? Shall we have a drink and catch up? It's just . . . it's been so long.'

For a moment I just blink at Penny. She wants to see me again? Why? Penny surely doesn't want to sit around gossiping about the good old days. Her eyes are wide, earnest. There is a low, creeping voice urging me not to say yes. Not to fall back into that place, when I finally have some semblance of a life. It might not be the one I imagined, but it is something. Connor is waiting for me. *But he's going to leave, too. Everyone always does.*

I find myself nodding.

'A drink sounds good.'

'Who was that?' Connor asks, as I return to the booth. I have forgotten to order any food, but my appetite is gone.

'Penny. An old school friend.'

'I've not seen her around, before.' Typical, observant journalist. Connor thankfully grew up in the next town over and doesn't appear to know the ins and outs of what happened all those years ago.

'She moved for uni. I've not seen her since the summer we finished sixth form.'

I look down at the menu, not reading the words, but not wanting to continue the conversation.

'What's she doing back here?'

'She's visiting her gran. I don't think she'll be around long.'

I don't mention that I am seeing her tomorrow: I don't want to go into any more detail with Connor. Thankfully, he gets distracted by the menu and goes to order, leaving me to my thoughts of Penny and the strange feeling I have that she hadn't been quite honest. Then again, nor had I.

Chapter Eleven

Penny

Now

I walk away from Morley's, still reeling in shock at seeing Rachel Kingston, after all these years. The dull thud of awkwardness between us still lingers, like a bruise. *Rachel.* I'd barely recognised her. After all, we haven't lain eyes on each other since that summer. Since the night at the old fairground. I had waited for Rachel to speak – she always spoke first, always led the conversation – but she didn't, she just looked wide-eyed back at me, her eyes too large for her face. It is almost impossible to reconcile the girl I once knew – my brash, confident best friend – with the woman I just saw. It has thrown me off balance. I didn't expect to feel so rattled. The memories of what happened that night had risen between us, the police, everything shattering. Guilt twists inside me. Guilt for leaving town without a word. Not reaching out, even after I heard about Rachel's dad. *And who was to blame for that? Rachel was the one who . . .* I stop myself, biting back the thought. My phone, always glued to my hand, starts ringing and I check the screen to see it's Clem.

'Hey,' I say, relief at this reminder of my normal, every-day life. At Clem, my adult, uncomplicated, best friend.

'Hey babe,' Clem says. 'Just checking in. The flat is super quiet without you.'

My chest aches. I already miss our flat in Highgate. I can picture her in the kitchen, her long, tanned legs on show in her gym shorts, stirring some delicious home-cooked French cuisine.

'Thanks, Clem. I'm okay.' I debate telling Clem about Rachel, but decide I need to get it off my chest. 'I actually just bumped into an old school friend.'

'Oh yeah? Replacing me already are you?'

I force a quick laugh.

'Impossible. But . . . well, it's the first time I've seen her since sixth form. We've got a bit of a messy history. Seeing her again was just really strange.'

'Okay . . .' Clem said, her voice softening in response to my own tone. I've never told Clem anything about Rachel, or what happened back then. 'And how do you feel after seeing her?'

'I don't know. Confused. I asked her to go for a drink. I thought maybe we could have a chat, sort of clear the air?'

'And . . . are you going to tell her?'

'Tell her what?' I ask, even though I know exactly what Clem means. I accidentally kick a pebble on the pavement and watch it skitter across the tarmac.

'The truth,' Clem presses. 'About why you're back in town. About everything.'

'No. It's not . . . I don't need to tell anyone about that.' *Especially not Rachel Kingston, of all people.*

Clem sighs on the other end of the phone.

'You know you're going to have to face reality eventually? Stop pretending it isn't happening?'

'I know,' I murmur, barely hearing Clem's response as my mind drifts back to Rachel. Something isn't sitting right. I can't place it, but the encounter has stirred up more than I expected.

'I'll talk to you later, okay?' I say.

'Sure thing, babe,' Clem says, though she sounds concerned.

I glance back towards Morley's terrace, but I can't see Rachel in the crowd. The unsettled feeling clings to me, like cobwebs. Inviting Rachel out for a drink had seemed like the right thing to do at the time, a spur of the moment decision that might help clear the air. Only I can't shake the feeling that I've opened a door I should have left closed.

Chapter Twelve

Rachel

2005

*T*he air inside the shop was thick with the smell of burning incense: spicy and sweet, with something darker beneath it. Music was playing, some sort of soft gong sound. The shelves were crammed with crystals in bowls, candles, strange books with cracked leather spines. I walked over to a corner where bowls of beaded bracelets apparently represented different properties: success, wealth, healing.

'Why are we in here, again?' I asked Penny, who was holding up a necklace with a small charm hanging from it shaped like a crescent moon.

'I told you, I want a dreamcatcher to hang over my bed. I kind of love it in here though, don't you? It's so weird.'

I mumbled something, but I didn't feel the same. Something about the shop felt . . . off. It felt like a different world to the sunny one outside, where people bustled past with supermarket shopping bags.

As Penny browsed the dreamcatcher, I spotted a sign next to the counter, above a pair of heavy, black velvet curtains. Written in swirling gold letters were the words: 'Fortune Reading: £5'. I grinned and went over to Penny, nudging her and pointing at the curtains.

'Dare you to get your fortune read.'

Penny looked up at the sign and shook her head, with a giggle.

'Fine. But you have to go after me.'

'Fine.'

We went over to the velvet curtains and Penny tugged them open. Behind it was a small, dimly lit alcove, with a circular table covered in a purple cloth. On top of the table lay a deck of Tarot cards, face down, surrounded by flickering candles in mismatched holders. I jumped when I realised a woman was sitting behind the table. Her face flickered eerily in the candlelight. She wore heavy rings on each finger, her dark hair twisted into thick braids and her eyes – sharp and knowing – met mine. She smiled slowly, her deep red lips curving as if she already knew something we didn't.

'Sit,' she said in a low voice, motioning to the chair opposite her.

'She's going first,' I said quickly, pushing Penny forwards. Penny widened her eyes at me as the woman gestured for me to go back outside. I ducked hastily back through the curtains into the main shop, trying to stop myself from giggling at the look on Penny's face.

About ten minutes later, Penny emerged from the curtain, her face flushed.

'I can't believe you left me in there on my own!' she hissed.

'What did she say? Are you going to meet a tall, dark stranger?' I sniggered.

'Actually,' Penny said quietly, trying not to look too pleased, 'I got the Sun, the Nine of Cups and the Wheel of Fortune. Apparently that means good things are on the horizon, I just need to be open to the opportunities coming my way. I've got a bright path ahead.'

'Funny that, after she took your fiver.'

'Your turn, off you go.'

Penny gave me a gentle shove. I rolled my eyes and pulled the curtains back, taking my place in the small alcove opposite the fortune-teller.

'Five pounds,' she said softly, once I was seated. I fished the five-pound note from my handbag and handed it over. I could sense Penny hovering behind me, peeking between the curtains.

The woman shuffled the Tarot cards slowly, her eyes not leaving mine. 'The cards know what you've come here for,' she whispered, spreading them out in a perfect fan across the table. 'Pick three.'

I glanced back at Penny with a grin, though my heart was suddenly fluttering in my chest. I selected the cards, one by one. The woman's ring-adorned fingers brushed over the first card and turned it over. It was the Moon: a pale, glowing orb hanging over dark waters, with creatures rising from the depths.

'Deception,' the woman murmured. 'Things are not as they seem. Beware of a lie. Beware of what is hidden in the darkness.'

I swallowed, my heart now thudding in my chest. This was meant to be a laugh . . . but something about the woman's tone was making me uneasy. She flipped over the second card. The Ten of Swords. A figure lay on the ground, pierced through by ten swords, their blood pooling beneath them. My stomach turned.

'Betrayal,' she whispered. 'Someone will tear you apart, piece by piece. And when they do, your world will collapse. Something precious will be taken from you. Someone you love, gone.'

I shivered, feeling cold sweat break out across my spine. What did she mean? What was she talking about? Was it

Mum? Dad? I realised my fingers were gripping the edge of the table. Behind me, Penny shifted.

'Isn't this a bit much?' she said, trying to laugh, but her voice was tight. The woman ignored her and turned over the third and final card. The Tower. I stared at the image: a towering structure engulfed in flames, people falling from its heights as it crumbled. The air in the alcove seemed to tighten. The fortune-teller's eyes grew dark as she studied the card.

'The Tower,' she said, her voice even softer than ever. 'You are walking towards destruction.'

I tried to shake off the chill that began to creep up my spine, but it was impossible. I couldn't take my eyes off the card. The flames.

'The life you know,' she whispered, 'will all come crashing down. Everything you believe to be solid will be reduced to ash.'

Behind me, I heard Penny shift again and clear her throat uncomfortably. But she didn't say anything.

'And here is the truth you do not want to hear,' the woman continued. 'You are the one pulling on the thread. You will make a choice. But you are ensuring your own destruction. You are the one who will light the flame.'

'You're wrong,' I blurted, my voice shaky. 'This is just made up nonsense.' This woman was nothing but an old fraud.

The woman smiled: another slow curl of her lips. 'You have already started down this path. The cards do not lie.'

'Come on, Rach,' Penny muttered behind me. 'Let's go.'

I stood up and turned to leave, but the woman's voice followed me, haunting and soft as I pulled apart the curtains, revealing the overly warm but bright shop once again.

'There is no escaping your destiny. The chains are already wrapped around you.'

Chapter Thirteen

Rachel

Now

On Sunday I find myself back at Morley's, anxiously jiggling one leg under the bar stool as I wait for Penny. I overthought my outfit before I left home, changing five times and throwing things on the floor in frustration before settling on a long cotton dress that skims, rather than hugs, my stomach and hips. I used to be confident in my outfit choices. Full of myself. Beneath the dress, my stomach flutters with nerves.

I think I have longer to wait, but Penny walks in five minutes early. That is another thing I remember about her: she was always punctual, always put-together. I was always the one turning up late, laughing it off. Nostalgia sweeps momentarily over me.

'There you are.' Penny smiles broadly when she sees me. Today, another warm day, she wears a long skirt and a silky pink camisole that moves like liquid against her pale skin. She looks stunning and I try to ignore the little bobbles all over my own dress. Jealousy bites at me. *Stop comparing yourself.* But how can I not? Penny represents what I could have, perhaps, become, had I left town all those years ago. Had I succeeded. After all, I was once the louder of the two of us, the one who spoke first, drank first, decided what we should do on a weekend. She used to rely on me. Now confidence radiates from her, whilst I feel like a plant that has stopped growing and slowly withered in the dark. I try to stop the resentment from distracting me. Penny is here now, seemingly wanting to put the past behind us. The trouble is, how can I? How can any of us?

I stand up, unsure how to greet her, but Penny leaves no room for questions and wraps me up in a hug. I return it, her embrace catching me off guard, an unfamiliar rush of emotion swelling in my chest. We break apart and Penny slides onto the bar stool opposite me. She gestures to the girl behind the bar before raising her eyebrows at me.

'What are you having?'

'Umm,' I stammer, flustered at being put on the spot, 'a G&T, please.'

'Two double G&Ts,' Penny says smoothly, 'with Indian tonic, ice and fresh lime; juniper berries if you have them.'

I blink at her: who *is* this slick confident person? Has so much changed in fifteen years? The girl behind the bar looks like she has been gifted a special task and hurries to make the drinks. The difference between us feels sharper than ever. I don't know how to act, what role I now play in this dynamic.

'I'm not supposed to be drinking before the wedding,' Penny sighs, 'but a drink is all I want at the moment. *Anyway*,' she swivels back on her stool to face me, effortlessly casual. 'Tell me everything. What have you been up to all these years? Where are you living? You haven't changed a bit, your skin is amazing. I'm in the middle of a skin fast for the wedding. You *need* to tell me what your skincare routine is. And that *boyfriend* of yours. Wow.'

I flush. The rush of questions leaves me momentarily speechless. The smooth skin would be down to staying indoors with a boxset, not any fancy routine. I struggle to catch up with her barrage of words.

'He's not . . . we're just . . . early days,' I finish, lamely. I don't want to talk about myself, or Connor. 'Do you still live in Durham?'

'Oh no, I moved to London, god, ten years ago, now. Since I got my first job.'

There it is again: that bitter twinge of jealousy. I have always wondered what life in London would have been like, what my classmates at drama school went on to do. It's one thing thinking about it, however: quite another having it thrust in front of me in the form of Penny, even more perfect than she always used to be.

'I've lived with my best friend since we moved to London,' Penny continues. 'She has this amazing flat in Highgate, of all places.'

Penny's face shifts slightly, her expression tightening, her mouth tugging down at the corners. The change is so quick that I almost miss it. Before I can ask if something is wrong, she seems to recover herself, her smile back in place.

'How about you?' she asks brightly. 'Are you still in London? And still acting? What was drama school like?'

I hesitate, feeling my stomach churn. *Tell the truth.* But instead I find myself talking as though the words belong to someone else.

'I'm between shows at the moment, but yes, I still love to perform.' I sit up straighter, trying to mirror the bouncy inflections in her voice. 'You know how it is.'

'That's wonderful!' Penny claps her hands in delight. 'I knew you would be. You've always had that *thing* about you. Something special. Have you been in anything I would have seen? Surely I haven't missed you in anything?'

'Well . . . I'm mostly Broadway, not much TV.' The lie rolls off my tongue, my heart racing. But there's something else too . . . a fleeting moment of enjoyment. Pretending to be someone who performs, who lives in a flat somewhere edgy in London with Connor, my handsome boyfriend. Then reality pulls at me and I catch myself. I should have learnt a long time ago about where lies can get you.

I open my mouth to tell Penny the truth, but at that moment the girl behind the bar sets the drinks down in front of us. Grateful for the distraction, I pick up my drink, my hands shaking slightly.

'And how's your mum?' Penny asks, already onto the next topic. I reason that it doesn't matter that I haven't told her the truth; we aren't going to see each other again. What is one more little lie?

'She's fine.' I am about to leave it at that, but I remember that Penny used to know my home life better than anyone else. 'She's . . . the same, really. As she was before.'

Penny looks down at her drink, her face softening.

'Listen, Rach, I've been thinking about all this ever since I saw you yesterday. I know it's been fifteen years, but I wanted to say how sorry I am about your dad. It must have been so tough, especially with you going off to drama school.'

'It's fine,' I say, woodenly. 'It was a long time ago.'

I curled up on my bed as tears poured down my cheeks, soaking into the fabric of my pillowcase. I clutched my stomach, the uncontrollable sobs coming thick and fast. How could he be gone? I just saw him, the air was still warm with him. Gasping with grief so big, so terrifying, I fumbled for my phone. I couldn't do this on my own, I wasn't strong enough, I couldn't look after Mum by myself.

I dialled Penny's number. She was my number two on speed dial, right after Dad. She still wasn't talking to me after everything but surely, despite everything, she would answer?

The phone rings.

It rings and rings, and no one answers.

Penny unexpectedly reaches forward and touches my hand, the band of her engagement ring cold against my skin.

'I've thought about you a lot over the years, Rachel. I felt awful about the way we left things. That we never even said goodbye.'

'There was a reason we didn't say goodbye,' I say, my voice tight. The elephant in the room looms between us, as it always has done. It was only a matter of time before it showed itself. Penny chews her lips, choosing her next words carefully.

'I've thought about all that, too, obviously. But . . . we were all so young. People do stupid things, things they regret later. It was all so awful. But I think it's time that we all put it behind us.'

She pulls her hand away and runs it through her red hair: a loose curl springs up at her crown. Deep down, I know it's not that simple. Too many years have gone by, too much silence, too much brooding resentment. But I suddenly realise that, at least for this moment, I don't want to dive into the past. Right now, I'm just a normal person, having a drink with an old school friend, something I never do. For a moment, I can almost imagine Penny is still the girl with the scrunchie around her wrist and blue mascara, as though no time has passed. It's just one drink. Then she'll be gone.

The girl behind the bar comes over and sets down a small terracotta bowl of bar nuts, breaking the spell. I glance at her in irritation, but Penny immediately reaches out and scoops up a handful.

'Thank *god*, I've been practically starving myself to make sure I fit into my bloody wedding dress.'

She pauses, the nuts halfway to her mouth, and her face goes still. But she doesn't say anything else.

'How did you meet this lucky man, anyway?' I ask, starting to relax as the gin settles in my system. 'Is he not visiting your gran with you?'

But Penny doesn't respond. Her eyes are fixed on something behind me, widening slightly.

'Penny?'

Penny's gaze snaps back to mine, and she forces a smile.

'My fiancé and his best man have actually just walked in. I didn't realise they were coming here. I told them I was doing wedding stuff.'

Before I can say anything, Penny slips off her stool and disappears behind me. *Strange.* She seems all over the place. Perhaps – the thought makes my stomach twist uncomfortably – she is regretting meeting me, after all.

Someone is calling Penny's name. Out of curiosity, I glance over my shoulder to see two men entering the bar from the terrace. It takes me a moment to register what I am seeing. When I do, the world seems to slow, so that all I can sense is the thickness of my tongue against my dry mouth. Tom, Penny's high school boyfriend. My old school friend. The same lanky frame, the same freckles. None of the weight he once carried. And standing next to him . . . taller, broader. More handsome. Liam Haughton. My teenage boyfriend, my entire universe, once upon a time.

Suddenly, it is as though we are all back on the beach that night, again. I can smell the seaweed on the shore, hear the cackle of Sasha's laughter, the ominous creaking of the old Ferris wheel. I have wished, so many times, I could rewind that summer and the events that followed. Now the ghosts of my past are all standing in front of me.

Chapter Fourteen

Rachel

Now

Blood pounds in my ears as Penny approaches Tom and Liam.

Liam. Here.

He and Tom both look effortlessly put-together, a world away from the teenagers I last saw. They are laughing with each other as Penny approaches them, joking around like they hadn't all left town, like my life hadn't been ruined.

Penny reaches them and starts talking quietly to them, her hands gesturing as though she is trying to explain something. Explain *me*. The hum of chatter around me fades to a low buzz. The bar suddenly becomes too hot, just like the stifling summer heat that year, when all the grass turned yellow and the metal of the Ferris wheel flashed blindingly in the sunlight. Tom suddenly looks over, his face a mask of surprise and I quickly spin back round on my stool, my cheeks numb and my heart racing. *What's going on? What are they all doing here?*

I feel like I've been winded. I tighten my grip on my glass, hearing the ice rattle. Why are they still friends? And Penny and Tom, still together, after all this time. Why didn't she tell me? Anger prickles at my skin at the sight of them all together. Still connected, still moving through life like I never mattered. And I try to stop my mind racing back through the fragmented memories of that night. Why are they suddenly all back on the same weekend?

I can't stay here any longer. The walls of the bar feel as though they are closing in on me, the air thickening with the weight of seeing them again, of everything that went unresolved.

I push my stool back, the legs scraping against the wooden floor. Penny turns towards me and sees me picking up my handbag. Without looking at Liam or Tom, I give her a quick wave and gesture at my watch, like I need to leave, even though my hands are shaking. Then I turn and leave the bar through the exit in the opposite direction to them. The urge to flee overwhelms me as I walk, and I have to stop myself from running. I race down the steps into the warm afternoon air and start walking down the road, my pace quickening with each step, desperate to put as much distance between me and Morley's as possible. Then I hear footsteps behind me.

'Rachel! Wait!'

I don't have to turn to know who it is. I keep walking, not wanting to face him, but I hear his footsteps quickening behind me and know it is inevitable. He catches up with me easily, and takes my arm, gently.

'Rach, wait. Please.'

I jerk my arm away, spinning around to face him.

'What do you want, Tom?'

His face, still slightly boyish with the same old freckles, contorts into something that looks like guilt. Or perhaps that's just what I want to see.

'I just wanted to . . . say hi,' he finished lamely.

'That's it?' I ask. 'After fifteen years?'

He hesitates.

'That was hardly my fault, Rach. Or Penny's. It was complicated.'

'What part of it was complicated?' I ask, bitterly, unable to stop the words falling from my lips. 'The part where you all left town and stayed friends with each other?'

'It wasn't like that,' Tom says gently, taking a step towards me. 'Remember what you did, Rachel. How were we supposed to react?'

'You could have spoken to me. You were supposed to be my friend.'

The loser and the fatso. Only Tom is no longer fat.

'It's not that simple and you know it. Plus, Penny just explained to us that she bumped into you and wanted a drink, to clear the air. She wants to put it behind us.'

Put it all behind us. It sounds so very neat. The hurt wells up in my chest, threatening to spill over. The sharp sting of them all standing there, in their little group.

'How does Liam feel about that?' I ask.

Tom's face says it all: a slight wince.

'That's what I thought. I can't do this, Tom. Good luck with the wedding.'

'Rach . . .'

69

But I don't let him finish. I turn and walk away, leaving him standing alone in the street, knowing that he will not follow.

Chapter Fifteen

Rachel

Now

My phone rings twice as I walk home: Penny's number, still saved in my phone as *Bestie* from all those years ago, lights up the screen, but I ignore it. It was stupid of me to think that we could have a drink together, when there are still so many unanswered questions. When they still don't know the whole truth of that night.

The night is long, insomnia keeping my aching eyes open until the pre-dawn light of Monday morning. I finally drift off, only to wake from a fitful doze to a message from Penny.

> *I'm so sorry I didn't tell you. I just wanted to focus on catching up. x*

I hold my phone in my hand for a moment, staring at it, my eyes roaming over the contact name being on my screen for the first time in so long. Then I drop the phone onto my bed and start getting ready for work. I try not to think about Penny, Liam, or Tom, but it's impossible. Over and over again I replay the moment I saw them all together, Penny gesturing to them from behind me. The moment I realised Penny was marrying Tom. And each time I feel the bitter sting of that revelation. They had all stayed friends. Not one word to me for fifteen years and yet there they all were with one another. *Don't think about it. Don't think about them. They don't matter.* But my jaw is tight as I check on Mum and then leave the house.

When I arrive at my desk, there is a small gift bag and card sitting in front of my keyboard.

'Happy birthday, Rach,' Didi says, beaming from behind her own desk. Today she is wearing a lime green dress to match her new nails.

'Thanks, Dee.' I force a smile.

'What are you doing tonight?'

'Nothing much,' I say. 'Just a quiet one.'

Mum won't remember, of course. I sit down in my chair and pull the gift bag towards me. I open the card first and read the scribbled inscription. *Rach, Happy Birthday. Thanks for another year of keeping me sane. Lots of love, Didi.* Inside the gift bag are two bottles of my favourite wine.

I smile and put the card up next to my desk. *Who needs Penny?*

'Where's Charles?' I ask, popping the wine into my bag.

'In a meeting.'

'That's early.'

'He's marked it as private so even we can't see what he's up to.'

'I dread to think what he's up to if he's marked it as private to his own secretary.'

We start discussing the many things Charles could be up to and I start to cheer up slightly, settling back in my normal routine. Didi laughs loudly at my latest suggestion, just as the front door to the office opens and a woman walks into the room in a cloud of overly-sweet perfume. I have to bite back a groan, my momentary good mood suddenly dissipating.

'Morning ladies,' Charles's wife says loudly as she approaches our desks. 'Quiet morning, is it? Having a little catch-up?'

'We don't start work until eight thirty,' Didi says, brusquely.

'And not a moment before, right?' Charles's wife says, in a sugary-sweet tone. She puts her expensive leather handbag down on my desk and I grit my teeth. Her eyes stray to the birthday card on my desk.

'Oh, Rachel, is it your birthday? God, how time flies. Why aren't you all going out for drinks? Charles didn't mention a thing.'

'I don't like to make a fuss,' I say, fighting to keep my tone polite.

'Well, you certainly used to.'

Sasha Kennedy, now Mrs Sasha Rowland, loves to remind me that we used to go to school together. Almost as much as she loves to remind me how far she has come – and how far I haven't.

'Where's Charles?' she asks, with a toss of her long blonde hair, looking around for her latest husband.

'In a meeting,' Didi says. 'Might be a while.'

'That's okay, I'll wait.'

Sasha sits down in a spare chair, crossing her long legs, and watches Didi with a smug expression as we turn to our computers. I can feel her waiting for something, feel the tension building. And then, just as I expected:

'Guess who I saw this weekend,' Sasha says, her gaze trained on me. 'Penny, Tom and Liam. The old gang, back in town.'

I don't respond, but my fingers freeze on my keyboard. Sasha's lips curve into a smile, clearly satisfied by the flicker of emotion she's stirred in me.

'Must be strange, seeing them all still friends. But not with you, anymore.'

I try to focus on my screen, ignoring Didi's confused look, but her words cut through me. For as long as I live in this town, there will always be reminders of what happened back then.

The door to the main office opens and I exhale in relief as Charles enters, speaking over his shoulder to someone just out of sight. Thank *god*. Hopefully now Sasha will leave.

' . . . delighted to have you on board for the year,' he is saying as he enters the office. 'We've not found any decent candidates; this is a godsend. Oh yes, the bathroom is just down there.'

Charles steps into the room, his smile broader than I've seen it in a long time.

'Well, we've found Justine's replacement,' he announces, 'She'll be lucky to have a job to come back to, based on what I've just seen.' He laughs and Didi shoots me a look. 'Thankfully they've agreed to an immediate start, so you can stop working quite so hard, Rachel.'

Sasha leans back, her eyes on me. 'Oh, don't worry darling, Rachel seems very relaxed to me.'

'Ah, excellent,' Charles says, turning around and waving through the open door, 'come on in, you can meet our two secretaries.'

Ignoring Sasha's smirk, I arrange my face into a polite smile, wondering who the newcomer might be. It makes a difference in a firm this small. A man steps into the office, tall and dressed in a smart suit.

It takes me a couple of seconds to register what I am seeing, to understand why my stomach has plummeted. *No. Not him. Not here.* But there is no mistaking him. The room seems to tilt, the edges of my vision blurring. His eyes sweep the room, locking with mine for a moment and I feel my breath catch in my throat. The past rushes back with such force I can barely breathe.

'Rachel, Didi,' Charles beams, 'meet Liam Haughton, our newest lawyer.'

Chapter Sixteen

Rachel

2005

*I*smoothed down my denim skirt and glanced around the restaurant with a surge of delight. We never went out to eat and especially not at one of the nicer places on the seafront. It felt different: people were talking more quietly, so it was like a muted buzz, rather than being able to hear them shouting at each other like they did at the local diner.

'Can I get you something to drink?' the waiter, who had quietly appeared out of nowhere, asked.

'A bottle of house white,' Mum ordered, just as Dad opened his mouth to speak. He closed it again, with a resigned look.

'Can I have a vodka and coke?' I asked eagerly.

'Absolutely not,' Dad said, firmly. 'You're not eighteen until August.'

I slumped back in my chair, furious.

'She'll just have a coke,' Dad ordered. 'And two wine glasses, thanks.'

The waiter left and Dad looked around at me and Mum. They had both made an effort tonight: Dad was wearing one of his 'fun' shirts, which had a tree pattern on it, and Mum was wearing lipstick and a nice dress. I had noticed, however, her clothes were starting to hang off her a bit more than they used to.

The wine arrived and Dad made a show of tasting it and then nodding to the waiter that it was okay.

'Nice place this,' he beamed when the waiter was gone. Then he turned to me. 'We actually have some news to share with you, Rachel.'

As he spoke, the door opened and another family walked in. My eyes widened. It was him, behind his parents. Liam Haughton. He looked incredible in a black shirt, his hair gelled. Immediately, I slipped my Nokia out of my back pocket and sent Penny a message under the table.

Omg @ Seasons with M&D & Liam H just walked in! What do I do?!

'Rachel, put your phone away,' Mum hissed. 'Your dad is trying to talk to you.' I looked up to see both her and Dad looking at me. Dad looked a bit hurt.

'Sorry.'

'Like I was saying,' Dad continued, 'We wanted to bring you here for a reason. You know that . . .'

A voice cut across Dad's announcement.

'Johnny boy!'

We all looked up at the man standing by our table and my heart nearly stopped. It was Gerard Haughton, Liam's dad. The Gerard Haughton, the richest man in town. Large, tall, with a thick head of wavy, greying hair. What was he doing talking to us? Behind him stood Liam's mum, Janet, who had black hair and wore an expensive-looking silver dress . . . and Liam. His hands were shoved in his pockets and he was looking around the restaurant with a bored expression.

*I immediately tried to rearrange my face to look the same,
like I was super annoyed to be there.*

'Gerard, hi,' Dad said, looking a bit flustered. 'This is my
wife, Lizzy, and our daughter Rachel.'

'Lovely stuff,' Gerard said loudly in his posh, booming
voice. 'Out celebrating, are we?' He gave Dad a meaningful
look that was lost on me.

'Well yes, actually, we are.'

'Well then, why don't we join tables? Makes sense, don't
you think? In the circumstances.'

*I saw Janet's eyes widen at Gerard, but she didn't say any-
thing. Mum looked flushed and happy, her wine glass already
empty. I couldn't believe it. It was like one of my many day-
dreams, but it was actually happening. Gerard clicked his
fingers at a waiter who immediately came over and helped
drag another table across the thick carpet. Janet and Gerard
sat down on my right and Gerard directed Liam to the chair
opposite me. My heart was beating like mad and I desperately
wished I could have checked my hair and make-up somehow.
My phone buzzed in my pocket but I ignored it. Penny could
wait. Liam Haughton was sitting in front of me.*

'I think this calls for some champagne,' Gerard said, clicking his fingers again at the waiter, who scurried away to fetch
some. I looked over at Dad, confused.

'What calls for champagne?' I asked.

'Well, that's what I was trying to tell you, sweetheart.
Gerard and I are going into business together,' Dad said,
proudly. 'We're opening a restaurant. This restaurant in fact.
Seasons is closing and I'm buying it. I'll be running it, but
Gerard will be part-owner.'

'The real work begins now, Johnny boy,' Gerard said, with a look of someone who had just presented Dad with a gold medal.

Wow. For a moment I was distracted even from Liam. Dad had always wanted to open his own place on the seafront. Mum was beaming as she topped up her wine glass with a shaky hand. She had always wanted Dad to do something more than be an IT man at the local council. And he was going to be doing it with Gerard Haughton? This night could not get any better.

'That's amazing, Dad. Really.'

Dad looked thrilled. The champagne arrived and the four adults put their heads together and started discussing the business. I looked across from me at Liam. To my surprise he was looking right at me.

'Hey, Rach.'

'Hey,' I managed. Next to Liam, Mum suddenly laughed too-loudly and a couple of people on a neighbouring table looked over. I cringed and looked down at my lap.

'I hear you're going to drama school in London,' Liam said. I looked up, taken aback that he knew.

'That's right.' My face was burning. I had never spoken to him alone, before.

'I've applied to do History at UCL,' Liam said. *'So maybe we'll be headed in the same direction.'*

'Wow, UCL,' I said, impressed.

Mum laughed loudly again.

'I'm dry over here, Gerard,' she cooed at Liam's dad, holding up her champagne flute. Her eyes were starting to look glazed and I swallowed.

'Hey, you wanna see the view from the balcony outside?'
Liam suddenly asked.

Anything to get away from Mum. I nodded.

'Sure.'

Mum's loud voice followed us out of the restaurant to the long terrace that wrapped around the restaurant. It was windy this close to the shore and my hair whipped around my face.

'You've got a tonne of hair,' Liam said, watching me try to smooth it down.

'I know, it's a pain.'

'It's nice. I like long hair.' He dug into his jean pocket and pulled out a pack of cigarettes, offering them to me.

I knew I would be in trouble if I went back inside smelling of smoke, but there was no way I was saying no to Liam Haughton. Especially not when he lit his cigarette and then took a step closer, raising the lighter so that he could light mine for me. I tried not to look too deeply into his eyes.

'Your mum's kinda crazy,' he said, taking a step back and dragging on his cigarette.

'I know,' I muttered.

'Guess that's where you get it from,' Liam said, looking at me with a grin. 'Or so I hear from Isaac.'

Fucking Isaac, *I thought angrily.* What had he been saying?

'It's why I hadn't spoken to you earlier,' Liam said, leaning against the terrace railings. 'He's still super into you. Bro code and all that. But . . . here we are.'

My brain was struggling to fathom what he was saying. Liam . . . had wanted to talk to me? From inside, came the sound of a glass breaking and peoples' shocked voices. I glanced behind me and saw through the terrace doors Mum standing by the table and waiters helping clear up a broken wine glass. Mum was laughing. Anger rippled through me. How could she, tonight of all nights? In front of Liam's family? That would put him right off me. But when I looked back at him, he looked unfazed. He dropped his cigarette on the ground and took a step towards me.

'Looks like you could do with a distraction, Rachel Kingston,' he said quietly.

Before I knew it, he was right in front of me, his lips moving across mine, his tongue pushing into my mouth. It was happening, it was actually happening. I forgot that my cigarette was in my hand until the embers burnt down to my fingers, pain jolting through my hand. I flicked it to the ground, trying to ignore the pain sizzling across my skin. Liam Haughton was kissing me.

And suddenly the Nine of Cups card popped unbidden into my mind, and I heard the fortune-teller's words. 'Someone will tear you apart, piece by piece. And when they do, your world will collapse.'

Chapter Seventeen

Rachel

Now

There is a long, suffocating silence as Liam and I stare at one another, the shock on his face surely mirroring my own. Clearly, he hadn't expected me to be here any more than I was expecting him. My heart pounds through my shirt, so violently I can hardly think straight. *Liam. Here.* Nothing is making sense, why is Liam talking to Charles about a job? Liam had chosen to study History at uni; I had no idea that he had become a lawyer. Had he changed his mind at some point? He never seemed quite sure on what he wanted to do. When they first left town, I checked each of their Facebook pages multiple times a day, feeling a hot, sick burn in the back of my throat whenever I saw them on nights out, arms around their new friends. How dare they laugh and joke and do shots? When I was still here? But after a while, I simply stopped looking. I couldn't stand to see them anymore. And in that time, it seemed he had gone on to become a lawyer, of all things.

Charles, oblivious to the tension, chats away loudly about how lucky the firm is to have someone like Liam stepping in. But all I can do is sit there stupidly, the blood draining from my face. I never imagined he would come back to town. Now here he is. He looks so much like the boy I once knew: taller, more polished, but the same jawline, the same dark eyes.

Sasha looks utterly delighted.

'Liam Haughton!' She stands and crosses the room, air-kissing his cheek. 'You're covering Justine's maternity leave? I thought you lived in London.'

Liam blinks at her, like he's struggling to get his bearings.

'I did . . . I mean, I do. It's just temporary.'

His voice. It's like listening to an old tape recording of yourself from years ago, one that makes your insides knot uncomfortably.

Sasha's brow furrows a little in confusion and Liam shifts on the worn carpet.

'There were . . . cuts at my firm. I took voluntary redundancy.'

'Oh,' Sasha replies, though it's clear she isn't really interested in why Liam has returned, only that he has returned. 'Well, we'll just have to make the most of it whilst you're here, won't we?'

Charles, looking slightly irritated at Sasha's enthusiasm, clears his throat.

'You two know each other?'

'Yes, darling,' Sasha simpers, one hand still on Liam's arm. 'Liam and I went to school together.' I know what's coming. She turns to me, her eyes glittering malevolently. 'So did Rachel. In fact, Liam and Rachel were *very* close, weren't you? Isn't that right, Rachel?'

I can feel Didi and Charles's gazes swivel toward me, but I can't get my mouth to work. I manage a stiff nod, hoping it will be enough. There's a slight pause. I glance at Didi out of the corner of my eye and see that she, too, looks less than enthused about Liam's arrival. Her jaw is tight, her expression as forced as mine. Charles's comments about Justine not having a job to return to have clearly pissed her off.

'Well,' Charles says, after a beat, 'I hope that doesn't mean too many late nights catching up with one another about old times.' He turns to Liam, who looks like he has something lodged in his throat. 'There's plenty to do now Justine is off.'

'No problem,' Liam says, stiffly. 'I'd, uh, better get going. Thanks for meeting with me on such short notice, Charles.'

'Not at all, we're thrilled to have someone so distinguished joining us. From a Magic Circle firm, no less,' he says, looking around at us with his eyebrows raised impressively. 'I'll get one of the girls to email you the final contract and details,' he adds, waving a hand dismissively towards me and Didi.

Liam offers a small, tight-lipped smile, and nods once more before heading for the door. I slump back in my chair, staring blankly at the card Didi gave me this morning. The pattern on the front blurs and I clench my fists under the desk, trying to steady my shaking hands. Why didn't Penny tell me? Why did she make out they were just visiting her grandma?

Sasha follows Liam out, her heels clicking on the entrance floor, clearly having forgotten whatever it was she came to talk to Charles about. I let out a shaky breath once the door is closed, but my chest is still tight.

Didi leans forward, her brow furrowed. 'Are you okay? You look pale.'

'I'm fine,' I lie, turning back to my desk so Didi doesn't ask any more questions.

The rest of the day passes in a blur. Neither Didi nor I talk much. I operate on auto-pilot, going through the motions as my thoughts continue to spiral. At five thirty I mumble a goodbye to Didi and hurry out of the door.

I walk quickly along the promenade, not wanting to think, wanting to keep moving. I don't have my swimming things with me, but I decide to head home and get them. I need to distract myself.

As I pass the familiar red-and-gold awning of Morley's I glance up, out of habit, before something makes me stop. Through the railings, at the far end of the terrace, I spot a small group of people sitting at one of the tables in the sunshine. I freeze. It's Liam. He is sitting there, his back to me, but I know it's him. He even moves the same way as he did when we were younger. Beside him, shaking her head, is Penny. Tom sits across from them, his hands gesturing in the air, as though he is in the middle of telling them a story. But there is something else that stops me, something not quite right about the scene, like a jigsaw puzzle piece jammed into the wrong place. It's something about the way Penny's chair is angled, the way Tom is sitting opposite her, not beside her. The way Penny's hand is on Liam's arm and he leans in close to her, for a moment. I feel a sickening twist in my stomach as realisation dawns on me.

Penny . . . and *Liam*.

My mind races, the pieces slowly falling into place. Penny never mentioned Tom specifically by name. She had been vague about her fiancé, vague about everything. Because it is Liam she is marrying. Not Tom. She was lying to me the whole time. All of a sudden, my legs feel weak and I stumble back off the kerb, desperate to get away from the sight of them.

Chapter Eighteen

Rachel

2005

*O*n *Saturday morning I woke to the sound of a loud crash coming from somewhere downstairs. I shot up in bed, my heart racing. My first thought was Mum. I jumped out of bed and ran downstairs towards the kitchen. When I entered, I found Mum clutching Dad's arm: both of them were laughing.*

'Sorry, sweetheart,' Dad said, his face pink. 'Your old man nearly killed himself falling off a chair.'

I blinked, my heart slowing as I took in the room. There were balloons strung up along the picture rails just beneath the ceiling and the kitchen table was covered with the birthday party tablecloth Mum used whenever she remembered to decorate. Presents were piled neatly in one corner and in the centre was a clumsily made birthday cake with a big number '18' candle in the centre. The room felt brighter than it had in a long time.

'Your mother made the cake,' Dad said, still laughing and nudging Mum. 'That's why it's wonky.'

'Don't be so rude, John,' Mum said, coming over and giving me a hug. She smelt like baking and soap. Not her usual smell. My heart swelled. 'Happy birthday, darling.'

'Thanks, Mum.'

We spent the morning together, eating cake and opening presents – a new webcam for my computer, some eyeshadow palettes, money, and a necklace. We hadn't had a day like it in a long time. It felt like fate that it had coincided with my eighteenth.

That evening, Mum and Dad went out for dinner and I got ready to go over to Liam's. I didn't know what to expect: we had only been sort of boyfriend and girlfriend now for nine weeks, and half of that time we had spent revising and taking our final exams. He had told me it would just be the two of us, and to wear something nice. I wondered whether tonight was going to be the night. I couldn't decide how I felt about it: I had made excuses up until now, every time he had tried to go further. I wasn't about to give it up that easily, not to Liam Haughton. I wanted more from him first, I wanted to hear him tell me he loved me. I wanted this one to count.

I arrived at Liam's huge house at seven o'clock and waited for him to answer the door, smoothing down my tight pink dress. He opened the door, wearing a light blue shirt and shorts, and my heart did a little flip. His hair was still damp from the shower and he had caught the sun. God, he looked perfect.

'Happy birthday, Kingston,' he said, grinning as he pulled me inside. Almost straight away he pushed me against the wall and pressed himself against me, giving me a long kiss that made me go weak at the knees. Almost as quickly, he moved away from me and started walking down the hallway.

'Where's your mum and dad?' I asked, rearranging my dress.

'Out. Come on.'

I followed Liam down the hallway and, just as we entered the kitchen, I half-screamed as an explosion of noise greeted us. Everywhere I looked, people were jumping out of corners, party hats on and shouting happy birthday at me. My mouth fell open as I realised that Penny, Tom, half our year and all our parents were here. Liam squeezed me close to him.

'Happy birthday,' he whispered in my ear.

Before I could even process what was happening, Penny bounded over to us, throwing her arms around me in a massive hug. 'Happy birthday!' she squealed, as Tom elbowed his way through the crowd of people and hugged me, too. 'We've been planning this for weeks!'

'No way guys,' I said, looking around at Penny, Tom and Liam. 'I can't believe you did all this for me.' Tom grinned and wrapped his arm around Penny, giving her a kiss on the cheek.

'You know what Pen's like when she gets an idea into her head.'

Out of nowhere, my parents appeared, followed by Gerard and Janet Haughton, who were holding glasses of champagne.

'Surprise!' Dad called out, beaming at me. I glanced across at Mum: she was holding a champagne glass, but her eyes didn't look glazed. I let out a sigh of relief. This really was turning out to be the perfect birthday.

'Happy birthday, Rachel dear,' Janet said in her clipped accent, bestowing a couple of air kisses on me. Gerard followed, squeezing my shoulder.

'Lovely to have you here, Rachel. Might as well get used to our families being together, now the restaurant is about to open, *hadn't we?' He grinned at Mum and Dad, but Janet frowned and shushed him.*

'Let's not talk business now, Gerard.'

The next moment I was swept along by a sea of friends from school wishing me a happy birthday and shoving shots into my hand. I threw them back, laughter bubbling out of me. Everything was perfect. Even the sight of Sasha Kennedy did nothing to dampen my spirits. Someone handed me a birthday princess tiara which I tucked carefully into my hair. I looked around the room, soaking it all in. Penny and Tom were dancing together, his hands wrapped around her waist. My eyes sought out Liam across the room and my chest swelled when I saw him, chatting away to a group of friends. We could be that perfect, too. Just like Penny and Tom.

The night blurred happily: dancing, drinks, laughter, Liam. A makeshift dance floor had been created in the lounge and someone turned the music right up so we all piled in there. I stood in the centre, dancing and twirling with Penny, Tom and Liam, running my hands through Liam's hair. Thrilled that he had done this for me.

After an hour or so, I left the lounge to pee. The downstairs toilet had a long queue outside so I slipped out of the hallway and made my way up the thickly-carpeted stairs, looking for another bathroom. The house was huge and as I reached the top of the stairs, I realised there were doors everywhere. I approached the door at the far end of the corridor, my footsteps muffled on the carpet, before realising that it was ajar. Inside, the voices of Janet and Gerard drifted out, low but sharp. Instinctively, I stopped, something cold settling in my stomach. I knew I shouldn't be listening but I couldn't move.

'. . . all of the best champagne,' Janet was saying, 'and she was asking for more. That woman is an embarrassment. And frankly, the way Rachel knocks back drink herself, she's going down the same path.'

I froze. I was still clutching a shot glass. The tiara on my hand suddenly felt too tight, pressing against my scalp.

'I don't know what Liam sees in her,' Janet continued, her voice full of disdain. 'Always drinking, always talking back at school, apparently. She wants to be an actress, for god's sake.'

'He's young,' Gerard said dismissively.' Every boy has their bit of fun before they settle down. He's just sowing his wild oats and all that.'

My grip on the glass tightened, my breath catching. Just a bit of fun.

'Well, he wouldn't be the first one. Susan Lance told me she's been with all sorts of boys. Surely you want better for Liam than the loose daughter of the town drunk?'

It was as though she had physically slapped me. The town drunk's daughter. My ears rang loudly, but not loudly enough to drown out the rest of the conversation.

'They're just kids, Janet. It's not going anywhere. And her dad is a good bloke.'

'You're only saying that because you think you're going to get some money out of him.'

Gerard chuckled.

'Maybe. If all goes well. But I do happen to like the man. Even if he's never picked up a golf club.'

'Oh for Christ's sake, Gerard.'

I backed away from the door, blood roaring in my ears. I stumbled down the corridor and finally found a bathroom. I shut the door quietly behind me with shaking hands. I turned and gripped the edge of the marble sink, staring at my reflection in the mirror, my eyes glassy and my tiara askew.

Chapter Nineteen

Penny

Now

I pay for my drink and carry it outside, to where Liam and Tom are already sitting at the bar. The salty sea air brushes across my face as I walk towards them, the early evening sunlight shimmering off the waves. It is beautiful, but I can't help comparing it to the leafy buzz of Highgate, the only place I want to be right now. Yesterday still feels like something of a blur, almost making me question if it even happened. I haven't seen Rachel since she left the bar so suddenly, and she hasn't replied to any of my calls or my texts. I guess she's already back in London: I imagine her at home in her flat, with her handsome boyfriend. My stomach knots with jealousy.

Tom glances up as I sit down, the freckles dancing across his nose.

'We've been wedding planning I promise. We were just saying how concerned we were that the peonies might clash with our ties.'

'Oh very funny,' I say grumpily. I am too tired to laugh, too tired to pretend. 'I'm amazed you even know what a peony is.'

'I'm a learned man.'

'That's Tom-speak for "one of my girlfriends went on about them",' I shoot back.

'Isla did insist on fresh peonies in the flat, yes. But I thought they were lovely.'

Tom is trying to keep a superior look on his face and I can't help but laugh. I am still grateful that he is here. We broke up towards the end of university, yet we always stayed close, helped by the mutual friends we had both made. Liam, on the other hand, had drifted from us both, floating in and out of contact, until a few years ago when he and I reconnected at a uni reunion.

'So,' I say, turning to Liam and trying to sound casual. 'How did the talk at the law firm go?'

Liam and Tom exchange a look. Tom is no longer smiling. The air between us shifts; tightening.

'What?' I ask, suddenly on high alert. 'Don't tell me you didn't get it?'

This can't be happening. Liam had been at one of the best firms in London, how could he not have been offered a job at some small-town firm? This was a last-ditch attempt, before his dad, Gerard, can insist on him joining the family business. I don't want Gerard and Janet Haughton getting any more involved in our lives. Rowland & Associates was the only firm with a job going and apparently willing to offer Liam an interview. We need this.

Liam sighs. 'I got offered it. They're desperate to have me,' he adds in a mutter.

Relief washes momentarily over me. *Thank god.*

'Then what's the problem?'

Liam and Tom exchange another glance, which irritates me. Like they think I can't handle what they're about to say.

'Rachel Kingston works there,' Liam says finally, his voice flat.

My mouth falls open.

'What are you talking about? Rachel doesn't work there, she lives in London . . . she's an actor.'

Liam looks at me, his expression tight with frustration.

'Whatever she's told you is a lie. She's still here. In town.'

My stomach knots painfully.

'That doesn't make any sense. I looked at the firm's website. She's not on there.'

'She's a secretary,' Liam says bluntly. 'They aren't on the site.'

I slump back in my chair, the knot in my stomach tightening into something painful. She was lying?

'I told you, you shouldn't have met up with her,' Liam mutters, taking a long swig of his drink. 'I still can't believe you snuck off to see her. Rachel, of all people.'

'She did say she was between roles . . .'

'She's worked there for years, Pen,' Liam says. 'Hardly a break between roles. She lied to you.'

I fall silent, trying to process it. All this time, I thought Rachel was visiting town, just like I had told her I was. Neither was true. I had been stupid, caught up in Rachel Kingston once again. Tom lights up a cigarette, shaking his head.

'I thought she might have changed, you know? But it doesn't sound like it.'

'What did the guy you interviewed with say? Charles?' I ask. 'Did he know?'

Liam shakes his head.

'Charles moved here from Herne Bay and took over the firm about ten years ago. It's obvious he doesn't know . . .' Liam looks around for the right words, ' . . . what happened.'

'Which is weird, really,' Tom says, 'considering he's married to the one and only Sasha Kennedy.'

'You're not serious.'

Liam sighs and nods.

'Yep. Was there in the office with Rachel when I finished interviewing with Charles. I forgot how damn small this town is.'

'Is Sasha still hot?' Tom asks.

'I thought you were seeing someone?' I say indignantly. 'We've given you a plus one for her!'

Tom gives me a fake innocent look.

'I was just *asking* . . .'

'So the job . . .' I begin cautiously, turning back to Liam.

'I don't know what I'm going to do,' Liam says, shaking his head in frustration. He shifts beside me, rubbing the back of his neck. 'The last thing we need is Rachel Kingston involved in our lives. Not right now.'

Despite my anger and my frustration at the position we are in, I reach out and take his hand, desperate to prevent the feeling that everything is slipping out of our control. As I open my mouth to reply, a flicker of movement catches my eye from across the street. My heart skips a beat.

Is that . . . ? For a second, I swear I see her. Rachel. Standing there, half-hidden behind a lamppost, watching us. Her long brown hair gleaming in the sunlight. But then I blink, and she's gone. Yet I can't shake the uneasy feeling in my gut. *Was that Rachel?*

I force myself to look back at Liam. I think about everything that is riding on this. The empty savings accounts, the house deposit, our beautiful wedding. The last thing I want is to be back in this town, with the memories of our past thick in the air, and Liam working with Rachel. I want to be back in my flat with Clem, back at my office in Holborn. But we are out of options.

'You have to take it,' I say, eventually, the words heavy in my mouth. 'You don't have a choice.'

Liam stares down at his pint glass, his hand gripping it tightly. *How did we get here?*

Tom clears his throat, looking more serious than usual.

'You're just going to have to be careful,' he says, looking between me and Liam. 'I mean it. Rachel Kingston is complicated. We all know that.'

'Complicated?' Liam asks in disbelief. 'She's a hell of a lot more than complicated.'

Chapter Twenty

Rachel

Now

The sound of creaking wood echoed in the distance. The air, hot and humid. I remember that, I remember the air. Ahead of me, the Ferris wheel loomed, I could hear its metal arms creaking softly in the wind. Somewhere in the darkness, laughter echoed. My heart pounded in my chest as I moved. Looking for him. Looking for Liam. Then – glass breaking, a bottle smashing on the floor. More snatches of laughter. Until the air was broken by the sound of sirens.

I wake with a start, gasping for breath. *That night, always that night.*

The house is quiet as I get dressed and go downstairs. I find Mum asleep on the sofa in the lounge. The TV is still on, its flickering blue light casting shadows across the room. Her head lolls to one side, her mouth slightly open. Slowly, I pick up the empty bottle from beside her on the floor. I wonder how many more mornings we will do this dance for, until the day she doesn't open her eyes again.

It is another sunny day, but it does nothing to lift my spirits as I walk to work. My thoughts spin endlessly. Penny marrying *Liam*. The betrayal still feels fresh, like an open wound. Seeing them all together at Morley's yesterday. A spare chair next to Tom, empty. Were they talking about me? Surely Liam won't accept the job, now that he knows I work at the firm? My thoughts repeat on a loop, over and over.

By the time I arrive at work and settle behind my desk, I am in a foul mood.

'Everything alright?' Didi asks frowning across her desk at me.

'Fine,' I mutter. 'Just tired.'

Didi's eyes linger on me, sharp with interest.

'Nothing to do with the new recruit?' she asks, raising an eyebrow, her voice just a little too casual to me.

I glance quickly at her, my heart racing.

'What do you mean?'

Does she know something? Has she heard what had happened back then? She grew up on the other side of town, had never indicated she knew anything.

'Nothing,' Didi says, but I am sure there is still something probing in her gaze. 'I just thought . . . you acted a bit odd around him yesterday, that's all.'

'I was just pissed off at Sasha,' I half-lie, turning back to my computer so that Didi will stop talking. I am never usually this rude to Didi, but I have no capacity to be polite this morning.

'It's not anything to do with you knowing him?' Didi presses. 'Sasha said you went to school with him?'

My stomach tightens.

'We barely knew each other. It was just Sasha being Sasha.'

'Right . . .' Didi says slowly, still looking at me. 'But you have to admit, he's pretty impressive, right? You know, for someone choosing to return to this town. Don't you think?'

Her tone is light, but I can't shake the feeling she is fishing for something. *You're just being paranoid.*

'Sure,' I reply stiffly.

There is another pause after which Didi finally turns back to her own desk.

'By the way, Charles was asking whether you had finished going through the latest CPS disclosure in the McKenzie case yet.'

'Finished going through them?' I splutter indignantly. 'They only arrived yesterday!'

Didi grimaces sympathetically. Scowling, I pull my in tray towards me, where a stack of new documents arrived from the CPS the day before.

'He should have instructed a barrister by now,' I say irritably. 'What's the hold up?'

'Guess he wants to prove himself at all the hearings for as long as possible,' Didi says, rolling her eyes.

With a sigh, I pull the latest documents toward me and start sorting through the stacks of CCTV footage and surveillance evidence gathered from neighbouring properties, losing myself in the task. After the chaos of the past few days, the meticulous work of indexing feels almost soothing. I know the case inside out, know exactly what to look for, and the task demands my full concentration. Perhaps I'll be able to help find something that shows Shelly leaving on her way out to walk the dog.

A few hours later, Didi hands me a coffee, which I accept gratefully. I pause for a moment, arching out the cricks in my back and neck, before returning to the last few documents. So far, none of the neighbouring cameras have apparently shown anything from that night; the angles are all wrong, all unhelpful. As I near the bottom of the pile, something catches my eye. A corner of something sticking out at an odd angle. Not a legal document. I pull it out and my breath sticks in my throat.

It's a postcard. The vintage black and white photo of the town, looking out over the beach. The old fairground sits at the centre of the shot. The image is faded, the details almost blurred, as if time has worn the photograph down. The carousel is there at the heart of it, its once-vibrant horses frozen mid-gallop. The Ferris wheel dominates the skyline. Even though it is from a time when the fair was open, the image has an empty, abandoned look to it. The sky is too grey, the beach beyond too barren.

I flip the postcard over.

The back of it is blank. Bone white. The emptiness of it sends a chill down my spine.

'Rachel?'

I jump at Didi's voice, realising she has been watching me. Her expression is curious.

'Did you . . . did you go through these documents yesterday?' I ask, my throat dry.

'Not forensically, just enough to know they were for you. Why?'

I hold out the postcard to her, my hand shaking slightly. Didi frowns down at it.

'I don't remember this being in here. But if it was part of the post, I missed it. Maybe it's a marketing thing?'

'Maybe.'

She turns it over, examining it closely.

'Weird that there's no message. You would think a company would put an ad or something on here. And it must have been hand delivered. Maybe a friend?' she asks, handing the postcard back to me. Not wanting her to think I'm freaking out over nothing, I make a humming noise and shove the postcard into my desk drawer. I try to go back to my work, but it is almost impossible. My heart is beating, hard.

I know it's not from a friend in town: I don't have any.

The postcard is a reminder.

Or a warning.

Chapter Twenty-One

Rachel

2005

*T*he sea breeze tugged at my hair as Liam and I walked along the promenade. After the boiling hot sunshine of the past few weeks, the sky was now overcast and I couldn't shake the heaviness that had settled on my chest. I had been waiting since my birthday for Liam to do something to make our relationship official: ask me to be his girlfriend, change his MSN status, anything. But instead it felt the same as before and I kept replaying the moment I heard Janet's words at my birthday: the loose daughter of the town drunk. I hadn't told Liam about it. I didn't know if his parents had said anything to him. I glanced over at him, hoping to see some sign that things were all good between us. He looked perfectly relaxed, kicking a stone ahead of him like boys do, as if he didn't have a care in the world.

'I can't believe it's results day tomorrow,' I said, trying to break the silence. 'London is so close, now.'

Liam smiled, but I couldn't tell whether it reached his eyes.

'Yeah, it's crazy.'

I waited for him to say more, to share my excitement, to pick up the thread of the conversation, but he just kept walking, his hands in his pockets. The silence stretched on and I felt a familiar unease creeping in. I had thought that if I could get Liam to notice me, I would be the happiest girl alive. That it would secure everything for me. It never occurred to me that keeping him would be as hard as getting him.

'You're excited, right? About UCL?' I asked, though I already hated myself for asking more questions.

He shrugged, his voice casual.

'Yeah it'll be fun. A change, you know? Getting out of this town.'

The word change hit me like a punch. My stomach knotted and I had to fight to keep my smile in place.

'Yeah, I mean . . . we'll still be super close which will be cool. Just a tube journey. It'll be like now, but more exciting.'

Liam chuckled, but I was convinced the sound felt hollow.

'Sure it will.'

I waited for him to say something more, something sweet. Something reassuring. But instead he stopped and reached out, brushing a strand of hair away from my face, his fingers lingering against my cheek for just a moment too long.

'I had no idea you were such a worrier,' he said, softly. 'I thought Rachel Kingston was a bad girl. I didn't think you gave a shit.'

Was it a compliment or a criticism? I couldn't tell. But he was looking at me with a soft smile and the warmth of his touch against my cheek made everything else melt away. My heart lifted a little; but just as quickly, he pulled away.

'We've got to come back for the restaurant opening, too,' I said, having to hurry slightly to keep up with him. 'It's the first weekend of Sep—'

'Hey!'

We turned to see Penny and Tom walking towards us, arm in arm. They were laughing about something, their heads close together. So natural, so easy.

I forced a smile.

'Hey guys! What are you up to?'

Tom grinned.

'Liam told us you were here.'

I glanced at Liam, my heart once again sinking. He had told them to come meet us? I thought we were on a date. Just the two of us.

'Ready for results day?' Liam asked. He sounded more cheerful than before.

'I guess so,' Penny said, shrugging. I knew how anxious she was and I reached out to give her a reassuring squeeze, but Tom was already there, his arm wrapping around her shoulders.

'Don't be nervous, you'll have done great. You'll be saying yes to Durham in no time. And then I can visit every weekend,' he grinned. Of course. Tom had applied to Newcastle, just a short distance from Penny. I swallowed the bitterness crawling up my throat.

'And you guys will be in London together,' Tom said, punching Liam on the arm. 'Good luck squeezing into a single bed in halls, huh?'

Liam's smile wavered for a second and I tensed. But then he wrapped his arm around my waist and pulled me close, planting a kiss on my temple. 'We'll manage.'

His touch once again sent warmth through me, but it was fleeting, and I couldn't help but notice the slight awkwardness in his voice. Was I imagining it? Was he just being polite in front of Tom? Maybe Penny sensed the tension, because she reached out and linked her arm through mine, pulling me away from Liam and Tom.

'Hey, I meant to talk to you about something,' she said as we walked, her voice dropping into a soft, conspiratorial tone. 'Remember when we used to plan out the flat we'd share together? You wanted a water bed and I wanted beaded curtains across all the doors.'

Despite my anxiety over Liam, I couldn't help but laugh.

'Pretty sure you also wanted an inflatable sofa.'

Penny smiled, her eyes warm and excited.

'Well, if you wanted . . . I'm still up for it. I mean, as soon as I finish at Durham I'll move to London and we can get a flat together. We could maybe even find a house-share, that could be fun. Just like something out of Friends. What do you think?'

Penny's words caused a sudden lump to form in my throat. We had been so caught up in our own relationships recently I hadn't realised just how much I missed her and the comfort of our friendship. I blinked, trying to keep the sudden rush of emotion at bay. I suddenly felt hopeful about the future again.

'I'd love that, Pen.'

She gave me a quick hug and we walked slowly back towards the boys. When we reached them, Liam took my hand in his and gave me another quick kiss on my temple. Maybe I had been imagining his distance. Maybe I just needed to change my perspective and how I was interpreting things. Maybe everything was fine, after all.

Chapter Twenty-Two

Rachel

Now

'Everything alright?'

I tear my eyes away from my third check of the room to see Connor watching me, his eyebrows pulled together. Behind him, the seafood restaurant is noisy with Friday night chaos: waiters ferrying large silver trays of golden battered cod, scampi and chips to various tables. Every time the door opens, I glance up, my body tensing, relaxing only when I see it isn't Liam or Penny walking through the door.

'Oh. Yes, sorry. Miles away.'

'You've been miles away this whole time,' Connor says, putting his menu down and propping his elbows up on the jaunty fish-themed tablecloth. The single candle stub flickers between us as he moves. 'What's going on?'

'Nothing,' I say, quickly. Below the table, my knee is jiggling: I force my leg to be still. 'Just a long week at work.'

I don't want to discuss Liam, Penny or Tom, with Connor. Or with anyone.

'McKenzie trial still causing you grief?' he asks, his tone light but curious.

Despite my edginess, I raise an eyebrow at him.

'I told you, I'm not going to give you an inside scoop, Connor.'

He chuckles.

'I wasn't asking you to. You know as well as I do that she's guilty.'

'That's not true,' I say, frowning at him. Though I have always been firm about not discussing the case with Connor, I find myself seizing on the distraction, my bottled-up emotions needing an outlet. 'It's always the same old story. A younger woman has the nerve to marry an older man with money and she's immediately a gold-digger.'

'Only when the older man with money is attacked whilst he sleeps and there's no sign of a break-in,' Connor shoots back.

'It's not that simple and you know it,' I insist angrily, leaning forwards. 'It's about people making snap judgements. It's about her hair not being the right colour, or her clothes being too tight. People take one look and decide they know everything there is to know about a situation, without ever bothering to probe their own opinions. Their own prejudices.'

Connor looks surprised and I clamp my lips together. I've said too much. At least I didn't reveal her lack of alibi.

'Sounds like you believe her.'

'I don't have a view,' I say, trying to sound more professional, pulling back. 'I just want to do a good job on the case.'

The waiter comes over and motions to my empty glass.

'Another large white wine?' he asks, and I nod.

Connor declines a refill, his beer bottle still half full.

When the waiter has brought me a fresh glass, there's a lull in conversation. I try to think of something to say, but my mind keeps drifting back to Liam. To the postcard. It feels too bizarre to explain; childishly, I don't want to mention it out loud in case it seems more real.

'I forgot to ask, how was the old school friend you saw the other day?' Connor asks, taking a sip of his beer. 'Penny, right?'

I nod, surprised he remembered her name. Then again, he's a journalist: his mind probably works like a steel trap.

'She was fine,' I say, evasively. Then, before I can stop myself, I add, 'She's back in town for a while, actually.'

I don't say any more. Not that she's marrying Liam. Or that he is about to join the firm.

'Were you close, the two of you?'

'We were best friends,' I admit.

'How come you lost touch?'

'We just did,' I say, my tone suddenly sharper than I intended. 'Haven't you ever lost touch with a friend?'

'Sorry,' Connor says, letting out a soft laugh. 'I didn't mean to pry. I was just interested.'

There is another moment of silence, the space between us filled only by the dance of the candlelight. Then Connor reaches across the table, his fingers gently closing around mine. It's a simple, grounding gesture, that tugs me away from the spiral of my thoughts, but there's also an unfamiliarity to it that makes me hesitate.

'Actually,' he says, his dark eyes almost black in the low light, 'I think new relationships are far more interesting than old ones.'

Chapter Twenty-Three

Rachel

Now

The following Monday dawns in a haze of anxious fatigue. When I get to work, I spend the first hour jumping every time the door opens or the phone rings. I can feel Didi's eyes on me, but she doesn't say anything. Every time I open my desk drawer, the postcard with the image of the fairground pulls my gaze to it.

The office feels tense, as if something is hovering in the air just out of reach. I hear footsteps approaching, and I tense, but it is just Didi returning from grabbing a coffee. She gives me a curious glance before settling back at her desk.

'The new guy, Liam, was in early,' she comments, nodding upstairs towards the offices. 'Looked like he was already getting settled.'

My heart skips. Liam's here. Already. My stomach knows, a mix of dread and something else I can't quite place. The phone starts ringing and I quickly answer it before Didi can, needing a distraction.

'Rowland & Associates, how may I help you?' I ask, my voice tense.

'Is that you, Rachel? It's Shelly.'

'Yes, it's Rachel, Mrs McKenzie. How are things?'

There is a long pause and I start wondering if the phone line has gone dead, when I hear Shelly speak in a whisper.

'Awful.' I can hear the tears, thick in her voice. 'Someone's leaked some old photos of me, they're all over the internet. There are reporters outside Mum's house, I already feel like a prisoner. My brother Sam is the only person who's come to see me in days. All my so-called friends have gone quiet and I can't even speak to my own husband.' Shelly's breathing starts building, heavy into the receiver.

I know it's a case, I know it's a job, but anger suddenly floods through me at what she is going through. The case is spiralling into a full-blown media circus, all because Shelly is younger and more attractive than her husband. All because people love to demonise, to create a soap opera from people's actual lives. Her entire world is coming apart at the seams, being destroyed, and no one writing articles about her, or reading the articles, cares.

'Listen, Shelly,' I say firmly, my hand slightly sweaty on the receiver as I grip it painfully hard, 'everything is going be okay. Trust me. We're going to help you prove you're innocent, I promise you.' I know I shouldn't be making promises but I can't help myself.

'*How?*' Shelly asks desperately, and I can almost picture her free hand, running manically through her bleached hair. 'Charles doesn't seem like he has a clue! He just keeps asking me for proof of my alibi, which I don't *have*. Everything I've tried has been a dead end and the police are being fucking useless. It's like they don't want to help. No one *believes* me.'

'I'm going to go through the evidence we've had so far from the CPS,' I say, my own voice sounding almost as desperate as hers. 'There's inconsistencies, things that need looking at again. There *will* be something, okay? You have to trust me.'

I'm making promises I might not be able to keep, but I can't stand the desperation in her voice. At least she has family on her side, I remind myself. A mum and brother. It's more than I had.

'Can you just put me through to Charles?' Shelly says, her voice flat all of a sudden. 'I really need to speak to him.'

'Of course,' I say quickly, and I put her straight through to him. Her tone sounded like the fight had gone out of her. That wouldn't be good news; Charles needs her to fight.

'Imagine how scared that woman must be,' Didi says. I jump; I had almost forgotten Didi was even there.

'I know,' I mutter back, though on some level, I know exactly how scared she must be. Of what is to come. Of prison: that faraway place you think exists only on a TV screen. It's the kind of fear that keeps you up at night, gnawing at your insides. Keen to speak to Charles about Shelly, I pick up my completed index of the prosecution materials as soon as I see his phone line is no longer engaged and make my way upstairs. When I reach the top floor, I see Charles's door open slightly, but it's the other door that catches my eye. Just knowing he is in there sends a shiver down my spine. I walk quickly past his office and knock on Charles's ajar door.

'Come in,' Charles's loud voice echoes through the hallway.

I step inside. He is sat back in his chair, rubbing a hand across his forehead. I hand him the index I've painstakingly created.

'I've been through all the latest materials,' I say breathlessly, 'and I checked Street View on Google Maps. I think there's a couple of houses that could be worth double-checking with the neighbours to make sure they don't have any footage. I *think* they were missed, so if we can just . . .' But Charles hands the document back to me with barely a glance.

'Can you give this to Liam? I'm handing the McKenzie case over to him.'

'You're . . . you're what?'

At the tone of my voice, Charles glances up, irritably.

'Why do you think we hired someone of his calibre?' he says. 'The McKenzie case is the most important case we've had for years. A lawyer as skilled as Liam could be a lifeline.'

'But . . . Charles, I've done all the work on it,' I say, my voice high and sharp. 'You said I could attend all the hearings . . .'

'I'm sure if you want to attend, he'll let you go with him. All that matters right now is that we win this case.'

'But . . .' I begin again, knowing I am pushing it but unable to let it go. Liam of all people, swooping in and taking over. What does he know about defending a woman like Shelly McKenzie? 'Charles, surely with your qualifications . . .'

At this Charles finally looks at me properly, his eyes boring into mine with something like surprise. I never talk back to him. Finally he gives a low sigh and leans forward on his elbows.

'Rachel, Shelly McKenzie just threatened to instruct another firm.'

My mouth falls open. That doesn't sound anything like Shelly.

'W . . . why?'

'Her family seems to think that she needs a more . . .' he scowls and does quote marks in the air, ' . . . *prestigious* firm. A London firm. Not some high-street firm in a town no one has heard of. She says she doesn't want to go elsewhere, but unless we can come up with something to help her with her case, we're going to lose her. And frankly,' he gives a short, sharp cough as though the words are causing him physical pain, 'the firm can't afford to lose her. It's not been the best year. What with paying for Justine's maternity leave and Liam's salary . . . well, let's just say he might be our last hope.'

I stand there, unable to think of anything to say. I knew things had been tough the last year or two, but I had no idea the firm might be in trouble. And now Charles is pinning all of his hopes on Liam solving the McKenzie case before Shelly McKenzie takes her business elsewhere. After the work I've put into the case from the beginning.

'I just think,' I say slowly, 'that you should be careful. Liam might not be all he says he is. Anyone can impress in interview.'

'I think I can tell when someone is bullshitting, *thank* you,' Charles says, shortly. 'Was that everything?'

Seething, but realising there's nothing I can do, I turn and leave the room, clutching the index I made to my chest. I head to Liam's door, my heart beating louder with each step. I knock, my pulse quickening.

'Come in,' Liam calls.

When I open the door he is sitting behind his desk, looking immaculate once again. He looks startled to see me for a moment, then composes himself.

'Charles asked me to give you this,' I say, holding out the index.

'Rachel,' he says, his voice cautious. He takes the index but doesn't look away from me. The room is thick with tension. 'I don't know what to say. I had no idea you were still here. We all thought you'd be in London.'

You never thought about me at all. None of you did.

'You thought wrong,' I say coldly.

Liam's face tightens sightly. He rubs his hand over his jaw.

'Look, I don't want to make this difficult, Rachel. What happened . . . was a long time ago. Penny and I are just here trying to move on. We don't want any trouble.'

'From me, you mean?'

Liam studies me for a moment, as though he is trying to work out what to say.

'If you won't do it for me, at least do it for Penny. She's been through enough recently.'

The words sting, making me want to scream at him. *She's* been through enough? What about me? What about the last fifteen years? I swallow the anger, trying to keep my face impassive.

'Why here? Why this firm?'

'You don't own this town, Rachel. I've got every right to be here,' he says, his voice taking on an edge.

I want to ask him about the postcard, about so many things, but I don't know how. And even if I did, he would deny it.

Liam presses his lips together in frustration.

'Look, I know this is awkward. But I'm here to work, nothing else. So please,' he says, and this time his voice takes on a hard, warning, edge, 'leave us alone.'

Chapter Twenty-Four

Rachel

2005

*I*woke on A level results day with a thick head and a dry mouth. Checking my alarm clock, I saw it was past midday. Shit. I was late to meet Penny. One thing had led to another yesterday and me, Liam, Penny and Tom had joined up with some people from school on the beach, riding the end of the summer high. I swallowed back bile that tasted like cider and climbed out of bed. Thankfully I didn't have to worry about my grades. My place at drama school was set. This was just the final part.

When I eventually dragged myself to school, everyone else was already inside the library. It was weird walking through the school on a weekend, seeing people in jeans and trainers. I could hardly believe this was it. No more school. Inside the library, there were long trestle tables set up for results day and only a few brown envelopes left.

I spotted Penny with Liam in the far corner, and I hurried over to them.

'Rach!' Penny said immediately. She held out a brown envelope with my name marked on it. 'Where have you been? I picked yours up for you.'

'Thanks,' I said breathlessly, taking the envelope from Penny. Then I reached up and wrapped my arms around Liam, pulling him down for a kiss.

'Christ, you stink,' he laughed, pulling his lips from mine. 'How long did you stay out for last night, you piss-head?'

'A bit later than you guys,' I admitted. I pointed at the envelopes in their hands. 'Well? How did you both do?'

Liam looked happier than I'd ever seen him.

'I got three A's and a B,' he said, his face jubilant.

'Wow!' I squealed. 'You only needed three B's! That's amazing, babe.' I kissed him again.

'Not quite as good as this one,' he said when we broke apart. He shook his head at Penny who ducked her head, looking proud but embarrassed. 'Four A's, of course.'

As I watched him, something hot flickered inside me. His face was full of admiration, something Liam Haughton did not give out easily. Had he ever looked at me like that? I realised Penny was watching me and I reached out to give her a hug.

'Well done, Perfect Pen.'

Penny pulled away from me, her face red, and flapped her hands.

'Open yours!' she demanded.

'Can't I do it on my own?'

'Don't be daft!' Liam said. 'We've both done it here.'

'Fine.' I suddenly wasn't quite so keen to open mine, but I did as Penny asked and tore open the envelope. I slid the paper out with slightly shaky hands, nervous all of a sudden. It took me a few moments to register what the paper said. Liam and Penny were both watching me avidly and I thought again of the impressed way Liam had looked at Penny, with her four A's.

'Two A's and a B,' I announced, proudly. Penny's mouth dropped open.

'Seriously? Wow!' She craned her neck to look at my paper but I stuffed it back inside the envelope.

'You barely revised,' Liam said, laughing and putting his arm around me. 'Well done, babe. Not just a pretty face.'

I glowed under his praise.

'Are we still going out to celebrate?' I asked, feeling lighter. 'What time shall I be at yours?'

Liam's face dropped and his arm went loose around my shoulders.

'Oh, sorry Rach, did I not say? It's just family. I mean . . . my parents wanted to celebrate just us.'

'Oh.' I pulled away from him, my stomach doing small, uncomfortable flips. 'I thought it was both of us going?' I was sure he had originally invited me. I'd bought a new dress for the fancy restaurant Gerard had mentioned, on the outskirts of town. Penny caught my eye and pulled a sympathetic face.

'No babe, I never said that.'

I thought about what his parents had said about me the other day in their bedroom. Had they changed their mind? Told Liam not to invite me? Liam looked awkward.

'It's fine,' I muttered, still stung. 'Don't worry about it.'

I thought Liam might say sorry again, but instead he glanced at Penny, before letting out a long breath. For some reason this look made me feel uncomfortable.

'Actually, there's . . . something I need to tell you, Rach.'

Penny suddenly looked down at the floor, shuffling her feet. I tensed, suddenly wary of what was coming.

'What is it?'

Liam ran a hand through his hair, avoiding my eyes. 'I, uhh, actually applied to Durham as my first choice. I didn't tell anyone because I wasn't sure I'd get the grades, but . . . I did.'

It took my brain a second to register what he had said.

'I don't understand. You're not . . . going to London?'

'No, Rach. I'm going to Durham. It's a big deal, getting the grades. I just didn't think I would manage it.'

I blinked. We'd been talking about London for weeks. Now he was saying he was going to uni . . . with Penny? My chest felt tight, but I forced a smile, even though everything inside me was spiralling out of control.

'I know that. I just . . . I just didn't know.'

'I didn't tell anyone. Not even my parents. And well . . . we've not been together long, have we?'

'No. Of course. I get it,' I said, but I couldn't meet his eyes. Just then, Tom's voice cut through the library.

'Oi! You lot!'

He came bounding over, a huge grin plastered across his face.

'I got an A and two B's!' he announced proudly. 'Ready for Newcastle, baby!'

Liam clapped Tom on the back. 'Nice one, mate.'

Penny and Liam shared their results, and Penny threw her arms around Tom. Their enthusiasm was palpable but I barely registered it. Penny and Liam would be at uni together, close to Tom. I was going to be in London, far away from them. From Liam. What did this mean for us?

Liam, clearly sensing my mood shift, turned towards me, his eyes softening. He cupped my cheeks in his hands.

'Hey, listen,' he said in a low voice, 'London isn't that far. I'll come and visit all the time. And you'll be at Durham seeing Pen. It'll hardly be any different.'

Even though disappointment still churned in my stomach, the way he was looking at me made it harder to hold on to my upset.

'I promise,' he added, leaning forwards and kissing my forehead.

I wanted to believe him. I wanted to believe that even at Durham, I could hold on to him. But he had already pulled away, back to the others.

'Come on, let's grab a drink before we go home,' Tom said. 'Practice for Freshers' Week.'

Liam and Penny nodded eagerly and they started talking about pub crawls and fancy dress nights. They were all standing so close together and I couldn't help but feel like I was watching something unfold that I wasn't a part of.

Chapter Twenty-Five

Penny

Now

I shift on the armchair, trying to get comfortable, but the muggy air is making my head pound. Gran's conservatory is the coolest room in the house, yet it is still stiflingly hot. I think longingly of the cool interior of the kitchen at Clem's and my face screws up in a scowl. I am not used to being this hot, this *angry*. I always have it together, take satisfaction in things being logical, organised. Some people might say it's boring, but I have never understood how other people run around, constantly caught up in stresses they create for themselves that could easily have been avoided. Yet here I am, with everything completely slipping out of my control, trying to re-organise my beautiful, perfect, wedding, from London to *here*.

I reach for my ice-cold lemonade and check my emails. Nothing new. Nothing on our team chat, either. I hate being quiet at work and I have a suspicion it's because my team all went out for drinks last night. I would usually be there too, without fail. But this new situation means I'm temporarily working from home most of the week and already I feel disconnected from everyone else in the London office. They try to remember to dial me in for the team meetings but it's awkward and stilted being the only one and they forget I'm even there most of the time. I keep rewinding back through the last few months, trying to identify the point at which it all went wrong, the point at which I agreed to moving back here.

I reach for my phone and text Liam.

Head still hurting. Can you get me some painkillers on your way home? Xx

As I am holding my phone, a notification pops up on my screen: the cancellation charge from the London ballroom we had booked the wedding for. I baulk at the amount for something that never even transpired. I know we could have asked Janet and Gerard for the money for the wedding, but Liam and I both agreed we didn't want to owe them. It's bad enough that we're now around the corner from them.

I pick up my drink and take a sip, the ice cubes clinking in Gran's crystal-cut tumbler that all grandparents own. My thoughts drift to Liam as I await his response. He's not been himself at all since we returned to town, though that's hardly my fault. I know he misses our life in London as much as I do, and even though Tom has been trying to cheer him up by staying in town for a few days, I know he resents the fact that Tom still has a job and flat in London while we are stuck here. I take another sip of lemonade, thinking of Gran's usual 'When life hands you lemons, make lemonade.' But how are we supposed to do that, when nothing is going as we – as I – planned?

Liam has been in a doubly foul mood ever since he discovered Rachel was working at the same firm. *Funny, that we are all back here again*, I think. We all tried to escape, all planned bright and shiny futures, and yet some malevolent force has meant we're right back where we started, again. Like landing on a snake and dropping right back down the board.

I curl up tighter in the armchair, massaging my fingertips into my aching temples. My phone lights up on the small glass coffee table and I reach for it. Liam has replied.

Will get some after work x

That's it. No *'hope you're feeling better'*, no *'love you'*. What the hell is wrong with him? After everything I have sacrificed because of choices *he* has made, the least he could do is act grateful. Irate, I throw my phone onto the sofa, where it bounces and then disappears between two floral cushions. I should text Tom, he's still in town, and he normally gets me what I need. Then I stop, feeling a pang of guilt. Liam is my fiancé. Not Tom.

Only right now, my fiancé is holed up in a small crappy office with his school girlfriend. I think of the police interview fifteen years ago, just before I was due to go to Durham. The relentless stream of questions asked by the beak-nosed detective, the fear. My mum's stress. All caused by the hurricane that is Rachel Kingston.

Chapter Twenty-Six

Rachel

2005

The evening air was warm, the last streaks of sunlight fading into the horizon as we made our way down to the beach, the alcohol in our plastic bags clinking. The sound of the waves mixed with the distant laughter of the party ahead. I couldn't believe that everyone had their results and that we were onto the next part of our lives. Penny walked beside me, her voice trailing off as my thoughts drifted back to Liam. He hadn't messaged all day. Not a single text. I knew he was out with his parents, celebrating his results, but that gnawing sensation in the pit of my stomach hadn't left since he told me he was going to Durham. I hated admitting that I had planned a future in London with him, of meeting each other's friends, of parties, of seeing the city together. Handsome, popular, Liam, who had finally noticed me. I couldn't shake off the feeling that once he was at Durham he would forget all about me. How could I stop that from happening?

'You've barely said a word, Rach,' Penny said, her voice cutting through my thoughts. She was looking at me with a worried expression.

'I'm fine,' I said, quickly, not wanting to share what was going on inside my head. 'It's just been a bit of a mad day, that's all.'

'It'll be okay,' Penny said, gently, sensing my unease. 'I'm sure you and Liam will work things out, even if he's not in London. And anyway, there'll be plenty of guys at drama school. Hot guys. Liam Haughton is not the only boy on the planet.'

I nodded, though it did little to soothe my unease. What would Penny know? Her relationship was stable, secure.

My phone buzzed in my pocket and my heart leapt. Finally. But when I pulled it out, it was just a message from Dad.

Night going okay sweetheart? Don't forget, text when you're on your way home and try not to make too much noise, your mum's gone to bed early x

Annoyed that it wasn't Liam, I shoved my phone back into my pocket without replying.

'Who was that?' Penny asked, glancing over at me.

'Dad,' I said, trying to sound casual. I didn't want to think about Mum and her hangovers. 'Just . . . asking about the car he's thinking of getting me for my results.'

Penny frowned, slightly.

'I thought your dad said you didn't need a car in London?'

Shit. I shrugged, trying to keep my voice light.

'Yeah, but he's impressed with how good my grades were.'

Penny didn't have to know that Dad would never buy me a car right now regardless of where I was going; not with Mum's drinking spiralling out of control and the restaurant's finances on shaky ground until it finally opened in a few weeks.

The party came into view ahead, the flickering light of a driftwood fire casting long shadows across the sand, and the *sound of the latest Usher album playing from a set of speakers drifting across to us.*

'That's going to get the police called on us,' Penny muttered at the sight of the fire. 'I bet that's Isaac and his mates.'

We approached the fire where bottles of cheap cider and beer were being passed around. Sasha Kennedy's grating laugh filled the air. She was standing near the edge of the group, her blonde hair catching the firelight as she stood in front of a couple of guys from our class along with her best mate, Tara. When she spotted us, her eyes narrowed slightly.

'Oh hey you two, you made it,' she called out, as though it was her exclusive party.

'Afraid so,' I replied, sarcastically sweet. Her eyes narrowed. 'I thought maybe you would be busy practising how to play roles for drama school,' she said, her tone equally as sugary. 'I can give you some tips, if you like, on how to play a classy character. You might need the help.' Tara and the boys next to them sniggered. I felt heat rising in my chest.

'Thanks, Sash. I'll send you tickets to the premiere, one day. If you think the supermarket will let you off work?' I could feel Penny's warning beside me, but I didn't care. Sasha had always known how to push my buttons and tonight, I wasn't in the mood to play nice.

Before she could reply, Sasha's eyes flickered past me, and her expression changed, her smile turning coy. I followed her gaze and my stomach flipped when I saw Liam walking towards us. He hadn't noticed me yet, but his casual stride and the way he greeted everyone made my heart ache. He looked so good. I hated how much I wanted him to look at me the way he did that first night, on the restaurant terrace.

When he reached the group, he shot me a smile, but he didn't come over to me. Sasha sidled up to him before I could move. She flashed him a playful smile.

'Well, if it isn't the man of the hour,' she purred. 'Durham University. Impressive.'

Liam grinned, his arm brushing hers.

'Not as impressive as Penny's four A's, right?'

Was he trying to deflect Sasha's attention? Or was he complimenting Penny, again? Beside me, Penny laughed nervously, but my eyes were still locked on Liam and Sasha as she moved closer to him and he didn't pull away.

'Oh come on, don't be modest,' she said, her voice low and flirtatious. 'We all know you're going places.'

My skin prickled with irritation. I grabbed the nearest bottle of cider and twisted the cap off, taking a long drink to steady myself. Penny glanced at me, her expression uneasy, but she didn't say anything. Liam hardly seemed to have noticed that I was there. Or maybe he just didn't care. Tears welled in the back of my eyes.

My phone buzzed again: another message from Dad. I didn't even bother reading it, shoving my phone back into my pocket, my pulse racing with a mix of anger and hurt. I wanted to yell at Liam, to drag him away from Sasha and remind him that I was his girlfriend, not her. The laughter around me felt distant, hollow. Even with Penny by my side, I felt alone. I couldn't shake the feeling that everything was slipping away, out of my control.

I watched as Sasha leaned in closer to Liam, whispering something in his ear that made him laugh. Was he doing this on purpose? I threw my head back and took another long drink.

'Rach,' Penny said softly, nudging me. 'It's just Sasha. You know how she is. She's just trying to wind you up.'

But I wasn't listening. My eyes were still on Liam, watching the way he smiled at Sasha. And then he looked up for a moment and gave me a wink across the fire, his eyes flashing in the light. My heart leapt and I waited for him to pull away from Sasha, to come over to me. But he didn't.

Furiously, I turned away from them, bringing the bottle to my lips once again. In the distance, the rusted Ferris wheel loomed against the sky, its skeletal frame creaking in the breeze. Sasha laughed loudly again and I gritted my teeth. I wasn't going to stand around watching this. I grabbed Penny's hand and pulled her away from the group, taking out another cider bottle from our plastic bags.

'Come on, Pen,' I said loudly. It was time we had some fun.

Chapter Twenty-Seven

Rachel

Now

The heat of the fading sun warms my face as I stand looking out across the waves. To the right, further along the beach, the new fairground construction is well underway: lorries and vans are parked haphazardly in front of the old metal barriers that separate the fairground from the beach, and some of the scaffolding has already been taken down, revealing shiny new rides. They aren't messing around. I suppress a shudder.

To the left, a group of after-work swimmers are already in the water, their heads bobbing up and down like seabirds. Most of them wear caps and proper swimsuits, but I never bother with anything but my old swimming costume that is now worn in various places. I walk along the beach until I find a secluded spot, away from the main stretch of beach, but not too close to the fairground. Leaving my bag and dryrobe on the pebbled sand, I pick my way across the seaweed left by the slowly receding tide and walk straight into the shallow water without stopping. The water is colder than I expected, biting at my skin as I wade deeper. I welcome it. It's why I'm here.

As soon as I am out far enough, I dive beneath the waves.

The sounds of the beach are replaced with the familiar, disembodied quiet of being underwater, the only real noise the muted current. It is close to bliss, something I have relied on ever since Dad died, to heal my mind. It hasn't always been this way: the first time I discovered open-water swimming, I was so desperate to quiet the voices in my head that I hadn't cared whether I even made it back to the shore. But instead of drowning me along with my thoughts, it had proven an icy, desperately needed distraction. It's been my lifeline ever since.

I push myself forwards, focussing on nothing but my front crawl, letting everything else fade away. I know that as long as I keep the pier behind me and swim parallel to the shore without getting caught in any tides, I will be fine. I come up for air, taking a large gulp, before diving back under. The sunlight shimmers against the surface of the water and my muscles quickly begin to burn as I continue to kick my legs out behind me, my jumbled thoughts slowly untangling themselves with each new stroke. I try not to dwell on thoughts of Liam, or Penny. I have to concentrate on my own life, I have to somehow pretend that they do not exist. Penny already said the job was only temporary. And although I am angry about the McKenzie case, Charles does have a point: it makes sense to give it to Liam. It only really stings because it's him. *And what about the postcard?* An innocent mistake, perhaps. Something caught up in the post. That's all.

I turn my head, coming up for air and checking I am still parallel with the shore. That's when I see it. A figure, in my periphery. I freeze. A wave slaps me in the face, but

I barely notice it. The figure is standing right by my bag and towel. Too close. I blink a couple of times, convinced it is a trick of the light as the sun begins to sink below the horizon. But, no: the figure is real. *Just someone out on a walk. Admiring the view.* Yet something feels wrong. Something about the way they are standing, perfectly still, their head angled towards where I am treading water.

They're watching me.

A chill crawls down my spine. No, I must be imagining it. Someone has just stopped for a moment. Telling myself I am being stupid, I begin to turn back towards the sea, but as I do so, the figure moves. I pause, awaiting the relief that comes from the person calling to their dog, or moving on, but instead they bend down. My pulse spikes as I watch them reaching toward my bag.

'Hey!' I shout, but a wave crashes into me and I splutter, spitting out seawater. 'Hey!' I yell again, but I am way too far away and my voice is lost in the wind. The figure doesn't give any sign they have heard me, doesn't react.

I turn and begin swimming as fast as I can towards the shore, my heart pounding against my ribcage. I lift my chin to check where the person is. That's when I see them slowly straighten up and look back in my direction, as though they know I am watching. I put my head down and kick harder, my stokes frantic as I try to reach the shore.

After a few minutes, I finally reach shallow water and drag myself into a standing position. My breathing is ragged as I stagger up the beach, looking around wildly; but the figure is gone. I scan the beach. No sign of anyone: just a few people further down the shore, walking their dogs, their heads down as if nothing has happened. Was it one of them? My bag lies exactly where I left it.

I rush over to it, my feet slipping on pebbles, and drop to my knees beside it. I open it with cold, shaking fingers, and go through it, my hair dripping across the canvas fabric. My phone is still in the side pocket. My house keys are there. My purse. Everything is still there. I sit back on my heels, breathing hard. Did I imagine it? My phone screen lights up as I pick it up. No messages, no missed calls. It feels strangely warm beneath my hand, but perhaps that is because my skin is so cold. I am hit by the sudden urge to change the pass-lock for my phone, which I do with trembling hands. I straighten up and pull my dryrobe over my head, letting the adrenaline slowly ebb away. Despite the warmth of the evening, I am freezing, my swimming costume clinging to my skin. Shivering, I look around me: there are various sets of footprints, but they mingle with countless others. It is almost as though the person was never there.

Chapter Twenty-Eight

Rachel

Now

The office feels stifling today, the summer heatwave making the air thick, despite the two desktop fans Didi has set up to cool us down. All they do is push the warm air around, their low hum making my head feel even more sluggish, despite the two coffees I've already had. Neither of us speak much.

Just as I am staring, glazed, at my computer screen, willing my brain to focus, the door to the office swings open. Charles strides in, talking loudly, his tanned hands gesturing as he explains some legal point or other. He looks more relaxed than he has done for months. Liam enters behind him, looking as sleek and self-assured as ever, his tie perfectly knotted and straight. I once again notice, however, the circles under his eyes, his distracted expression. I stiffen and quickly turn back to my computer, pretending to be engrossed in something important. Didi, who has otherwise been quiet all morning, smiles brightly, tucking her hair behind her ear with a flash of her bright nails.

'You came back then,' she says to Liam, with an almost teasing smile. 'More fool you. Can I get you anything? Tea? Coffee?'

I glance at Didi with thinly-veiled disgust. What has got into her? Since when she did offer to make drinks for the lawyers? We have never been those types of secretaries.

'I'm fine thanks, Didi,' Liam says. 'Do you think you could help me with my calendar later, though? A couple of my meetings seem to have disappeared.'

'Of course,' she says brightly.

'Rachel,' Charles says, turning to me, 'can you dig up the Steven Larkins file from the basement for Liam? His appeal's been granted. Given Liam's credentials, I think this one will be a slam dunk for him.'

I nod stiffly.

'And make sure he's got everything he needs for the McKenzie case,' Charles continues, his face slightly flushed as he turns to Liam, 'he thinks there are some neighbouring properties that need a second look, don't you?'

Liam shrugs, his face the picture of humility whilst Didi gasps in admiration.

'I just noticed one or two houses where the owners were away and the police haven't done much to follow up. I'll call Shelly McKenzie today about it.'

'That's what *I* said,' I snap without thinking. All three of them look at me but I look at Charles, avoiding Liam's eye. 'I *told* you there were neighbouring properties missed.'

Charles frowns at me.

'This is an attempted murder trial, Rachel. It's not about point-scoring.'

I clamp my lips together furiously, angry tears stinging my eyes.

Charles sweeps from the room and Liam makes a move to follow him, but as he passes Didi's desk, he pauses. He gestures to one of Didi's many photo frames, a photo I know shows Didi with a group of school friends in Amsterdam.

'Hey, I know that guy. I used to play hockey with him.'

Didi blinks in surprise.

'Really? Damien?'

'Yeah, he went to the private school a few towns over. Rushmore House? Is that where you went?'

'For most of secondary school,' Didi says shrugging, though her face has gone a little pink. 'I changed to a state school on the other side of town after my parents divorced.'

'Oh, sorry,' Liam says, looking a bit awkward at this, but Didi waves her hand.

'Don't worry. We've all got past baggage, right?'

Liam glances at me, then just as quickly looks away. *Was that some sort of threat?*

'Right.'

Didi smiles at Liam as he leaves the room and I turn back to my own desk, taking a deep breath to calm myself. Everyone seems completely enamoured by Liam, none more so than Charles and his constant references to Liam's perfect credentials. He has swept into the firm like some sort of knight in shining armour . . . but still, something about all this doesn't seem to make sense. Why is such a seemingly talented lawyer back here? My thoughts race, frustration bubbling beneath the surface. Then an idea hits me.

I pull out my phone and unlock it. I am surprised to see that the battery is down to 25 per cent: I must have forgotten to charge it last night, I was so freaked out by the person watching me on the beach. I open my work email app. I don't want to do this on my computer and risk Didi seeing. Quickly, I search the recruitment email for Liam's previous firm and draft a message.

Subject: Personnel File
Good morning,
I hope this finds you well. We have a new joiner called Liam Haughton starting with us, however due to an IT systems error, we have lost his personnel file. Could you please re-send the reference you gave him, including the dates of his employment with you, up until his redundancy? We do apologise for the inconvenience.
Kind regards,
Rowland & Associates

I hit 'send' before I can second-guess myself, my heart pounding. It's reckless, but I need answers. There has to be something. And if I find it, maybe I can get him out of this firm and my life can return to normal. I fish in my drawer for a spare charger and plug my phone in. Then I stand and head towards the basement.

I pause for a moment at the entrance to the basement, steeling myself, before taking the narrow staircase down into the cool, musty air. The fluorescent lights flicker slightly as I make my way along the alphabetised rows to the section where the Larkins file is stored. I scan the labels for the right files, running my fingers along the dusty spines, until I find the right one. It is heavy and I have to heave it off the shelf. As I walk back along the row, my eyes flicker inadvertently to the far end of the shelf, where the 'K' files begin. I stop. My heart begins to pound as I walk slowly forwards, towards the spot where my own legal file should be. The file containing my statements from fifteen years ago and the things that I said. The things no one else should ever have been allowed to see.

It's gone.

Chapter Twenty-Nine

Rachel

2005

*T*he taste of cheap vodka burned my throat as I sat on the sand, but I didn't care. I was already countless drinks deep, the warmth spreading through me, so that everything was blurry and just a little bit brighter. My head spun with every movement. I laughed loudly at something Isaac said, even though I didn't really hear it. Liam and I still hadn't spoken and I was determinedly ignoring him. Not that he seemed to care: Sasha had been near him all night. That gnawing feeling had turned into something darker, more desperate, and I needed something to take the edge off.

I watched Isaac rummage clumsily through his backpack for more vodka. That's when I saw them: small cylinders wrapped in plastic. Fireworks.

'What are those?' I asked, pointing.

Isaac grinned.

'Just a bit of fun to end tonight in a bit of a bang.'

I stared at the fireworks for a second. Suddenly, a wild, reckless energy surged through me, fuelled by the drink, the rage, the fear of what was next, everything that was simmering beneath the surface. This was perfect.

'What are we waiting for?' I said, standing up too fast and staggering on the sand. Isaac caught me. 'Let's do it . . .' I looked around and my eyes alighted on the old Ferris wheel above our heads, ' . . . at the fairground.'

'The fairground?' Isaac raised an eyebrow, glancing nervously towards the others by the fire who were listening. 'You mean, break in?'

'It's hardly breaking in if it's been shut for years,' I said, my voice louder now. 'What's the point of doing them here? We can really let them off in there. Let's climb up the Ferris wheel and do it.'

Isaac blinked, but after a beat, he grinned.

'You're fucking insane, Rachel Kingston. I love it.'

I laughed and grabbed his arm.

'Come on then!'

Isaac shouted at the others and we started walking towards the old fairground, the rusted gates coming into view further up the beach. My footsteps felt too big, too fast, and I kept stumbling.

Behind us, other voices called out. 'Hey! Where are you guys going?' I heard people shouting to each other, gathering friends and following us, the excitement and danger of the fairground reeling them in.

When we reached the gates, I turned to the others, grinning; but they were all suddenly looking more hesitant. Rolling my eyes, I spun around and started climbing up the gate first, gripping the cold metal bars with shaking hands, the adrenaline surging through my veins. My dress rode up and there were a few wolf whistles, which I laughed at. Isaac swung his backpack on and started scaling the gates, too, faster than me. The *others all hesitated for a moment, but one by one they followed, laughing and yelling to everyone else to follow.*

Inside, the fairground was eerily quiet, the rides looming in the darkness like long-forgotten graves. The Ferris wheel stood tall and broken, its metal frame rusted and swaying slightly in the wind.

'Get the music!' someone yelled and, before I could react, the sound of pounding bass erupted from a speaker. Suddenly, everything became more electric, the darkness vibrating with energy.

Isaac had already made his way through the weeds to the base of the Ferris wheel. He grinned at me, his face dimly lit by the glow of the moon.

'Ready?'

I put my hand on the Ferris wheel frame, when a voice cut through the night.

'Rachel, stop!'

I turned to see Penny running towards me, her face flushed, her eyes wide with panic. Tom followed close behind her. 'You can't be serious. This isn't funny, anymore. You're going to get us all in trouble setting those off.'

'Oh come on, Pen, it's just a bit of fun.'

'This isn't about fun, Rachel. You need to stop this,' Penny insisted. 'You're going too far.'

Suddenly, Penny's rational, self-righteous attitude made me want to scream. I could see it in her face: that same disapproving look she always used. The one that said she was better. That her boyfriend, her grades were better.

'Oh please, afraid to break a rule for once in your life, Perfect Penny?' I said, my tone dripping in sarcasm.

Penny took a step towards me.

'You're just doing this to get Liam's attention. And for what? He was never planning a future with you. You know that right? Just let it go.'

Her words cut through the vodka-induced haze like a punch to the gut.

'What did you say?' I asked, slowly. 'What do you mean, he was never planning a future with me?' Penny's eyes widened, and I realised. 'You knew, didn't you? About Durham?'

I looked over at Tom, who was looking just as guilty.

'And so did you? You're both supposed to be my friends and you never said anything.'

'I'm sorry, Rach,' Tom said quickly. 'You just . . . you can just be a bit. Caught up in Liam. We thought it was best coming from him, not us.'

'We were just trying to protect you,' Penny said, taking a step back. 'We knew you were thinking about the future with Liam, about London . . .'

'Protect me?' I spat. 'I can protect myself and I can plan my own future, thank you very much. You're not the only one who got good grades, Penny.'

'I know you failed, Rachel,' Penny suddenly snapped. 'I saw your results. Stop lying.'

Her words hung in the air between us, sharp and cutting. I stared at her, my chest heaving, the heat of anger and embarrassment mixing with the alcohol in my blood.

'Please, Rach, don't do this. Don't you remember what that fortune-teller said? You're the one pulling the thread. You cause your own destruction.'

The Funfair

Through the vodka-induced haze I registered a sense of fury at Penny I'd never experienced before. Perfect Penny, going to Durham with Liam.

'So now the stupid fortunes are real? You've got a bright shiny future, and my life is going to be ruined? Thanks, Pen.'

'That's not what . . . I didn't mean . . .'

Tom grabbed Penny's arm.

'Come on, this isn't worth it. You're both drunk.'

But I wasn't listening anymore. I just shrugged as Tom pulled Penny away and turned back to Isaac.

'Let's light them up.'

Isaac hesitated for just a moment before nodding. We began to climb the broken, rusted frame of the Ferris wheel, and all the while I tried to drown out the pain of Penny's revelation.

As we reached the top, I could see the beach and the sea stretching out below us, the dark water glittering under the moonlight. Isaac fumbled for a moment with the fireworks and then, with a loud crack, the first one shot into the sky, exploding in a burst of red and gold. The sound echoed through the night and the fairground was suddenly illuminated, casting long, eerie shadows over the abandoned rides, as everyone below cheered. I looked down at them all and that's when I saw him. Liam. His face was lit up in a golden burst of light. The image of the fortune-teller's tower of cards suddenly flashed into my mind, everything teetering on the edge of collapse. And then, just as quickly, the moment was gone, swallowed by the crackling fireworks and the darkness.

Chapter Thirty

Rachel

Now

I struggle through the rest of the day until five thirty finally rolls around. Didi chatters on in the background but all I can do is grunt back at her. I can't stop thinking about my legal file. It's been down there for years; Liam is the only person with any motive to take it. Why? What is his plan? I knew, I *knew* that there would be trouble if he ever came back to town. And now he's here in the same office with me, with people who know about me, about my life.

I rinse mine and Didi's tea mugs and begin packing up my bag, just as Charles walks into the office, followed by Liam. My gaze roams over his bag, slung over his shoulder, but of course I can't see any indication as to whether he has my file.

'Oh good, I've caught you,' Charles says, when he sees me. 'Can you leave my papers out for tomorrow? The Jameson trial has been moved to nine a.m. because they're a judge down in the afternoon. Typical.'

I pause, my hand on my bag handle. None of the papers are ready for the Jameson trial: I should have done it today, but I was too distracted, and thought I had all of tomorrow morning.

'Sure,' I say, forcing a smile. 'No problem.'

As I sit reluctantly back down again, Didi jumps up and grabs her bag.

'I'll walk out with you both.' She waves goodbye to me and falls into step with Liam and Charles, letting the door swing shut with a sharp click. I grit my teeth as their voices start to fade away.

It takes me all evening to get the papers ready for Charles and when I eventually stand up to leave in the deserted office, my back aches from being hunched over for so long. The office is completely silent now, the dim evening light casting long shadows across the room. I trudge upstairs to leave the bundles on Charles's desk before locking up.

By the time I get home, the house is shrouded in darkness. When I open the door, the house is eerily silent, and the familiar feeling of dread steals over me. I flick the hallway light on, but the switch clicks impotently, none of the bulbs coming to life: the trip switch must have gone, or else something has messed with the power. The heavy air clings to me as I walk into the lounge, expecting to find Mum passed out on the sofa, but the room is empty. My skin prickles with unease as I move through the darkened rooms. In the kitchen, the curtains are pulled back and I can just about make out the shadowy garden beyond. There is nothing here, either, just stacks of dishes and glasses on the side by the sink. The house seems to be holding its breath, waiting for me to find her.

I walk upstairs, my footsteps creaking on the stairs. The dread I felt when I first opened the door increases, pressing against my chest as I reach Mum's room. I expect to find her in bed as she so often is, dead to the world, sometimes with her shoes still on. But when I enter the room, it's as dark and empty as everywhere else. *It's fine*, I tell myself firmly, *she's often out late*. Not that this thought is of any comfort: I hate knowing she might be sat, drunk, on a bench somewhere, or worse.

I return downstairs and check the fuse box using the light from my phone, but it all looks fine. A power cut, then. Power cuts are disorientating: the air feels too thick, too still. I walk slowly into the kitchen, feeling the habitual pull of small motions that are momentarily pointless: reaching for a light switch, using the kettle, turning the TV on. It's like the walls are pressing in; everything too dark, too quiet.

I pour the remnants of an almost-empty bottle of wine into a glass and pace the kitchen, unsettled by the dark, the silence, and my own racing thoughts.

Suddenly, there is a noise from somewhere outside the house and I freeze, my grip around the wine glass tightening. A fox shriek, I think. It shrieks again and the sound goes straight through me, high and screeching. I glance towards the back doors, trying to shake off the chill the shriek sent through me. I lift the wine glass shakily to my lips and as, I do so, there is a loud *snap* from somewhere beyond the kitchen. *What was that?*

Putting my wine glass down on the table with a soft clink, I walk towards the kitchen door and peer down the hallway, to see the shadow of someone on the other side of the glass. I know immediately that it is too tall to be Mum and my mouth goes dry. I try to locate the source of the snapping sound, but it is quiet, again. Just the shadow on the other side of the door. Had they knocked? Had I missed it?

Against my better judgement, I walk down the hallway on slightly weak legs. Taking a deep breath, I turn the latch and open the door. Muggy, pre-thunderstorm air greets me, warm as the heat from a hairdryer. But otherwise, the porch is deserted. The lack of streetlights makes the shadows more impenetrable than usual. I take a step outside and peer around, but there is no one to be seen. Exhaling loudly, trying to cleanse myself of my irrational nervousness, I close the door firmly. I take a step and hear a soft rustle on the doormat. Bending down, I see a flyer beneath my shoe and release a shaky laugh. It was someone out flyering. The snap was just the snap of the letterbox. *A bit late, to be doing it at this time*, I think, but relief still courses through me, until I turn the flyer over and stop smiling at once. My hands tremble as I look down at the brightly coloured print.

The Funfair Returns! Grand Reopening!

My breathing comes in short, sharp breaths and I suddenly worry I am about to have a panic attack. I've not had one in a long time. Not since a therapist taught me how to breathe through them, from my abdomen like a balloon, and not through my chest. *Is this a coincidence? Someone posting this flyer through the door this late at night?* I can feel my mind taking me somewhere I don't want to go, not here, not now, in this already dark hallway. Back to that summer, where the grass turned yellow in the heat, back to that night where we were supposed to be celebrating exam results but some insidious force changed all that. *The neighbours*, I think. I can ask them if they had a flyer. Just to put my mind at ease. I turn around and once again wrench open the door. Too late, I realise there is someone standing there: I stumble back, heart pounding.

'Woah, Rach,' Connor says, his face appearing out of the shadows. 'It's just me.'

I back away into the hallway, letting Connor through the door.

'What are you doing here?' I ask, trying not to let my fear sound in my voice.

Connor holds up a packet of long, tapered candles.

'I thought you might need power-cut supplies. I brought wine and a battery pack, too, in case you need to charge your phone.'

'Thanks,' I say, surprised at his thoughtfulness. I lead him down the hallway and into the shadowy kitchen where I bin the flyer and then fetch a dusty candelabra from the days when my parents had actual dinner parties, and a box of matches. I plug my phone into his charger and we sit down at the table with a glass of wine each, the candles between us. Connor's face looks ghoulish in the flickering light. I try not to think about the flyer in the bin.

'You seem jumpy,' he says.

'I'm fine.'

'Are you? You don't seem yourself.'

'Just been busy at work,' I lie. 'The McKenzie trial, you know . . .'

'Really? It seems like you've been off ever since you bumped into that old friend of yours.'

I glance swiftly at Connor but his face is hard to read in the candlelight. He has always been straight-talking, but this divergence into my past has thrown me off course. We have never gone here, before.

'I really don't know what you're talking about.'

Connor sighs.

'And what about Liam Haughton?' He circles the rim of his wine glass, then looks up at me. 'Your ex-boyfriend? What about him?'

Chapter Thirty-One

Rachel

Now

Connor's eyes look black in the candlelight, the skin beneath them sunken. There is a sudden tension in the air, that seems to press like a weight on my chest.

'What do you mean?' I ask, my voice sharp. This is not Connor's territory, not his right. For once, I find myself wanting my mum to come home, to end this conversation. 'There's nothing to tell you about Liam Haughton.'

Connor shakes his head, his eyes never leaving mine.

'I know, Rach. I know what happened back then. When you were eighteen. Why you acted so strangely when that Penny girl showed up at Morley's the other day.'

My mouth has gone very dry. The events of that night, the days after it, are etched into my brain like carvings in a tree, weathered over time, yet the deepest scars remain.

'How do you know?' I manage. My voice sounds distant. Not my own.

'I'm a journalist.'

Suddenly, I am angry: the stress of the last few days, the lack of sleep, the paranoia that someone has been watching me, all come crashing down upon me like a wave. I am on my feet before I know it, the feet of the chair scraping loudly in the silence.

'And you think being a journalist gives you the right to invade my privacy?' My voice rises. 'How *dare* you go around poking your nose into my past.'

Connor's eyes widen and he looks taken aback.

'It wasn't like that,' Connor says, quickly. 'Someone at work mentioned it when they heard Liam Haughton was back in town. They assumed you had told me about it. So I looked into it. I just wanted to know what they were talking about.'

'Then you should have *asked* me,' I say, my voice now practically a hiss. 'Like a normal person. Not gone behind my back and looked it up.'

It's happening again. It doesn't matter how hard I try to keep the past locked away, eventually it always comes out. And when it does, they all look at me differently. But with Connor, I find it hurts more. It isn't until now – faced with the possibility of him walking away – that I realise I have begun to feel things I never wanted to feel.

Connor gets to his feet too, facing me across the table. I wait for him to pick up his battery pack and leave. To look at me the way so many others in town do. But he doesn't. He comes over to me and unexpectedly wraps his arms around me.

'I can't believe everything you've been through,' he murmurs against my hair.

The shock of his sympathy runs through me. It is the last thing I expected. I pull away and look up at him.

'You don't . . . blame me? For what I did?'

His eyes soften in the light of the candles.

'Not everyone in this town is small-minded.' He leans forward and plants a kiss on my forehead. 'What happened?' he asks, gently.

'If you've looked it up you already know what happened,' I say, wearily. 'You already know why I don't have any friends. Why Charles was the only one who would hire me. I'm the town's pariah.'

Connor gently tugs me back over the table and we sit down.

'I want to hear it from you. If you're willing.'

There is a long silence as I try to work out whether I am ready to tell him. Part of me wants to run, to lock this part of my life away and never think about it again. But how can I? Liam and Penny are back and ever since then, things have shifted. I can't pretend that nothing is happening. If Connor is going to hear it, I want him to hear it from me. Not rumours from people who weren't there, who don't know the whole truth.

Connor is waiting patiently, his expression calm. He isn't judging me. At least, not yet. I exhale, my hands trembling again, and fold them in my lap, gripping my own fingers tightly.

'Fifteen years ago,' I begin, each word feeling like it's being pulled from some deep cavern. I pause, my throat tightening, my mind already swimming back to the fragments of that night. 'I had it all. Then I lost everything.'

Chapter Thirty-Two

DC Rainer

1 September 2005

*D*C *Andrew Rainer was tired and irritated. It was the hottest summer he could remember and the damn shirt he was expected to wear as a DC was straining at the collar and, if he was honest, around the gut. He was starting to resemble the oft-depicted cliché of detectives in films. All he needed now was to start eating donuts. Not that he would get a chance at a snack any time soon: he already had two suspects to interview, their lawyers clamouring about holding times and unfair arrests. But first . . . he entered Interview Room 3 and sat down next to PC Marina Thompson who had already set out a jug of water and plastic cups. Unlike the other, more clinical interview rooms in the station, this room had a window and the walls were painted a soft beige. The chairs were cushioned, set loosely around the table to feel less formal. It was designed to be calming, comforting, but it was still an interview room and the two-way mirror on the wall behind them reminded everyone of that.*

There were three other people already in the room: a thin-faced lawyer called Richard Sanders that DC Rainer had met countless times; a lean, middle-aged man with a kind, but anxious, face and finally, a teenage girl with thick, dark brown hair that gleamed and reminded Andrew of a horse he used to pass in the field near his childhood house. The girl looked to be around the same age as his Charlotte and sat with her hands twisted in her lap, her eyes constantly darting to the mirror on the wall. Her expression was difficult to read, which was saying something, given how many interviews he had conducted.

'. . . is DC Andrew Rainer,' PC Thompson was saying in her low, calming voice. She was already known for her skills in the Sexual Offences Investigation Team: people trusted her, opened up around her. He got the feeling it would be needed today.

'Right then,' DC Rainer said, ignoring Richard Sanders and focussing on the girl. 'Shall we get started, Rachel?'

Once Rachel Kingston confirmed that she was happy to be recorded, they began. DC Rainer watched her as she spoke, trying to take in every detail, every movement. She glanced over at her dad constantly. They had offered to speak with Rachel alone – it was unusual to have a lawyer there, though parents often stayed – but she had said no, she wanted him to stay. She spoke in a quiet, but steady voice.

'It happened on results day. It's a tradition to celebrate down at the beach.'

DC Rainer knew exactly what night Rachel was talking about: the night that a group of teens had broken into the old, abandoned fairground. They had had to send a few officers down after complaints of some fireworks being set off. PC Thompson gave an encouraging nod, to indicate Rachel should continue. She seemed better now that she was talking. More comfortable.

'Everything was normal, at first. Just drinking down at the beach. Then we . . . ended up in the fairground.'

'Whose idea was it to enter into the fairground?' PC Thompson asked.

DC Rainer caught Rachel's eyes flicker towards the two-way mirror, then. Just for the merest of moments. Her first tell.

'I don't know.'

Rainer said nothing, knowing that silence was golden whenever it came to interviewing.

'I guess it was just one of those stupid ideas that seemed really funny at the time.' She shivered and appeared to rub the goosebumps on her arms. 'Later on in the night, my boyfriend Liam said he wanted to talk to me. We were messing around, being silly. We went into the old Funhouse. We found this room, which had an old bed in it.'

'What's Liam's full name, Rachel?' PC Thompson asked, gently.

'Haughton. Liam Haughton.'

PC Thompson glanced quickly at DC Rainer and he knew why. This wasn't good. Gerard Haughton was what some people called a 'hard-nosed businessman'. Others called him a bully. Whatever the label you chose, he owned half the rental properties in town and had serious influence over its residents. The lawyer now made sense to Rainer, too.

'Please, continue, Rachel,' PC Thompson said.

'Liam and I somehow ended up on the bed. We were kissing. I told him I loved him. It was the first time I'd said it. He started saying stuff . . . like he was sorry for being such a dick. Sorry for lying to me. He had lied about the uni he was going to. And he was always doing thoughtless stuff. He'd been out with his family all day and he hadn't messaged me, so I'd been upset. He'd been flirting with Sasha Kennedy all night, *too. I thought maybe he was finally realising what he had. He said other stuff too . . . his hands were on me . . . but then my head started spinning and I began to feel sick. It hit me out of nowhere and I just wanted to go home.'*

Dread stole over DC Rainer, or perhaps it was intuition. He had the sudden desire to walk out of the room, to just get up and leave. Not have anything to do with what he was about to hear, because he was still human, no matter how many cases he had dealt with, and his daughter Charlotte was still the same sort of age as Rachel. But he remained where he was, trying to ignore this shift in the atmosphere.

Rachel took a deep, shuddering breath, and her dad reached out and took her hand.

'You can do this, sweetheart.'

'We can break whenever you need. No rush,' PC Thompson said swiftly, but Rachel shook her head.

'No, I'm fine, I want to get this out. I told him that he didn't need to say sorry, that everything was fine. I guess I was still upset but I wanted to make up. Go back to normal. He started being all sweet then, cuddling me and kissing my neck and at first I tried to go along with it. But I was starting to feel really dizzy. I had drunk about half a bottle of vodka and I just . . . I told him no, that I needed water. I stayed where I was, just like staring at the wall, curled up, trying to breathe, to stop myself from throwing up. But then I suddenly felt him behind me and he suddenly started doing it again. He pressed my face into the bed and held me there. I could barely breathe. The mattress smelt foul. And I kept trying to say no, but he said I wanted it. I tried to push him off, but he was so much stronger than me and in the end, I just froze. I waited for it to stop . . . and

eventually it did. He just left me there and walked off. I came out of the Funhouse and he acted like nothing had happened, as if I might not have remembered. But I do.'

She looked up then, and her eyes were narrowed.

'I told him I loved him. And then he did that.'

There was a long pause following Rachel's story. She picked up the plastic cup of water next to her and took a sip. Out of the very corner of his eye, Rainer could see PC Thompson was looking quietly impressed. She was fast forwarding, as she always did, planning the way this might go down. And Rainer could tell that she thought Rachel would be an impressive witness. Articulate. Strong. But there was a hell of a long way to go between now and a possible trial. Not least the prospect of interviewing Liam Haughton, with Gerard Haughton no doubt breathing down their necks.

DC Thompson glanced, very briefly, at him. Her expression mirrored his own. This was going to be an incredibly difficult case to prove. A classic he said / she said. Against the most powerful family in town.

Chapter Thirty-Three

Rachel

Now

Connor's face is still over the candles, but his eyes are open a little wider than normal, his gaze intensely focussed on me. The candlelight sharpens his expression. Finally, in the ensuing silence, he speaks and his voice cracks a little.

'Jesus. I mean, I heard the general . . . but hearing it from you, like that . . .' He lifts a hand to rub his forehead, as though trying to make sense of what he's just heard. 'So you took on the Haughton family?'

'I tried to.'

'What do you mean?'

'Well, if you've been speaking to people, you know that I dropped the charges. It never went anywhere.'

Connor frowns. 'My colleague said that you didn't just drop them. That you claim to have made them up. Why would you have said that? You made the town turn against you.'

'They were against me anyway, Connor. Everyone who heard about it thought that I was some jealous girlfriend. That's what Liam told everyone. Drunk Lizzy's psycho daughter,' I say, not even bothering to suppress my bitterness.

'But, still, telling the police you made it up when you didn't . . .'

'Why does it matter?' I ask, sharply, anger flaring up within me. 'None of that matters anymore.' My head is starting to throb from the wine and the lateness, the sheer emotional exhaustion. I am spent: I don't want to go into it anymore. I don't want to think about what happened after that police interview, after word got out, the parts I haven't told him. The parts I've never admitted to anyone. I've told him enough.

'Sorry, I just . . . I'm just trying to make sense of it all. What you went through.' Connor pours himself more wine with the air of someone trying to distract themself. My heart is thumping. I can't decide whether I want him to stay or whether I want him to leave. Reliving it all is exhausting.

'And Penny and Tom,' he continues slowly after a pause. 'They didn't believe you?'

'No,' I say, feeling the weight of their betrayal all over again. 'I dropped the charges and the next thing I knew, they were gone, off to university. My so-called friends disappeared without a backwards glance. Not a word from either of them, even after Dad died. Nothing.'

'And now Penny is marrying Liam.'

I nod and close my eyes for a moment. The silence hangs between us.

'What are you going to do about work?' Connor asks, eventually. 'You can't stay there.'

'I can't just leave.'

'Rachel . . .' Connor leans forward, his voice urgent. 'He's a predator. A criminal. You can't . . . I mean, surely you want to be as far away from him as possible?'

'Of course I do,' I snap, pressing the heels of my palms against my now aching temples. I debate telling him about the postcard, the legal file . . . but he's already looking so horrified, I decide against it, for now. 'I hate every moment of it. It's not that simple, though. The bills need paying and I've almost paid the mortgage off. Mum doesn't work. I can't just drop everything.'

'What about your dad? Didn't he leave you any money?'

I let out a soft, humourless laugh.

'No. Quite the opposite.'

'What do you mean?'

'He left us with nothing. He quit his job and re-mortgaged the house just before he died. Sunk everything into a restaurant that never even opened. It wasn't his fault,' I say defensively, seeing the look on Connor's face, 'he was always sensible. A bit too sensible, Mum always said to him. But opening a restaurant was his dream and when I turned eighteen, he finally decided to go for it, funnelled most of his savings into it. He died days before the grand opening.'

'And all the money he put into it was lost?'

I nod.

'Mum went to see Gerard Haughton about it,' I say. 'Liam's dad.'

'I know who Gerard Haughton is. Why did she go to see him?'

'To ask him whether he would give us some money. Seeing as he was Dad's business partner.'

'What did he say?'

'He said no. Told Mum it wasn't his fault that Dad had been irresponsible with all his money, not taking out any protection. Mum asked Gerard why he hadn't told Dad to do that at the time. Dad had been relying on Gerard to be the one who knew what to do when it came to the business. Gerard just said that Dad's naivety wasn't his concern. Acted like he was some idiot who got himself in trouble.' I clench my fists, a fresh wave of anger crashing over me. 'As though Dad would have known what he was doing; he worked in IT at the council all his life. Gerard was the one who persuaded him to open the business in the first place.'

Connor slowly shakes his head, his face filled with sympathy.

'Jesus, Rach. You must really hate the Haughtons,' he says, quietly.

The rage that has simmered for years surges to the surface and I nod.

'I do.'

Chapter Thirty-Four

Rachel

Now

That night I lie awake staring up at the ceiling, the humid air clinging to my skin. Though it is not here yet, I can sense the storm is coming, creeping closer by the hour. Connor lies next to me, his breathing steady and deep, in contrast to my racing thoughts. It is the first time I have ever let someone stay over, and it's strange having him here in the bed beside me. So close. I cannot tell if I am relieved or terrified by it. I let out a slow breath and roll over, trying not to wake him. The house is quiet, save for the faint creaks and groans of the old walls in the wind. Then I hear it: the unmistakable sound of the front door creaking open. I tense immediately, listening.

Mum's home.

I hear her shoes clatter against the wooden floor in the hallway, the uneven shuffle of her steps. She stumbles, muttering something under her breath; I hear the thud of something being dropped. I squeeze my eyes shut for a moment, trying to block it out, hoping Connor doesn't wake up. He doesn't know this side of my life. How deep mine and Mum's damage runs. I hold my breath as Mum staggers up the stairs . . . then, at last, the door to her room creaks and closes. Connor shifts beside me, but he doesn't wake up. I close my eyes again, willing sleep to come.

When I finally drift off for a few hours, I wake to find Connor propped up on one elbow, watching me.

'Morning,' he says, his voice husky from sleep.

I give him a tired smile, my head thick from the wine last night and lack of sleep.

'Morning.'

'Sleep okay?'

'Not really,' I admit. 'It wasn't you, or anything. I'm just . . . not used to sharing a bed.'

Now he is awake I don't know what to do with myself. He brushes a strand of hair off my forehead. His touch is gentle, but I still feel the awkwardness lingering between us from this new intimacy.

'It's nice waking up with you,' Connor says, as though he can read my thoughts and is trying to reassure me. 'I didn't realise your hair was so curly.'

'It's just the heat.'

He stretches, looking around the room. I try not to think about how my bedroom must look to him: the yellowing woodchip wallpaper peppered with holes from old posters, the corkboard full of old ticket stubs and cards I never even glance at anymore, the dusty piles of CDs on my school desk. The room is frozen in time. Like me.

'You don't have a sister, do you?' Connor asks, pointing at a photo on the corkboard that is just visible from behind an old birthday invitation. I almost laugh.

'That's Penny. She dyed her hair dark brown for a while.'

I hadn't even registered that photo was still there: I hid all my frames after it happened, not wanting to be reminded of my old friends. The photo shows me and Penny on holiday with her parents when we were fifteen, head-to-toe in knock-off brands from the Spanish market, our noses burnt. A deep sense of longing steals over me. Penny and I had laughed constantly on that holiday, getting tipsy from sangria her parents let us have at dinner, seeing who could handstand the longest in the water. I loved going on holiday with Penny. It was like being part of a normal family.

'Are you close with your family?' I ask, not wanting to think about these happy moments with Penny. Connor and I haven't spoken much about our families: he seemed to take my lead when I never mentioned Mum or Dad.

Connor shrugs.

'Relatively.'

I wait, but he doesn't say anything else.

'Is that it? You go off and google my past, but I don't get to hear anything about yours.'

Connor looks sheepish at this reminder.

'I don't mind telling you, it's just not very interesting, that's all. I'm close with my mum. Less so with my dad, but we still get along. I didn't see him very often growing up. He was always working.' He rolls over and checks his phone. 'We'd better get going. Come on, I'll drive you to work.'

Connor drops me off on the way to his office. He leans in to give me a quick kiss, and I catch Didi watching through the window. She raises her eyebrows suggestively as though I have done something scandalous. I half-smile back at her, allowing myself to enjoy this small flicker of normalcy.

But as soon as I enter the office, reality hits. Shelly McKenzie is standing in the main reception area with Liam and Charles, holding something small in her hand. I approach slowly, trying to understand what's happening. Shelly's face is flushed, stripped of her usual make-up.

'I've done it,' she's saying breathlessly to Charles and Liam. 'I've found my alibi.'

She glances over at me, her face full of wild hope. Closer, I can see that the object in her palm is a small SD memory card.

'How?' I ask in disbelief.

'One of my neighbours.' She looks back at Liam. 'I did what you said, I went and spoke to them all, again. When he was originally asked by police to review his CCTV, it was all wiped. Held in the cloud or something, he said, and he only has a seven-day recording subscription. But I made him double-check it yesterday and when he did, he realised that the camera comes with a physical memory card, too. Which holds footage from the past six months. The police totally missed it.'

'You're saying there's footage from that night?' Liam asks.

Shelly nodded.

'Yes. I've only glanced at it, I was so desperate to get it here, but it shows me leaving the house the back way, just like I said. And then someone entering the house at the time of the attack, just after. It's a bit dark, it'll need that enhancing thing, but it's clearly not me, it's so much taller.

And they use the spare key we hide around the back.' She frowns for a moment, a look of concern crossing her face fleetingly. 'I don't know how they knew about it.' Then she shakes her head and her trembling smile returns. 'I can't believe it was missed.'

'Excellent work, Mrs McKenzie,' Charles says, looking like he is fighting to keep his delight under control. Shelly beams but shakes her head.

'It's all thanks to Liam. You were right to make me speak to everyone again. I think you might have just saved me from going to prison, I really do.' Her eyes fill with tears.

'That's why we hired him,' Charles says proudly, clapping Liam on the back. 'I knew he would solve this case in a heartbeat. It barely took him a day!'

Liam shakes his head as though he is being modest and a hot spike of anger bursts through me. *Of course. The hero.* I should be pleased for Shelly – and I am – but I can't stand to see everyone beaming at Liam in admiration. He takes the memory card from Shelly and promises to sort out the next steps. She leaves the office, looking tired but elated.

'Great,' Charles says, clapping his hands together. 'Let's get on with it, then, shall we?'

They leave the room and I walk over to my desk, my good mood from this morning evaporating as quickly as it came. For one moment, I had felt normal. Almost happy. But there is nothing normal about my past or my present and being back in the office is a reminder of all the things that are wrong. Including what Liam is doing with my legal file. I glance at the dark, looming clouds, watching as the first few raindrops begin to spatter against the window.

The storm has arrived.

Chapter Thirty-Five

Rachel

Now

I have never felt so intensely relieved to get to five thirty. I cannot believe it has only been a week since Liam joined, less than two weeks since Penny unexpectedly appeared at that bar. I am exhausted, both mentally and physically. Connor is out of town this weekend, seeing friends. I decide to go home, cook something from scratch for once, and have an early night. I normally hate weekends spent rattling around the house with Mum: now, I am craving the two days away from the office.

As I pack up my things, Didi, who already has her bag over her shoulder, makes a move towards the door.

'I'll see you tomorrow at the party, right?' she asks. My stomach knots with dread. It's the last thing I want to do, but her expression is hopeful and I can tell she really wants me there. Maybe it would be good for me; maybe meeting new people from a different part of town who know nothing about me would be healthy. Didi is still waiting for my answer, lingering by the door.

'Sure, I'll be there, Dee.'

A smile breaks across her face.

'Great! Bring an umbrella.'

I leave the office a few minutes after. It feels much later than five thirty due to the dark storm clouds: fat raindrops intermittently drop onto the pavement and thunder rumbles in the distance. I put my head down and hurry in the direction of home. When I pass the row of shops halfway along the promenade, I can't help but glance at Dad's old restaurant, the familiar knot tightening in my chest. Lost in thought, I don't see the person coming towards me until we almost collide.

'Sorry,' I say, before realising who it is. 'Oh. Hey.'

Penny does a double-take when she sees me, her perfectly styled eyebrows lifting in surprise.

'Hey,' she replies, breathlessly. 'I didn't see you there, sorry.'

There is an awkward pause. My heart is still beating from being so close to Dad's old restaurant, and the memories of him stir up memories of that summer, of Liam, of Penny. I've not seen Penny since the day I met her at Morley's, or since Liam started at the firm.

Penny shifts her weight.

'Are you okay?' she asks after another long moment. I nod, but it is clear she doesn't believe me. 'Listen, I don't suppose you fancy a drink? It's Friday night, after all.'

I hesitate. I have a choice. There is a line being drawn in the sand and for some inexplicable reason, this feels like a pivotal moment; as though I am deciding whether or not to step into the old fairground all over again. I could decline and go home, cook dinner. Have an early night free from the ghosts of my past. Or I could let whatever this is between us play out. I think of everything that has happened since Liam returned, the unanswered questions. My legal file.

I smile at Penny.

'Where shall we go?'

We choose a small pub tucked down a side road off the promenade. It's a slightly run-down place I wouldn't normally go to, but there aren't many options around and the impending rain drives us inside. Penny orders a bottle of rosé and we retreat to a small corner table. She pours us both a glass.

'Cheers. To no plans on a Friday night,' she says as we clink glasses. There is a small pause.

'So . . .' Penny begins. 'I guess . . . we're both back here.'

'Looks like it. Not exactly the plan, was it?'

Penny's mouth twitches.

'Not *exactly*.' She looks up at me with an indecipherable expression. 'So, you're not an actor?'

I shake my head. I can't exactly lie, anymore.

'I stayed in town.'

'I . . . I didn't know. I always thought you'd gone to drama school. That you were living in London.'

'No, I never made it to drama school.'

'I'm sorry, Rach,' she says, her voice barely above a whisper. 'For everything. For the way that night turned out. For leaving town. For Liam. Everything.'

I swallow, remembering the hurt. The betrayal of her leaving. But I don't want her to know how deeply my scars still run. Not when she's marrying *him*.

'I'm sorry, too.'

'Do you . . . regret what happened?' she asks, tentatively.

There is a pause.

'Every day,' I say quietly.

We both sip our wine for a while, lost in thought.

'What about you?' I ask. 'Why have you moved back?'

'Well . . . Gran's not well, like I said. And Liam was made redundant. All things considered, we thought it would be a nice change. A bit of a recharge, you know?'

She shrugs, her smile bright. I watch her as she takes a sip of wine. She was always the planner, the one who had everything perfectly laid out in front of her. To hear her allude to things not going to plan feels off. But isn't that what happens to most of us? Things don't work out the way we expect them to?

'How's Liam finding things?' I ask, trying to make it sound casual.

'You probably know better than I do,' Penny replies. 'He's been working late all week, I've barely seen him. I thought his new boss would go easy on him the first week, at least.'

This pulls me up: Liam has left the office before me every day. I know, because I've been waiting for him to go before I leave, not wanting to accidentally walk out with him. Has he been telling Penny he's been staying late? Why would he lie? Knowing that whatever I say might get back to Liam, I shrug.

'Guess he just wants to make a good impression.'

'I'm glad. He needs . . .' she stops midway through her sentence. 'He's really pleased to have the job, I mean. London was so high-pressure.'

She suddenly throws back the rest of her glass and grins at me.

'Didn't you drive here?' I ask dubiously, knowing that her Gran's house is the other side of town.

'So?' she replies, with a laugh. 'Since when did you worry about drink-driving?'

It hits me in that moment just how little I know about thirty-four-year-old Penny. I have stored a snapshot of her in my mind, something to refer back to. She was the one who wore glasses when she first arrived at school, the quieter, more sensible one. The one who asked me what we should do each weekend, who checked the lip gloss shade with me before she bought it. Sitting here, however, I am suddenly caught by an unsettling feeling of change; that things have shifted and I am hanging on to an old, teenage version of Penny that no longer exists. Adult Penny suddenly sits outside the framework I have for her, having lived fifteen years without me.

We talk about mundane things for a while: Penny's job, Connor, the weekend's storm. Our glasses of wine disappear quickly.

'Look who just walked in,' Penny suddenly whispers.

I crane my neck, just in time to see Sasha Kennedy weaving her way through the throngs of after-work punters. Though she always takes care in her appearance, she is even more dressed up than usual, in a tight blue dress and deep red lipstick, her hair blow-dried in blonde waves. She looks around expectantly before heading to the corner of the bar closest to us.

'Wonder who she's meeting?' Penny says. 'Date night with her husband?'

'Charles wouldn't be seen dead in this pub,' I reply.

Sasha looks around again and her eyes alight on us in the corner. She does a double-take, her eyes flickering between the two of us. Then she gives us a look that can only be described as a sneer and turns back to the bar.

'Did you see the look on her face?' I ask.

'She's *so* weird,' Penny replies, leaning forwards. Suddenly we are eighteen again and gossiping about people in our class. She gasps. 'Maybe she's having an *affair*.'

I take another sip of wine, my head happily woozy.

'She wouldn't dare. In a town this small? It'll be all over the hairdressers by the morning,' I giggle.

'Maybe she's just scouting the place out for husband number four?'

'I think that guy next to her was interested? Drinking the bitter.'

'He's at least ninety, he'd have a heart attack if she even looked at him.'

We both dissolve into tipsy giggles. When we've stopped laughing, Penny gets up and orders another bottle of wine, though I am only on my second glass. She smiles at me, her pale cheeks flushed in the warm pub.

'I've been meaning to ask you, Rach. Is it . . . weird, me marrying Liam? When he was your . . . you know. You were together.'

I don't know what to say to this. Surely the weird part was my allegation, not the fact that we were together?

'I mean . . .' Penny continues, her eyes a little glazed. 'You were just so into him. Your first love and all that. Remember all the secret missions we went on to stalk him?' She giggles and takes another drink of her wine.

An odd feeling passes over me.

'I don't remember.'

Penny smiles benignly at me.

'God, I've missed you Rach. I know everything got fucked up back then. But can we just . . . start again? We've got so much to catch up on.' She pours yet more wine into our glasses.

'I want to know *everything*.'

'So do I,' I reply, the odd feeling still lingering. 'So do I.'

Chapter Thirty-Six
DC Rainer
2005

*D*C Rainer and PC Thompson arrived at the front door of the three-storey Victorian townhouse. It was the exact kind of house that young buyers were going mad for, with large bay windows and stained glass in the door. They featured a lot on Homes under the Hammer, where the buyers would pull up red swirly carpets to expose the original wooden flooring underneath. Old, draughty, but it was the character that was important, apparently. This particular house was clearly well cared for, with a neat front lawn and modern guttering in place of the old lead style on other houses along the street.

PC Thompson knocked using the round brass knocker, then took a step back.

'Not looking forward to this,' she muttered under her breath. He didn't reply, but internally he agreed. It was a sticky part of the job.

After a minute, the door opened to reveal a middle-aged woman who was clearly beautiful, but the effect was marred somewhat by the ratty pink dressing gown she wore and her bloodshot eyes.

'Can I help you?' she asked in a croaky voice, looking the two of them up and down. It wasn't most peoples' reaction *when they found two officers on their doorstep. They usually asked if anyone was hurt.*

'Mrs Kingston? Can we come in?' PC Thompson asked, in her most polite voice. Elizabeth Kingston hesitated: Rainer knew it wasn't her first dealing with the local police force. She was well known to them, mostly for minor disturbances. Disorderly conduct, that sort of thing. Sad, really.

'It's about Rachel,' PC Thompson added. At the mention of her daughter's name, Elizabeth Kingston sighed and took a reluctant step back.

They followed her down a long hallway and into a large sitting room with the same outdated, matching three-piece suite his own mother had had, with frilly skirts at the base. Elizabeth gestured at them to sit down and then went to call Rachel. She didn't return to wait with them. A few moments later, the eighteen-year-old Rachel walked in, closely followed by her dad, with Elizabeth bringing up the rear. All three of them sat down together on the sofa, Rachel on her dad's left. It was obvious, as it had been when she gave her first interview, that Rachel's dad John was the protective parent. His jaw was tight but he made an effort to give Rachel's hand a reassuring squeeze. She stared directly at Rainer, but did not speak. He once again had the impression of a teenager far older than her years. Or at least, the look in her eyes was. Rainer looked away first.

'Well?' John Kingston asked, looking between the two officers. 'What's the update? Have you arrested him?'

Rainer cleared his throat. 'I'm afraid not, Mr Kingston. It's not that simple. We did interview Liam, in the presence of his father and uncle.' His uncle, some hot-shot lawyer from

London, had made life very difficult indeed, not to mention Gerard Haughton's omnipotent presence. He had prowled back and forth, barely concealing his snarl. Rainer had found him every bit as arrogant as everyone always said. He still wasn't sure what he thought of the boy, Liam.

'And? Did he admit anything?'

'He was mostly advised to answer no comment. However, he did give a prepared statement about his side of the story. He accepts that he did enter the Funhouse room with Miss Kingston – Rachel – as she describes that night and that they did kiss and cuddle on the bed. He also confirmed Rachel told him that she loved him.'

Rainer watched Rachel's parents look at one another. Rachel continued staring at him, unblinking.

'However, Mr Haughton states that things went no further than that. He is alleging that Rachel was extremely drunk and he began to feel uncomfortable when she said she wasn't feeling well. He left the Funhouse to find her best friend, Penny, but that shortly afterwards the police arrived, following the reports of trespassing on the fairground.'

Rachel continued to stare at Rainer, but she began picking her thumb cuticle repeatedly.

'And . . .' *Rainer hesitated.* 'He also stated that you were not his girlfriend.'

At this, Rachel suddenly moved for the first time. Her face coloured.

'He said . . . I wasn't his girlfriend?'

'He stated that it was very early on in the relationship, but that in his opinion . . . the emotions were somewhat one-sided.'

There was a long pause. Rachel's eyes had gone oddly blank, Rainer thought. As though of all the things that Liam Haughton had reported, this had affected her the most.

'That's it?' John Kingston asked, his face going red. 'So he just denied it? Said nothing happened?'

'That is his version of events at present. We've also spoken to,' he checked his notebook, 'Sasha Kennedy and Isaac Evans, who both confirmed that they were with Liam just before the police turned up and that he was looking for Penny to go and help Rachel. There is no available CCTV from the night, so I am afraid we have nothing to corroborate anyone's version at this stage. We are also aware that everyone was inebriated to some degree or other.'

To John's right, Elizabeth Kingston gave a small snort.

'Inebriated. Can't you lot just say drunk? They were all off their faces.'

John gave his wife a sharp look, but didn't say anything.

'So what are you saying?' Rachel Kingston finally spoke, her voice hard and emotionless. 'Is that it? It won't go to court?'

'Well, not necessarily. We still need to finish investigating. Interview both you and Mr Haughton again, more formally. We need to go over every detail of that night in far more detail. Make sure there is nothing missed.'

Rachel's eyes flickered for a moment, before her face became a mask, once more.

'However,' Rainer continued, 'we want to be open with you. At the moment, there is very little to go on, very little that the CPS would consider if we presented the case to them. Because of the time that passed between the night in question and your report, there is no medical evidence we can use. There are no eye witnesses, apart from those who claim to have been with Liam and who say he showed no signs of having just committed an assault. No forensics from the beach. The reality is . . . it's his word against yours.'

'And who's going to believe her word?' Elizabeth Kingston said in her hoarse, slightly-too-loud voice. 'Against the town's golden boy? This is the Haughtons we're talking about.'

Rainer couldn't exactly disagree with her. The Haughton name was enough to tilt the scales, before anyone looked at this family that was clearly strained before any of this started.

'It is, unfortunately, the reality of many of these types of cases,' PC Thompson explained softly. 'But that's not to say we aren't going to continue our investigation and ensure we've not left a stone unturned.' Even to Rainer's ears, she didn't sound hopeful. The mood in the room was grim: he was keen to get out.

They were just standing up to leave when Rachel blurted out: 'Wait.'

They all turned to look at her. Her face was pale and she was moving her jaw back and forth, as though she was building up to say something. Eventually, she spoke.

'That wasn't the first time. He's done it before.'

Elizabeth Kingston briefly closed her eyes. Rainer and Thompson glanced at one another. Then, wordlessly, they sat back down again.

Chapter Thirty-Seven

Rachel

Now

I wake on Saturday after my evening out with Penny to an acrid smell that I know immediately is something bad. Panic sharpens the groggy haze of my hangover as I sit up and look over the edge of the bed. I recoil when I see a pile of watery sick on the rug, with undigested chips in it. *Chips?* I don't remember getting chips. My mind scrambles back over the night before. I remember a third bottle of wine: but everything after that is a blur, and that scares me. I don't normally black out. Not anymore, not like when I was younger. Now I pride myself on knowing when to stop, on keeping things clear in my mind. Only things are slipping, like I am coming apart at the edges, and I don't know how to stop it. My thoughts snag on Penny marrying Liam next week. Unease coils tightly. *Liam.* Is he the figure on the beach? The shadow I keep seeing behind me? Or am I just being paranoid now he is back?

A wave of nausea surges and I curl up on my side, riding out the nausea with my eyes squeezed shut until it passes. Is all this stemming from what happened back then? I picture Liam's eyes roaming over the pages of police interviews, taking in the truths, dissecting the lies. *He said / she said*: that's what the tall, large-nosed detective had called it back then. But that made it sound almost equal: two opposing statements, and that wasn't the truth. The truth was that the Haughton name would always carry more weight than the Kingston name in this town. Something is going on. Is Liam just trying to mess with my head, make sure I don't try to cause some sort of trouble? Or is there more to this? My head spins with questions, theories piling up one after the other.

After another twenty minutes of dozing, I finally peel the duvet off me, wincing at the pounding in my skull. My mouth is bone dry and grainy, as though I have swallowed a mouthful of sand. The curtains are still wide open and the clouds that have been gathering over the past few days look blacker than ever. The room feels hot and oppressive.

As I swing my legs out of bed, I am surprised to see that I am still wearing my work trousers from yesterday. A sense of unease tightens in my chest: it has been a long time since I had a night I couldn't remember, a night I had to piece together from morning-after clues. I wonder if Penny knows anything.

Avoiding the pile of sick, I stand up and cross the room, relieved to see my handbag on the floor by my desk. I fumble inside and am even more relieved to find my phone, which is nearly out of charge, but seems to be intact. The time on the screen is almost one o'clock in the afternoon. I have lost a whole morning. My pulse quickens as I unlock the phone. My banking app shows an online transaction to the local kebab shop at one fifteen in the morning. Urgh. There is also a message from Penny, sent at eleven twenty:

The Funfair

Just got home, let me know when you're back. Had a great time!!!! Xxx

I stare down at the message, my stomach knotting. If Penny got home just after eleven, where was I until one fifteen? Self-loathing steals over me and I toss my phone on the bed, my stomach roiling. I know better than to try to replay the events from the night before – it never helps the hangover – but it's hard not to start raking over everything that I might have said to Penny in the pub, to wonder who got the third bottle and when. Did I say too much? *Stupid. You lost control.*

For the rest of the day, I lay low. I hear Mum moving around the house and the clink of a bottle against a glass but I keep my door firmly shut. I ignore my phone and clear up the sick, then take a long, hot shower, trying to shake off the unease. Outside, the thunder rumbles ominously in the distance and rain begins to patter heavily against the windowpane, but I keep the curtains open. Inside, I curl up in bed re-watching *Emily in Paris* on my laptop, trying to sink into a shinier world full of fresh pastries and new clothes, where people's only concerns are their tangled love lives.

By the evening, my stomach feels settled enough to eat something. I walk downstairs in my pyjamas to the dark kitchen and flick on the light. Outside, there is a rumble of thunder and rain lashes against the glass of the patio doors. I start making myself some cheese on toast and am slicing the cheese when Mum stumbles in. I know immediately, with a sense of dread, that she isn't in a good place. Her eyes are slightly out of focus and she looks erratically around, as though she has lost something.

'Where is it?' she snaps.

'Where is what?' I ask wearily, the knife hovering over the block of cheddar.

'The photo of me and your dad. At the beach. The one I was looking at the other day.'

'That was of me and dad,' I correct her.

'No,' Mum says insistently, her voice rising, 'the one of *me* and him. I showed it to you. It was in the photo albums.'

Her voice is slurred, her face blotchy. The rain intensifies, hammering against the glass.

'I don't know the one you mean, Mum. But I'm sure it'll be there somewhere. You're just not looking properly.'

'It's not!' Her voice is sharper now, more accusing. 'I know exactly where I keep it. You've taken it, haven't you?'

'Don't be ridiculous,' I sigh. 'Why would I do that?'

'Because you were always jealous of me and your dad. Couldn't stand that he loved me so much. You hated that photo of us because it was special.'

I grit my teeth, gripping the knife harder.

'So special it wasn't in a frame?'

Mum's eyes narrow. She takes a step towards me.

'Your innocent act might have fooled your dad, but it never fooled me,' she snarls. 'Trust me, I'll find that photo.' Then she turns and storms out of the room. I hear her stomp back into the living room and begin rummaging around once again. I return to my measly tea, my heart beating uncomfortably.

Ten minutes later, I finish my toast and sit at the table, staring out of the back doors at the storm-darkened gardens, as dark and impenetrable as the blank spots in my memory from last night. My thoughts seem to swirl in the blackness outside, caught within the wild brambles that have grown so high in Dad's absence. Then, I freeze. For a moment, I am sure I saw a flash of light.

I blink, then lean forwards, my heart thudding. It was faint, like the flicker of a torch. I hold my breath, but the night remains as black as ever. Then comes a loud knock on the front door and I jump, my hand clattering against my plate. *Who could that be?* Mum hasn't gone out: she's been in the lounge the whole time. I get up to answer it, dread prickling at my skin.

When I open the door I find two male uniformed police officers standing in the porch. Their hats gleam wet with rain under the porch light.

'Good evening. Is this the Kingston residence? Do you live here?' one asks. I nod, my mouth dry.

'Yes, I live here with my mum. Why? What's going on?'

'We've had a report of a domestic disturbance. The caller reported witnessing an argument between two women.'

My mouth drops open.

'I think you've got the wrong house. It's just me and my mum here.'

'The report mentioned one of the women was brandishing a knife.' The officer looks up from his notepad, his eyes steadily fixed on mine. 'Have you and your mum had an argument tonight at all?'

'Well . . .' I falter. 'Well no, not exactly. Just a bit of a bicker. It was nothing serious.'

'Was a knife involved?'

'No! I mean, I was holding a knife, but it wasn't like that, at all.'

'Mind if we come in? Just for safety reasons you understand, to check you're both safe.'

I nod, helpless, and let them in. I stay in the hallway as they search the house, their boots wet and heavy on the wood floors. They move through the house, inspecting every corner. They enter the lounge and I hear them questioning Mum, who sounds as confused as me. She doesn't like the police. Five minutes later, they re-emerge from the lounge. They are too big and hulking for the hallway, that only ever contains me and Mum.

'Everything seems fine. Looks like your mum's had a bit to drink, so just keep an eye on her, yeah? And call if you need anything.'

I nod, unable to speak, embarrassed beyond belief.

'Oh, and this was on your doorstep.'

He holds something out to me. When I see what it is, my stomach turns. It is another funfair flyer. *Is this just a coincidence?*

The officers leave with a sharp click of the front door. I walk slowly back into the kitchen, my heart pounding, the flyer clutched in my cold hands. I know Mum didn't call the police, I would have heard her and she would never call them voluntarily, given how often they piss her off when they find her drunk in town. My gaze drifts to the back doors leading out to the garden. The garden that is completely blocked from sight from the neighbouring properties. So that the only way that someone could have seen the argument between us is if they were standing right there in the back garden. Watching us.

Chapter Thirty-Eight

Rachel

2005

*A*s soon as I opened my bedroom door, I could hear them. Their voices echoed from the kitchen, where the door had been left open, just enough for their words to drift through.

'This was a mistake. You should never have called the police.' My mother's voice, sharp and bitter.

'Keep your voice down, Lizzy.' Dad's tone was low, but firm. 'It was the right thing to do. You're her mother, you should know better than anyone . . .'

'It's because I'm her mother that I know it was the wrong thing to do. What good has it done her? Done us? She was just about to leave home for god's sake. Why couldn't you just have let it be?'

'Let it be? She deserves justice, he deserves to be locked up.'

A sharp clink: the sound of a glass being set down too hard.

'You think it's that simple don't you, John?' Mum's voice is filled with disbelief. 'Typical man. Do you have any idea what they'll do to her in court? Any idea what it takes for a woman to come even close to justice?'

'Of course I know it's not easy . . .'

'Not easy?' Mum laughed again, even more sarcastically. 'If this case even gets to court, they will tear her apart. Pick *apart her entire life. Have you thought about that? About the cross-examination from Liam's lawyers? It will be brutal. They will take every single thing that girl has ever done or said and put it on display. And Rachel . . . well . . . she's not exactly reliable, is she?'*

There was a long pause. I froze by the door, feeling like the air had been sucked out of my room.

'What's that supposed to mean?' Dad's voice was soft, defensive.

'You know exactly what I mean, John. She has a way of . . . rewriting things. Of making things suit her narrative even when things . . . aren't so clear.' Mum's voice lowered, but somehow it cut even sharper. 'You know what she's like. She believes what she tells herself, even if it isn't always the truth.'

A hard lump formed in my throat all of a sudden that made it difficult to swallow. That wasn't true. How dare she talk about me like that to Dad?

'She's our daughter, Lizzy,' Dad said firmly, after a tense silence. 'She wouldn't lie about something this serious. Not this.'

'I'm not saying she's lying,' Mum shot back. 'Not exactly. But she twists things. She's always been so intense about Liam, so . . . invested. In that whole family. You remember how it was. She was obsessed with him, always following him around, even before he noticed her at that restaurant. Remember how she used to hang around outside his house, watching him, when she said she was at netball? And now . . . this? And why didn't she mention that it had happened before?'

I heard Dad make some sort of noise, a grunt.

'*All I'm saying,*' Mum continued, her voice rising, '*is that it might not be as black and white as you want it to be. She believes what she's saying, I'm sure of that. But believing something doesn't make it true.*'

'*Lizzy, she's upstairs.*' Dad's voice was urgent.

'*Exactly,*' Mum said, speaking in a slightly lowered voice. '*She's upstairs, and she's oblivious to what she's set in motion. And the Haughtons, John. Don't forget about them. You've signed the contracts. Re-mortgaged the house. The restaurant opens next month. You really think this won't destroy us?*'

'*The business is safe. Gerard Haughton can't touch us. We are standing by her, Lizzy.*'

'*At what cost?*'

'*She's our daughter. At any cost.*'

The floor creaked, along with the scrape of a chair being pushed back. Panic surged through me and I quickly retreated back into my bedroom, my stomach churning.

Chapter Thirty-Nine

Rachel

Now

Sunday arrives with the tail-end of the storm. I wake to find the wind howling around the house, rattling at the windows as though it is trying to break through them. My body feels heavy, as though I am hung over, but I haven't touched a drop since Friday night with Penny. The thought catches me again: the blank spots. *What happened?*

I sit up, but my head is pounding. It is still early, the light outside grey and sickly looking. Forcing myself out of bed, I creep out of my room and up the stairs to Mum's room. I hesitate. I didn't check on her last night, after the police came around, but the guilt is gnawing at me now, as it always does. I push the door open gently and peer inside.

Through the grey gloom, I see Mum asleep on top of the duvet, her body curled in on itself, as though she is protecting something fragile. There is an almost empty wine bottle on the bedside table and photo albums are scattered across the floor. I step back out of the room, closing the door quietly before she wakes up. Suddenly, I feel the overwhelming urge to escape the house and the oppressive weight of Mum, of the garden where someone might have been watching us, of all of it.

Returning to my own room, I pull my swimming costume and dryrobe off the radiator. I don't even think about what I am doing until I am already out of the door, the wind whipping against my face.

I glance around as I walk down the hill, wondering if someone is watching me, feeling my skin crawl. My phone vibrates in my pocket and for a second, I think about ignoring it; but then I wonder if it's Penny. When I pull it out, I see a missed call from Didi. Scrolling back, I see another two missed calls from last night, whilst I was wallowing in bed. A wave of cold guilt washes over me. *Didi's party.* I swipe further through my phone, seeing a number of messages from her: starting off as cheerful reminders, followed by question marks. *Didi won't mind,* I tell myself. *It's just one party: she'll understand.* I shove the phone back in my pocket and carry on walking. I've got bigger things to worry about, like whoever called the police last night.

The beach looms ahead, cold and grey, the waves crashing harder than usual. I drop my things onto the dark, wet sand and wade quickly into the water, welcoming the shock of the cold against my skin. It is a relief, cutting through the noise in my head. *If I just keep moving, I'll stop thinking.* As soon I am deep enough, I dive beneath the waves, letting the water numb me.

Almost immediately, I know that this time is different: I need more strength than usual to propel myself through the water and the waves throw me up and down with more force than I was expecting. I push myself through the water, trying to get into a rhythm, but my arms begin to burn and when I come up for air, I can hear the rumble of renewed thunder. Panic blooms in my chest. I've made a mistake. I should have respected the weather and stayed put, no matter how much turmoil my thoughts were in.

Breaking back through the surface, I look around to orientate myself and see that I am far further left and far deeper than I realised. The pier looms closer, its concrete struts covered in slick green algae. I can feel the pull of the tide dragging me further out, and suddenly I am afraid. Taking a deep breath, I dive back under and start swimming as hard as possible but I am lifted impotently by the waves and it feels as though I am barely moving. When I next look around, I am ever so slightly closer to the shore, but the pier is looming over me, and I know if a wave throws me against the concrete struts I could be seriously injured. Trying not to panic, I start swimming again, my heart pounding from the exertion and the fear. Waves hit me in the face and water shoots painfully up my nose, but I carry on, not looking to my left, not wanting to see how close I am to the underbelly of the pier. At last, with a final push, my feet touch the seabed and I wade through the shallows, vaguely registering a shout in the distance. I squint through the sheets of rain to see someone in the shallows, fully dressed and waving their arms in the air.

As I stagger towards the shore, the person comes wading up to me.

'Are you mad?' they yell. It is a man's voice, a voice that I immediately recognise, but I can't place. I feel their warm hands on me, guiding me to the shore. I try to resist, but I am too tired. The next thing I know, my blue dryrobe is being pushed into my hands. I take it gratefully and start drying myself, shivering all over. As I begin to calm down, I finally take a proper look at the man, and realise it is Tom.

Tom doesn't look surprised in the slightest: he must have already realised it was me. His hair is wet, sticking to his forehead. He surveys me incredulously as I start drying my hair.

'What in god's name were you thinking, swimming in this weather?' he demands, his voice breathless. The bottom half of his jeans are soaked. 'You could have drowned!'

'Nice to see you, too,' I say sarcastically, through my chattering teeth.

'You weren't . . . trying to do anything stupid were you?' he asks, eyeing me warily.

'Of course not!'

'Right . . . so you're not suicidal, you're just completely insane?'

'I just needed to get out,' I mutter as I continue drying myself, rigid with cold. Tom looks at me for a moment, his concern clear in the set of his jaw. But instead of pushing, he just gives a small nod and wraps his jacket tighter around himself against the wind.

'Come on,' he says, once I have pulled my robe over my head, 'let's get inside. You look like you're freezing.'

Before I can argue, he picks up my bag and shoes. With no energy left, I follow him up the beach.

Chapter Forty

Rachel

Now

Tom heads straight for a chain pub restaurant right on the seafront and orders drinks whilst I get changed in the toilets and attempt to dry my hair under the hand dryer. When I emerge and find him, he has a small two-person table by the steamed-up window that looks out over the pier.

'There you go,' he says, gesturing to the mug in front of me, 'an Irish coffee.'

I don't really want any alcohol after Friday night, but I wrap my hands gratefully around the hot cup, letting the warmth leach into my numb fingers.

'Thanks. Sorry about your jeans.'

Tom shrugs and takes a drink of his own coffee.

'I thought I was about to play the hero, rescue some damsel in distress. Instead it was just my old mate from school who was going for a dip.' His mouth twitches. Of the three of them, Tom appears the most unchanged; I can almost see the quiet but funny, overweight nine-year-old I first got sat next to in class. What, I wonder, do they think of me? Do they think I have changed?

Or will I always be – in Janet Haughton's words – the loose daughter of the town drunk, who turned a town against her?

'So,' Tom says, studying me as I drink my coffee, 'why did you need to out get so badly you almost drowned?'

I scowl.

'I didn't almost drown,' I retort.

'Really? Because that's what this . . .' Tom suddenly waves his hands about frantically, drawing a few stares, 'looked like.'

I shake my head at him. To my surprise, however, I feel the corners of my mouth lift ever so slightly. Perhaps Tom senses it too, because he smiles.

'So, come on. Why did you go for a swim today? In a storm?'

I sigh, and take another sip of coffee, thinking about what happened last night. I'm not about to tell Tom about my fears of being watched, but he seems to sense what I am thinking.

'You don't trust me, do you? Because I'm still friends with Liam.'

'That's one of the reasons.'

'What are the others?'

'I told you the other day, Tom. You were my friend. And you just left. I can't just act like that didn't happen.'

'Rach,' Tom says, leaning forwards. 'Come on, you made a false allegation against Liam. The worst kind. And you could have got half of us kicked out of uni before we'd even started, with breaking into the fairground that night.

I'm sorry I didn't ever get in touch. But surely you can understand why?'

I grit my teeth. I want to tell him that I didn't make the allegation up. I am so desperate to, the words are on the tip of my tongue. After all, he needs to know, Penny needs to know. But I can't . . . not yet. If Tom doesn't believe me, he'll tell the others. And then Liam will know. I need to wait until I know more about Liam, until I can prove to them who he really is. For now, I need Tom to trust me. So, instead I shrug and drain my coffee. Tom nods towards it.

'How about something stronger?'

He returns a few minutes later with two pints.

'How come you're not back in London yet?' I ask.

'I've been helping Penny and Liam with a few wedding things this weekend. Plus my mum loves it when I visit, which isn't very often,' he adds, sheepishly. 'Work gets in the way a lot.'

'What do you do?'

'I work in the City. In HR.'

'Oh,' I say, trying to stem that familiar flow of bitterness that pools in my lower stomach at the thought of them all with their London lives and jobs. 'Sounds cool.'

Tom looks at me incredulously.

'I promise you, it's not. They don't even call it HR, they call it *Talent Acquisition*.'

He grins at me and I find myself smiling back.

'I'm training to be a police officer though,' he says, straightening his back proudly. 'I'm just having to do it part-time so I can still pay my rent.'

'Wow, a police officer?'

I can't help but wonder how Liam must feel about his best friend becoming a police officer. Is he nervous? Tom starts talking about his training and before I even realise where the time has gone, he is bringing another two pints over. I need to be careful: I need to keep my head, not drink too much. After Friday night with Penny and the police turning up last night, I can't afford to let my guard down. I glance out of the window. Could Liam be watching, now? He would surely hate the idea of me sitting here with Tom. Unless . . . a thought suddenly occurs to me.

'What were you doing out on the beach earlier, by the way? When you saw me?' I try to keep my voice light, casual. 'Hardly anyone was out in that weather.'

'I don't have a car and my mum's working the weekend shift at the hospital. I went to pick up some groceries,' he gestures to a plastic bag on the floor, 'and had to walk home.'

He raises just the slightest hint of an eyebrow and I can't help but feel he knows exactly what I am getting at, but he doesn't say anything.

'That's nice of you.'

He shrugs.

'It's no bother. She's always worked every shift she can. It's the least I can do.'

I feel a sudden rush of empathy for Tom. He, like me, came from humble beginnings: he was raised by a soft, gentle single mum who was a nurse.

'I had better get back, actually,' he says, checking his watch. 'Promised her a roast dinner. And I've got some stag-do things to sort before I head back to London tomorrow. If I don't go back soon, my girlfriend will think I've left her.'

'When's the stag?'

'Next week, just before the wedding.' He doesn't sound particularly enthused, perhaps because it's such hard work. Tom stands up. 'I'm going to the toilet, no rush on your drink.' Then he hesitates, standing by the table for a moment.

'Rach . . . you are, you know, okay after what happened, right? You've moved on?'

I look up at him, feeling my blood heating. I force a smile.

'Of course.'

Tom looks satisfied and walks away, leaving me to finish my drink and mull over our conversation. For a moment, it had been nice, seeing Tom again. Like he was *my* friend, again, not Liam's. Tom's phone, left on the table, lights up with a message. Keeping my eye on the stairs Tom has just disappeared up, I lean forwards. My stomach flips when I see the message is from *Liam H.* Glancing quickly up at the stairs to check Tom isn't walking down them, I pull the phone towards me and tap the screen.

Have you spoken to your mate on the force yet? About the intruder we saw on Friday night? Penny's still freaking out that whoever it was followed her home.

Friday night? Penny was with me on Friday night. There was an intruder at their house after Penny went home? Is

Liam making it up? I can't think why he would. For some reason, a faint alarm sounds at the back of my mind. *The blank spots.* No, I assure myself, that isn't anything to do with me. I wouldn't do something like that; I would know if I had. As Tom reappears, I quickly sit up and try to act normal.

Chapter Forty-One
DC Rainer
2005

*T*he Haughton residence was set along a private road where
each of the huge houses had sweeping driveways and tall
gates covered in CCTV cameras. He wondered why anyone so
rich wouldn't want to live with a view of the sea, something that
Marie had always dreamed of. Buying her a new-build exactly
seven minutes' walk from the seafront was the best he could do.

He pulled up to the gate and looked around for a moment,
until PC Thompson pointed out a small black buzzer by the
gate. Rainer reached out and tried to press the buzzer, but
he had parked too far over and couldn't reach. He rolled the
window down further and stretched half his torso through the
window, just managing to press it with enough force to hear a
ring. He ignored Thompson's smirk as he settled himself back
in the car, red-faced, and waited for the gates to open.

The door was opened by Gerard Haughton's lawyer and
Rainer wondered if this was some sort of power move by
Gerard Haughton, not answering the door himself. The lawyer, Rupert Fairfax, showed them straight through to the study
without any niceties.

'My client and his father will only be giving agreed
responses and will not be consenting to any further voluntary

interviews at this time until there is some sort of evidence in this investigation, beyond that of Miss Kingston's malicious allegations.' Rupert Fairfax opened the study door and gestured them inside.

When Rainer and Thompson entered, they found Gerard Haughton, tall and broad-chested, pacing up and down the expensive-looking rug. On a chair in the corner sat eighteen-year-old Liam Haughton. Rupert sat himself down discreetly in the far corner and opened a legal pad.

'Officers,' Gerard said in his usual, commanding voice. 'I want to know where you are with this farcical investigation.'

'Mr Haughton,' Rainer replied, trying not to match the volume of his voice to Gerard's, knowing that Thompson would pick up on it. 'We are at the same stage as we were yesterday when Mr Fairfax here called us. We are still collecting evidence in this investigation. Now, we came here because you asked us to come in order to discuss new evidence?'

Gerard ground his teeth and, for a moment, Rainer felt a fleeting thrill of fear. He had come across many different types of people before, but there was something about Gerard Haughton that put him on edge. He was charming enough when he wanted to be, but there was something unnerving about him when things weren't going his way.

'My son was asked to find an alibi for the additional day that that . . . girl . . . is claiming he assaulted her. He's found it.'

Rainer and Thompson both looked over at Liam Haughton. He seemed to shrink under their gaze, looking pale and terrified. Nothing like his father. He held out a piece of paper with shaking hands.

'That's the friend I was with all afternoon,' he said in a voice that was barely above a whisper. 'Penny Adams. We were doing some Durham research.'

Rainer took the paper from Liam, and saw that Liam had written Penny Adams's details.

'It should be a simple matter of confirming her alibi and wrapping all this up, wouldn't you agree DC Rainer?' Rupert Fairfax said in a bored voice from the other side of the room.

'For the specific day in question, perhaps,' Rainer said, irked at Gerard and this fancy lawyer trying to put pressure on him.

'What are you trying to say?' Gerard Haughton barked. 'That it doesn't help him with the damn fairground night?'

Liam Haughton suddenly opened his mouth to speak.

'Officer, I . . .'

'Quiet, Liam,' Gerard barked. 'You are not under police caution.'

Liam glanced at his dad and then fell silent. His face was paler than ever and Rainer found himself wondering, once again, what he made of the young man. It was hard to know, with his dad overshadowing everything.

'If your son wants to say something . . .' Rainer began but Gerard cut him off.

'He doesn't.'

There was a long, painful silence. Rainer watched Liam, but the teenager didn't say anything else.

'Thanks for this,' Thompson said after a while, in her usual calm voice. 'We'll take it away and look into it, alright?'

Gerard looked like he wanted to shout at them some more, but his lawyer shot him a look. Rainer and Thompson made their excuses and left as soon as possible.

'What the hell was that?' Thompson muttered to him as they walked back to the car. 'Couldn't they have just dropped this information off at the station?'

'That's not how people like Gerard Haughton work,' Rainer replied. 'They like to control the situation.'

'Well, if this Penny girl backs up Liam's alibi for the first occasion Rachel says it happened, it does throw Rachel's account into question.'

'Maybe. Seems a bit coincidental that he's managed to pluck alibis from school friends for both nights, doesn't it?'

They climbed into the car and Thompson frowned at Rainer as he manoeuvred the car around and waited for the gates to re-open.

'What is it? You think there's a cover-up going on?'

'I don't know. I really don't. Liam Haughton seems afraid. I just don't know whether it's of jail, or his dad. Or both.'

'And Rachel Kingston?'

Rainer shook his head.

'No idea.'

'Well, one of those kids is lying,' Thompson said, glancing in the wing mirror at the Haughton house as it got further away. 'I just don't know which one.'

Rainer looked grimly in the rear-view mirror.

'Yet.'

Chapter Forty-Two

Rachel

Now

On Sunday night, I sleep poorly. I have never slept well but tonight is especially hard. I keep picturing the message on Tom's phone from Liam, then racking my brains to remember what happened on Friday night. I roll over and look up 'blank spots in memory after drinking'. I click through a few different articles, my heartrate increasing with each one: 'Researchers link alcohol-induced blackouts to criminal behaviour'; 'The dark dangers of alcohol-induced amnesia: man convinced of hit and run claims he "remembers nothing".' My heartbeat increases from a steady drum to full palpitations and I put my phone down again. I can't spiral like this: I have to trust myself.

I drag myself bleary-eyed to work on Monday, my stomach churning from lack of sleep. The roads are quiet and gleaming silver with rain. The poster advertising the funfair flaps in the wind as I walk past the section of the railings it is attached to. The scaffolding covering the new funfair has been taken down now, the new rides glinting in the light.

I am in the office early and it is silent when I arrive, just the way I like it. For a moment, I fantasise about the way things were, before Liam and Penny arrived back in town. Before I began feeling like every movement I make is being watched. Revelling in the quiet, I make myself a coffee and then start organising the post. A few minutes later, the office door opens.

'Hey Dee,' I say automatically. 'Can you sort the switchboard, I'm having to deal with . . .' but I trail off, because when I glance up it is not Didi standing there, but Liam.

I swallow. The whole room seems to go still and I can feel my heart racing beneath my top, my hands sweaty. I search for some hint, some acknowledgement from him, of what he has been doing to me: but there is nothing. He simply puts his still-rolled-up umbrella down by the coat stand in the corner and nods at me.

'Morning,' he says, as though he is the world's politest man. If he thinks that I was at his house on Friday, his expression gives nothing away.

The last thing I want to do is respond to him, but I have to try: if I don't act normal, he could warn Penny and Tom to stay away from me and I might need them. Acting was once my dream: I can do this. I hear myself saying hello before going back to the post. I don't see the words that are written on the letter in my hand, every sense is heightened as I wait to see what he does next.

'I've, uhh, got a last-minute dentist appointment at midday,' he says, 'so can you move my twelve o'clock to tomorrow?'

I nod and he is gone with a swish of his expensive trench coat. As soon as the sound of his footsteps on the stairs fades away, I let out a sigh of relief. Begrudgingly, I rearrange his twelve o'clock client.

When Didi arrives a short while later, she is unusually quiet and sits down at her desk with a stiff 'Good morning'.

'Didi,' I say, after a moment's awkward pause, 'I'm really sorry I didn't make it to your party on Saturday.'

She looks up at me, her mouth a thin line.

'How come you didn't make it?'

'I wasn't feeling well,' I say, quickly.

'A bug?' she asks, one eyebrow raised in challenge. I flush.

'Something like that. A twenty-four-hour thing. I was in bed all weekend.'

'Right,' Didi says, her tone sceptical. 'It's just that you've said no to the last three things I've invited you to, so I thought maybe you just decided not to come and didn't bother telling me.'

'I was just ill, Dee,' I say, as my head throbs sharply. 'I'll be there next time, okay?'

'Okay,' she says quietly. 'Don't worry about it.'

Thankfully, the morning is too busy for either of us to chat much and by the time the lunchtime lull approaches, Didi seems to have returned to normal.

Just before midday, Liam re-enters the office, picking up his umbrella.

'Good luck at the dentist,' Didi smiles at him.

'Thanks,' he replies shortly and hurries out of the door. For a second, I watch him through the glass . . . then something comes over me and I find myself standing and grabbing my bag.

'I'm just going to get an early lunch, I'll be back in ten,' I say quickly to Didi.

As soon as I leave the office I turn right, following in Liam's footsteps up the high street. There is only one dentist in town, right towards the top of the street. As soon as I turn onto the main section of the high street, bustling with workers out getting lunch or having a cigarette, I spot Liam up ahead, striding along with his umbrella tucked under his arm. I hang back slightly, afraid that he will turn and see me, but I keep my eyes on him as he walks. He reaches the dentist and stops outside. I let out the breath I've been holding and feel the disappointment flood through me . . . he really was going to the dentist. Who did I think I was, Sherlock Holmes? I am about to turn around and head back, when Liam pulls his phone out of his pocket and starts walking again . . . right past the dentist. My stomach flips and I hurry after him, keeping myself hidden behind two women pushing prams and chatting.

He continues up the high street, towards the very top where the shops start petering out, just before a large supermarket and multistorey car park. He comes to a stop and looks left and right. I hunch a little lower behind the women to stay hidden. Then he takes a step forward and disappears. My heart begins to race. *What is he doing?* Whatever it is, it was apparently worth lying about.

The women in front of me peel off, towards the supermarket. Now alone, I approach the place where Liam disappeared and see it is a long, brick alleyway. I've not come down here before. Liam is already halfway down the alleyway, his broad frame blocking out most of the light filtering through. I hesitate in the entrance: every sensible fibre of my being is screaming at me not to follow him, but a compulsion carries me forward. I need to know where he is going. I take a step inside the dark alley and wrinkle my nose at the smell of urine. By now he is almost at the end. I walk slowly and softly behind him, praying that he doesn't turn around; I have nowhere to hide if he does. After a few moments he reaches the end and disappears. I hurry softly to the end where he vanished, then stop at the alleyway exit, pressing my back against the cold brick. Slowly, I peer around, my heart in my mouth.

The alleyway opens out onto a small industrial estate that looks as though it has been completely forgotten about by the rest of the world. Dilapidated red-brick warehouses loom oppressively on all sides, their broken windowpanes staring like blank eyes. Graffiti covers most of the walls and rusted metal barrels and pieces of machinery sit in dirty rainwater puddles.

I can hear my pulse loudly in my ears. There are two figures near one of the warehouses, standing half in shadow. Liam. He has his umbrella up, his posture alert and tense. Opposite him stands a man I don't recognise, though something about him sends a shiver down my spine. The man is burly, his features rough, as though they have been hewn out of his face. His coat hood is pulled low over his eyes and, though he seems to be speaking to Liam with intensity, his whole body remains perfectly still. I watch as his eyes flicker around the warehouses, checking. Checking no one is listening. Adrenaline pulses through me, making my whole body tremble. Liam responds, but I can't hear what is being said, their voices are too low. The scene feels wrong, tinged with an ominous darkness. As though the façade of normal life has been peeled away, exposing something far more sinister beneath.

Carefully, I slip my hand into my bag and pull out my phone. With my heart in my mouth, I open the camera and slowly point it towards the two men. Zooming in on their faces, I take a photo. Too late, I realise my phone is on full volume and the camera shutter makes a loud clicking sound. The man Liam is talking to suddenly looks around and I jerk back into the alleyway, my heart thudding. Clutching my phone in my hand, I turn and race as quietly as I can back down the alleyway. I hear footsteps but I can't turn around. As soon as I reach the end of the alleyway and emerge back out into the rainy high street, I hurry back to the office.

Chapter Forty-Three

Rachel

Now

L iam arrives back in the office half an hour later and I try to act as naturally as I can, though my heart is still beating furiously. Here, at last, is proof that Liam is up to something. And I have the photo to prove it.

'How was the dentist?' Didi asks when Liam enters the office. Liam looks flustered, his face red.

'Fine, thank you.'

'Oh, and Liam,' Didi continues, 'Mr Phelan left a message. Apparently you were supposed to be at a hearing this morning?'

'What?' Liam's head snaps towards Didi, who shrinks slightly in her chair. 'There wasn't a hearing in my diary this morning.'

'There seems to be,' Didi says in a quiet voice. 'It's in your calendar.' She turns her screen slightly to show Liam the 8.30 a.m. hearing. Liam's lips move slightly as he reads the diary entry. His face goes a deep shade of red.

'That wasn't there this morning,' he says, in a low voice. Didi glances at me, looking panic-stricken. Neither of us says anything and there is a long silence. Eventually, Liam straightens up.

'I'll call him now,' he says abruptly and leaves the room. Didi looks at me again in disbelief.

'What's his problem?' she asks, her eyes wide.

'I've noticed he can be a bit temperamental,' I say, shaking my head. 'Maybe he's missing his big London firm.'

'Maybe.'

I return to my computer, my mind still on Liam and the meeting he just had in the industrial estate. It can't have been anything to do with work or else he wouldn't have lied about going to the dentist. I slip my phone out of my bag and, checking over my shoulder that Didi is occupied, open the photo of Liam and the craggy-faced man. Just seeing his hooded face again sends a chill down my spine. How can I find out who the man is? Then it hits me: I pull up Connor's number and attach the photo with the message:

Can you find out who this man is for me? Will explain later.

The office door opens again and Sasha waltzes in, wearing a tight-fitting pair of white jeans, despite the rain, and her usual superior expression. I hurriedly drop my phone back into my bag.

'Charles in?' she asks me without bothering to say hello. *You really are a bitch*, I think.

'Yes, but he's on a conference call right now and then he's due in court,' I reply, knowing how petty I am being but getting a kick of satisfaction, nonetheless. 'I'm not sure he'll have time to see you.'

'I'm his wife, I *think* he'll manage,' Sasha replies with a sour expression. 'Let him know I'm here and get me a coffee whilst you're at it, would you?'

I stare at her. She has always acted superior to me, but she usually knows better than to treat me like staff. She returns my look with a challenging expression and I know that I have no choice. Furious, I get up and go to the kitchen to make her a coffee, making sure to put too much milk in it, knowing she hates dairy. When I return, she is leaning against my desk, frantically typing on her phone. Didi's head is down, clearly trying to avoid a conversation.

'You and Penny looked very cosy on Friday night,' Sasha suddenly says, glancing at the coffee I've set down for her, but not making a move to pick it up. 'Catching up on old times?'

In my periphery Didi goes still over her paperwork.

'Not really, it was just a quick drink,' I say. 'Your coffee is there.'

'It didn't look like a quick drink, when she was ordering the second bottle,' Sasha said, with a snort, ignoring my attempt to stop the conversation. 'You both looked just like you always used to. Totally hammered.'

'I thought you said you had a bug this weekend,' Didi says, quietly.

'I did,' I say, hurriedly, before Sasha can make things worse. 'I got it the next day.'

'That's not called a bug,' Sasha interrupts, 'that's called a hangover. You should be able to recognise them better than anyone.'

Didi looks at me, her eyes wide with hurt.

'Didi, I didn't . . .' I begin, but before I can say anything else, the office door opens and Charles walks in, briefcase in one hand and his silver hair windswept.

'Hi darling,' Sasha trills, though I detect a slight wince in the way she says it. I wonder if she even likes him. She makes no move to kiss him, but Charles doesn't seem to notice.

'What are you doing here?' he asks Sasha abruptly. Sasha colours but acts like he hasn't just spoken to her so rudely.

'I just came to say goodbye. I'm staying with my friend Rosie in London tonight, remember?'

Charles looks confused.

'I don't remember you mentioning that. On a Monday?'

Sasha looks like she is trying to stop herself from rolling her eyes at his old-fashioned approach to days of the week.

'Yes, darling. On a Monday. I told you this. Rosie works from home so it's easy to hang out.'

Charles looks as though he has never heard of the concept 'working from home'.

'Right. Well then, I'll see you when you get home.' Charles is already turning away from her, the conversation finished. It's clear Sasha knows this and with a last look of contempt at me, she sweeps from the office. Charles collects his bundles from Didi and then leaves the office, too. Once the door swings shut, there is a long silence. I look over at Didi: she is staring determinedly at her computer, but I can see her eyes are fixed on the screen and there is a pink tinge to her cheeks.

'Didi, ignore Sasha. I did start feeling unwell on Saturday.'

'It doesn't matter, Rach,' Didi says abruptly. 'I get it. I shouldn't have tried to push you into doing things outside work with me.' Before I can respond, she has stood up and walked towards the door. Just before she reaches it, she turns and looks back at me.

'You know, you can talk to me. You don't always have to be on your own.' Then she leaves the room, her coffee mug in her hand.

I sit there for a moment, trying to work out what she means. Whether to feel angry or not. I am about to get up and go after her, when my phone dings from my bag. I swivel quickly in my chair, and fish it out. It is a message from Connor. When I see what it says, I freeze.

Call me. Now.

Chapter Forty-Four

Rachel

Now

The local newspaper offices are right at the edge of town, next to a small square, the grass yellowed by dog pee, and overflowing bins on either side. The building is a squat 1960s block, out of keeping with the rest of the older town. In the grey aftermath of the storm, it looks even more depressing. It's a building I have only ever visited once, with my dad when I was small and he wanted to drop off a letter to the paper about protesting a new development on the seafront.

I push open the frosted glass doors and down a short hallway, find myself in an open-plan office. There are cheap uPVC windows across the full length of the back wall, the deep windowsills covered in large potted houseplants which make the whole place feel a bit like a greenhouse. Though it is only five forty in the afternoon, it is quiet: Connor is the only person at his desk. As soon as he sees me, he waves me over, pulling a chair away from a colleague's desk and gesturing to me to sit down. I look around. Connor's desk is perfectly neat: a giant *Best Grandson Ever* coffee mug is clean and back on his desk, his pens all in a plastic stationery holder. No papers lying around or scribbled Post-it notes, something I always imagined of a journalist. Just one newspaper from two days ago neatly folded in the corner of his desk: I catch a photo of Shelly McKenzie on the front page.

'Where is everyone?' I ask.

'Covering stories or gone home.'

I look back at Connor to see his face is sombre.

'What's going on, Connor? Why was it so important that we talk?'

Connor sighs deeply, before clicking his mouse: his screen comes to life, showing a different image of the man I saw earlier.

'That's him!' I say, pointing to the screen. 'That's the man I saw.'

Connor angles his computer screen away from the rest of the office, even though we're alone. He leans forward and drops his voice.

'Rach, this guy . . . his name's Wayne Stephens. He's not exactly someone you'd want to run into on a dark street at night.'

Something about Connor's expression, the ominous tone of his voice, sends a chill through me.

'And Liam? What would he be doing with him?'

Connor hesitates, as though trying to gauge how much he should say.

'I don't know for sure. But the people Wayne associates with . . . they're not the kind of people you deal with unless you're mixed up in something bad. If Liam's meeting with him, that's a serious red flag.'

I sit back in the desk chair, my mind racing. Why would Liam be involved with someone like that? With the Haughton name and money, why would he need to?

'What exactly has this Wayne guy done?' I ask quietly.

Connor hesitates once again.

'Mostly intimidation, a bit of extortion,' Connor says, running a hand over his short hair. 'He's the sort of person you call when you need a message delivering.'

I feel the blood drain from my face. *The blank spots on Friday night.* What if it *was* me? What if Liam saw me outside and thought I was spying on them?

'Do you think . . . maybe he's going to use this guy to scare me off?'

Connor's face tightens for a moment.

'Honestly? I don't know. But Rach, you have to be careful. Whether or not it's to do with you or something else entirely, if Wayne Stephens thinks you're snooping around . . .'

He doesn't finish his sentence, but he doesn't need to. I know what he's getting at, and my heart is pounding in my chest. This whole thing is spiralling out of control. This isn't just about the past anymore, suddenly there is something equally dangerous going on in the present.

'There's something I've not told you,' I say to Connor. I tell him about the postcard arriving at the office, and about my police file going missing. Connor's face grows more and more concerned as I speak. When I'm finished, he leans forward.

'Rach, I don't know what Liam is up to, but promise me you'll be smart about this. Stay out of it. Stay away from Liam, Penny, Tom . . . all of them. Okay?'

I nod.

'And you'll let me know if anything else comes up?'

I nod again and get up, my hands trembling slightly.

'Let me drop you home,' Connor says. 'Can you hang on for half an hour? I just have to send a report before seven.'

'It's fine. It's not far. I'll be careful.'

Connor sighs, his gaze flickering between me and his screen.

'Okay,' he says, eventually. 'But set your phone so I can see your location and text me as soon as you get home, alright?'

I nod.

'And Rachel?'

I turn to look back at him.

'Don't talk to anyone.'

Chapter Forty-Five

Rachel

2005

I walked slowly back up the road towards home. It was another hot day, but there was something different in the air. A crispness that hinted at autumn coming. At the turn of a season where fresh terms began, new adventures, sharp pencils and different friends. My phone was in my pocket, but I had increasingly stopped looking at it. There was no point. The screen would be as blank as it had been the day after the funfair and every day since. I had tried calling Penny. And Tom. But neither of them had answered. Were they with him? Or had they gone quiet on us both, stepping away from the whole thing and planning their journey north together? What about when Penny saw Liam at university, what then? Would he even be going to university? My stomach knotted. It was all such a fucking mess. How did we get from there to here? When did it happen? How could Penny not have called? All I wanted was for Liam to want to be with me.

I opened the front gate. It creaked, like it always did, then clinked as it swung back on itself. As I walked up the front path I saw Dad on the porch, bent over with what looked like a dustpan and brush in his hands. It took me a moment to understand what I was seeing. Then the sunlight flashed off something on the ground and I realised there were pieces of glass scattered on the ground in front of the house. I looked up and saw a jagged hole in the front window to the lounge.

'Dad?' I asked, running up the front path. 'What's going on? What happened to the window?'

Dad turned around, blinking in surprise.

'Oh, sweetheart. I thought you would be longer.'

'What happened?' I asked again.

'Nothing, really. Just some kids no doubt. They threw something through the window. Thankfully your mum was asleep upstairs.'

'What did they throw?' I asked, looking around. 'Like a football, or something?'

'No . . . a brick,' Dad sighed.

My blood ran cold.

'A brick? Someone threw a brick through the window?'

Carefully, Dad put the dustpan and brush down and walked towards me.

'Don't start worrying,' he said reassuringly, putting a hand on my shoulder. 'You're dealing with enough. It was just some petty vandalism, that's all. When me and your mum first moved in, a load of kids destroyed the daffodils out front. These things happen.'

I took a deep breath and nodded. For some reason the brick had completely freaked me out, but Dad's words were reassuring. If he wasn't worried, I shouldn't be. Right?

For the next ten minutes, I helped Dad clear up the rest of the glass and put it in the bin. He had already cleared up and hoovered the glass inside, though I was still paranoid about stepping on any shards buried in the carpet.

Once everything was cleared up, I made us both a cup of tea and we sat at the kitchen table with the back doors open, letting the warm air in. I kept looking at Dad for some sign that he was more scared than he was letting on, but he seemed fine, like he always did. I thought it was funny that people like him were described as rocks. That made me think of someone hard and unmoving and Dad was none of those things. He was more like water. Flexible, strong, calming.

'Stop worrying, sweetheart. I can see it all over your face. Now, we need to talk about drama school. Am I still driving you up there?'

My stomach clenched. We hadn't spoken about drama school, or next steps. Nothing beyond what had been happening right now.

I opened my mouth to say something, but Dad's phone began to ring. He always set it to maximum volume in case he missed a call from Mum and the sound rang loudly in my ears.

'Two secs, Rach, it might be important,' Dad said, pulling the phone from the little belt he always kept it in that Mum hated.

I sat with my hands wrapped around my tea as Dad answered the call, my thoughts still on the broken window. Dad was going to board it up until the window company could get out here, but I knew that another expense was the last thing he needed, right now.

'What do you mean, it didn't go through?'

I turned around to look at Dad, sensing immediately that something was wrong.

'The paperwork was all submitted weeks ago. I was assured it was approved.' Dad was standing completely still, the phone

pressed against his ear. My heart began to beat very fast. What was happening?

'I don't understand,' Dad said, his face turning a dark red. 'I spoke with the inspector personally! We need that licence, we open in less than a week.'

He listened for a moment, his expression growing more and more strained.

'Well, there must be a mistake. How long will it take to sort?'

I felt sick seeing him like this. He was never like this.

'Alright . . . yes, I understand. I'll follow up again tomorrow. Just please, do whatever you can.'

Dad hung up the phone and exhaled shakily. He leant against the kitchen counter, staring down at the phone as though the person was going to suddenly ring back and tell him it had all been a mistake.

'What happened, Dad?' My voice was barely more than a whisper.

'It's the health and safety licence for the restaurant. They're saying it wasn't approved. Something about missing paperwork, but I double-checked everything before I sent it in. I don't know what's happened.' He rubbed his forehead, his face lined with worry. 'I had better try and sort this out.'

He left the room and I heard him climbing the stairs to his study. I stayed in the kitchen, the sick knot of worry still in my stomach. Whatever Dad said, the things that were happening didn't seem like they were a coincidence, to me. They seemed deliberate. The brick, the licence issue . . . they were all messages from the Haughtons. With a sinking feeling of dread, I wondered how far they would go.

Chapter Forty-Six

Rachel

Now

As I leave the newspaper office, the sky is an oppressive grey, threatening more rain. My thoughts whirl, like leaves caught in the wind. I try to tell myself that whatever Liam was doing with this Wayne Stephens person has nothing to do with me. But that thought isn't particularly reassuring: what if it's to do with the firm? What if that's the reason he is back? And what does Penny know about it all? Is she in danger, too?

Connor's warnings echo in my head as I walk. I keep glancing over my shoulder as I walk through the quiet streets, my skin crawling with the sense of being followed. A couple of times, I am sure I hear footsteps – soft, measured – but whenever I turn around, there's no one. The street is deserted, nothing there but glistening puddles.

I quicken my pace, reaching the part of town where the roads become quieter and more residential. A car pulls up at the curb just ahead of me, its headlights cutting through the dim light and I freeze for a second, my breath caught in my throat. I wait, feeling my pulse in my throat. The car idles for a moment longer, then drives away, the sound of its engine slowly fading into the night. I exhale shakily and keep walking, trying to fight the panic that keeps rising like a snake.

With relief, I turn onto my street and hurry up the hill, my breath sharp and loud in the silence. That same image I sometimes entertain flashes cruelly across my mind: someone waiting for me to come home, the lights in the kitchen on, peering out of the lounge window to see if I'm approaching the house. Instead, I open the gate and see the house shrouded in darkness, the curtains firmly pulled across the lounge window. But I am, at least, home. Safe.

As soon as I enter the house, I see Mum's keys are in the thick conch that doubles as a hallway bowl. This doesn't necessarily mean she's home: she's been out without keys and come back banging on the door so often I had to install a key safe outside. Even then she often forgets the code, though it is the one we have always used, the first two digits of my birthday.

'Mum?' I call softly, praying I'm not about to find her in the kitchen again, poring over old photos and memories. Or worse. To my surprise, however, a voice calls out from the lounge.

'In here, love.'

Love? I can't remember the last time she used a term of endearment towards me; I hate the immediate childlike leap of pleasure in my stomach. I walk cautiously down the hall and into the lounge. The room is lit by the soft Tiffany lamps and it's been tidied: cushions straightened, curtains tied back with their fabric ties. No empty bottles to be seen.

Mum is sitting neatly in an armchair, her hair washed and brushed. She is holding a cup of tea, in her favourite china teacup, a wool blanket across her lap. She looks pale and tired and the cup shakes a little; but her eyes are alert. For the first time in a long while, she appears completely sober.

'You remember Katie, don't you?' Mum nods across the room to where a woman I don't recognise sits. She is around the same age as Mum, slim, with neatly styled blonde hair and wearing a silky pashmina. Her posture is relaxed, comfortable. As if she belongs here.

'Katie and I bumped into each other in town today. It's been what, twenty years?'

'Closer to thirty, I think,' she says, smiling at Mum, with a voice like soft caramel. 'Your mum and I used to be friends. We used to wait around outside ballet for you and my daughter Sabrina.'

I nod slowly, but inside my mind is racing. This all feels far too convenient. Mum, suddenly sober, reconnecting with an old friend out of nowhere? After everything that has been happening – after what Connor told me about Wayne Stephens – I can't help but feel suspicious. Katie's appearance feels too neat, too coincidental. Did Wayne or Liam see me, in the entrance to the alleyway, after all?

'Nice to meet you,' I say carefully, but I don't sit down. Instead I hover by the doorway, my eyes flickering between them both.

'We just got to talking,' Mum continues, seemingly oblivious to my state. 'Katie's been through a lot, like me. But she's doing really well for herself, now – she even volunteers for a few charities.'

Katie chuckles modestly.

'Oh, Liz. It's nothing really. Just trying to give back a little.'

I force a tight smile.

'That's great. Can I get either of you anything? More tea?'

'We're fine, thank you,' Katie says, before Mum can answer. I grit my teeth and leave the lounge, heading for the kitchen, feeling rattled. Mum never has friends over. And yet the idea that Katie might have been sent to keep an eye on me, or dig up information, seems almost laughable.

I enter the kitchen and sling my bag onto a chair and hurry straight over to the cupboard above the sink where, predictably, I find a bottle of red wine. The unusual thing about it is that it's unopened. I slosh some into a glass, then begin to pace up and down the kitchen, my thoughts jumbled, confused. It seems impossible that only a few days ago, I experienced a moment of happiness the morning I woke up with Connor. More unexpected laughter emanates from the lounge and I glance towards the door, scowling – then freeze. *Not again.* On the kitchen table is a brightly coloured flyer. The same flyer that has been posted twice through the letterbox twice already.

The Funfair Returns! Grand Reopening!

I grab the flyer and hurry back into the lounge, my heart racing. Katie and Mum are laughing about something, but they stop when I walk in and look at me expectantly.

'What's this doing on the table?' I ask, my tone abrupt. I hold the flyer out to them.

'Oh, I spotted it on the doormat when we came in,' Katie says in her smooth voice. 'I thought you might want to see it. A funfair.' She smiles at me, showing a row of straight white teeth. 'Looks fun, don't you think?'

Chapter Forty-Seven

Penny

Now

The door opens and Gerard stands there in a loud silk shirt, his thick hair swept to one side.

'There she is. My favourite future daughter-in-law,' he says, with a wink. 'What a pleasure. Come in, come in.'

'Thanks,' I say, following him into the wide, echoing entrance hall. We walk through to the kitchen, which is even more vast. It's not my taste at all: everything is black and glossy, the kind of cabinets that show every fingerprint.

'Drink?' Gerard asks. I nod, not wanting to seem rude. I hover by the spotless kitchen island as he pours me a glass of wine and gets a beer for himself. I feel a little awkward: even though Liam and I have been together for four years, I have never spent much time around Gerard and especially not one on one.

'Sit, sit,' Gerard insists, settling himself down at the island. I pull out a stool, leaving one between us. 'Janet is sorry to be missing you. Said she doesn't see you enough as it is.'

I bet she did. Janet has a knack for sly digs, dressed up as innocent comments.

'I just needed to pick up a few things for the wedding and it was the only time I could do,' I explain.

'Don't you work from home?' Gerard asks. 'Surely you've got all the time in the world?'

I flush. I hate the inference that my job isn't as important as Liam's, just because it's not on the same level as being a lawyer. Gerard must see the look on my face because he throws his head back and laughs.

'I'm just kidding, girl. Liam's always telling us how hard you work.'

I force a smile. I've never been able to work Gerard out, never sure what he's really thinking. 'Speaking of being at home,' he continues, 'have you set up those security cameras I told Liam to get?'

I shake my head.

'It was just one person outside, Gerard, really. I know I was freaked out at the time, but nothing happened, after all.'

'Maybe not this time, but if they were casing the joint, something will happen next time.'

'It's not going to happen next time,' I say firmly. When I had first seen the shadow of someone looking through the window the previous Friday night, I had been completely terrified. But now I am not sure whether it was the just the wine I had drunk with Rachel making me overreact. Things are bad enough without being afraid of being in my own home. Or Gran's.

Gerard eyes me for a moment, and I wonder if he's annoyed that I've stood up to him. I can't imagine many people do, let alone women. Then his mouth twists into a smile and he raises his beer in my direction.

'That told me,' he says, with a chuckle. He takes a long drink and then sets his beer bottle down on the marble countertop with a soft clink. 'In fact, I'm glad we've got a chance to talk. I wanted to say how impressed Janet and I were at how you handled the . . . situation. Before you moved here. Can't have been easy.'

I swallow.

'No,' I say, fiddling with the stem of my glass and not looking at Gerard. 'It wasn't.'

'Well, we all make mistakes. I'm glad you were able to see that. Stand by him.'

I don't know what to say. I don't want to talk about this, about what happened before we moved here, but I also came to see Gerard for a reason. And being on Gerard's good side will hopefully help.

'I believe in second chances,' I say, carefully.

'Atta girl,' Gerard says, giving me a pat on the knee. 'You might not be married just yet, but you're one of us, now. And us Haughtons stick together.'

I take a long sip of red wine. Like the kitchen, it isn't to my tastes. Too dry.

'Actually, I wanted to talk to you about something,' I say, my eyes still on the work surface.

'Oh yes?'

I swallow the embarrassment that is creeping hotly through me at the thought of what I am about to say.

'Things are . . . a little tight at the moment. Liam's taken a pay cut and with the wedding and everything . . .' I take a deep breath. 'Do you think you could . . . you and Janet could . . .'

'Say no more, Penny.' I look up at Gerard. 'I wondered how long it would take you to come to me. I know how stubborn Liam is.'

'He doesn't know I'm here,' I mumble, feeling a twinge of guilt. For all Gerard's talk of the family sticking together, Liam has consistently refused to approach his parents for help. I don't want to be here either, but each wedding payment that comes out is inching us further and further into the red.

'Well, let's keep it that way, shall we?' Gerard says, with one of his winks. 'How about we give you an early wedding donation to see you through the next few months?'

Relief rushes through me.

'Thanks Gerard,' I say, gratefully, my face going red. 'I wouldn't have asked if we didn't need to . . .'

Gerard shakes his head, but he looks pleased with himself.

'Not a problem.' He reaches out and puts his hand on my knee again. This time he doesn't move it. I swallow. 'Like I said, us Haughtons stick together. You're family now, Penny.'

'Thanks, Gerard. I really appreciate it.' Suddenly desperate to get away, I say, 'Maybe a cheque, then? Or . . .'

'Well actually,' Gerard says. His hand hasn't moved. 'Now you're here, perhaps first . . . you could do a little favour for me?'

Chapter Forty-Eight

Rachel

Now

I lie awake, long after I have showered and climbed into bed, long after Katie has left and the front door closed. Long after Mum goes up to bed, her footsteps measured for the first time in months, perhaps years. I should be glad that I won't find her in her usual state tomorrow, but I'm not; I'm angry at this Katie woman for invading our space with her presumptuous air, worried that her presence in the house is somehow connected to Liam. I thump my pillow to get more comfortable, desperate for sleep. Perhaps I should just leave, hand in my notice. Get away from Liam and any danger I may have found myself in. It's what any sensible, sane person would do. *Then why aren't you?*

The next morning I arrive bleary-eyed at my desk, my teeth still coated in fuzzy red-wine plaque and my head aching.

'Morning,' Didi says as I sit down. Her tone is frosty, but at least she is talking to me. I had almost completely forgotten about Sasha's revelation that Penny and I went out drinking at the weekend. I mumble a good morning back. Didi is holding her usual yoghurt pot and she eyes me warily, her expression softening ever so slightly.

'Everything alright?'

I nod.

'Didn't sleep well, that's all.'

'Maybe you should take some time off? You've got about three months' worth of leave you've never taken.'

I almost laugh at this. Where would I go? With whom? For one mad moment, an image pops into my mind of drinking white wine and eating seafood in some French fishing village with Connor. Then I remember Mum. And Wayne Stephens.

'Maybe,' I mumble.

As Didi and I settle down to work, low voices begin to rumble from upstairs. A moment later the sound grows louder, punctuated by the thud of footsteps on the stairs. We both look up as Charles and Liam stride into the room. Charles's deeply tanned face is creased with tension, whilst Liam's face is flushed, his jaw tight. He avoids looking at me and I feel anticipation pulse through me.

'What's wrong?' Didi immediately asks.

'The memory card,' Liam says, his eyes sweeping across the office. 'Shelly McKenzie's memory card. Have either of you seen it?'

'The alibi memory card?' Didi says, quickly.

'Yes, the alibi memory card,' Liam replies, with barely contained frustration. 'The one that's crucial to the whole case. The one that might keep her out of a jail cell. Have either of you seen it?'

'Of course not,' Didi says, swiftly, her voice tight.

'Rachel?' Charles barks. His face is growing redder and redder.

'No,' I say, immediately. 'I've not been working that case since you gave it to Liam.' My tone sounds too quick, too defensive.

There is a long, suffocating silence.

'Mrs McKenzie is coming in this afternoon,' Charles says, his voice tight. He turns to Liam. 'We have to find that memory card.'

'Are you sure you didn't move it?' I ask Liam.

'Of course I didn't,' he shoots back and I feel a thrill of fear as he glares at me. 'I locked it in my filing cabinet. Now it's gone.'

The tension in the air tightens even further, like a noose.

'The McKenzie case is hanging by a thread,' Charles says. He looks as though he is trying to stop himself having a heart attack. He levels a tight gaze on Liam. 'Find it. Now.'

Charles leaves the office and Liam follows him. He looks almost panicked. Didi and I look at one another. My heart is racing.

'If Shelly McKenzie finds out that evidence is gone . . .' I say.

'I know,' Didi says. Her face is pale. 'I haven't touched it. Have you?'

I shake my head.

'. . . then Liam is in real trouble,' Didi says.

We both begin performative searches of our desks, opening drawers and then turning to the filing cabinets behind our desks. During our search, the office buzzer goes and we both look up. To my surprise, I see a flash of familiar red hair.

'Penny,' I say quickly, as she walks in. 'If you're here to see Liam, it's not a good time . . .'

'Oh?' Penny asks, immediately looking concerned.

'Just . . . something from a case is missing. It's a bit stressful at the moment.'

'Oh dear,' she glances towards the office door and the stairs to Liam's office, then turns back to me. 'I actually came to see you, anyway.'

I blink in surprise. Penny looks over to where Didi is standing next to her desk and smiles.

'I'm Penny, Liam's fiancée,' she says.

'Oh,' Didi says, looking surprised. 'Nice to meet you.' For some reason Didi's voice isn't as bright as it normally is. She is eyeing Penny in a funny way. I turn back to Penny.

'What did you want to see me about?' I ask. 'Do you want a drink, or anything?'

'No, that's okay, I can't stop long. I just wanted to give you this.' She fumbles in her bag and pulls out a small A5 piece of paper. For one awful moment, I think it's another funfair flyer, but when Penny hands it over to me, I see that it's a brightly-coloured invitation.

'My hen-do,' she says. 'I know it's last minute, but I really want you there.'

My eyes widen.

'Your hen-do?'

Penny smiles and nods.

'You have to be there. You're my oldest friend. My maid of honour has reorganised the whole thing so it's here in town. Do you think you could book the Friday off? I won't take no for an answer.'

I open and close my mouth a few times. I don't know what to say. Is it weird, going to Penny's hen-do, given our history? Or is this yet another olive branch from Penny?

'I know what you're thinking,' Penny says. 'And Janet won't be there. I'm doing an afternoon tea with the *older* women this week.' She giggles. 'So, you're coming, yeah?'

'Sure,' I say, not knowing what else I can do. 'I'll see if I can get the day off.'

Penny claps her hands.

'Great news! Can't wait to see you there.' She straightens up and hoists her handbag back onto her shoulder. 'I had better go before Liam thinks I'm checking up on him. See you both later.'

She waves and leaves the office, her red hair swinging behind her. Didi doesn't say anything about this visit from Penny, she just goes straight back to looking for the memory card. I'm sure it's because of the hen-do invite, given that I missed her party last weekend. I don't want to fall out with Didi – she's one of my only friends – but I also don't have the capacity to reassure her right now.

Connor told me to stay away from Liam, Penny and Tom. Deep down, I know he's right. And yet there is something that is drawing me to Penny. A desire to find out more about her life, about Liam. It's like a compulsion I can't seem to fight. And after all, a hen-do with just Penny and her friends won't be dangerous, I reason. It's not like anything could happen.

Chapter Forty-Nine

Penny

Now

I return home after stopping by the law firm and go back to my makeshift desk in Gran's conservatory. It is bright and sunny, the summer sunlight pouring through the glass, bathing the small table in a white-yellow glow. My fingers drum on the keyboard, though I don't type anything. My thoughts – normally so calm, so organised, reflecting my outer being – are now tangled, snagging on unwanted thoughts. Rachel. Gerard. Liam. It's all become such a mess. Even Rachel seemed tense when I went in, as though she was hiding something. Telling me that it wasn't a good time. Had something happened between her and Liam? I realise I am gnawing at the nail on my index finger and pull my hand away from my mouth. I mustn't have chewed nails for the wedding photos. With no nail to chew, I stare blankly at my laptop screen. New emails are waiting in my inbox, but I don't see them, see only the whiteness of the screen.

Should I tell Liam what happened when I went to see Gerard? My stomach lurches. I can't. The thought of his reaction turns my stomach. Meanwhile, the cheque Gerard wrote me burns a hole in my pocket. I haven't decided whether to cash it into my own account, or into our joint account and simply wait for the inevitable fallout. Of how to explain to Liam that I went to Gerard and now . . . now I am caught in a net I have no way out of.

Chapter Fifty

Rachel

Now

The rest of the afternoon is beyond tense. The office is searched, but there is still no sign of the memory card. I avoid going upstairs, hearing from Didi that Liam has cancelled his afternoon appointment with Shelly McKenzie. Charles comes down on his way out to court whilst Didi is in the kitchen getting coffee. His hair is sticking up on one side, as though he has been running his hand through it, and his jaw is clenched.

'Any sign of the memory card?' he asks immediately.

I shake my head.

'I'm sure it'll turn up, Charles.'

He makes an odd sort of hissing noise through his lips, one hand on the door handle.

'I can't understand it,' he says. 'We hire a lawyer with an exemplary background and then for the first time ever, crucial evidence goes missing.'

'What are you getting at?' I ask, carefully.

Charles makes the hissing noise again and shifts his weight.

'I'm saying, I took a chance on him. He impressed me. But I'm starting to question my decision. Justine never lost anything.'

I almost laugh at this: Charles was desperate to hire Liam. It was hardly taking a chance on him.

'I wonder . . .' Charles begins pensively, his hand still clutching the door handle, 'this couldn't be a set-up, could it? From his old firm? Wanting Liam to poach clients for them?'

'It could be,' Didi says unexpectedly, looking thoughtful. I glance at her in surprise: she seems so taken with Liam; is she now doubting him, just like Charles?

With a final scowl, Charles leaves and I sit there, thinking about the memory card. For the first time ever, it looks as though Liam might have to face the consequences of something going wrong. *Until Gerard steps in and fixes it all for him.* I glance out of the window, feeling the urge to go for a swim to release some tension, but I am hesitant. It isn't just about what happened last time – when the current caught me in its clutches. I haven't forgotten about this Wayne Stephens character. What if he's still watching me? I would be making myself a sitting duck. So instead, when the end of the day finally arrives, I say goodnight to Didi and head home.

The sunlight has broken through the tail end of the storm and the town is suddenly much brighter as I walk the familiar route home. All along the beach, people are emerging again after the past few days, walking along the promenade with their dogs, queuing up for ice cream or chips at the vans parked by the pier. There is a buzz about the place, like this is just a normal, seaside town. Like bad things have never happened here.

The house is empty when I get home. As soon as I enter the kitchen, I see a note on the table from Mum.

The Funfair

*Katie has a spare ticket to a show in the city tonight –
will be home tomorrow. Mum.*

I read and re-read the note, trying not to panic. I can't
remember the last time Mum went out with a friend, let
alone stayed overnight anywhere. She's far too dependent on alcohol to be able to do that kind of thing without it going wrong. Does this Katie woman know about
Mum's drinking? None of this feels right. They only
bumped into each other yesterday. What if she's in danger? I pick up my phone and call Mum. She is useless
with her phone, but if she's going away for the night,
surely she would have taken it with her? The phone
rings and rings but Mum doesn't answer. I type a message to her to call me back, then switch my phone to full
volume and put it on the table. Not knowing what else
to do, I fetch one of the wine bottles Didi bought me for
my birthday and pour myself a glass, the glugging loud
in the silent kitchen.

The house grows steadily darker as the evening draws in
and I remain pacing around the kitchen, still in my work
clothes. I look out across the back garden, where for the
first time in a few days, everything looks golden and peaceful as the sun sets over it. No sign that there was anyone
watching us the other night, when the police came around.
No indentations in the grass, nothing.

My phone dings loudly on the table and I lunge for it,
hoping it is Mum: but then I see it's an email. It takes me
a moment to register who it's from.

Subject: Employment Status Confirmation – Liam Haughton
Dear Ms Kingston,
Thank you for your request.
Mr. Liam Haughton left Ashford Langley LLP on January 12th of this year. In this case, we are unable to provide any further reference due to the nature of his departure which was not, as your email states, as a result of a redundancy. We encourage you to reach out to Mr Haughton directly for more details.
Kind regards,
Human Resources
Ashford Langley LLP

I have to re-read the email to double-check what I am seeing. Liam wasn't made redundant? *Due to the nature of his departure*. That makes it sound like . . . Liam was fired. Almost six months ago. Charles's comment earlier makes more sense now: *'I took a chance on him.'* Is that why Liam ended up back here? Because he couldn't get a job anywhere else?

There is a noise outside the house: I hear the gate creak slowly. I freeze, listening. Could Mum be back early? Could it be – I swallow – Wayne Stephens? Here as soon as Mum was out of the way? I wait, my phone clutched in my hand. Then the doorbell rings.

Chapter Fifty-One

Rachel

Now

I walk slowly down the hallway, my heart hammering. As soon as I open the door, I find Connor on the doorstep. Relief floods through me.

'Oh,' I say, letting out a breath. 'It's just you.'

Connor grins.

'Who were you expecting? I feel sorry for them, already.'

I shake myself, trying to rid myself of the paranoia. It's just Connor.

'Can I come in?' he asks. I nod and step back to let him through the door. It's a relief to have someone here, to have a reassuring presence in the house.

I close the door and follow him into the kitchen, where he's already taken his shoes off, as though he has been here many times. For a moment, the sight of him so relaxed catches me off guard. It's almost . . . normal.

'Sorry for just dropping by, but I wanted to check how you're doing after yesterday.' His voice is soft, concerned. 'Has anything else strange happened? Any sign of Wayne Stephens?'

'Funny you should ask.'

I tell him about the memory card going missing, the abrupt arrival of Katie, and Mum's overnight trip with her.

'And,' I finish, holding my phone out to show Connor the screen, 'I just got this from Liam's old firm. Penny said he was made redundant, but this email pretty much says he was fired.'

Connor frowns down at the screen.

'Whatever it was, must have been bad not to have got any reference at all. Do you think . . . he did it again? What he did to you?'

'Maybe.' I chew my lip for a moment. 'Do you think you could find out?'

Connor nods slowly and hands my phone back.

'I can't promise anything. But I can try.'

'Thank you.'

Suddenly exhausted, I sink down into a chair and reach for my glass of wine. The emotional toll of the past few days presses down on me. It's like everything has been freshly stirred up, like swirling sediment at the bottom of old wine: the past, Liam, Mum.

'I just don't understand,' I say. 'I don't get why Penny and Liam came back . . . why Liam is watching me, trying to mess with my head.'

'Well, if he's lost his job, the last thing he's going to want is you looking too closely at him,' Connor says, then raises an eyebrow, 'which is *exactly* what it sounds like you're doing. If he's got more recent skeletons in his closet, he might have more reason than ever to keep you quiet.'

'If he has, Penny can't know about them. She would never marry him if she did.'

Connor looks up at the ceiling, still thinking.

'Could there be something about that night – something you haven't maybe remembered yet – that he's afraid might come out?'

As unpleasant as it is to think back to that night, I rack my brains for something I might have missed. But it's so hard to separate the facts from my nightmares anymore. My memories keep snagging on the gaps, like wool on barbed wire.

'I don't think so. I would have to go back over my police statement to try and remember.' This reminds me that Liam has my police statement. How could I have been so stupid, leaving it down in that basement?

Unable to sit still any longer, I get up and cross over to the back doors again. Outside, the garden is bathed in a soft twilight. It looks so peaceful, so far removed from the turmoil in my head.

'None of this is a coincidence,' I say, more to myself than Connor. 'He's planning something, I just don't know what. But I have to figure it out before it's too late.'

Connor stands too, his expression darkening.

'Look . . . maybe you shouldn't be getting yourself caught up in this, Rach. It's not for you to figure out.'

'You just said you were going to help me look into it,' I say, indignantly. I need Connor.

'I know I did. But I'm not so sure you should be getting involved. Remember Wayne Stephens? Maybe it's best if you stay away from Liam. Stay away from all of them.'

'Penny's invited me to her hen-do on Friday,' I admit.

'You aren't thinking of going?' Connor asks, his face taut with disbelief.

'I think it's a good opportunity,' I say, crossing my arms defensively. 'Think about it, some of these girls will have been at uni with Liam. They might be able to shed some light on the last few years of his life.'

Connor shakes his head vehemently.

'You're walking right into the monster's lair, Rachel.'

'If no one goes in,' I say, 'no one ever destroys the monster.'

Connor sighs and takes a step closer. His hands settle gently on my shoulders, his voice soft but urgent.

'Listen, I know you want answers, I get that. But let's not get too carried away before we know more. You don't necessarily know that all this is even connected to what happened back then. Maybe your mum really is just out with an old friend, maybe the memory card really has just been misplaced. None of these things are exactly a direct threat, are they?'

'And the person who was watching me whilst I was swimming the other day?' I challenge, feeling a fresh wave of frustration rising in my chest.

Connor's eyes remain calm, though there is a flicker of something unreadable in his eyes.

'It could have been a dog walker. Or someone worried you were in trouble. I'm just saying, not everything has to necessarily be suspicious.'

I stare at Connor. Realisation slowly dawns on me.

'You don't believe me, do you?'

'Of course I believe you, Rach,' Connor says, his voice immediately softening. 'I've been here for you this whole time, haven't I? All I've wanted since the moment I met you is to be there for you.' He runs a hand through his hair. 'What I'm saying is that we all see the world through our own lens, through our own perspective. You went through something traumatic fifteen years ago and now Liam is back. Of course your view of things is going to be influenced by what happened. But that doesn't necessarily mean every little thing is connected to him.'

'That's just a fancy way of saying I'm being paranoid,' I snap, feeling the heat rising in my cheeks. *Not him, too.* 'I knew I shouldn't have trusted you. Christ, I bet your damn paper is funded by the Haughtons.'

Now it is Connor's turn to go red.

'How can you say that? I believe every word you've ever said to me. But that doesn't mean there can't be another explanation. Having tunnel vision never helped anyone.'

'Because journalists are so open-minded,' I snap back, turning away from him and pouring myself another glass of wine so that I don't have to look at him. I can't believe he is saying all this. I thought he was supportive, believed in me. I hear footsteps behind me and wonder if he is leaving, but instead he turns me around, taking the wine glass from my hand and putting it down on the table. He cups my face in his hands and looks beseechingly at me with his dark brown eyes.

'Rach, listen to me. I really care about you,' he says, gently. 'But I'm scared that you're going to put yourself in real danger because of all this. I'm just asking you to take a step back.'

I blink back the tears threatening to spill over. I hardly ever cry.

'I can't. Not until I get answers.'

Connor sighs and pulls away. Frustration is etched across his face but he seems to sense not to push it.

'Fine. I get it. But at least let me stay here tonight, okay? We can cook something together. It'll help take your mind off things whilst you wait for your mum to call back.'

I nod, feeling exhausted all of a sudden. It isn't just the argument with Connor, the fear of him not believing me . . . it's more than that. It's the fact that I still haven't told him the full story.

Chapter Fifty-Two
Rachel
2005

I was upstairs when the doorbell rang. Dad was downstairs and Mum was in bed even though it was only three o'clock in the afternoon. I stayed curled up on the window seat, ignoring the cardboard boxes and suitcases in the corner, only half-packed to take to drama school. I couldn't believe how excited I had been about it all, the way I had pictured the parties with Liam in student houses, the pubs we would get to know, the train rides back home together on weekends and holidays. I wondered what he was doing now. Was he talking excitedly to Penny about Durham? My best friend, who hadn't called or text once. It would be them on the train together, instead, coming back at Christmas with full suitcases, drinking next to each other on the cheap off-peak seats.

The doorbell rang, longer this time. I suddenly wondered if it could be the police. They said they were checking out the details of my statement. My stomach churned with anxiety. I climbed off the window seat and crept out to the landing, peering through the window that overlooked the front porch. I couldn't see the familiar blonde hair of PC Thompson, but before I could make out who it was, I heard Dad opening the front door.

'Gerard,' Dad's voice was surprised but wary.

My stomach lurched. Liam's dad was here? I pressed my back against the wall, my heart pounding.

'John,' Gerard's loud voice carried through the hallway. 'I think we need to talk, don't you?'

'If it's about the investigation, I don't think that's a good idea. It's a conflict of interest.'

'Oh for god's sake, get off your high horse. This is about our kids.'

There was a long pause. Tell him to go away, Dad, I thought. Don't let him in. But he must have done, because a moment later the door clicked shut and two lots of footsteps walked down the hallway into the lounge. Their voices grew muffled once they entered the lounge. My mind whirled with anxiety. I chewed anxiously on my lip, not sure what to do, torn between hiding back in my bedroom and finding out what they were saying. Making my mind up, I crept carefully along the landing and down the stairs, avoiding all the areas I knew would creak. Eventually I made it downstairs and tiptoed along the hallway to where the lounge door stood ajar.

'You have a choice, John,' Gerard was saying. 'Do the right thing.'

'What choice?' Dad's voice was thick with anger. 'What you're offering isn't a choice. It's a threat.'

I held my breath. A threat?

'It's not a threat. It's business,' Gerard said. 'You and I both know Rachel's allegation is baseless, though no one seems to know why she would do such a thing. I can't do business with someone whose daughter is accusing my own son of something so heinous.'

'It was you, wasn't it? You spoke to one of your contacts at the council,' Dad's tone was suddenly bitter, 'and got them to revoke the restaurant's health and safety licence.'

There was a horrible, swooping sensation in my stomach. The licence? I thought Dad had sorted that out with the council. He had told me everything was fine.

'And I can just as easily get it approved again,' Gerard said smoothly, 'but only if Rachel drops the charges and leaves no room for ambiguity that my son is innocent. I will not have this hanging over his head for the rest of his life.'

'That restaurant has been my dream,' Dad said, his voice quieter now. 'You were the one who persuaded me to go for it. I've re-mortgaged my house. Left my job. Poured everything I have into it.'

'Then be a man,' Gerard said coldly. 'Don't just stand by and let these things unfold like you do with your wife at every party. Because when it all comes crashing down, you'll be the one who loses.'

'You've got some nerve,' Dad said. His voice was shaking. 'The arrogance to think that it's Rachel who's lying and not your precious son.'

'Emotions aside, John, the facts of her story don't add up.'

There was a shuffling sound, as though someone was getting up. Panicked, I half crept, half-ran down the hallway and hid in the kitchen, blocked from view, but listening in the doorway. The lounge door creaked open and Gerard's voice rang through the hallway as if he was shouting in my ear.

'She's lying to you, John. I think somewhere deep down, you know that.'

There was a long silence.

'I'll wait until this evening,' Gerard said, his voice like steel. 'If I don't hear from you that the charges have been dropped and a full apology issued, you can say goodbye to the restaurant. And good luck getting another job in this town.'

The front door slammed and the house fell silent. I stayed frozen in the kitchen doorway, my heart pounding. Gerard's threat hung in the air like a black cloud. It never occurred to me that he would go this far, that he would interfere with Dad's restaurant. His dream. And then Gerard would stop him getting another job? I felt sick. This was big, scary, adult stuff and I was drowning beneath it.

There was silence from the hallway. After a few minutes, I heard the sound of Dad going upstairs and his study door opening and closing. I clenched and unclenched my fists, trying to decide what to do. Everything was completely out of control now, and Dad was being pulled into this nightmare. He was the only person I cared about in the entire world. I couldn't stand it any longer. I knew what I had to do.

I walked quickly to the phone in the hallway, my hands trembling as I picked up the receiver. With shaking fingers, I pulled DC Rainer's card from the drawer and dialled the number printed on it.

When it was done, I hung the phone up and slumped against the wall, breathing heavily. I had done it. It was over. Now I just had to worry about being charged for making a false complaint.

I walked slowly upstairs towards Dad's study. I was even more nervous about telling him than I was about telling the police. I was scared to see the disappointment in his eyes. But I kept telling myself at least it was over, now. The restaurant *would be safe. I stood outside his study and took a deep breath. Just as I took hold of the door handle, I heard a noise from the other side of the door. A strange, heavy, thud. Pushing the study door open, my blood ran cold. Dad was slumped over his desk, one hand gripping his chest, his face pale and contorted with pain. The radio hummed innocently in the background, completely out of place in the scene of panic unfolding before me.*

'Dad!' I cried, rushing to his side. His breathing was laboured, his eyes wide with fear.

'Ambulance . . .' he wheezed, struggling to get the word out. I got up and tore back down the stairs to the hallway phone. I grabbed the receiver, my fingers fumbling over the buttons as I dialled 999. Tears blurred my vision as I fought to stay calm, trying to explain to the operator what was happening. Please, please, let him be okay. He was all that mattered in that moment, all that had ever mattered to me.

The phone operator kept asking questions, questions I couldn't answer about 'was he pale' and 'was he in pain', and when I couldn't stand it anymore I shouted at them that the front door was unlocked and raced back upstairs, almost falling over twice. I tore back into the study and fell to my knees beside Dad.

'Dad,' I whispered urgently, 'Dad, someone's coming.'

But he didn't respond.

Chapter Fifty-Three

Rachel

Now

When Connor and I arrive at his place, I can't help but blink in surprise. I'd never been over before, but I had always pictured him living in one of the modern flats so common in the town; something practical and minimalist, to match his neat desk. But he takes us to the other side of town and down a narrow winding road, emerging beside a small, stone-built cottage. In the fading light, I can see worn wooden furniture out front and pink sea thrift bobbing in the breeze. It sits on a secluded spot right on the edge of a stretch of pebbled beach, facing the sea, tucked away from the public part of the path. The sound of the waves is close, soothing, almost lulling me out of my anxious thoughts. Almost.

'This is where you live?' I ask, unable to mask my surprise.

Connor chuckles and nods.

'It belonged to my grandad. My mum inherited it and my sister didn't want it, so I live here. Thought I could rent it out, when I . . . you know. Move out of town.'

I can't help but feel a pang at the reminder that he's planning to leave as soon as he can. Don't think about

269

it. *Not right now*. We climb out of the car and Connor grabs my overnight bag from the back seat and waits for me to follow.

Inside, the cottage is even more pleasantly surprising. The ceilings are low, with dark wooden beams, and grey slate flooring underfoot. The decor is cosy and mismatched, though not without thought: a beautiful ash-wood chair sits in the corner by the window, a big cosy throw is spread across the sofa, and a faded but warm rug takes up almost the entire space. The walls are a soft white and on them hang framed photos, including one of what must be Connor's grandparents standing proudly on the beach out front, perhaps decades ago. The place smells faintly of wood and saltwater, a scent that reminds me of childhood holidays and long-forgotten days spent on the beach with Penny. It's a world away from my mother's house, the tension of the town, and everything that feels so heavy right now. For one brief moment, I feel like I've stepped out of the chaos and into somewhere almost dreamlike.

'This is . . . really lovely,' I say softly.

Connor glances around, a small smile tugging at his lips.

'Yeah. It's a bit old-fashioned and the signal is crap. But that's why I like it.' He drops my bag by the sofa and heads into the kitchen, calling back over his shoulder 'Make yourself at home. I'll get us some drinks. Red wine okay?'

I nod and follow him into the kitchen, which is as cosy as the rest of the cottage, with green cabinets and wooden worktops. I can imagine a life spent curling up with a book, listening to the waves just outside the window. As I stand by the counter in the small kitchen, my eyes drift to the back door, which opens directly onto the pebbled beach. The kind of beach I could walk straight out onto in the mornings, for a swim that would be completely private.

'Why don't you go and get changed?' Connor asks. 'I'll get a fire going, it can get a bit cold in here at night, even in summer.'

I follow his directions up the narrow wooden stairs to the bathroom. Just like the rest of the house, it's painted white, with sloping ceilings and a view of the dark waves. I get changed into some trackies and a sweatshirt and look at myself in the mirror. But I barely see the pale-faced, brown-haired woman in the reflection. All I see is a woman tangled in a mess that she doesn't know how to escape from. Even here, in this homely seaside cottage, the threat lingers. I have to tell Connor the truth, before he finds out some other way.

I walk back downstairs to find Connor on the sofa, the fire in the wood burner already crackling happily. He hands me a glass of wine and I sit beside him on the worn sofa, pulling the throw up around me. We sit in silence for a moment, the sound of waves just audible above the sound of the fire. I am reluctant to break the spell of this peaceful cottage, to ruin it with my confession, but I don't have a choice. Not if I want to finally figure out what Liam is doing back here and why he is watching me. I have to separate the fact from the fiction.

'There's something I haven't told you,' I begin. Connor looks up at me but doesn't say anything. I know he is waiting, letting me talk. I take a deep breath.

'Not all of my police statement was true,' I say quietly. I feel Connor shift next to me, but I can't look at him. 'I . . . knew the police didn't believe my story. I could see it in their eyes, they weren't going to do anything about it. It was the Haughtons we were talking about . . . you should have seen the way the police were looking at me. Like I was mad. So I . . . I told them that it wasn't just that night at the fairground. That he'd done it before.'

There is a long pause. I can feel the weight of my confession hanging between us. Connor still hasn't said anything.

'I didn't think it through,' I say, my voice slightly breathless. 'Once I'd said it, there was no going back. And part of me . . .' I hesitate, glancing across at him, ' . . . part of me thought that maybe that's what it takes. Maybe this is how I get them to listen. To take me seriously.'

It was justified. They didn't believe me. I know they didn't. I had to make them listen.

Sometimes the ends justify the means.

I look at Connor again, waiting to see how he is going to react.

'So . . . the other time didn't happen?' Connor asks.

I shake my head.

'No, I . . . made that part up. But that doesn't mean that what happened at the fairground wasn't real. It was.' My voice catches in my throat as I say it. 'I just . . . I was afraid they wouldn't do anything about it. They'd let him walk away, and that would be it. And he would congratulate himself on being Liam Haughton. Untouchable.'

Connor looks back at me with a mixture of thoughtfulness and something else I can't place. Is he judging me?

'And now Liam has your statements, you think? Because your legal file is missing?'

I nod, swallowing. If Liam has seen my statement, he will have seen just how much I said . . . how detailed and elaborate the accusations became. Not only that, but he will also have seen the parts from the fairground night where I stretched the truths, know the gaps where my memory failed me. It would be like looking into the cracks of my mind, the parts I tried to paper over with lies.

'He knew the basic accusations but . . . not everything. It was too early in the investigation. But if he's seen it all now . . . maybe this is his way of telling me that if I try and raise it again, no one will believe me. Why would they?'

Connor reaches for my hand, squeezing it gently.

'Well, you've got me on your side this time,' he says, firmly. 'We'll figure this out.'

I squeeze his hand back.

'You're not going anywhere?'

'I'm not going anywhere.'

He looks at me, the air between us suddenly heavy with something else. A realisation that we are completely alone. Then my phone rings from my bag. I jump up and run across to get it out. My heart leaps when I see Mum's name on the screen.

'Mum? Where are you? I've been worried.'

'I'm fine, Rachel,' Mum says, her voice surprisingly bright. The signal is patchy, but she doesn't sound drunk. In the background there is a low hum of voices. 'Still at the show. It's the interval. We're having a lovely time.' She giggles. She actually giggles. Mum, happy. Mum, out with a friend. 'Don't worry about me. Have a good night. I'll see you tomorrow.'

She hangs up before I can say anything more than a quick 'Bye'.

Connor comes up behind me as I'm still staring at my phone and wraps his arms around me. The fire crackles softly behind us, flickering shadows across the wall.

'How about we forget about it all for tonight?' he asks softly. 'Your mum is safe, you're safe.'

I lean back against him.

'Okay.'

Chapter Fifty-Four

Rachel

Now

When I wake the next morning, the first thing I notice is how the light is different to the light in my bedroom: it filters softly through the thin curtains, reminding me I am in Connor's bedroom. The room smells like the sea – briny and fresh – and for a few blissful seconds everything that has been happening in the past few days is kept at bay, beyond the walls of this cottage.

Connor stirs beside me, his hand brushing my side as he stretches like a cat. I turn to look at him and see a soft smile tugging at the corners of his lips.

'Morning,' he murmurs.

We lie in comfortable silence for a few moments, neither of us rushing to get up. Like a child, I wish I could just stay in this bed, with the duvet tucked under my chin, and not face the day. Eventually, Connor rolls out of bed and pulls on a pair of shorts.

'Coffee?'

'Yes please.'

By the time I reluctantly push back the duvet and get up, Connor already has two steaming mugs of coffee on the worn wooden counter. I wrap my hands around one, letting the warmth seep into me, then wander into the lounge and start looking at the photos on the wall. Connor comes to join me, pointing out different family members who are now long gone, but who had once lived in this cottage.

'That's my favourite one,' he says, pointing to a black and white photo of a man with large bottle-lens glasses, proudly holding up a fish. 'That's my grandad. He loved to fish. I think that's the biggest haddock he ever caught.'

'It's a sea bass.'

Connor glances at me in surprise.

'What?'

'The fish. It's not a haddock, it's a sea bass.'

Connor blinks for a moment, then laughs.

'You know fish?'

'A little. My dad was obsessed with seafood. Opening a seafood restaurant was his dream. He almost did it, too.'

Connor's eyes widen with realisation.

'Wait . . . John's Catch . . . the restaurant on the promenade. That was your dad's place? The restaurant that never opened?'

I nod, the memories flooding back, bittersweet.

'I'm so sorry, Rach. What awful timing that he died right before.'

'I don't know if it would have opened, anyway.'

'Why not?'

'After I made the allegation against Liam, Gerard threatened Dad. Told him the restaurant would be ruined if I didn't drop the charges. But knowing Gerard Haughton, he still would have ruined the restaurant one way or another.'

Connor lets out a heavy breath, his face a mixture of anger and pity.

'So that's why you said you made it up? To appease the Haughtons?'

I nod.

'I didn't think I had a choice.'

I also knew, though I don't tell Connor this, that it was only a matter of time before my lies came out, once the police started digging. I had wanted to make that call, in the end.

There is a heavy silence. I watch Connor's expression as he pieces together the puzzle of my life, connects all the dots he didn't have before. I'm not sure how I feel about everything I've told him now. Whether I should have told him quite so much.

'I'm going to get changed,' I say, moving towards the stairs. I leave my coffee on the side in the kitchen as I make my way back up to the first floor. When I reach the top of the stairs I notice, for the first time, another door, other than the bathroom and bedroom. It's closed, but I'm curious. We've spoken so much about me, I want to know more about Connor. Glancing over my shoulder to make sure he isn't about to come upstairs, I slowly walk towards the door and turn the handle. The door creaks slightly as I open it and I pause, listening . . . but there is no sound from downstairs. Slowly, I open the door the rest of the way and step inside.

It is another small, bright room, with a window overlooking the beach. There is hardly anything in here: just a chest of drawers on the left and a desk and chair in front of the window. I walk over to the desk, conscious of my footsteps creaking on the wooden floorboards.

The view through the window is serene: the water shimmers in the pale morning sunlight. I can see why he would position the desk right here. Unlike his desk in his office, this desk is covered in papers; articles, photos, clippings. I glance down – and my heart stops. There are images of the funfair scattered across the surface. The same flyer that has been posted repeatedly through my own door, old newspapers articles and – my stomach turns – a piece of paper with a name written at the very top. *Rachel Kingston.* Below is a list of scribbled notes. *1 Sep 2005 – accusation made against LH. Three witness statements from fellow school friends from that night – Penny, Isaac, Tom. Assault reportedly happened at 11 p.m. Rachel – drunk.* I swallow. He's been . . . looking into the case? Into me? *Rachel – drunk.* My eyes sweep across the newspaper clippings: they are all about the fairground, old photos from times when it was open, even photos from when it was abandoned. The image is visceral and catches me unaware: the old, rusting roller coaster, the broken Ferris wheel. I can almost hear the shouts, the creaking of the Ferris wheel in the wind. A cold dread creeps over me.

There is a noise behind me and I spin around to find Connor standing in the doorway.

'Connor . . .' I say slowly. 'Why do you have all this?' I pick up the piece of paper with my name on it. 'And what the hell is this?'

Connor walks into the room. His expression is unreadable.

'I was looking into the case. Trying to help you,' he says, sounding wary. 'I needed a bit of background, that's all.'

'And what about all the funfair stuff?' I demand.

'It's just work stuff,' he says calmly, picking up one of the clippings and studying it for a moment. 'A puff piece on the re-opening of the fairground. Front-page news.'

'This flyer . . .' I say, unable to shake off the feeling that something isn't right. Or am I just being paranoid, again?

'Yeah, it's part of the marketing campaign, you must have seen them around?' Connor asked. 'They're plastering them all over town.'

' . . . And postcards? Are they part of the campaign?' I ask, slowly.

'Yeah, they've printed a load of new ones,' Connor shrugs. 'I guess the funfair is a huge deal for the area. I'm sorry,' he says suddenly, brushing my fingers with his own. 'I closed the door so that you didn't see any of this. I thought it was the last thing you would want to see right now.'

He tugs gently on my arm and leads me out of the room.

'Come on, your coffee is getting cold.'

I let him lead me out, but my temporary feeling of safety has gone with the images of the funfair, the reminder of that night. It's as though I will never be able to escape.

The fortune-teller's lips curved into a smile.

'There is no escaping your destiny. The chains are already wrapped around you.'

Chapter Fifty-Five

Rachel

Now

The wind whips at my hair as I sit on the old wooden bench along the promenade that evening, looking out over the sea. The brass plaque fixed to the centre of the bench reads *In loving memory of John, who loved this view*. My fingers trace the worn engraving, and I wish that touching his name could somehow bring him back, even for a second. This was our spot. After he died, the plaque became a way to keep it that way.

The beach stretches out in front of me, the early evening light blanketing the horizon in a soft glow. It's peaceful, with the crisp smell of salt and seaweed mingling with the coolness of the coming evening. It helps calm my thoughts slightly, the anxiety of the past couple of weeks momentarily at bay.

As I sit looking out over the horizon, a couple makes their way, unhurried, along the beach. I don't pay much attention to them until they cross my eyeline; then I realise there is something familiar about the way one of them moves. With a jolt, I realise it's Mum and Katie. Katie looks as elegant as ever, her hair in a low bun. They are walking slowly: Mum isn't really used to going for walks, and not along the sand.

I watch them as they pass, chatting to one another. It's strange, seeing her socialising. I feel like I'm spying somehow. Yet that same concern creeps over me, that fear of why Katie has suddenly appeared. Who just befriends an alcoholic out of nowhere? Does she think she's some sort of hero? Or is it more dangerous than that? Mum doesn't even look over at Dad's bench as they pass and I have to suppress a strange, hurt feeling. Everything in my life is suddenly changing.

I pull my phone out of my pocket and type Katie's name into the search bar, before remembering I don't know her surname. I try *Katie, Hollow Bay*. Then, *Katie, charity work. Katie, Liam Haughton. Katie, Wayne Stephens*. Predictably, nothing comes up on Katie. All I can see about Wayne Stephens are a couple of old articles about him committing ABH and some petty thefts years ago, when he was only a teenager. His more serious crimes aren't mentioned and I wonder if that's because of the organised crime circles Connor said he now moves in. I shiver, despite the warmth of the evening. I keep scrolling through the results anyway, just in case there is something buried further down. My eyes alight on an old article towards the bottom of the page that looks interesting, and I hurriedly skim it.

Local business mogul Gerard Haughton in bitter legal battle: Stephen Chapman brings a fresh case against the property and finance tycoon after a fight that has waged for three years.

The article is dated almost twenty years ago and I click off it again in irritation. It's not helpful, after all. I am about to tuck my phone back into my pocket when it rings: Connor's name appears on the screen. Despite my jangled nerves, I feel my shoulders relaxing at the sight of his name. It's a sense of protection I've not had before. Not since Dad died.

'Hey,' I say as I answer.

'Hey. You not at home?'

'No, I'm at the beach. How did you know?'

'Heard seagulls. You're not planning on swimming, are you?'

'No, I didn't think that was a good idea right now.'

'I agree. You can always come to the cottage and swim near here, so I can keep an eye out.'

'Thanks. That's sweet.'

'Any sign of the McKenzie memory card?'

My stomach gives a small, uncomfortable jolt at the reminder. I forgot that I had told Connor about it after the first glass of wine last night. The tension in the office today had been palpable: even Didi, ever the chatty one, kept her head firmly down and barely spoke.

'No, nothing. I've never seen Charles so stressed. Liam rescheduled his meeting with the client until next week to buy the firm some time, but it's only putting off the inevitable shitstorm.'

'Okay, well just keep your eyes peeled. If Liam is trying to frame you for something, you want your wits about you.'

'Have you found anything out about his job, yet?' I ask, wanting to change the subject.

'Well . . . I've managed to confirm what you suspected. It wasn't a redundancy, he was fired. One of their rising stars, too.'

I sit up straighter.

'And? What else?'

'That's it,' Connor says, and he sounds frustrated. 'I've not been able to find anything about what happened. It's weird . . . dead end after dead end.'

'Oh,' I say, disappointed, scratching at a splinter on the bench.

'That's information in itself though, in some ways,' Connor continues.

'How do you mean?'

'Well, normally when that happens it's because they kept it all internal. Confidentiality agreements signed, that sort of thing. Often it's when a firm doesn't want its reputation damaged.'

'Really?' I ask, thinking of the cagey email from HR. 'So if there was some kind of accusation against him? Maybe from a client?'

'Yes, or a colleague. There's definitely something weird going on. It's all very secretive.'

'Why does everyone always protect him?' I ask, frustrated. 'How does he always get away with everything?'

'I'm sure he won't this time. Are you still planning on going to the hen-do on Friday?'

I nod, then remember he can't see me.

'Yes. It's a good opportunity to get behind the scenes.'

'It's also a good opportunity to get yourself in trouble,' Connor says, dubiously. 'Just be careful okay?'

'I will.'

Chapter Fifty-Six

Rachel

Now

When Friday arrives, the day of the hen-do, I anxiously pace around my room, trying on make-up and then smearing it off again with cotton wool. I have to fit in today, but I don't know what I'm doing. I don't know what 'festival couture' even means. A quick internet search shows lots of images of girls wearing bindis, sequins, and glitter, whilst standing in the mud at festivals. I would have loved this theme, once; would have made sure I had the best outfit at the party. But now I stand in front of my open wardrobe, my heart racing. I am playing dress-up in someone else's world.

I pull out the closest things I can find to 'festival couture': an old pair of Dr Martens and a puffy three-tier gold skirt I once wore in a play. The waistband is tighter than the last time I wore it, and it digs into my skin uncomfortably. I add some shiny eyeshadow I got for Christmas from Didi last year and, for once, take the time to carefully blow-dry and style my hair. When I finally look in the mirror, I almost don't recognise myself. A surge of something unexpected – something almost giddy – runs through me. I look like one of the girls I am about to go and meet. Like I so often do, I picture a girl who isn't me in my grey life.

This girl lives in a cool London borough and goes to art festivals in her sparkly skirt. This girl belongs.

With an odd spring in my step, I walk downstairs to get my bag and find Mum in front of the freezer: it takes me a moment to register what she is doing. Then I spot the bottle of vodka in her hand, the glass frosted over.

'What are you doing?' I ask, sharply.

Mum glances over her shoulder, her expression caught between guilt and defiance. She closes the freezer with a loud snap.

'What does it look like?'

Disappointment crashes unexpectedly through me. It's the first time I've seen her with a drink in her hand for a few days now.

'I thought you were trying to stop.'

'I am,' Mum says, defensively. 'It's just one drink. It's the afternoon, isn't it? I haven't had one all day.'

I bite my lip, feeling the sting of anger mixed with helplessness. It was always going to come back to this, wasn't it?

'Don't,' I say, holding out my hand. 'Give it to me.'

There is a long silence. Something flickers in Mum's eyes, something fragile; I have never actively tried to stop her drinking before. She grips the bottle harder. Condensation drips off it and onto the floor. Then she snorts and the spell is broken.

'Don't be so melodramatic. You're hardly one to lecture me on drinking. Like mother like daughter, eh?'

'I am nothing like you,' I say through gritted teeth.

'That's what you tell yourself,' she says coldly. 'I see the truth. You leave this house to go to work, you come back again, you drink.'

'I drink a normal amount, a glass or two at most.'

'Listen to yourself!' Mum cries. 'You actually believe that, don't you? That's what is so terrifying. What about last weekend, Rachel? When you came home gone one in the morning and threw up everywhere? Do you think I didn't notice?'

I feel like I've been slapped. Mum, sensing the fight is won, turns away and begins pouring a glass. I stand there, torn. I am suddenly gripped by an overwhelming urge to stay and try to stop her, to pour the vodka down the drain and watch her all day if I have to. But I know I can't. Not today. Not when I've finally been invited to Penny's hen-do. I am caught between the past and the present, the path I want to take and the path I know I'm going to take. But what is the point of even deliberating? All paths lead to Liam, in the end. With a sick feeling in the pit of my stomach, I leave the house, just like Dad did so many times.

The hotel, like everything else in town, was once magnificent. It is an imposing, Victorian building with a sweeping entrance flanked by thick, intricately decorated columns and tall stained-glass windows. The brick is a deep red, and ivy tastefully covers the front of the building, hanging over the old sign that reads *The Belton Hotel*. From a distance it still appears grand, but the closer you draw the more neglected its visage becomes. The ivy is brown and out of control, obscuring half of the windows. The paint is flaking from the columns so that pock-marks of plaster are visible. It is just like the town itself: once beautiful, now fraying at the edges.

I step inside, the thick red carpet muffling my footsteps. It smells of mothballs and warm wood.

'Can I help you?' A young, blonde girl smiles from behind the reception desk.

'Oh, thanks, I'm with a hen-do today. Penny Adams?' Despite my edginess, and my churning anger at Mum, I experience a small thrill when her name touches my lips.

'Of course! Right this way. The rest of the bridal party has arrived.'

The bridal party. It sounds so grand. I smooth my gold skirt and follow the girl down a wide corridor and to a heavy wooden door. As she opens the door I am greeted by a wave of noisy chatter and laughter.

'Can I get you a drink?' the girl asks. 'There's wine and champagne in here already, but would you like a speciality cocktail?'

'A cocktail, please.'

The girl disappears, and I am left staring into a room full of women standing chatting around a long banquet-style table decorated with eucalyptus and tall champagne glasses. In the corner, I spot Penny, but she is deep in conversation with a group of friends, her back to me. I suddenly realise that no one else is in 'festival couture': they are all wearing elegant dresses or high waisted jeans. Casual, stylish clothes. *Fuck.* The outfit I had carefully curated, been almost proud of, suddenly makes me look like a kid in a dressing up box raid. Did I misunderstand the invite? I'm sure I read it properly. I stand awkwardly for a moment, feeling sweat pool under my arms. I didn't know what to do with myself. All around the room, someone has used string and mini pegs to hang up blown-up photos like glossy bunting. I pretend to look interested in them so it's not so obvious I am standing on my own. As I am looking, one of them catches my eye. In disbelief, I walk over to it and peer closer. It's of that night. The night of the funfair. There's a whole group of them, standing in front of the Funhouse. My stomach turns. Penny is at the front, Liam, Tom, Isaac and Sasha all behind her. Their soft, youthful faces are pale from the flash and they are all laughing, their arms around each other. I am not in the photo. Had he done it already? Or was this before? As I stand, staring at the photo, something niggles unpleasantly at me. I can't work out what it is. It's as though something is knocking at a door I can't open. What *is* it?

Not wanting to look at the photo any longer, I turn away and approach the long table at the back of the room which is piled with presents and bottles of champagne. Without checking if anyone is watching, I pour myself a glass, but I pour too fast and the bubbles froth and spill over the rim, dripping onto the pristine tablecloth.

'Rachel!' a voice rings out, startling me. I quickly step away from the wet tablecloth, to see a tall blonde woman approaching me. This can only be Clem, Penny's maid of honour. 'You made it, then,' she says, brightly.

I try to decipher what she means by this. Was she hoping I wasn't going to come? She makes it sound like something exclusive I have intruded on.

'I'm Clemence, by the way. Clem. It's so lovely to meet you. So funny, last week was the first time I had ever heard of you from Penny.'

'Oh yeah we sort of, umm, lost touch,' I say.

'Well, it's great to have you here.'

I wonder if I can detect sarcasm in her voice or it's just the way she speaks. The blonde receptionist appears at my side then, holding a cocktail. She glances at the champagne in my hand.

'Oh, I forgot I ordered that,' I say, putting the champagne flute down and taking the cocktail.

'Glad to see you getting in the right spirit,' Clem beams, her teeth so pearly they look moonlit. 'I love your outfit too, by the way.'

'Thanks,' I say, self-consciously. 'Did I misunderstand festival couture?'

'Oh no, everyone's just getting changed upstairs later on.'

Clem smiles benevolently at me and I decide to take the opportunity whilst I have it.

'So, you've known Liam and Penny for . . .' I begin, but Clem glances over her shoulder.

'Sorry babe, I've got a few things I need to attend to. Maid of honour, you know?' she jokingly rolls her eyes. 'Will you be okay? All the girls are super friendly.'

'I'll be fine,' I say, my stomach sinking at the thought of being left alone again. 'No problem.'

I sip my cocktail as Clem glides away. She is everything that a maid of honour should look like. Everything I would have wanted to be, when Penny and I planned our own weddings. *It's not fair*, I want to scream, looking around at this room full of stylish, laughing women. *I should have been one of you. I would have been one of you.*

If it wasn't for Liam Haughton.

Chapter Fifty-Seven

Rachel

Now

It takes Penny a good twenty minutes to realise I have arrived, by which time I've finished my cocktail and two more glasses of champagne, hovering at the back of the room.

'Rach!' she beams as she walks towards me. She looks so polished and poised, her silky white jumpsuit gleaming under the soft light of the hotel room. So at ease in this crowd of people. I can't help but feel a pang of jealousy.

When Penny reaches me, she pulls me into a tight hug. Her touch sends a shameful warmth rushing through me, like someone starved, and I want to hang on for longer, but she is already pulling away.

'I'm so glad you came,' she says, looking at me happily, her hands finding both of mine. 'It always seemed so tragic, the thought of not having any school friends here. It feels complete with you here.'

Her words trigger a confusing swell of emotions. I am, after all, here for the wrong reasons. If I can help it, she won't be having a wedding at all, I realise.

'I'm glad I could be here,' I reply, forcing a smile. 'Although you're missing the strippers you so desperately used to say you wanted.'

Penny bursts out laughing.

'You're right, I think Clem is a bit classier than that, sadly. Come on, everyone's sitting down.'

Clem has sat me amongst a group of friends who have all clearly known each other for a long time. Over lunch and headband making, they chatter away to each other, laughing at in-jokes and sharing life updates. They talk about their lives in the city, Instagram trends, bottomless brunches. I laugh when they laugh, nod when they nod, but none of it feels real to me. Can they sense how out of place I feel? *You're here for a reason. To get answers. To find out more about Liam.* But the longer I sit in this room, the more I feel like a fraud. The photo hangs tauntingly on the wall, just on the edge of my vision.

As I try to thread another flower onto my crown, I turn to my left, where Sonja and Anabelle, two of Penny's friends I remember from the WhatsApp group, have their heads together, whispering about something. I seize my moment.

'So, how do you know Penny?' I ask, trying to keep my smile bright as I finish my fifth glass of champagne and attempt to copy the way Sonja is doing her headband. Hers looks perfect.

Sonja laughs, as though the question has surprised her.

'God, we've been friends since *halls*,' she said, rolling her eyes as if to say, *aren't we old*. 'It was the first day and one by one these flatmates arrived and each time, my heart just *sank*. I just knew that they weren't my kind of people, you know? Then the door opens and this girl walks in with these gorgeous red suede boots.' Sonja touches the arm of Anabelle next to her. 'You remember those boots don't you, Bells? And after about twenty minutes, we bailed on the rest of the flat and got horrendously pissed at the student union on peach schnapps. And here we are.' Sonja raises her glass in the air.

'How about you?' I ask Anabelle, who has been listening to our conversation.

'I was on Liam's course, we sat next to each other in our first lecture. To be honest, I fancied the absolute pants off him, I was trying to get his attention forever.'

Sonja laughs.

'Oh my god you *did*.'

'You both must know Liam really well then,' I say. I try to sound casual, but my words come out slower than I intend, a slight disconnect between my thoughts and my mouth.

Sonja nods.

'Yeah. I mean, we've known him as long as we've known Pen, really.'

'And what was he like? At uni?'

Anabelle gives a small laugh, glancing at Sonja.

'Well, he was the life and soul of the party, really. Good at sport, fun. But he could be a bit distant, sometimes, too. A bit . . . hard to pin down.'

I lean in, my heartbeat picking up in anticipation.

'How do you mean?'

I take another sip of champagne. It goes down easily and I refill my glass. Anabelle shrugs.

'He was just . . . mercurial, I guess. He had these moments where he'd pull away, go a bit off-grid. But Penny brought out the best in him. They've always had this special connection, even when they were just friends.'

I feel a pang of something like envy, but I push it down.

'And him and Penny didn't get together until they moved to London?'

'That's right,' Sonja says, glancing at Anabelle. 'We didn't see him for a bit, he took a gap year or two and then turned up at a reunion a few years ago.'

'A gap year?' I repeat, my words slurring slightly. I take another gulp of champagne, feeling it burn a little at the back of my throat. I drop my voice conspiratorially. I'm teetering now, the alcohol clouding my judgement but also pushing me forward. 'What do you think he was *really* doing?'

Sonja and Anabelle exchange another glance. Sonja gives me a small smile.

'I don't know what you mean. He just went travelling around Australia. Finding himself. The usual stuff.'

I work to cover my frustration at this mundane response. Is there anyone Liam hasn't got convinced?

'And how do you know Penny?' Anabelle asks quickly.

'We went to school together,' I say, pleased to be the one with the deeper connection, this time. 'We were best friends.'

Anabelle claps her hands together.

'No way! So, you already know Liam? And Tom?'

'Oh yes, Tom and I were friends before I even met Pen. We go way back.' I take a sip of champagne as the girls glance at one another.

'Oh my god, so you must know about Liam's crazy ex, right?' Sonja asks, leaning forwards in excitement.

My stomach knots.

'Excuse me?'

'He had this ex he used to talk about. Said she was, like, obsessed over him in this really scary way. But he never went into detail. Just said it totally messed him up.'

I can barely hear the noise of the room over the roar of blood in my ears.

'I don't really remember,' I manage to say through the acid in my stomach.

'And what do you do?' Anabelle asks.

'Oh. I work in a law firm.' Then I see another opportunity. 'With Liam, actually.'

Anabelle and Sonja both raise their eyebrows in polite interest.

'Oh really?' Anabelle asks. 'That's cool.'

I nod, my neck feeling weirdly rusty.

'Big change, though, right? After his last firm. It's not quite London around here.'

I wait for them to give something away, perhaps exchange a knowing look about Liam's disgraceful exit from his last firm, but all that happens is Anabelle's face creases in sympathy.

'I know, it must be so difficult for him. Being made redundant is so tough.'

My insides burn with frustration. He really has everyone fooled. Sonja, next to her, tuts.

'He's making a good go of it here, though, isn't he? I'm so impressed with how he's handled everything.'

Anabelle nods effusively.

'So true, he's so impressive.'

The anger builds inside me, reaching boiling point.

'He wasn't made redundant, he was fired,' I say, before I can stop myself. There is a beat of silence as the words hang in the air, and I realise, through my tipsy haze, I've said too much. My stomach lurches, but before I can back-track, Anabelle speaks, in a whisper.

'He was fired?'

'I . . . I didn't mean that,' I stammer, but the damage is done. Anabelle and Sonja are exchanging wide-eyed looks, and I feel a cold sweat break out on the back of my neck.

'I really don't think that's true,' Sonja says, after an awkward silence. 'I think you might have misunderstood. There's no way Liam was fired.'

I force a laugh, the sound brittle and shaky.

'Of course . . . I think I was thinking of someone else.'

I take another long sip of champagne, trying to drown out the rising panic inside me. My head feels foggy, the room too bright, the air too thick. I laugh again, too loudly, as Sonja and Anabelle turn away from me.

Chapter Fifty-Eight

Penny

Now

I sip my espresso martini and look around the room at all the women gathered there, trying on their headbands and chatting. It's amazing to me how they all have their own background, history, their own story to tell. Their own secrets, too. I look across at Anabelle, who I know is cheating on her pig of a husband; to Effie, who outwardly looks happier than anyone, but is drowning in debt. We all put forward our own version of the truth, our own version of ourselves. You would never guess half the darkness in this room. My phone buzzes in my pocket and I slip it out. My stomach churns when I see it's from Gerard.

Have a good time this evening, Penny.

Clem suddenly leans over, putting her arm around my back. I quickly slip my phone back into my pocket, forcing all thoughts of Gerard away.

'Are you having a good time?' she asks.

'It's perfect, Clem.'

She knows that the day is faultless, but she likes to ask anyway. Sonja comes to join us then, crouching between mine and Clem's chairs. She looks up at me with her wide brown eyes.

'Seriously mate, where did you find that one?' She nods over at Rachel who is chatting animatedly to some of the other girls. She suddenly laughs a bit too loudly and Sonja winces.

'What do you mean?' I ask, though I have an inkling.

'Oh come, Pen. I know you're a good friend, but she's a bit . . . intense, isn't she?'

'I think she's just a bit drunk,' Clem says, fairly.

'What did she do?' I ask.

'She just started asking all these questions about Liam, wouldn't let it go. And she was hanging off every word we said, it was a bit weird.'

'What sort of questions?' I ask, with a fissure of unease. Why would Rachel be quizzing them?

'Nothing really specific, mostly just what he was like at uni, what he was doing during his gap years . . . she mentioned something about his job.'

I blink.

'What about it?'

Sonja looks like she is deciding something. After a moment, she shakes her head.

'It was nothing. I think she was just, I don't know, kind of shit-stirring? The weirdest part was her face when she was talking about you and Liam . . . it was so weird.'

'Oh well, I think I might know why that is,' I say. 'She was Liam's girlfriend in Year Thirteen. She's probably just feeling a bit awkward about it.'

Sonja suddenly claps a hand across her mouth.

'*She* was Liam's girlfriend?'

'Yeah. Why?' I ask, seeing the look on her face. 'What's the matter?'

Sonja moans softly, looking horrified.

'Oh fucking hell, we asked her if she knew Liam's crazy ex from school.'

My mouth drops open and Clem, next to me, gasps.

'Son, you *didn't.*'

'I bloody did. You should have seen her face.'

For a moment, me, Clem and Sonja look at one another. Then suddenly, Clem bursts out laughing.

'Clem!' Sonja hisses at her, but Clem just shakes her head, her eyes watering.

'I can't believe you did that. Oh god, I just keep picturing it, I'm sorry.'

After a moment, Sonja starts laughing and suddenly I'm laughing too. I can't help it: their laughter is infectious. I glance over to where Rachel is sitting, then immediately stop laughing. She has stopped talking to the other girls and is watching us, her mouth pinched.

Chapter Fifty-Nine

Rachel

Now

The rest of the day passes with me fighting my panic about what I told Sonja and Anabelle. Why did I tell them Liam was fired? Not that it looked like they believed me. But what if they say something to Penny? I watch them carefully throughout the day, looking for any sign that they've told her.

After lunch, everyone troops upstairs for games, espresso martinis and face-painting as the other girls get ready. I sit in a corner with my gold skirt and my drink, trying to smile through it all, but apart from Sonja applying some glitter to my cheeks, hardly anyone talks to me. I look over at Penny constantly, but she is always engrossed in one conversation or another, the princess of the party. I think of her, Sonja and Clem, looking over at me earlier and laughing. *Liam's crazy ex.*

My head starts to swim from all the champagne and espresso martinis as the day drags on. I feel as though I am in a fog, everything just a little too bright and a little too loud. The other girls are loud, vibrant, carefree: a world away from me.

By the time the group is ready to leave the hotel for the night, I'm struggling to walk straight in my Dr Martens and

I have to focus on not slurring my words. The night is dark and warm as we leave the hotel, ready in face-paint and bright outfits. For this section of the evening the itinerary simply said: 'Night out'; there are rumours of live music on a roof-top bar somewhere. Given there is no roof-top bar in town, I assume we are going further afield; but when we leave the hotel, I register through my fuzzy head that there are no taxis waiting and Clemence starts marching the group straight down the hill. I don't care; I just follow.

Everyone walks down the hill in a laughing, stumbling mass of glitter and sequins, the group moving as one, sweeping me up with them. Penny stumbles into me in her terrifyingly high heels, her freshly-donned white sequinned dress reflecting the orange glow of the streetlights as we pass.

'Rach!' she giggles, linking arms with me and leaning into me for support. She looks completely hammered, her face-paint smudged slightly. 'Come on, slow coach.' She pulls me to the front of the group, alongside Clemence, and links arms with her, too. Clemence is the only one who still seems to have her wits about her, her maid of honour performance flawless all day.

'I'm so happy you came, Rach,' she says, squeezing my arm even tighter. 'You've been the only good thing about moving back here.'

She has no idea. No idea what them moving back here has done to me.

'Not the in-laws?' Clemence asks, laughing.

'Definitely not.' Penny's face darkens for a moment before she shakes her head, as though clearing it. 'Where are we going, Clem? Why won't you tell me?'

'We'll be there in a moment. It was all I could do on short notice but you're going to *love* it!'

Penny looks happily confused, but my gut suddenly twists with unease. I force myself to take deep breaths, but the alcohol is making it increasingly harder to focus, harder to think clearly. I stumble a little on the pavement, the dizziness making the ground feel uneven beneath my feet. I blink against the neon glow of the streetlights as we reach the bottom of the hill and turn left, hoping I'm wrong. Hoping we are about to walk straight past, to somewhere, *anywhere*, else.

We don't. I feel a sickening jolt as Clem stops at the entrance to the brand new fairground, which has a huge red and yellow banner outside reading *GRAND OPEN-ING!*

I stare at the place in front of me. For the first time in decades, the fairground is alive again: lit up in a dizzying array of colours, the helter-skelter already full of people, the sounds of the new roller disco blaring from inside the newly refurbished amusement arcade. The bright lights and the sounds of laughter feel like a slap to my senses.

Ding-ding-ding! You've won a prize!

Clemence turns to beam at me and Penny.

'Isn't this *so* retro? I thought we could re-live some childhood nostalgia.'

Penny gasps and claps her hands together drunkenly.

'Is this where we're going? It's not been open since I was little!'

She doesn't even look at me: there is no sign that she thinks this would be a traumatic place to come. *Why would she? You said you made it up, remember? Nothing happened here.*

'Hope it's alright,' Clem says, as she begins digging in her bag and pulling out tickets. 'I know it's not exactly a weekend in Paris, but it's still cute.'

'It's perfect, Clem. Absolutely perfect. Right on the beach, too.'

Clem begins gathering the other girls together, sharing the news that the funfair is the night out. There is lots of cheering and laughing whilst my head continues to spin horribly, made worse by the bright lights. No one seems to have noticed that I can't breathe; that an iron hand has clamped around my throat. I have done everything I could to avoid walking too close to the old funfair for all these years, always a dark blot on the horizon. And now it has a new, noisy technicolour layer to it. I am swept forward by the group of girls as Clemence hands the tickets over to a man on the front booth.

'You won't find any butlers in the buff in there, girls,' he says, with a yellowy leer. Clemence ignores him and marches past, and before I know it, I am through the gates.

I am back inside the fairground.

Why hadn't he said he loved me? My head was spinning. The old, musty mattress dipped as he moved. Outside, there were snatches of laughter from the others. More fireworks. He still hadn't told me he loved me.

Chapter Sixty

Rachel

Now

The other girls swarm inside the fairground, laughing and cheering as Clemence leads us to a VIP area she's booked, on a raised platform overlooking the fairground below. It is roped off, with a canvas roof and a private bar, giving a perfect view of the rides, the stalls, the swarming masses of people. I stand to the side, my heart pounding in my chest, the thick glitter Sonja applied earlier suddenly feeling too tight on my face.

The fairground is a confusing mix of old and new, of that night and this night. The huge Ferris wheel that has stood stationary for so many years is now finally rotating, its red compartments already full and its spokes lit up with bright yellow and pink bulbs. I remember Isaac and I climbing up the old, rusted frame . . . but now there is a line of people waiting to ride it, their laughter filling the air. Screams come from the roller coaster as it dips and swoops over the crowd milling around below. And there, at the end of the pier, looming large over the scene, is the old Funhouse, the squat two-storey structure with a large clown face in the very centre, its painted mouth stretched grotesquely wide to allow people entry through it. I can remember the eerie quiet of the old fairground, punctuated only by our shouts and music coming from the speakers. Now there is circus music pumping through the fairground, loud and jolly, chilling me to my bones. *Do do dodododo do do do do.* The sweet smell of donuts and popcorn from the many food vans invades my nostrils, making me feel sicker still. It's as though the old fairground from my memories has come alive, loud and crawling with people. Everywhere I look there is something else, something bright and new: a long, tropical-themed bar called *The Coco-Not-Shy* where groups of people stand around drinking brown-bottled beers and cocktails out of coconut shells; the restored amusement arcade has axe-throwing, bowling, a diner. There are food stalls, too, selling burgers, jacket potatoes, pizzas. A crazy-golf course. The place is heaving: everyone seems keen to grab a small slice of nostalgia. I want to run as far away as possible from it.

Ding-ding-ding!

The noise of another prize being won explodes behind us. I am starting to feel claustrophobic, the muggy summer air thick in my lungs. Clemence has gathered everyone in the VIP area and calls me over. I approach robotically: I have lost the ability to think. She reaches into her large white tote bag emblazoned *Maid of Dishonour* and pulls out a stack of what looks like . . . masks?

'Here we are girls! Pop these on for a photo!' I take one automatically as it's passed to me. It feels flimsy in my hands. When I turn it over, I nearly drop it: Liam's face is staring back at me, two grotesque-looking holes where his eyes once were. The alcohol swills in my stomach, threatening to rise to the surface. I look up, seeing that all the other girls have covered their sparkly faces momentarily with their masks: a crowd of Liams surrounds me, their eyes blank, their faces frozen in grotesque grins. I feel sick. The memories are starting to swirl, the way the night first started out, the breaking into the fair, the laughter, then his hand over my mouth, the darkness.

'Rach . . . I'm not sure about this . . . you're too drunk . . .'

The fragmented memory hits me out of nowhere, like a snippet of a dream that returns just after you've woken up. I haven't heard Liam's voice in my memories before, not like that. Not those words.

The sea of Liams bobs up and down as the group of girls all laugh hysterically and pass shots of sambuca around. I take one, two, three, automatically, waiting for oblivion. In a daze, I find myself pulled onto the first ride by Penny, the bright pink roller coaster. It's a bad idea, it's too high, but the safety bar is clicking into place across our laps and the compartment is lurching forwards. Penny is laughing, her eyes glazed, her mask now sitting on top of her head. She reaches out a hand to mine, squeezing it tightly.

'Isn't this brilliant?' she squeals. 'Are you having a good time?'

'Penny, why did you invite me tonight?' My voice feels sluggish, thick with alcohol. 'I mean . . . after everything that happened between me and Liam . . . Why would you want me here?'

Penny's smile falters as the roller coaster starts making its ascent and the fairground starts to drop away. She turns to me.

'I told you before, I want to be friends again. I want to make things right with you. I should never have left you behind when your dad . . . I loved John. He was such a good man.'

She looks wide-eyed at me. Behind her, the lights of the fair reflect on the surface of the water as we continue to rise further and further.

'I'm not sure the Haughtons feel the same way you do,' I say, unable to stop myself from saying what is in my head. My inhibitions are lowered and it feels like the walls between Penny and I are finally gone; it is just the two of us in our rising compartment, no Liam, no one else. She is still holding my hand and I cling onto it. 'I think they would rather never see me again.'

Penny leans forward and a devilish grin comes over her face.

'Fuck the Haughtons,' she whispers. Suddenly, we are giggling, just like we did the last time we were together, before we argued and everything went wrong. But then Penny's face turns serious again. She leans further towards me, straining against the bars holding her in place. We are high up now, the fairground spread out below us in a rainbow of flashing lights and colours.

'Rach, there's something I haven't told you. I haven't told anyone.'

Something in her expression makes me stop laughing. We are suspended at the top of the ride now, the world spread out beneath us, the lights of the fairground glittering like stars. For a second everything feels still, like we are on the edge of something big.

'What is it?' I ask, my heart pounding. Have I finally convinced her to trust me enough to tell me something? Is it about why Liam was fired? Maybe now is the time to finally tell her the truth about him. She has to know what he is. Before it's too late.

Penny opens her mouth to speak, but before she can get the words out, the roller coaster drops, sending us falling through the air. Penny's scream fills the night as the car turns upside down, the wind rushing past us in a dizzying blur of lights and noise. My heart is in my throat, my hands gripping the safety bar tightly.

When the ride finally slows, I turn straight back to Penny, desperate for her to finish what she was saying.

'Penny,' I say, putting a hand on her shoulder, 'what were you about to tell me?'

Penny looks at me, her face pale. She opens her mouth, and then vomits onto the floor of the compartment.

Chapter Sixty-One

Rachel

Now

By the time we step off the roller coaster, Penny has been swept up by Clem and taken to the toilets and my head is spinning worse than ever. I stagger away from the group, towards the far end of the fairground, closest to the beach. I hang off the edge of the railings that surround the fairground, gulping in fresh air. A few metres away, the beach is almost pitch-black, the waves rolling in softly, in contrast to the loud music and noise behind me. My heart is pounding; I feel sick. The screams and music fade away and I am back in that night, fifteen years ago. The night that changed everything. A therapist – Rueben I think his name was, I had asked for a woman and there was a mix-up – once told me that some people re-visit traumatic places as part of exposure therapy. Coming full circle. But none of this is giving me clarity, all it is doing is messing with the memories of the thing, so that it's like a film, clumsily spliced together from disconnected parts. I close my eyes, but the memories surface anyway, fragmented, jagged.

'*I love you, Liam Haughton.*'

'*I know you do. Maybe we should talk for a minute.*'

'Shh . . .' *My hands on his chest. Clumsy movements. His minty breath hot against my ear.*

'*Rach . . . come on. You're wasted.*'

His hands, pushing me away from him.

No, no that's not right. That isn't what happened. And even if that part of it *were* true, something I had forgotten until now, that doesn't make what happened afterwards untrue. I push away from the barriers. There is no way that being here could lead to any kind of closure for me, there will never be closure until I hear Liam admit what he did . . . until I can show Penny the truth about who she is marrying. For as long as she thinks I made it up, she won't believe me. I need proof. I need to get out of here, to sober up.

I stagger through the crowds, the smell of churros and chocolate sauce turning my stomach. Everything is so loud, too loud. Blaring music, clattering rides, overlapping voices. Everything is spinning. I can't find the exit. Where is the exit?

My phone buzzes in my skirt pocket. I pull it out and check it, seeing my phone is down to 15 per cent battery. It's a message. From an unknown number.

I click on it, the screen fuzzy through my drunken haze. It is an image, not yet downloaded thanks to the poor signal. I wait as the download circle creeps slowly towards completion. When the image finally appears, my breath catches in my throat.

It's a photo of me. Right here. Right now. At the fair. The back of my head, my gold skirt. Taken moments ago, as I walked off the roller coaster. Whoever took it was close. My heart races as I whirl around, scanning the crowds for anyone who might be watching me. But I can't see anyone: no one seems to be looking at me, nothing seems out of place.

The sound of the fairground music pounds in my ears. *Do do dodododo do do do do.* I need to move, I need to get out of here. Whoever sent me this is messing with me. But my feet are rooted to the spot.

And then I see him. Liam.

He's a few feet away, walking past a popcorn stand. I freeze, my phone in my hand. It can't have been him. *Can it?* I blink and he disappears into the crowd, like a ghost. Is he here, watching? Did he send the photo? I stand frozen, unsure what to do. Then suddenly – I see him again. Walking towards the entrance of the Funhouse. I look around, and finally spot the exit sign in the far corner . . . then look back towards the Funhouse. Before I know it, something inside me, some dark force, is propelling me forwards towards the Funhouse. I move as though in a trance, as if the ghost of my eighteen-year-old-self is leading me back towards the Funhouse. Back to the place where it all began. It occurs to me that I have only half existed since that night, only half present in everything I have ever done. I walk through the crowds, unseeing, and arrive at the entrance to the Funhouse as though I am trapped in a loop of my past.

The Funhouse looms over me, looking almost exactly the same as it did back then. It's been so meticulously restored that it could be the very same one, untouched by time. Memories swirl, but they are confusing memories, because now I am back here, I am suddenly no longer sure what is real and what is my own version, colouring in the lines over the past fifteen years. Kaleidoscope memories. *You do know what happened. Don't let him confuse you.* Why else would he have been tormenting me these past few weeks? The photo on my phone is proof enough. There has to be a reason.

The clown's mouth across the entrance yawns widely to let people through. I am shaking all over, the alcohol making it impossible to think clearly. But it isn't the Funhouse, or the fairground, that is the threat: they are nothing but the shells that house the memories. *He* is the threat. Anger flares inside my chest, suddenly, overpowering the fear. *This ends now.* The clown's mouth grins down at me, a grotesque reminder of everything that happened here. But I can't turn back now. I have to know what Liam is doing – what he wants. I need the answers I have been searching for all these years.

I take a deep breath . . . and step inside.

Chapter Sixty-Two

Rachel

Now

As soon as I step inside the Funhouse, the world shifts. Everything dissolves into shapes and shadows that stretch long across the sawdust-strewn floor. The air is thick with the acrid smell of cheap smoke machines and stale popcorn. The music – an eerie, repetitive circus tune – rings loud in my ears, too jolly, too aggressive, grating against my skull. I take a few shaky, uncertain steps forward as my eyes adjust to the dim lighting.

'Keep moving!' someone shouts from behind, a group of rowdy teenagers shoving their way forward. I stumble a few more feet and come to a wooden rope-bridge that sways underfoot.

I pull Liam along the old wooden bridge, the ropes fraying under our hands, the planks swaying wildly from side to side. He laughs and it makes me giggle, too, clutching on to him to stay upright.

'I thought you were ignoring me, tonight. You've been flirting with Sasha.'

'Is that why you pulled the stunt with the fireworks? And why you were flirting with Isaac?'

I giggle.

'Maybe.'

My legs are shaking but my mind is in a state of complete numbness, constantly straining through the darkness for a sign of Liam. I am more convinced than ever that I saw him walk in here. Is he spying on Penny? On me? I force myself to take step after step, gripping the ropes tightly.

Though the building is the same, being inside the Funhouse now that it is actually open is disorientating, causing jolting hiccups in the memories that have solidified over the years. Somehow, it is scarier now, with its loud music and crowds of people pushing through the foggy corridors. The jarring realness of the place now muddles with the memories of that night, of the boy I had loved, of the secrets I kept hidden for so long, I don't know what's real anymore.

I push myself onwards, until I come to the next corridor, this one a rotating cylinder with smooth sides, like the inside of a washing machine. The group of teenagers are right behind me: I can't turn back. Carefully, I navigate my way through the moving corridor, scrabbling to stay upright, even as the alcohol swimming through my bloodstream causes me to lurch clumsily forward, my limbs heavy and useless. Behind me, the teenagers tumble to the ground, howling with laughter.

The cylinder finally spits me out into a room of mirrors. In every direction, I see myself: my face contorted into different shapes, horrible, stretching expressions, my mouth twisted and my eyes hollow. I half-expect Liam to appear in the mirror behind me, watching. Waiting. My chest tightens and all of a sudden I am struggling to breathe as the choking crawl of a panic attack overwhelms me.

Thick smoke pours from a hidden machine, curling into the space between the mirrors. I cough, my throat raw, as the group of teenagers arrives behind me and I am forced deeper into the maze. I feel my way around a corner, my breathing becoming laboured. This was a horrible mistake. I am trapped. The memories of that night are closing in on me, confusing me. *What happened?*

I need to get out. The route behind me is blocked by groups of people pushing forwards, oblivious to my panic. The rooms twist and turn into each other, no clear exit in sight. Fake doors mock me at every corner, and those that are real lead to dead ends or tight crawlspaces I won't go near.

At last, I push on a door that is actually real: the room ahead is a blur of shapes and flashing lights. I can just about make out other people already inside, moving around. A low moan escapes me. The more determined I am to get out, the more the panic builds. I try feeling my way along the wall, but the floor beneath me shifts unexpectedly and I almost lose my balance. People behind me start laughing and screaming as the floor moves beneath their feet and starts carrying them to different areas of the room. *Surely there has to be an emergency exit in here?* Then, out of nowhere, everything goes pitch black. Screams pierce the air and I stand frozen, my breathing loud and heavy in my ears. I wait, heart thumping, for the lights to come on, but nothing happens. A few seconds later there is a bright burst of strobe lighting, enough to sear my retinas with light; then the blackness returns.

It takes me a few seconds to realise someone is standing close to me. Breathing near me. *No, no, no.* The next strobe lights up the room and my blood runs cold: Liam is standing right in front of me. I open my mouth to scream, but it mingles with the other screaming people and then everything is dark again. Panicked, I take a rapid step back, but the floor moves again and I stagger sideways, landing on another moving section. *This isn't happening. This isn't real.* The room lights up for yet another moment and there he is: a foot away from me, looking around. Looking for me. I didn't imagine it.

'No, please no,' I moan. I try to feel my way away from him, try to find a wall to hang on to, but there is nothing but thin air. The next moment, something bumps against my mouth, as though someone is trying to find my mouth to put a hand over it.

We are on the bed. How did we get here? His hands are on me. My blinking feels slow and heavy. His hand moves . . . one minute it is on my hip. The next it is across my mouth.

Adrenaline courses through my veins and I let out a scream that goes on and on, cutting through the music and through the laughter of the other people.

'Get off! Get the fuck off me!'

The music stops and dim lights flicker on. As I blink in the light, I look wildly around for Liam, but he is nowhere to be seen. Nearby, however, I spot Tom and a group of other men, wearing T-shirts bearing Liam's face and the words *FBI, Female Body Inspectors*. They are all staring at me with their mouths open. The floors are no longer moving. I hear a staff member calling to see if everyone is alright.

'What are you doing here?' I ask, angrily. 'Why . . . why was Liam here?'

'We're here for the joint stag and hen. Clem and I planned it as a surprise,' Tom says.

'Was it you who put your hand over my mouth? What were you doing?'

Tom looks bewildered, but I don't care.

'I didn't touch you.'

'You're lying!' My voice breaks.

Tom glances behind him, at his friends, then back at me. I hate the look on his face.

'Rach, I swear, we were just having fun. Liam . . . he's hammered. If he touched you, I'm sure it was just a mis-understanding.'

'No, he . . . I saw him. I felt him do it, he . . .' my voice falters. I'm not sure, anymore. My breathing is slowing. Embarrassment starts to settle on me now, with the lights on and everything quiet. My face begins to burn. A door opens and a large man walks into the room with a long ponytail and a bright torch.

'Right you lot, get out, there's a queue around the block and we need to restart.' He points his torch to a door hidden in the far corner with a small glowing exit sign above it. I don't want for anyone to say anything else. The embarrassment burns like acid on my skin. Without look-ing back, I turn and run, stumbling through the exit and into the warm night air.

Chapter Sixty-Three

Rachel

Now

I don't stop running until I have reached the brightly lit bar area, which obscures the view of the Funhouse and the suffocating darkness beyond it. I find a quiet spot on a bench, overlooking the waves. My chest heaves as I gulp down the fresh sea air, trying to slow my heartrate. I press my hands against my knees to ground myself, the sheer gold fabric itchy beneath my fingers.

Out of the corner of my eye I see movement. I quickly look up and there is Tom, hovering at the end of the bench, holding two coconut shell drinks with stripey red and white straws.

'Are you alright?' he asks, setting the drinks down on the bench.

'I'm fine,' I mutter, my throat dry. I don't want to look at him. I don't want to see that same look in his eyes: the one that thinks I am mad. For something to do, I pick up the drink he's placed in front of me and take a long pull from the straw.

'Yeah, you look really chill,' Tom says, sitting down opposite me and taking a sip of his own drink. 'What happened back there?'

I don't know. I don't know what happened. Was Liam there? Was he trying to scare me?

'Nothing. I . . . I've just had too much to drink.'

'Why did you think Liam grabbed you? Rach, talk to me.'

Do I tell him? Tom is Liam and Penny's best friend. Which means he could either help me or hurt me. But he was also my friend, too. Once.

'Not here,' I say, glancing around. 'Will you walk me home?'

Now it's Tom's turn to hesitate: he glances behind him to where some of the other stags are wandering back towards the bar, shouting and heckling each other. For a moment, I think he is going to refuse, but then he sighs and nods.

'Yeah, alright. They probably won't even notice I'm gone.'

We both finish our drinks and get up from the bench. My limbs feel like they are weighed down with bags of sand. I wish I hadn't drunk so much. As we begin walking, there is a loud squeal and we both turn to see Penny running towards Liam. My stomach lurches at the sight of him, here in the fairground. I still haven't quite recovered from what happened back in the Funhouse, still convinced he did it on purpose. But now we are outside of that place, it is harder to be sure. Liam spins Penny around whilst everyone else cheers. I think back to what she was about to tell me about the Haughtons. It was something important, I'm sure of it.

I walk towards the entrance, not saying goodbye to anyone; I'm not likely to see them again and I didn't want to go anywhere near Liam.

We make our slow way out of the lights and noise of the fairground and start walking along the promenade and towards the hill that slopes up to my house. The sky is an impenetrable inky black, lit only by the orange streetlights and to our back, the rides still lit up along the pier.

'Sorry for dragging you away,' I mumble after a while.

'It's fine,' Tom says, shrugging. 'To be honest, I was surprised to see you there tonight. At the fairground of all places.'

I shake my head.

'I wasn't really thinking straight. I should have said no as soon as Penny invited me.'

'She's pretty hard to say no to,' Tom says, glancing across at me with a small, almost nostalgic smile. 'When she wants you to be her friend, that's usually the end of the discussion.'

I glance sideways at him and, for a moment, it's as though nothing has changed between us.

'You were my friend first, remember?' I say softly.

Tom looks across at me, and I think I see something flicker in his eyes, but maybe it's just the reflection of the streetlights.

'Yeah,' he says eventually. 'I remember.'

The silence stretches between us as we turn onto the hill that leads to my house. I know I need to say something, to tell him the truth, but the words feel like stones lodged in my throat.

'What is it, Rach? What's going on?'

I take a deep breath.

'I suppose . . . I'm trying to understand what happened fifteen years ago. I want to know what really happened.'

'Shouldn't I be asking you that question?'

'What do you mean?'

'Well, you made that allegation fifteen years ago, and shit hit the fan. Then said you made it up. Now you're suddenly back in Penny and Liam's lives. What's your game plan, Rachel?'

'I don't have a game plan,' I say, frustration bubbling up inside me. He was supposed to be the one who would listen. 'This isn't a game.'

We have reached my house. The gate is open and we walk through, along the path, and come to a stop outside the front door.

'Then what is it, Rach? What's going on?'

His voice is steady, but there's an edge to it. It's time. I can't back out now. I want to try to get my words out right, but my head feels muddled and tired.

'Some strange things have been happening to me recently,' I say, carefully. 'Ever since Liam and Penny came back.'

Tom looks at me steadily, silently, and I can suddenly see the police officer he is training to be. He is listening to me talk as though I am a witness. Will he believe me?

'It started a few weeks ago. Someone messing with me. Warning me, I think.' I explain about the postcard, being watched on the beach, the police turning up at the house. The feeling of being watched. Tom watches me closely, his eyes narrowing.

'And you think this has something to do with them?' he asks. 'Why would it?'

This is it.

'Because there's something you don't know. Something Penny doesn't know.'

I force myself to look him in the eye.

'I didn't make it up, Tom. What I said about Liam fifteen years ago . . . it was true.'

Tom takes an abrupt step back, as though someone has just punched him.

'What did you just say?' he whispers.

'It was true. What I said about what he did to me. I lied about what happened because Gerard Haughton threatened my dad's business. He said if I didn't take it back, he'd make sure my dad lost everything.'

Tom is shaking his head and panic flares within me: I need him to believe me, I can't let him go back and tell Liam everything I've just said.

'I don't . . . but . . . you said you made it up. You told the police that. You told everyone that. We all thought you just got confused . . . or just angry at him for ditching you to go to Durham.'

'I wasn't confused or angry,' I insist, my voice rising with desperation. 'I just did it to protect my dad.'

I am getting nowhere. Tom is backing away from me, still shaking his head.

'Liam said you would do this. He said that you might try and stir it up again. I told him he was being paranoid . . . but he said he thinks you might still be infatuated with him.'

'That's not true!' I say furiously. 'He's lying because he's afraid. I just need your help . . . to get some information, anything that might help prove I'm telling the truth.

I know he lost his job, was it for doing the same thing again? You must know something.'

'Does Penny know this is the real reason you've been spending time with her?' Tom demands, as though he hasn't heard me.

'No,' I admit, my voice high, pleading. 'No, I . . .'

'She thinks you're her friend. She's been defending you to Liam.'

'I *am* her friend,' I insist, 'that's why I'm trying to protect her . . .'

'I can't do this, Rach. She's about to get *married*. You can't ask me to help you with this.'

Tears well up in my eyes, but I blink them back. He doesn't believe me. All he sees, all anyone sees, is the same girl trying to ruin Liam Haughton's life. They don't see him as the monster, they don't understand what he's been doing to me, the way he has crept into my life, my office, my *mind*, in order to mess with me. Tom was my one chance to persuade someone in Liam's inner circle that he isn't who he says he is; but I realise now how foolish I have been. Tom and I aren't the same friends we were in secondary school.

Tom gets a crumpled pack of cigarettes out of his pocket and lights one up. As he takes a drag, his phone rings and he pulls it out, the glow of the screen bright in the darkness. The name on the screen says Penny and I notice an unguarded softness in his expression. And in that moment, it suddenly clicks. How had I not realised before?

'You're still in love with Penny, aren't you?'

Tom flinches, his eyes darting to me in surprise.

'Don't be ridiculous. She's one of my best mates. I've got a girlfriend.'

'I don't believe you. You still care about her. Does she know?'

'Rach, stop. Please.'

I am sure that I have got this right, sure that the look on Tom's face when Penny started calling him betrayed his real emotions. I'm also sure Penny has no idea.

'I just need some information; anything you can tell me that might help prove what happened. Or anything Liam might tell you.'

'I'm not digging into this mess for you, I'm training to be a cop, for god's sake. I can't get involved in all of this.'

I take a step closer, desperate now.

'Please Tom, think about what I'm saying. If I'm telling the truth . . . if Liam is who I say he is . . . can you really let Penny marry him? Are you so sure about Liam you won't even ask the question?'

My words hang in the air. He stands, staring at the end of the path, towards the road, his cigarette limp in his left hand. His phone rings again and he raises it once more to his face, the light casting shadows across his skin. It is Penny, again.

'I have to go,' he says, quietly. 'She might need me.'

'Tom, wait . . .'

'No, Rach. I'm sorry.'

And with that he walks away, back down the path.

Chapter Sixty-Four

Rachel

Now

I stand in the porch long after Tom leaves, long after his footsteps fade down the street. Frustration and fear wash over me in waves. I've told Tom everything, and now he's heading straight back to Penny and Liam, his best friends. He'll tell them. Of course he'll tell them. Panic flares within me, creating a sickly acidic feeling in my stomach mixed with the alcohol. They will shun me, Penny will have nothing more to do with me. And then? Then there will be no possibility of stopping her marrying Liam. I've ruined everything by opening my mouth, but I can't take it back now. I have to think. I *have* to think of a way to prove what happened or prove that he's been the one doing these things to me. *I have to prove that I'm not going mad.* The doubts from the fairground earlier, the fractured memories that suddenly appeared tonight for the first time, have confused me. *They weren't real. You know what happened.* It feels more important than ever to keep going, to catch Liam out. But how? I check my watch: it's eleven thirty. Much earlier than it feels. Chewing my lip, I open my handbag and pull out my keys. My fingers tremble. *Don't give up. Not yet.* Without fully knowing why, I turn and retrace Tom's footsteps back down the pathway and through the open gate.

The promenade is teeming with people, late-night revellers laughing and shouting, their faces blurred as I pass them. I stick to the other side of the road, hidden in the shadow of the shops and old townhouses that face the beach. I keep my head down, making sure nobody from the hen or stag sees me as I skirt along in the darkness.

After ten minutes, I reach the row of shops at the end of the road that turns onto the main high street. Two doors down, a kebab shop is full of life, its neon lights the brightest along the road. Teenagers stand outside the kebab shop holding cardboard boxes of fried chicken and chips, covered in bright red ketchup. The smell churns my stomach.

I keep walking, slipping past them, unnoticed, until I find myself standing in front of the law firm. I stare at the building for a moment, my heart pounding harder with each second. This is insane. Breaking into my own workplace? My fingers clutch my keys harder. Glancing around one more time, I slip down the side of the building. The shadows feel alive, crawling around me, closing in, but I grit my teeth and keep going. Something looms up at me out of the darkness, startling me. *Just a wheelie bin.* I hurry down the passageway, my footsteps too loud in the silence.

I reach the rear entrance to the building and fumble with the keys, my hands shaking. *Why am I doing this? Why don't I ever know when to stop? Is this what happens to Mum, when she has a glass in her hand?*

I suddenly think, inexplicably, of Connor. Of his cosy cottage on the pebbled beach, of his wooden countertops and fireplace. If I called, he would answer. Then the door opens and I step inside.

Almost immediately, the alarm screeches to life and my heart lurches. I rush to switch it off, my still-drunk fingers clumsy on the glowing keypad. It takes two tries before, thankfully, the noise stops and the corridor falls silent. The only sound left is my breathing.

The office has that Friday smell to it, the linger of cleaning products still in the air. My Dr Martens squeak on the polished floor as I make my way up to the second floor, each step feeling heavier than the last. My mind spins, thoughts tripping over one another: Penny's almost-confession on the roller coaster, Tom's reaction, the photo someone sent me. Despite the many dead ends the day has presented, I have the odd feeling that I'm teetering on the edge of something. I just don't know what it is.

I reach Liam's office door and grab the handle. I push down, but meet firm resistance. It's locked. Of course it is: if he's hiding something, he isn't going to leave it open for the world, is he? Anger flares hot in my chest. I stand there for a moment, unsure what to do next. Then I remember: Didi has a spare set of keys, somewhere, for emergencies.

I turn around and head back downstairs, emerging into the main part of the front office, where mine and Didi's desks sit, shrouded in darkness. I start opening each drawer in turn, looking for the keys, my movements increasingly frenzied. A security light flickers on somewhere outside, casting a little more light around the room, before flickering off again. I open the bottom drawer, tugging it out with impatience. That's when I spot Didi's photo frame, the one of her and her school friends that usually sits on her desk, now tucked away in the drawer. Odd. Why would she have hidden it? I pull the photo frame out of the drawer so I can look underneath and something small slides off the frame and falls to the ground. I kneel down, searching for whatever it is on the carpet. My fingers finally brush against it. It is small and metallic. I lift it up to examine it.

The memory card. The exact same one that sat in Shelly McKenzie's open palm the other day. I stare at it in disbelief. It's been here all along, tucked away in Didi's drawer. My head spins – did Didi take it? Or did someone else hide it here, knowing I'd find it? Liam? Is he watching me, right now? The photo sent to me from the fairground occurs to me and I feel the hairs on the back of my neck stand up. Have I just walked into a trap? I can't make sense of it, can't make sense of anything, anymore.

I am still clutching the memory card in my trembling hand when the office light turns on. I look up, bleary-eyed, to see Charles standing in the doorway, with a look of disbelief on his face as he spots the memory card in my hand.

Chapter Sixty-Five

Penny

Now

Oh god, I am completely wasted. I can feel the hangover already lurking on the edges of my periphery, threatening to suffocate me when I wake up. When did hangovers get so much worse?

'Here you go.' Clem comes over to me in the kebab shop and hands me an extra-large kebab and chips. I look down at the mess of meat and sauce, my stomach churning at the sight.

'You've got to eat,' Clem says, watching my face wrinkle with disgust. 'You'll regret it if you don't.'

I nod, not trusting myself to speak, and start to pick at some chips. There is a burst of noise and I look up to see some of the guys stagger into the shop wearing some of Clem's hen-do masks with Liam's face on them. It was a great idea of Clem's to combine the two nights out, but there is a part of me that wishes it had just been us girls. The men have disrupted the dynamic, the girls have spent half their time with them and Liam . . . I could have done with some space tonight, space from the Haughtons, but instead he was everywhere, including on those stupid masks and on the boys' T-shirts. Clem and the girls start shifting across chairs, making more room for the new arrivals.

'I hear you vommed on the roller coaster, wife-to-be,' Freddie, one of Liam's mates from his first house-share in Clapham, says in his loud voice. 'Nice work!'

He plonks down next to Clem, laughing loudly. His loudness, his overbearing presence, reminds me forcefully of Gerard. *Gerard.* God, how had I become entangled in this mess? *Don't think about it.* Then I suddenly remember that I was on the roller coaster with Rachel and a flash of a conversation returns to me. We were holding hands . . . I almost told her . . . my stomach lurches even more and I drop the chip I am holding. What was I *thinking*? If Liam had found out . . .

Tom appears then, looking exhausted, his freckles almost bleached out under the harsh fluorescent lights. He's quieter than Freddie: he just sits down on the red plastic chair beside me and starts helping himself to my food. His presence is comforting. Safe, almost.

'Where have you been?' I ask, as we both eat from my polystyrene box, like we have done on so many nights out before. 'I called you twice.'

'Sorry, I got back as soon as I could. I was, uhh, walking Rachel home.'

I look up at him in surprise.

'You were?'

'Yeah, she was a bit drunk, so thought I would make sure she got home safe.'

'That was nice of you,' I say. 'I'm sure her boyfriend would have picked her up.'

Tom shrugs but doesn't say anything. I watch him, the person I have known for so many years, whose every facial expression, every inflection has become easy to work out. Suddenly he is the opposite.

'Did you kiss? Is that why you're acting so weird?'

'Of course not!' Tom says indignantly. 'And you've got ketchup on your face.'

'Where?' I demand, embarrassed and fumbling for a napkin. He reaches out and brushes some of the sauce away from the corner of my mouth with his thumb, the lightest of touches. For a moment, we just look at one another. I see something in Tom's eyes I haven't seen in a long time. Something that surprises me. Has it always been there? Have I been so used to having Tom around as my friend, always, consistently there for me, that I missed the signs?

Suddenly, the kebab shop feels too small. Too loud. Too bright. The misery that has been simmering inside me for weeks – months, maybe – threatens to spill over. It was all okay, before. When it was me and Liam in the early years in London. Before he lost his job, before we returned to Gerard and Janet's clutches and moved down here.

'Are you sure this is what you want, Pen?' he asks in a low, urgent voice.

'What? Getting married?'

He nods, his gaze steady, searching mine for something. Something I can't give him. He doesn't know what's really going on.

I look down at his T-shirt, at the face of my fiancé above the words *Female Body Inspector*. I think about my doubts,

I think about everything that's gone wrong these past few weeks, months. The way Liam has been acting, the secret I've been keeping from him. I'm teetering once more on the roller coaster again, about to fall. But what's my alternative? Run away? No. I'm not giving up now. I've made my choices.

'Yes,' I say to Tom, wiping the ketchup from my mouth myself. 'I'm sure.'

Chapter Sixty-Six

Rachel

Now

As the sunlight filters through the gaps in the bedroom blinds and slowly pulls me into consciousness, the first thing I register is a pounding headache crashing through my skull. It builds as I come to my senses, sending waves of dizziness through me. Then the nausea hits, an awful, churning feeling in the pit of my stomach. I try to recall what happened last night. The noise and lights of the funfair. The dizzying, disorientating feeling of being back there after so many years. Suddenly the rest of the night comes crashing back and I inhale sharply. *Going into the office . . . finding the memory card . . . Charles standing there* . . . He had been alerted by the alarm system on his phone. The black spots are back in places, but I remember babbling, trying to explain that I was just picking something up that I forgot, but Charles heard the slur of my words, saw me holding the memory card. My excuses were irrelevant: he said we would talk on Monday, but I already know there will be very little I can say. Not to mention Liam will almost certainly know by then about me blabbing to Sonja and Anabelle about him getting fired. He'll do everything he can to get rid of me.

I push the duvet back and climb gingerly out of bed. The room seems to tilt, my stomach lurching. But I can't sit around. I need answers.

An hour later, I turn onto a neat street on the edge of town, furthest from the beach, where the large Victorian houses give way to smaller new builds. There are a number of people outside their houses, cleaning their cars, kids on balance bikes on the way to the park or beach. Normal, Saturday morning activities, in stark contrast to my own state. The sun beats down on me, and I can feel the alcohol seeping from my pores.

I walk up to a house with bright geraniums in the window box and a green front door. I ring the doorbell and wait. A few moments later, I hear a voice shouting on the other side of the door.

'I'm getting it!'

The door opens and Didi stands there in a baggy T-shirt dress, her hair piled on top of her head. When she sees me, her eyes widen. She looks almost panicked.

'Rach. What . . . what are you doing here?'

'I think you know, Dee.'

Didi shakes her head but a faint blush is creeping up her neck.

'I don't know what you mean . . .'

'The memory card. I found it.'

Didi's shoulders sag. She opens the door wider and steps back.

'You'd better come in.'

Inside, the house is an exact reflection of Didi herself: the walls are covered in bright, patterned wallpaper and every surface is covered in photos of her large circle of friends and family. Everything about the house is bright and cheerful, in contrast to the tension between us.

Didi leads me past the lounge, stopping in the doorway and leaning in.

'Dad,' she says, 'my friend Rachel is here, I'm just going to be in the kitchen with her, okay?'

An old man sits in an armchair bathed in sunlight, his thin frame hunched over, watching TV. He looks a lot older than I would expect Didi's dad to be, with an unhealthy pallor and a long, morose expression. He barely acknowledges me, just nods towards the TV without a word.

'I try and persuade him to come over on a Saturday morning so I can make sure he's eaten and had company,' Didi says, as we walk into the small, cream-coloured kitchen. 'Otherwise he'll just sit in his flat not doing anything. What kind of drink do you want? We've got tea but you look like you could use a coffee.'

She's rambling, trying to cover up the tension.

'Tea is fine, thanks.'

It is quiet between us as Didi boils the kettle and brews the tea. When we are both sat at the small two-person table in the corner, Didi chews her lip, her eyes darting between me and her mug.

'You said you found the card,' she says, finally.

I nod.

'In your desk drawer. What the hell is going on, Didi?'

Didi buries her face in her hands.

'I'm so sorry, Rach. I . . . don't know what I was thinking.'

'Does it have something to do with the photo that was in that drawer, too? Of you and all your school friends?'

'Sort of. I met those friends at Rushmore, when I used to go to private school.'

'But you've always said your family has no money. That your dad can't afford a new boiler.'

Didi nods, slowly.

'It's true, my family doesn't have any money. Hasn't for a long time. But we did, once.' She nods towards the lounge. 'My dad, Stephen Chapman, was an entrepreneur. He's a real tech genius. Mum always said he was born way before his time.'

Stephen Chapman? *Where have I heard that name before?*

'He made a fair bit of money from some software he created. We had a nice life, but it was never about that. He wanted to change the world. Be the first. He came up with an idea for an internet connection, basically an early router. But he needed funding to create it.'

'Gerard Haughton,' I say, with an ominous feeling.

Didi nods, again.

'Gerard and Dad went into business together. There was this really exciting time when Dad was convinced his vision was about to pay off, he was working day and night on it.'

Dread steals over me because I know already that there cannot be a happy ending to this story. Didi looks down into her tea and her shoulders sag. She looks upset.

'Dad finally cracked the design. It needed some testing but he knew it would work. He just needed a bit more money. He asked Gerard . . . but Gerard said no. That the

340

money was gone. He told Dad to shut up shop. And then
. . .' Didi grips her mug tightly and a dark shadow crosses
over her face. ' . . . and then Gerard Haughton sold the
designs. Made an absolute fortune. Dad spent years trying
to sue Gerard Haughton. Used every penny he had left,
but Gerard Haughton always managed to win. He left Dad
with nothing.'

The weight of this revelation crashes down on me.
I always knew what Gerard Haughton was, from my
own experiences. But hearing that he destroyed another
family's life in almost the exact same way makes me
angrier than I ever thought I could feel. It suddenly
dawns on me where I've heard the name Stephen Chapman before: the news article I read the other day about
Gerard Haughton being embroiled in a legal battle with
his business partner.

'And Liam?' I ask. 'The memory card?'

'When Liam joined, I just . . . I couldn't believe it. But I
thought maybe he would be different to his dad. I tried to
be nice to him, get him onside a bit, you know? But when
I tried to talk to him about his dad, he completely shut
me down. I tried to act normal, hoping he would open up
eventually . . . but when I saw him put the memory card in
that drawer I just . . . something came over me. I wanted
to punish him, punish every one of the fucking Haughton
family. So I took it. I was only planning on taking it for a
few days. I just wanted him to get in trouble, to see him
scared. To realise that he isn't as bulletproof as he thinks
he is. But then it all sort of snowballed. Liam started locking his office door so I couldn't return it, and I'd already

sworn I had searched everywhere. I was just trying to think of a way to put it back.'

'You messed with his calendar too, didn't you?' I ask. 'Made him miss appointments.'

Didi nods.

'It was all so stupid . . . so *risky*, but I couldn't see past my anger, not when Dad sits in that lounge every Saturday hardly saying a word.'

'Charles thinks it was me who took the memory card,' I tell her. 'I went into the office last night . . . to look for something. I found it and he caught me.'

Didi covers her mouth with her hands.

'I'm sorry, Rach. It's all my fault.'

'No, it's not. I shouldn't have been there outside of work hours. It's my own fault.'

Didi looks defeated.

'He's going to fire me.'

'That's not going to happen,' I say. 'Not if I can help it.' I reach into my bag and pull out my phone. I open the photo I took the other day of Wayne Stephens.

'Dee, do you recognise this man? I saw him with Liam the other day. He's apparently involved in some dodgy things. Do you know anything about him?'

Didi studies the photo for a moment, then shakes her head.

'No, sorry. Hang on, let me see if Dad recognises him. He's lived around here forever.'

She gets up and I follow her back into the lounge.

'Dad, can you look at this photo for me? Do you recognise this man? With the hood?'

Didi's dad takes the phone off her and frowns down at the screen. He zooms in on the photo with surprisingly dexterity, bringing it up to his face and cocking his head to the side.

'No,' he says after a while. 'No, I don't.'

I sigh and look at Didi.

'Thanks, anyway.'

'What's it about? Why was Liam with him?'

'I don't know.' My hangover throbs, coupled with the frustration at another dead end. 'I have a ton of questions and no answers.'

In the corner, Didi's dad suddenly gives a loud 'Har-rumph'. He is still frowning down at my phone.

'What is it, Dad? Do you recognise him, now?'

'It's not that,' Didi's dad says. He looks up at me, his expression thoughtful. 'But you might have another question to add to your list.'

Unease prickles through me.

'What do you mean?' I ask.

'Have you noticed your phone running slower?'

I nod, confused.

'Yes . . . and draining battery really fast. But it's an old model . . .'

'It's not the model. There's a spyware app installed on your phone.'

My stomach drops. *A what?*

'But . . . my phone was locked,' I stammer.

Didi's dad shrugs, dismissively.

'There are ways around it. Someone looking over your shoulder, someone who knows how to get past passcodes.'

I am stunned for a moment, thinking of the hundreds of times a day I type my passcode into my phone without so much as a second thought.

'What does that mean?' Didi asks, her eyes wide.

'It means,' he says, his voice heavy, 'that whoever installed that app has seen everything you've been doing. It means you're being watched.'

Chapter Sixty-Seven

Rachel

Now

I leave Didi's in a complete state of shock. How long have I been watched for? And how did whoever it was get access to my phone? But, I realise, it wouldn't be difficult: I always have my phone on me, or in my bag. Anyone could have messed with it. I think of the person watching me on the beach . . . remember my phone being warm afterwards. But who *was* it? Loath as I am to use my phone – it feels tainted and I don't trust that the app has gone, though Didi's dad assured me it was – I dial Connor's number. I am desperate to hear his voice, for him to help me make sense of this nightmare. But it goes straight to voicemail. I leave him a quick message, explaining everything that's happened since last night and tell him to call me as soon as possible.

My hands are shaking as I fumble with the key to the front door, feeling a creeping sense of dread seep into my chest. My thoughts are spinning out of control, fragments of information flying around my head like debris: Liam, Wayne Stephens, my missing police file, the spyware. Didi's confession explains away the memory card and her odd behaviour around Liam, but it doesn't explain the rest. Someone is trying to scare me and right now, they are winning. Does Penny know something? Is that what she was trying to tell me on the roller coaster last night? Nothing makes sense.

I push open the front door. The house smells faintly of lavender, as though Mum has been cleaning, but there is no sign of her as I enter the house. I glance up the stairs. I need to make sense of what is going on. Connor said that maybe I missed something. If I have, there is only one place that will help jog my memory.

Before I know it, I'm climbing the stairs, the wood creaking beneath my feet. My heart is pounding as I make my way past my room and up the next flight of steps, towards the room on the right of the landing. I stop outside the door to Dad's study. I haven't set foot inside since he died. It's been a closed-off part of the house, frozen in time. I put my hand on the smooth brass handle, hesitating for a moment, feeling the familiar ache rising in my chest. I can almost feel him inside: sitting at his desk, tapping away at his old computer, drinking a cup of tea. My best friend, my protector. Gone in an instant, leaving me to navigate the wreckage of my life without him.

Taking a deep breath, I push open the door. I expect the hinges to creak, to remind me of the passing of time, but it opens smoothly and silently, as though it has been waiting. As I step inside, the first thing to hit me is the smell: somehow, his woody aftershave still clings to the air in the room. It's like a punch in the gut. Smells are different from other types of memories: they are visceral, they get under your skin in a way that nothing else can, triggering a hundred snapshots of Dad.

Across the desk which overlooks the garden is a pile of opened post, left in a manner that suggests the reader has just stepped out of the room, for a moment. Which, I know, would have been the same day he died; the final day of his life, captured and preserved in this small room. *Focus. You can't think about it right now.* I have to help Penny. I swallow the painful lump in my throat and approach the desk. Immediately, I see a letter relating to his re-mortgage of the house to help fund the restaurant, an optician's appointment, a takeaway flyer, scooped up with the rest of the post.

After looking around, I crouch down in front of Dad's squat four-drawer filing cabinet that sits to the right of his desk. Dad was a meticulous filer: I know my police statement will be in here. I open the first drawer and my breath catches at the sight of his handwriting on the small, labelled sections of the folders. It is like a familiar piece of him, that I haven't seen in years. Ignoring the ache in my chest, I switch off my emotions completely and start rifling through the folders. They contain bank statements, household bills, mortgage statements. Not what I was looking for. I open the next drawer down, then the next, but there is nothing in any of them that would relate to me. Frowning, I look around and spot the under-desk drawer that runs the length of the desk. Sitting down on Dad's old leather chair, I wheel it backwards and pull the drawer open, towards me. There it is: a thin folder simply labelled 'Rachel'. I pull it out and flip it open. Right on the top is my police statement, my official version of events, typed out after my video interview. The statement that had shaped my entire life from that point onwards. The truth, the half-truths, the lies, all in black and white. I recall PC Thompson, whom I had liked, dropping it around for me to go over and sign. My teenage signature is at the bottom, awkward and over-choreographed.

Something has been nagging at me ever since last night . . . as though being back in the fairground stirred something within me that I forgot. Is it the fractured memories that came back? Surely they weren't real? I pull the statement towards me and begin to read. I realise, as I absorb the words, that I have forgotten a lot of the detail of that night, that my words from back then feel surprisingly unfamiliar, as though it is someone else speaking. One particular passage catches my eye.

It was exactly eleven o'clock when it happened. I know, because I got a new watch for my birthday and it beeps every hour, which was really annoying. It was beeping when he put his hand over my mouth. I felt his ring against my lip. He said something in my ear. He said . . . I wanted it. This is what you wanted, he said.

I pause, re-reading the passage. Had I really said it all like that? So confidently? I linger for a moment longer over the words, then carry on reading. I just need to find one thing. Anything. Details flood back, both sharp and blurred at once.

The awful smell of his breath in my ear. Hot. Stinking of beer and smoke.

I bury my face in my hands in frustration. There is something here, floating just out of my reach. Something I've missed, something that might unlock this strange, nagging feeling. That might explain what's been happening recently. I just need to work out what it is.

Chapter Sixty-Eight

Rachel

Now

I am still staring down at my police statement, my heart thumping, when I hear footsteps behind me. I turn in Dad's chair, the base squeaking, to see Mum in the doorway. She is wearing her old cream cardigan over her nightdress, the one that is threadbare at the elbows and the bottom of the pockets. There are bags under her eyes and it suddenly hits me just how much she's aged. She is only sixty-five, but in the last fifteen years she has changed beyond recognition. What would Dad think, if he saw us both now?

'What are you doing in here?' she asks, her voice low.

'Sorry,' I say quickly, half-rising from the chair, 'I just needed to check something.'

Mum doesn't seem to be angry: she barely seems to be listening. She looks around the room, clutching her cardigan to herself. She takes a slow step inside.

'I've not been in here for such a long time,' she says, softly. 'It still smells like him.'

'I know,' I whisper.

She walks over to the desk and I quickly stand to let her sit down. She does so, running her hands along the length of the desk as though it might suddenly disappear.

'I used to do the household receipts in here, when we used to have a ledger. And the Christmas cards. I used to pretend I was working. Not just a housewife. Not just a failed actress.'

I don't know what to say: I've never heard Mum talk like this before. Something in the air has shifted between us, something raw and unspoken. Mum looks out over the garden for a while whilst I hover next to her, unsure what to say. Then her eyes drift down to the pages spread across the desk. She reaches out and touches them, her lips mouthing silently, as though she is reading a script. Her fingers brush over my scrawled signature.

'I begged your dad not to take you to the police station,' she says eventually. Quietly.

'Because you didn't believe me,' I say.

Mum sighs.

'That was . . . one of the reasons.' She looks back down at the pages of my statement. 'Why are you looking at this, now?'

I hesitate. But I need to get it off my chest, I need to tell someone. Even if it is the last person I ever thought about opening up to.

'I think Liam Haughton is trying to scare me. I don't know why . . . but I think he's nervous about me bringing up what happened back then. As though there might have been something that was missed. I thought my statement might help me make sense of it all. Help me understand what he's so afraid of. Maybe even prove what happened.'

There is a long pause whilst Mum continues to look down at the desk, her fingertips still tracing the pages in front of her. I start to wonder if she heard me, but then she speaks.

'Did you know that each time you recall a memory, you're not actually recalling the exact same memory? You're actually re-constructing it. Like a painting you keep adding to, keep touching up. Until eventually, it's hard to know what the original event was. How the painting started. It happens a lot with the memories I have of John. I think over time I've filled in gaps . . . changed some of the details . . . so the original ones have almost completely faded.'

Her words sink in like ice. This is not what I need to hear. I should have known she was the last person who would make me feel better.

'So what now?' Mum asks. She turns the chair slightly, to look at me straight on. 'What's your plan?'

'I don't have one,' I admit, feeling a sense of panicked defeat creeping in. 'I don't know whether to . . . just leave it. Leave Penny alone. Find a new job, move on with my life. Hope that all the strange things that have been happening stop.' Even as I say it, I know I can't just walk away. Not after everything. There is something here that I've missed, or else why would Liam have been trying to scare me into silence? If I let go, I'll never be free of this . . . of Liam, of that night. Whatever Mum says about memories, I am holding a painting of a nightmare I can't let go of.

Mum turns her chair back again, towards the garden. Some of the ivy has grown too high and is starting to creep up the windowpane.

'I told you I didn't want you to go to the police back then, because even if what you were saying was true, I knew what would happen to you. I knew because the same thing happened to me.'

353

'The same . . . *what*?' I stare at Mum, unable to believe what I've just heard. My heart is suddenly beating painfully fast. I don't want to hear what she is about to say. I don't.

'I was assaulted. When I had just started acting. Oh, you hear about it all the time now, it sounds almost *vintage*? but I was one of those young women, full of dreams, who found herself on a director's sofa.'

I cannot move, I am frozen on the spot. Shock, revulsion and sympathy pulse through me. All this time, she's carried this secret and she never told me. Not even when I needed her most. How could she have gone through life without saying anything?

'I went to the police, like you. But it was a different time. They didn't do anything. Didn't seem to think it was a big deal. My housemates in London told me to leave it, that it was par for the course in the acting world.' She wraps her arms tightly around her cardigan again as though she is cold. 'But I couldn't just leave it, even if the police didn't care. I tried to tell others in the industry but no one wanted to hear it. It wasn't the done thing in those days, to make a fuss. Instead, they closed ranks. I was blacklisted. Dropped by my agent. I never acted again. Because of one man and his ego. His greed.'

'Mum . . . I'm so sorry,' I whisper. But it feels inadequate. Hollow.

She continues as if I haven't said anything.

'My life was ruined because I tried to get justice. The way people looked at me after I had reported it . . . after I had dared to stand up to a man they were all convinced was so wonderful, so *talented*. But it was more than that. They were afraid of him. They were afraid of all of those men. Because they ran the acting world. Just like Gerard Haughton runs this town. All I wanted for you was to get out of this town, get as far away from the Haughton family as possible. To heal. I didn't want you being looked at the way everyone looked at me.'

There is a long silence. Finally, I find my voice, though it is dry and scratchy.

'Why didn't you tell me?' I ask.

Mum looks as though she is considering this, thinking about how to formulate her response.

'Because I knew you. Even at that age, I knew exactly what you were like. So headstrong, yet so naive. I thought that telling you would make you even more determined to go to the police. Like some sort of campaign on behalf of all womankind.'

I look out of the window, trying to work out whether what she says is true, though already knowing that it is. I would have been sickened to know that the same thing had happened to my own mum, even more angry than I otherwise would have been.

'Do you believe me, now?' I ask. For some reason, the teenager in me still needs to know. Still needs the softness of a mother.

'I don't know,' Mum says, flatly. 'Do *you* believe you?'

'I . . . of course I do. All I've ever wanted is to see Liam suffer like he made me suffer.'

'Well then,' Mum says, getting slowly up from the desk chair, 'I suppose I can't stop you from doing what you need to do. But if you don't mind me saying so, Rachel, you're starting to look as bad as me these days.'

I stand there in silence as she leaves the room, shock coursing through me. How could she come out with something like this, just when I am on the brink of spiralling myself? Fifteen years more, of silence? Would I have done the same thing, if I had ever met someone and had a daughter? Would I have been the same as Lizzie Kingston? My phone, clutched in my hand, starts buzzing. I glance down, thinking it'll be Connor. But it's Penny's name flashing on the screen.

I take a deep breath and answer.

'Penny?'

'Rach? I need your help,' she says, her voice anxious. 'It's the rehearsal dinner tonight. Clem had to leave for an emergency, and I'm struggling to handle it all alone. Can you come?'

I stare at the screen for a moment, my mind whirring. The thought of being at that dinner, surrounded by the Haughtons, makes my stomach churn. But this might be my last chance, to speak to Penny, to confront Liam . . . whatever it takes.

'Yes,' I say slowly, determination settling in my chest. 'I'll be there.'

I need to end this. One way or another.

Chapter Sixty-Nine

Rachel

Now

Penny had complained over the phone about the last-minute venue compared to the 1940s ballroom they had hired in London, but as I turn off the coastal road into the pub car park an hour later, my first thought is that it looks absolutely perfect. Despite the skittish, exhausted state that I am in, it is hard not to stop and marvel for a moment as I climb out of my Dad's old Ford, my hair catching in the wind. The pub is a higgledy-piggledy stone building, with small windows, and stands slightly tilted, as though it has bowed in the wind. It stands on a small hill, with white-wash stone steps leading directly down from the patio onto the sand. It is one of the only properties around, right at the end of the stretch of coast. Lights are strung up across the patio, already glowing against the darkening clouds on the horizon. I can't imagine any London ballroom being better than this. But the surrounding beauty does nothing to ease the tension in my chest. Every part of me feels tightly coiled, ready to snap. I need Penny to listen to me.

Inside, the small pub has been laid out, ready for an intimate rehearsal dinner: one long banquet table is in the middle of the main room, decorated with thick cream linens, candles in jars and peonies. The sinking sun over the horizon temporarily filters through the dark clouds and lights up the walls in a soft orange glow. There is no one around. I stand, unsure what to do with myself, until I hear footsteps and Penny enters the room.

'Thank *god*,' she says, as soon as she sees me. She hurries over and then holds out her arms to me. I step towards her and she hugs me, tightly. We stand like that for a moment and I have no idea what she is thinking, but I am thinking *If only she hadn't chosen Liam to marry, of all people.*

Penny releases me. She looks every bit the bride-to-be in a shimmery satin peach dress that gives her skin a pearly glow. Her hair is loosely curled and clipped back on one side with a sweet white clip. Her eyes, however, look tired.

'Are you okay?' I ask.

'I'm fine,' she says, with a small smile. 'Just hungover.'

I glance around the quiet pub.

'Where is everyone?'

'They're on their way. I've been here since this morning sorting everything out.' She takes my hand and gives me a tired but warm smile. 'Thank you so much for dropping everything and coming tonight, Rach. You've been so supportive since we arrived back. It's still so easy between us, isn't it? Just like sisters.'

'Just like sisters,' I echo. *Say it. It's time.*

'Do you want to come upstairs?'

'Sure.'

Penny leads me past the bar and down a low-ceilinged, narrow corridor. She turns right up a winding staircase, with the same low-ceilings, and out onto a landing that is obviously the guest house part of the pub. The walls are decorated with delicate little embroidered handkerchiefs and paintings of vases.

Penny opens the second door along the corridor and we walk into a large bedroom. In the centre of the room is a mahogany four poster bed piled with white cushions and a lambswool throw. There is a thick, shaggy rug across the floorboards and an old roll-top bath stands directly in front of the low window that captures a breathtaking view of the sea. The entire room is bathed in a soft light, warm and inviting.

'It's beautiful,' I breathe, momentarily distracted by how perfect it all looks.

Penny walks over to the wardrobe and opens it. Inside is an ivory dress encased in a see-through gown bag. She pulls it out carefully and hangs it up on the back of the wardrobe door.

'What do you think?'

I have never paid any attention to wedding dresses before, but this one is something straight out of *A Midsummer Night's Dream*. It is soft and romantic and seems to be made up of a thousand tiny petals. Closer, I see the ivory has a hint of delicate pink to it, like the last whispers of a sunset.

'It's absolutely gorgeous,' I say, truthfully, though my stomach twists at the sight of it. I can't let her marry him.

Penny comes to stand next to me and she reaches out a hand to the dress, touching the gown bag lightly with her fingers.

'I still remember the day I chose it, so clearly. I was forced to take Janet and my mum along with me and Clem. They kept trying to point me in other directions, but it was just like they always say . . . when you know, you know. Just like with Liam.'

I turn to look at her, my pulse quickening. This is it. I need to tell her.

'Pen, what did you want to tell me last night?'

Penny frowns.

'Last night? When?'

'On the roller coaster,' I say, my voice thick with urgency. 'You said there was something you needed to tell me. Remember?'

Penny shakes her head, slowly.

'I don't remember saying that, Rach. We were wasted, remember?'

Frustration wells up within me. Is she lying? Or has Liam said something to her, to change her mind?

Penny crosses to the mirror and starts touching up her make-up, as the sound of loud voices can suddenly be heard as guests seem to be arriving. Time is running out. I have to do it now, no matter her reaction. She has to know the truth about that night fifteen years ago, before she marries Liam.

'Penny, I have to . . .'

I am interrupted by a knock on the door. It opens and Tom pokes his head around.

'Everyone's sitting down,' he says to Penny. He nods at me. 'Hey Rach. You coming?'

'You go ahead,' Penny says, twiddling a lock of hair through her straighteners. 'I won't be a second.'

'But . . .' I begin, but Tom is already holding the door open for me. I want to protest – this was my chance, I needed to tell her – but Penny has turned back to the mirror and Tom stands, waiting. I follow Tom out of the room, biting back the rising panic. If I don't get her alone again soon, it might be too late.

When I emerge into the corridor, I am surprised to find Tom looking stressed. He glances either way down the deserted corridor and then takes my arm and tugs me along it, away from Penny's room.

'What wrong?' I ask.

Tom looks at me seriously and lowers his voice.

'We've got a problem.'

Chapter Seventy

Rachel

Now

Tom holds a phone out to me, his expression grim.

'Liam dropped his phone last night when he was drunk. I picked it up for him and saw these messages. He's been seeing someone back in London.'

Stunned, I look down at the screenshots Tom has taken of the messages from someone called Hannah: messages thanking him for the night before, saying she can't wait to introduce him to her family. I swipe the next page and see explicit photos that I immediately jerk back from. I hand the phone back to Tom, my heart racing. Here, at last, is proof. It might not be a criminal offence, but it still shows exactly who Liam is.

'I can't believe this,' I say. 'Does he know you know?'

Tom shakes his head.

'No, and I've not had a chance to speak to him about it yet.'

'Penny?'

Tom glances nervously towards her door.

'She has no idea.'

'Christ, Tom, you have to tell her.'

'Not right now. It's not fair to tell her before I've even spoken to Liam about it. And it's their rehearsal dinner, it's hardly the right moment.'

'Tom, there *is* no right moment,' I hiss, indignantly. 'She's about to marry him! She deserves to know.'

I see Tom's resolve falter, see the hesitation in his eyes.

'Fuck's *sake*,' Tom mutters, pacing up and down the corridor. 'What was he *thinking*?'

'I told you, Tom. I told you what he was like, didn't I? You didn't believe me.'

My heart is racing. I haven't even had to say anything: Liam has done this all by himself. I can hardly believe that he's been so carelessly predictable. Penny's door handle turns and Tom quickly hisses:

'Don't say anything.'

I am about to snap back, but Penny emerges into the hallway.

'What are you doing?' she asks, when she sees us.

'Nothing,' Tom says, quickly. 'Just catching up on last night. I don't remember much.'

He gives me a look as he walks past and follows Penny downstairs. I follow too, but my heart is pounding in my chest. I'm still shocked that Liam would be so stupid, but it makes perfect sense. He doesn't even respect his fiancée. Hatred burns through me.

Downstairs, the guests are already seated at the table. The room is full of the gentle buzz of conversation and soft classical music in the background. There both the families are: Penny's grandmother Grace, who looks smaller than ever, Penny's mum and dad, her uncle, and right at the top of the table, Janet and Gerard Haughton. Neither of them smile at me as I enter the room behind Tom and Penny. And there, at the very head of the table wearing a navy shirt, is Liam. He smiles widely when he sees Penny and gives her a kiss which makes Penny's mum beam. When he sees me, his jaw tenses for just a split second. Then I blink and the look is gone.

'Thanks for filling in for Clem, Rachel. We really appreciate it,' Liam says. 'Thank god it's a bank holiday and we'll have a chance to recover before work, huh?'

Something in the way he says it makes me stop. Does he know what happened last night? Has he spoken to Charles? I search his face for a sign; but from the outside, he looks completely genuine. Before I have to answer, Penny ushers me into the seat beside her. She reaches out and gives my hand a squeeze before pouring me a generous glass of wine.

'I'm fine, thanks,' I say quietly, but Penny shushes me.

'We're going to need it to get through this dinner,' she whispers, with a giggle.

I am immediately opposite Janet and Gerard and try to avoid eye contact with them, but it is almost impossible. I keep my head down as Gerard spends the first course and main talking loudly, smugly, about the roaring success of the fairground opening night. Though it's the last thing I want, I find my hand reaching for my wine glass, just so that I can distract myself, drown him out. The tension in my chest tightens as the evening drags on. All I can do is continue to sip the wine and keep myself together.

'Bloody wise investment,' Gerard says loudly to Penny's dad as he puts down his knife and fork. 'Told you, Phil, you would regret it.'

I can't stand to look at him: all I can think about is my dad and his business, the threat that Gerard held over his head before he died. The stress that Gerard put him under. My hands tremble on my cutlery and clank my fork too loudly against the plate. Penny tops me up and I take another sip, trying to keep myself together, but it is almost impossible, I am wound tight as a bow. My chicken sits almost completely untouched on my plate. Over and over again, my eyes dart to Liam.

'Dad, can we not talk business at the table please?' Liam asks. 'Shall we go through some speeches before dessert? Tom?'

'Oh right,' Tom says, looking distracted and slowly getting to his feet. 'I'll, uh, go first. Don't expect much, folks, I took my best man duties a little too seriously last night.'

Tom's speech is charming enough, but it is obvious that he is distracted. He keeps glancing anxiously at Penny; I see Penny look over at Liam with a puzzled expression. I grip my wine glass tightly. *She can't marry him. She can't.*

The next thing I am aware of, Liam is standing to give his speech. As always, he is smiling, his white teeth gleaming. *My, what big teeth you have my dear.* His voice is smooth and his speech is charming as he begins to thank everyone for everything they've done. Then he turns to Penny.

'Pen. You're going to get the full earful tomorrow, but I can't let tonight go without telling you how much you mean to me . . .'

My heart is pounding. I can feel it against my ribcage. The anger rises inside me, reaching boiling point.

' . . . from the moment I met you, you erased so much of who I didn't want to be and helped me uncover all of the parts I never even knew existed . . .'

I down the rest of my glass with a shaking hand, blood roaring in my ears.

' . . . I can promise you, with or without wedding vows, that I will spend the rest of my life being the man you deserve . . .'

'NO!'

The words are out of my mouth before I can stop them. There are gasps as my chair falls back behind me: I am on my feet without knowing I have stood up, my bag falling to the ground and the contents scattering across the slate tiles. I am shaking all over. I can't take it anymore.

Liam stops abruptly.

'You . . .' I say, breathing heavily, ' . . . will never be the man that Penny deserves.'

'Rachel!' Tom says loudly, his eyes wide, but I am not listening. I can feel Penny tugging at me, whispering at me to sit down, but I can't: every shard of pain, every moment of hurt, of fear, of stress, of doubt over the past fifteen years is pouring out of me and I cannot stop it.

'I won't let you marry him, Penny,' I say, my voice cracking with emotion. 'Not without knowing the truth.'

'What truth?' Liam asks, his arms spread wide. As always, he manages to remain calm. 'What truth is so important that you would try to ruin our rehearsal dinner?'

'The truth about what happened in the fairground fifteen years ago,' I say loudly, the words ringing in my ears. I turn to Penny who looks horrified. 'Penny, I didn't make it up. Everything I said about what happened that night was true. I only told the police I made it up because *he*,' I point a shaking finger at Gerard Haughton, 'threatened my dad and his business.'

'Rachel . . .' Penny says quietly. 'What are you doing?'

'You have to be kidding me,' Liam says in a low voice. The rest of the table sit in deathly silence, looking shocked. 'All along, this was still your game? Nothing happened fifteen years ago and you know it. Or maybe you don't,' he says, throwing his hands up. 'Maybe you really believe that's what happened. That's the story you've told yourself. But it isn't true, Rachel. Now, if you don't mind . . . kindly get out.'

'No!' I shout, not moving. 'I know what you did! You've been stalking me ever since you got back to town. Harassing me. I know you've been watching me, messing with my phone. Following me. You're a *liar*.'

'Rachel, stop,' Tom says, his voice firm, but I don't listen. I turn back to Penny, my eyes burning, adrenaline coursing through me.

'Penny, listen to me . . .'

But there is a scrape of a chair and Gerard Haughton has stood up.

'You heard what my son said. Get out. You've done enough damage.'

'He's cheating on you, Penny,' I say loudly, urgently. 'Tom found the messages on his phone. He's been cheating on you.'

Liam pales and I feel a stab of satisfaction.

'What's she talking about, Liam?' Penny asks, her voice shaking.

'It's bullshit,' Liam says, the superior expression now wiped from his face. 'Of course I'm not cheating on you. How can you even ask me that?'

'What utter nonsense,' Gerard echoes. 'Penny, you can hardly—'

'Stay out of this, Dad,' Liam snaps. Gerard's eyes widen and beside him, Janet gasps. 'I can handle this myself.'

Penny ignores Liam's interruption, her eyes still flickering between me and Tom. 'One of you explain to me what the hell is going on. Right now.'

'Show her, Tom,' I say loudly, ignoring the aghast expressions around the table. 'Show her the messages.'

'Rachel, I asked you not to say anything,' Tom says, pleadingly, but Penny has turned to him, her face a mask of disbelief.

'Show me, Tom. *Now.*'

Slowly, Tom hands his phone over to Penny, the screen unlocked. I watch her face as she scrolls through each of the messages. Her faced drains of colour. When she reaches the explicit photos, she thrusts the phone back at Tom, with a nauseated expression.

'Penny, whatever is on that phone is a lie,' Liam says, firmly. 'It's probably just a wrong number.'

'She's calling you Liam. She's saved you as a contact,' Penny hisses. Her face has gone from very pale to red. There are blotches forming on her neck.

'Then *she* probably did it,' Liam says furiously, gesturing at me. 'No doubt to try and frame me.'

'Listen to yourself, Liam,' Penny says. 'When would Rachel have had your phone?'

369

'Penny, dear, let's all calm down, shall we?' Janet Haughton begins, but Penny whips around to look at her.

'Stay out of this, Janet,' she says, angrily. 'I'm not going to brush this all under the carpet like you do about everything.'

'That is *enough*,' Gerard says, suddenly slamming his palm on the table, making Penny's parents jump. 'We have paid good money for this dinner, money you begged us for. You are acting like a child.'

Liam looks at Penny now, his face mirroring the disbelief in hers.

'You . . . you went to them for money? After I told you not to?'

Penny lifts her chin defiantly, but tears are spilling down her cheeks.

'Yes, because you were too stubborn to do it, even though we needed help. And your dad was perfectly happy to do it, as long as I did a little favour for him, isn't that right Gerard?'

For a moment, Gerard's top lip curls into a scowl, but as quickly as it came, it is gone again.

'She just signed a document for me, that's all. Just a formality for the money she was so keen to grab from us.' His voice is cutting, dismissive.

'What kind of document?' Liam asks, slowly. His voice has taken on an even harder edge now, so that it is like solid steel. 'Dad, what did you make her sign? What have you got her involved in?'

Gerard says nothing. Janet looks around at Liam, Gerard, and Penny, her mouth open in shock, as Liam turns back to Penny.

'What were you thinking, Pen? Going behind my back, borrowing money and signing documents without telling me?'

With tears still falling down Penny's cheeks, she stands up to face Liam.

'I suppose that makes us both liars then, doesn't it?'

With a sob, she turns from the table and runs out of the room. I make a move to follow her, but the next thing I know, Tom is in front of me.

'No, Rachel,' he says, and he looks furious. 'You've done enough damage.'

'Tom, please, I have to . . .'

'No,' he says firmly. 'This wasn't the time or the place. Please, just go.'

I look around desperately, but quickly realise I will never be able to get past Tom, or any of the others, to speak to Penny. The other guests are all staring at me in shock, Gerard red-faced and furious.

With a hollow, empty feeling in my stomach, I duck down and grab my bag, before turning and walking out of the pub.

Chapter Seventy-One

Connor

Now

I check my phone again, but there's still no response from Rachel. I've not heard from her since her frightened voicemail earlier.

'Connor, please call me back . . . I've just found out someone installed some sort of spyware on my phone. It means they've been watching me. I think they followed me at the fairground last night. Please. Call me.'

I try calling her again, but it goes straight to voicemail. I put my phone down, frustrated. *Why isn't she answering?*

I hunch back over my desk, the low hum of the computer the only sound in the room. Scraps of paper and printouts litter the surface of the desk, information I've gathered on the Haughtons, the funfair, on Rachel herself.

I continue scrolling through the CCTV from the funfair the night before. By all accounts, it was a roaring success. Shareholders thrilled with the opening-night profits. Rumours that this is going to trigger widespread gentrification of the town, attract a new crowd of home-buyers.

The footage has been playing for hours now: endless crowds, faces blurred by motion, poor quality cameras. It's mostly useless. But I can't stop. I'm looking for something. Something in particular.

Rachel said someone was following her last night. If they were that close to her, perhaps there was a trace of them on the footage.

I click through frame by frame. Waiting. My eyes are dry and gritty from staring at the screen for so long. I keep going, the repetitive monotony gnawing at my patience. The hours of footage blend together in one bright blur, until . . .

I stop. Hit pause.

There is Rachel: her long hair falling down her back in waves, her gold skirt bright under the fair lights. The poor quality of the footage makes her limbs look jerky, like a puppet. And there, just a few feet away from her, hidden by a balloon seller . . . is a figure.

I zoom in, squinting at the screen. The resolution is terrible, but the figure's face is angled towards her, watching her. A chill creeps up my spine as I lean in closer. The quality might be terrible . . . but the person is easily recognisable. *Shit.*

I reach for my phone. My knee jiggles up and down as I put the phone to my ear and listen to it ring. *Come on. Pick up.* No one answers, so I try again. And again. On the fourth time, with one arm in my jacket and my car keys in my hand, someone finally answers.

Chapter Seventy-Two

Rachel

Now

I walk, numbly, down the steps and out into the gravel car park. I cannot drive: I have drunk too much, my head is all over the place, spinning with countless thoughts. Without caring where I am going, I leave the car park and stumble out onto the sandy beach. The lights of the pub patio flicker behind me, but soon I am swallowed by the darkness, with only the sound of the waves in front and the crunch of sand beneath my feet to distract me from my racing thoughts.

My stomach swirls, sickeningly, making me want to throw up. I should be pleased that Penny has seen a hint of Liam's true colours, pleased that this means the wedding might be on hold, if not cancelled altogether. But instead all I can see are the faces of those at the dinner table: the shock, the disgust, the way Penny had looked at me. Why hadn't I stopped myself? Why had I let it boil over the surface like that? Penny will never forgive me. I haven't won, I haven't got any closer to the closure I wanted.

It's over.

I stand there for a moment, completely defeated. The waves are black velvet, only distinguishable by the odd crest that catches the moonlight. *It's time to let go*, I think. I might never know the full truth about that night, might never get closure from Liam. A small part of me is still desperate to uncover the truth, to understand why he has been tormenting me. But perhaps it no longer matters. Exhaustion drapes over me like a heavy blanket, smothering the last flicker of anger, of determination. I need to find a new job. I need to process what Mum told me about her own assault. And more than anything, I need to get as far away from Liam Haughton as possible.

I lift my head, about to turn and head back up to the beach, when I hear it. The soft, sinking sound of footsteps in the surrounding darkness. There is someone behind me.

Chapter Seventy-Three

DC Rainer

2005

*D*C Rainer yawned and rubbed his eyes as he looked away *from the photo he had been gazing at. He and Marie had allowed Charlotte to have friends over last night, something she had called 'a gathering, Dad, not a party'. He couldn't stand the idea of having a load of seventeen-year-old boys in the house without any supervision so he had insisted that he and Marie would stay upstairs in their room, not bothering anyone, but there if Charlotte needed anything. That was all. In reality, he had stood with his ear to the door, listening for any sounds of couples sneaking off into bedrooms, or fights about to break out. He knew he was too protective of Charlotte, Marie always said it, Charlotte always yelled it, but how could he not? With the things he had seen during his time on the force?*

PC Thompson walked back into the office, a cup of tea in one hand and her phone in the other. She sat down at the desk opposite him and took a drink of tea, then immediately screwed up her face and put the mug back down, again.

'Gone cold. Can you microwave tea? Or will the milk go funny?'

'According to my mother-in-law you can microwave absolutely anything.'

Thompson looked down at the mug dubiously, then pushed it away.

'Think I'll just make another one.' She glanced at the photos spread out on Rainer's desk. 'What are you looking at?'

'The Kingston assault case. I know it's been dropped, but these photos from one of the kid's cameras were nagging at me.'

Thompson leaned forwards.

'What about them?'

Rainer picked up the photo he had been looking at. A blown-up, glossy photo of a group of teenagers messing around in the abandoned, derelict funfair, the flash making their eyes red and their faces eerily pale. In the distance, the Funhouse loomed over the scene, the giant painted clown leering down at the teens.

'Look at that. See the timestamp on the photo? Eleven exactly.'

Thompson took the photo off him and studied it.

'Okay, and . . .?'

'Rachel Kingston said that she knew what time it was because her watch beeped during the attack. She was adamant it was eleven, remember?'

'Right . . .'

'And Liam Haughton is in that photo. At eleven.'

'So he couldn't have been in the Funhouse with Rachel, then,' Thompson finished. 'Assuming the timestamp is correct.'

'Assuming that, yes. But she also said that his ring dug into her lip, didn't she? When he covered her mouth. But he's not wearing a ring in this photo and you can see both his hands clearly.'

'Well then, doesn't that prove what we already know? That she was lying? She admitted to lying.'

'*I know,*' Rainer said, more to himself than her.

Thompson looked at him with narrowed eyes.

'*What is it, then?*'

'*Nothing, just a gut feeling. Something doesn't sit right.*'

They were quiet for a moment before Thompson spoke again. '*It is a bit strange that we had that witness come forward – the one that said they saw Liam running away from the Funhouse at the exact same time as Rachel said the attack happened.*'

Rainer pulled the statement Thompson was talking about towards him, scanning it again. The witness was the one person who had corroborated Rachel's timings. They had also described Liam's panicked expression, the way he bolted from the scene.

'*So which is it?*' Rainer said, rubbing the top of his forehead, where his hair was starting to recede. '*Did Liam do it, and the timestamp on the camera is wrong? Or is the witness mistaken about seeing Liam running away from the Funhouse just after eleven?*'

'*Or,*' Thompson said, picking up the photo again, her brow furrowed, '*. . . was the witness lying?*'

Chapter Seventy-Four

Rachel

Now

'Hey, Rach.'

Tom's voice floats through the darkness. My shoulders drop slightly.

'What do you want, Tom?' I ask. My voice is hoarse. Defeated.

'I wanted to check you were okay.'

I feel, rather than see him reach my side. We both look out over the black waves.

'I'm sorry I told everyone about the cheating,' I say, my words hollow.

'No you're not,' Tom says, and there is just a hint of amusement in his tone. He isn't angry with me, after all.

'No, I suppose not,' I admit. 'But I wish . . . I wish it was different. For Penny.'

'This is the best thing for Penny,' Tom says firmly. 'She needed to know the truth about Liam. I've been making excuses for him for years. He cheated on his girlfriend at uni and I had to cover up for him. I was relieved when he went AWOL for a few years, to be honest. But then he came back and suddenly set his sights on Pen.' His voice tightens. 'I confronted him and he promised it would be different this time. That he had changed. Clearly, he hasn't. Penny is well off not marrying into that family. You know about Gerard, right?'

I am aware that there is water lapping against my feet and my shoes are wet but I don't move. I feel completely numb.

'I know he's screwed a lot of people over,' I say, thinking of Didi. 'My dad included.'

'It goes well beyond that. He's been stealing from people in town for years. He even persuaded my mum to put in some of her money to one of his schemes. She thought it would help her with her retirement fund after Dad left. When she panicked and tried to pull it out, he refused. Said the stock had tanked and it was gone.'

'Really?' I ask, but my tone lacks any real surprise. I'm not sure anything can shock me anymore.

'Yep. She only told me the other week, when I first came back with Penny and Liam. Asked me to have a word with Gerard.' Tom's voice is flat and hard. 'It wouldn't surprise me if he nicked your dad's money, too. The Haughtons think they can do whatever they want without any consequences.'

I remember the day Mum came home, her face streaked with tears after Gerard told her the money was all gone. The small, bare, funeral we had to have for Dad. I register a dull, sick feeling in the pit of my stomach but it is sedated, its sharp edge muted by my own numbness.

'Does Liam know?'

'Know? I think he's been in on it from the start. He lost his job signing off on some dodgy documents for Gerard at work.'

'That's why he lost his job?'

The information Connor and I had been so keen to uncover. Now I find I no longer care.

'Yes,' Tom's voice is slightly breathless, now. Almost eager. 'That must be the reason he was messing with you, sending that postcard and calling the police on you and your mum. He was trying to make you look unstable in case you pointed the finger at him for the rape, or stealing your dad's money, or both. You should have seen how worried he was when he got back to town and saw you working at the firm. I guess it all makes sense, now.'

'I guess so.'

There is a long pause.

'What happens now, do you think?' I ask.

'Oh, no doubt Gerard Haughton will try and wave his usual magic wand and sweep it all under the rug. But that's not happening this time. I'm going to make sure Pen comes back to London with me and Liam can clear up his own mess here.'

'Right,' I say, dully.

I hear the soft crunch of sand as Tom turns to look at me. I feel his hand in the darkness as it touches the side of my face.

'Rach, you should be happy. Pen is free. You helped stop her marrying him. And I can out Gerard Haughton to the town, make sure my mum gets her money back. Liam's been found out. They'll believe you about him, now. I thought this was what you wanted?'

His voice is quick, almost excited. I know he is right, that I should be happy. I may not have the closure I wanted, but everything makes more sense, now, and I am safe again. But at Tom's words, I feel a sharp jolt in my gut, a feeling of deepest dread, of painful uncertainty. Something isn't right; and as Tom's hand stays pressed against my cheek, it hits me like a bolt of lightning across the sky.

I thought this was what you wanted. And suddenly I am back on the bed in the old Funhouse and Liam is there. And for the first time that I can remember, the memory is sharp, as though it has been recorded in ultra-high definition.

'Rach, listen . . . no, you're too drunk.'

'Come on, Liam. Don't be such a pussy.'

'For god's sake, Rach. Rach? Are you okay?'

He shakes me and I blink.

'Huh?'

My eyes feel heavy and I feel sick. I drift in and out of darkness until I feel his arms around me again. Good. This is what I wanted. I allow him to nuzzle his head into my neck. It feels a bit funny. Different. The scratch of stubble. The smell of cigarettes recently smoked. Not Liam's usual smell. He keeps me on my side, his chest pressed against my back, his hands heavy and urgent. But they become too urgent and I start to feel sick. Maybe this isn't the best idea.

'No, Liam . . . I don't think . . .' I mumble. 'I've changed my mind.'

'Shh,' he whispers.

I try, hopelessly, to wiggle away from him, but my body is sluggish and I can barely keep my eyes open.

'No . . .' I mutter.

'Stop moving.'

'No . . . get off . . .'

'*I thought this is what you wanted.*'

I open my mouth to say no again, but suddenly there is a hand, smothering it. The cold pressure of a ring presses against my lip.

The same cold pressure of a ring that now lingers against my cheek. The same whiff of cigarettes. My stomach turns.

Oh god.

It wasn't Liam at all.

It was Tom.

Chapter Seventy-Five

Rachel

Now

Shock pulses through me as I stand there, the realisation finally dawning on me with terrifying clarity. All this time I had doubted myself. Wondered at the patches in my memory, began to question my own sanity. But it wasn't me who had twisted the truth – it was him: he had manipulated me, he had used me, he had tricked me in the worst possible way. My friend. Tom, with his freckles and sandy hair. Training to be a police officer and looking after his mum. His hand is still on my face and I jerk away from him, sickened.

'You,' I whisper. 'It was you.'

'What was me?' Tom's voice has lost its manic exhilaration: it's turned cold.

'That night at the fairground . . .' The truth hits me like a slap, stinging and raw. 'Liam left me in the Funhouse, and then . . . you. It was you, wasn't it?'

How could I have not realised it before? That Liam rarely smoked, and never that heavily. That the voice was different. My mum had been right, after all: I *had* altered the narrative, to make sense of what I thought happened. But I had never realised that there was another version of events. *This* version.

'You did all of this,' I say, backing away from him, my feet squelching in the wet sand. 'You made me think I was going mad. You made me think it was Liam.' My mind is racing, piecing together the events of the past few weeks. 'You put that spyware on my phone, didn't you? And . . . you made me think it was me outside Liam and Penny's house drunk that night . . .' I remember him going to the toilets when we were at the bar and the depth of his deception crashes over me like a wave. 'Liam never sent a message about a break-in, did he? You set it all up.'

Tom doesn't answer and I keep going, unravelling the awful truth like a scarf caught in the wind.

'Tonight . . . the messages on Liam's phone from that Hannah person. You sent them too, didn't you? You knew I would be desperate to tell Penny. You just wanted to make sure you didn't get your own hands dirty.'

There is a long, awful silence. I can't make out Tom's expression in the darkness, but I can feel the shift in the air between us. Then, at last, he speaks, his voice calm.

'Does it really matter, Rach? Really? I mean, Liam and Penny aren't right for each other, you know that. She should be with me. She just doesn't see it, yet. I actually love her, unlike *him*.'

'What you're doing isn't love,' I say, my voice shaking. 'None of this is love.'

'What would you know?' Tom snaps, his calm mask suddenly slipping, shocking me. 'You're pathetic. It's been so fucking *painful* being around you, pretending to be interested in your paranoid theories, watching you live your sad little life.'

'For fifteen years people have thought I was a liar.' Betrayal pounds through me and tears well up in my eyes. Thinking that Liam had betrayed me when we were eighteen was one thing, but this manipulation over the past few weeks is something else entirely. 'I thought you were my *friend*.'

'That's the trouble with you,' Tom says, and now he sounds annoyed. 'You just latch on. You latched onto Liam back in school and wouldn't let him out of your sight. Then you latched onto the idea of him assaulting you, then you latched onto Penny when she returned to town. You make it so easy for people to manipulate you.'

'You're a monster,' I breathe, backing away from him. 'You know it's just a matter of time before you're caught, right? People like you don't stop.'

'And what about you, Rachel?' Tom asks. I don't see him move but suddenly his voice is closer to me. 'Are you going to stop?'

'What do you mean?' I ask, stalling for time. In the darkness, I slowly inch a hand under the front flap of my bag, my fingertips searching for my phone, but meeting nothing. Panic flares in my chest as I remember my bag falling on the floor in the pub, the contents spilling out.

'Well, now you know it's me. So what's your plan? You've been like a dog with a bone since Liam got back, determined to out him to everyone. Are you going to do the same with me?'

'I . . .' He's baiting me, he knows that. 'No, I won't say anything.'

Tom laughs, loudly, a burst of high-pitched noise.

'We both know that isn't true. You'll go to the police as soon as we leave and I'm fucked. I can't have them looking into me, you see. I've got too much to lose.' His voice has taken on a new edge now, one I haven't heard before. Desperation.

'No, no I won't . . .' but before I can get any more words out, his hands are on me, grabbing my arms. My bag slips from my shoulder, falling uselessly into the wet sand as Tom drags me towards the water. The sea laps higher and higher against my legs and panic surges through me as he continues to force me into deeper water.

'No,' I gasp, trying to pull away from him, but he is too strong. 'No . . .'

Without a word he continues to drag me out into the deeper, blacker water. The water is ice-cold: it seeps through my clothes, pressing them against my skin like a layer of heavy film.

'Help!' I scream. 'Hel—'

But before I can get another word out, there is a hand on the back of my head and Tom shoves me under. Cold explodes inside my skull and I gasp before I can stop myself: seawater, salty, painful, rushes into my mouth, into the back of my throat. Tom's other hand is now on the back of my neck, holding me down. *He's going to drown me.* The thought sends panic screaming through me and I try to push back, but he is too strong. As I fight the instinct to inhale, my lungs begin to burn. The pressure builds, spreading like fire across my ribcage, every nerve in my body screaming for oxygen. I'm running out of time.

And then, as though he were right there next to me, I hear my dad's voice when he first took me out into the sea. *If you get stuck beneath a wave, don't panic. Panic causes movement, movement causes loss of oxygen faster. Stay relaxed. Ride it out.* I have to listen to him. Though all my instincts are screaming at me to do the opposite, I stop fighting and force myself to go limp. I focus everything on slow, intermittent exhales whenever I feel the overwhelming urge to breathe. Then, miraculously, the pressure on the back of my head lifts. Tom must think that I am unconscious: I can feel his hands splashing around, trying to check my pulse. I don't hesitate: kicking out as hard as I can, I connect with Tom's legs. Pain shoots through my foot and above the water, I hear a muffled shout, but I ignore it. Kicking out again, I start swimming as fast as I can.

Chapter Seventy-Six

Rachel

Now

All I can hear as I propel myself through the water is my heartbeat thundering in my ears. I don't know which way I am going, can't see anything through the oppressive blackness. My clothes and shoes weigh me down, dragging me further underwater. Through each frantic stroke, I gasp for air, waiting for Tom to grab me from behind, convinced every brush of seaweed is his hand on my ankle. The water around me is endless: I could be swimming in circles, or further from land, I have no idea. All I know is that I need to get as far away from Tom as possible. He is far more dangerous than anything out here.

As I come up for air, I hear a loud splash nearby. Panic surges through me as I gasp in cold air and swim harder still, away from the splashing behind me, willing my muscles to move faster, but I can already feel them slowing, the weight of the cold water pulling at them. After what feels like hours to my exhausted body, but could have been mere minutes, I slow down, trying not to make a sound as I tread water and look around in the blackness. My heart leaps when I see the pub's lights twinkling, closer than I'd first thought. Less than a hundred metres. I can do that. I still have enough energy. But the relief mingles with fear.

Where is Tom?

I listen for any sign of him – any splash, any breath – but the water is eerily quiet now. Is he hiding in the darkness, waiting? Keeping my head above water so that I can still listen out for any sounds of him approaching, I cut quietly through the water, my heart in my mouth, trying not to make a sound. The pub lights are drawing closer . . . only twenty metres to go . . . but the closer I get, the more aware I become of Tom's absence. Where is he?

At last, my feet touch the sandy bottom and I stagger through the shallow water, painfully aware of how loudly I am splashing. I am propelled forwards once again by my dad's voice. *Just get to the pub.*

I stumble heavily onto the welcoming, solid sand and run as fast as I can up the beach. My trainers are so water-clogged they feel like concrete but I keep running, not daring to stop and take them off. *Get to the pub, Rachel.* I am almost there: I reach the stone steps leading up onto the back patio and rear entrance. I race up them, my body close to giving up from exhaustion. I grab the double handles and pull. They are locked.

Somewhere behind me, I hear a sound and a panicked sob escapes me. I turn around, but there is no one behind me, just the empty patio lit by pretty, innocuous fairy lights. The perfect wedding venue. I race back down the steps and around the pub to the car park. Just as I reach the gravel, I hear a shout.

'Rachel!'

I look up and let out a cry of relief when I see it's Penny. It's over. I am safe. She is on the other side of the car park, running towards me. I stagger towards her, my knees almost buckling with the effort. Her arms are out towards me, shouting to me. We are only a few feet away from one another when the screech of tyres tears through the night. Headlights burst into view, and a car comes skidding towards us. I catch the look of horror on Penny's face, before there is a sickening thud and everything goes black.

Chapter Seventy-Seven

Rachel

Now

Liam's voice floats through the part-open hospital room door, as he stands outside talking to the doctor.

'Are you absolutely sure?' he asks.

'Yes, Mr Haughton, we're sure.'

There is a long silence before Liam speaks again.

'I can't believe it.'

I shift in my chair, wincing as the movement sends a sharp pain through my bruised ribs. The thin hospital gown is cool against my skin, in contrast to the heat of the pain radiating through the rest of my body. The torn and bloody clothes I wore to the rehearsal dinner are stuffed into a plastic bag at the foot of my own bed in the main ward, remnants of a night I want to forget but know I never will.

Liam re-enters the room, looking dazed. The hospital lights cast a dull glow over his face, deepening the shadows beneath his eyes.

'Are you okay?' I ask, my voice hoarse.

Liam nods absently.

'Connor's getting you a coffee,' I say. Liam nods again, his face pale and wan.

I am suddenly conscious that it's the first time Liam and I have been alone together in over fifteen years. I have to fight the urge to stop clenching my fists. *You're safe, now. It wasn't him.*

Liam's gaze shifts to the bed I am sat next to. Penny's red hair is more vivid than ever next to the sterile white sheets. Her eyes are closed, her breathing soft and steady, the delicate skin of her eyelids a soft purple compared to her pale face. One arm is in a plaster-cast, suspended in a raised pulley.

'I wish she would wake up,' Liam says anxiously, standing at the foot of her bed and looking down at her.

'She will,' I say. 'The doctor said everything would be fine, she's just had a lot of meds.'

Liam's face suddenly twists in pain as he looks at Penny.

'I can't believe what he did to her. To both of you.'

My insides churn at the memory of Tom's face behind the wheel, his eyes wild with desperation as the car hurtled towards us. It was Connor who had made the connection after seeing Tom watching me at the fair, and tried to call me to warn me. Thankfully, Liam had found my phone on the floor of the pub and answered it. As soon as Liam explained to Penny what Connor had told him, they had come looking for me and Tom, Penny running out to the car park, just as Tom was making his escape. I wonder if we will ever find out if hitting us was an accident or intentional. I am not sure I need to know. It is enough, for now, that he is in custody, tracked down by the police after he fled the pub car park.

Liam grips the end of the bed so tightly his knuckles whiten.

'How could I have been friends with him for all these years and never realised how dangerous he was?'

'Don't blame yourself,' I say quietly. 'None of us saw this coming. He did it to me, and I didn't even know.'

It feels surreal, sitting and having a normal conversation with Liam after all these years of hatred. The man I blamed for everything was never the real monster in my nightmares.

Liam lowers himself into the chair on the other side of Penny's bed, his head bowed as though he is in prayer.

'I'm sorry, Rachel,' he says after a while. His voice is laced with guilt. 'I was convinced you were this unstable liar and I shouldn't trust you. And you've been telling the truth for fifteen years. I still can't get my head around it.'

'Well, I was still wrong about you, too,' I say. 'Maybe if I hadn't been so fixated on the idea that it was you, I would have realised something was amiss. Realised that the second half of my memories felt different, somehow.'

Even though it is a relief to know what really happened that night, there is part of me that feels violated all over again, knowing how Tom had seized an opportunity the way he did. I push the thought away. I am not ready to face that trauma head-on just yet.

'There's something I haven't told you,' Liam says, raising his head. 'I took your police file. The one in the basement at work.'

'Why?'

He shakes his head.

'I just . . . I wasn't expecting to see it there. It shocked me. It brought up all the memories of back then. The fear that I was going to be charged and go to trial, you know? And I found myself taking it, wanting to know what drove you to accuse me all those years ago. I thought it might help me understand. It was a stupid thing to do.'

There is another long silence where we all watch Penny for a moment.

'Have you spoken to your dad?' I ask, tentatively, knowing this conversation will likely open another wound.

Liam's jaw muscles flex, and for a moment I suddenly regret bringing his dad up. He exhales slowly, as if he's trying to steady himself.

'Not yet. I didn't want to tip him off until . . . until I've reported him.' His voice falters and I can see the weight of the decision pressing down on him. What a terrible thing to have to do, report your own dad to the authorities.

'Did you ever suspect? That he might be committing fraud?'

'No, never. It was only when I signed some documents for him at work last year that all hell broke loose.'

'What do you mean?'

Liam sighs.

'My dad was a client of my old firm in London. I'm not supposed to have anything to do with his account, obviously. Anyway, he persuaded me to sign off a couple of financial reports. The firm found out I had signed documents without authorisation and fired me.'

So that's why he lost his job. Another piece of the puzzle, slotted into place. Forming a picture I wasn't expecting.

'What the firm didn't realise, nor did I at first,' Liam continues, 'was that the reports were fraudulent. But there was enough there to make me question my dad a bit, for the first time ever. So when we came back, with the story that I had been made redundant, I starting looking into his business dealings. Talking to people in town. That's when I realised how long this had all been going on for.'

I think of Liam's meeting with Wayne Stephens, how scared I was that he had instructed Wayne to come after me.

'And Penny?' I ask gently. 'What did Gerard ask her to do?'

'I don't know yet,' Liam says grimly. 'My dad is refusing to show me the documents. But he did admit it was linked to some shell company he set up in the British Virgin Islands. So he used her as a scapegoat in case anything went wrong. His own daughter-in-law.'

I don't know what to say: poor Penny probably felt she had no choice, after she had asked Gerard for money. My insides burn with anger at the thought of Gerard's greed and manipulation.

'I'm sorry for everything he's done to your family, too,' Liam says quietly. 'I'm so ashamed.'

I shake my head. The whole thing is a complete mess. Liam will carry the guilt over his dad's actions, and I now carry my own guilt, knowing that it was never Liam who attacked me. What if I hadn't retracted my allegation? What if the police, the CPS, had believed me, and Liam had been charged? Someone just as innocent as me. It all comes back to Tom. He is the reason that I lost my friends, lost my innocence. He is the reason I have spent fifteen years buried in pain, the reason we're all here in this hospital room.

Liam suddenly straightens up and looks down at the bed: Penny is blinking blearily around the room at us.

'Pen,' Liam breathes and he's on his feet in an instant, at her side. 'How are you feeling?'

'Rubbish,' she croaks. 'Everything hurts.'

'You've got a bad concussion and a broken wrist,' I say. 'The doctors said how lucky you were. We both were.'

She looks at me with large, terrified eyes.

'I can't believe what happened. Any of it.'

'Don't think about that just now,' Liam says, soothingly. 'Just rest. We can talk later.'

Penny nods, her face pale. She settles her head back down against the pillows, clearly still exhausted.

'I guess we'll have to postpone the wedding,' she sighs. 'All that organisation, down the drain.'

'Let's talk about it tomorrow,' Liam says. 'You might not want to leave it too late.' He reaches out and places a hand on the blankets covering Penny's stomach. 'When were you going to tell me?'

Penny looks at him, confused.

'Tell you what?'

Connor appears in the doorway and I get up: it's time to leave them to it.

Chapter Seventy-Eight

Rachel
Now

The early morning sun greets me as I step outside the hospital the day next day. The air is fresh and smells faintly of salt from the nearby sea. I wonder if I will ever be able to swim again. My body is still sore, my ribs aching with every breath, but the bruises are nothing compared to the memories. The night before feels like a nightmare I can't quite wake up from – Tom's hands, the suffocating cold of the water, the squeal of car tyres. And yet the nightmare is real. Penny is still lying in hospital and Tom is gone. The boy who sat next to me for most of secondary school, who wanted to fit in as much as I did. The fatso and the loser.

I walk through the hospital doors and glance back towards them. A part of me wants to go inside to check on Penny. Part of me feels like I owe it to her. But part of me also needs some time. Time away from them all, to let things settle. To begin to process. I look around for the taxi rank; Connor offered to get me before he left last night, but it's too early and I could use the time alone. The last thing I want is to feel dependent on anyone right now, not after everything that's happened. I've only taken a few steps away from the main reception, however, when I recognise someone sitting on a bench outside the hospital entrance, drinking from a Styrofoam coffee cup.

'Katie?'

Katie gets up when she sees me and smiles. Her hair is perfectly styled, another silk scarf around her neck.

'There you are. I wasn't sure where you might be, I was worried I might miss you.'

'What are you doing here?' I ask, completely nonplussed.

'Your mum asked me to come and get you. She wanted to do it, but her driving is a bit rusty. Come on, I'm parked this way.'

I am still opening and closing my mouth as she drops her coffee cup into a nearby bin and walks briskly off towards an old grey Volvo.

'It's kind of you to come and get me,' I say, as we climb into the warm car. It smells like sweet air fresheners and leather. I am both confused and touched at her thoughtfulness, this woman that I barely know. Katie waves her hand in the air.

'No trouble. How's your friend? Penny?'

'She's okay, thanks. They said she's got no long-term damage, just a few broken bones. She was lucky.' The mental scars will take longer to heal.

We pull out of the hospital car park and join the main road back to town.

'How's Mum?'

'She's fine, she met a few of my friends last night at a restaurant nearby and then I stayed over. I had to sleep in your room, sorry.'

It sounds nothing like Mum, to go out and meet other people.

'Did she . . . enjoy herself?' I ask, hesitantly.

'No, I think she had a crap time, actually. It was a bunch of recovering alcoholics drinking water and eating cheap Italian food.' Katie laughs. 'But she's asked when the next one is.'

'A bunch of . . .' I trail off and Katie glances across at me.

'I'm four years sober,' she says, her mouth twitching slightly at my surprised expression.

'Wow.'

I remember Mum saying that Katie had been through a lot, but I never would have suspected this woman, who seems so together, would have once suffered like Mum.

'It sounded like an awful ordeal, what you went through last night,' Katie says, her eyes back on the road. 'They've arrested the man, have they?'

I nod.

'I don't know what else has happened,' I say. 'I'm supposed to call the police so they can come and take my statement, later today.'

'Do you need to use my phone?'

'It's okay, I'll sort it when I get home. Thank you, though.'

I still don't know Katie very well, but now I am talking to her without the fog of suspicion that clouded my judgement before, I get the impression she is a completely selfless person.

'Thanks for everything you've been doing for Mum, Katie.'

Katie smiles in a comfortable but unassuming way, which tells me she is used to people thanking her, no doubt due to the charity work Mum mentioned.

'She really needs to get a handle on her drinking before her liver packs up. I should know.'

'I know. I'll be there for her,' I say firmly. I need to step up. Mum and I might not have the picture-perfect relationship, but she is all I have. I don't want to keep existing like two sad ships in the night, each on our own self-destructive cycles. Katie, however, shakes her head.

'You have your own life to live. You can't pause it for your mother, that's not fair. You're so young. I, on the other hand, have plenty of spare time.'

An unexpected warmth spreads through me. Katie is a reminder that perhaps there are good people in the world, after all.

We turn off the beach road, onto my road.

'I'll just drop you off, let you two catch up.' She suddenly looks nervous. 'I'm actually seeing Sabrina this morning.'

'Your daughter?'

Katie nods.

'We haven't spoken in a long time,' she admits. 'It was too hard for her, with me in and out of AA. I wasn't a very good mum in those days. Anyway, your mum got in touch with her. Tracked her down on social media, of all places. Told her all about how I'd been helping her with her own journey. That I was four years sober, now. Then Sabrina asked me if I wanted a coffee.'

Katie looks tearful for a moment and sniffs, loudly.

'I hadn't contacted her for ages because I wanted to respect her wishes and I felt so guilty about the kind of mother I've been. I never dreamed Liz would reach out to her.'

I would never have dreamed it either. Perhaps, like Liam, my own prejudice towards my mother has stopped me from seeing her as anything other than the villain.

Katie drops me off with another wave, and then she is gone and I am walking up the front path towards home. The familiar knot of dread starts to steal over me, a habit formed over a lifetime. I notice, however, that something is different. The lounge curtains are open and the sash window lifted . . . as though someone has let the summer air inside.

Epilogue

Five Weeks Later

The charcoal smell of the barbecue wafts through the air, blending with the fresh sea breeze. Connor's cottage is bathed in the golden glow of the late afternoon sun and the beach stretches out before us, endless and calm. There is a hint of autumn in the freshness of the breeze, and I tilt my face up to what I suspect will be the last bit of warmth before autumn fully arrives.

Liam flips the meat on the barbecue as Connor brings out fresh drinks to the table.

'One beer,' he says, handing it to me, 'and one mocktail.' He hands the pink drink to Penny who beams at him. She has been complaining about post-honeymoon blues since they got back, but she looks pretty happy from where I'm sitting, reclining in a garden chair in a light floral dress, with a sun-kissed glow. Her hand drifts absentmindedly to her stomach.

'How are you feeling?' I ask, nodding towards where her hand rests.

'I feel fine, actually. Just a bit sick and tired in the afternoons. We had an early scan this morning and everything is where it should be, thank god. I can't stop thinking about how lucky I was, after getting hit by that car.'

'I know,' I say softly. Penny smiles at me, but I see pain behind her eyes. Mocktails and honeymoons will only heal so much.

When Connor brings his and Liam's drinks out, we all raise our glasses.

'To the happy couple,' Connor says.

'Which one?' Penny grins and I roll my eyes.

'How's your mum been?' Liam asks me, as he and Connor sit down. The more time I spend with Liam, the more I realise how kind and attentive he is. He is nothing like the eighteen-year-old that I once knew: he is no longer arrogant or entitled. He is a genuinely nice person. My view of him had coloured my opinion to the exclusion of everything else.

'Better,' I say, surprised by how much truth is in the answer. 'She's been doing AA with Katie and they're even talking about going on a coach trip. Mum'll hate it, but she loves to complain so maybe it'll work well.'

Since Katie became Mum's sponsor, Mum's managed to stay sober for just over a month, now. Part of me wonders whether, if Mum had had help sooner, she might not have spiralled so badly. But I can't let myself think like that. I've been helping more, making sure there is no alcohol in the house, including for myself, cooking proper meals for us both. Keeping busy is helping prevent the nightmares about Tom and the panic that he is around every corner.

'I just adore Katie,' Penny says enthusiastically. 'The private carer she put us in touch with for Gran has been amazing.'

'Are you still going to be living with her?' Connor asks.

Liam and Penny both nod.

'It'll save us money and she'll have her independence, now she's got a carer.'

'And we need to save all the money we can get,' Liam adds. 'It's not like my parents are going to be much help when the baby comes.' Though he puts on a smile, I see a brief flicker in his eyes when he mentions his parents.

'How are things?' I ask, feeling a wave of sympathy.

'Dad's still under house arrest whilst they investigate. It's going to take a while. There's so much to untangle, decades of fraud. But they've already got enough to charge him. Thankfully they aren't going after Penny for signing those documents; they've accepted she wasn't involved, thank god.'

Penny squeezes Liam's hand, looking sad.

'What about your mum?' Connor asks.

'She's staying with my aunt, for now. She had no idea, she's still trying to come to terms with it all. She was pretty upset with me at first, for suspecting and not saying anything. But I couldn't, not until I was sure.'

'I'm so sorry, Liam,' I say. Gerard hurt so many people, mine and Didi's families included, but it must be so difficult to face the truth about your own father.

'So am I. He screwed over a lot of people. I just wish it hadn't taken so long for us to figure it out.'

I look up to see Penny watching me.

'Did you hear about Tom?'

I nod, but don't say anything else.

'We were on the flight home when we saw it,' Liam says. He seems to have taken Tom's actions particularly hard, convinced that he should have known. 'It's unbelievable. He had this whole other life we never knew about.'

After his arrest for hitting me and Penny with his car and driving off, the police took Tom's DNA for processing. It immediately brought up a match to the DNA of the perpetrator of a sexual assault committed in London five years ago. Tom is pleading not guilty, saying that what happened was consensual, but no one is buying it. It's all starting to come out of the woodwork: an employment history littered with complaints after staff parties and work drinks. He seems to have had an established MO: choosing girls who are already drunk and plying them with more alcohol to ensure they are compliant and – equally as important – unreliable. It is horrifying. Even more horrifying to think that he was making his way onto the police force.

'He never even had a girlfriend,' Penny says, shaking her head. 'He made that up too. I can't separate the lies from the truth anymore.'

'I wouldn't even try,' I murmur.

The talk moves to lighter topics, as we all try to push Tom from our minds. The sun warms our faces as we catch up over the next few hours. It is easy: as though the four of us have always been friends. Liam and Penny begin arguing about how many children Penny wants and Connor tells us about his latest story: a one-hundred-year-old resident who only eats Mars bars and drinks sherry. Talk then turns to work.

'It doesn't feel right, you not coming back to the office,' Liam says. 'Have you made up your mind?'

'Yep.' I have thought long and hard about it. After using my accrued annual leave to take time out to recover, Charles offered me my job back, with no disciplinary action, despite the memory card incident. Liam knows what really happened, but neither of us have mentioned Didi's involvement. And whilst the charges against Shelly McKenzie have officially been dropped thanks to the footage on the memory card, she now has to deal with the fact that it was her own brother, heavily in debt, who knew where the key was and broke in that night. Despite Charles's offer, however, I said no.

'I'm excited to start consulting,' I say, trying to push thoughts of poor Shelly McKenzie away. 'It's much more flexible.'

'*And* teaching,' Penny adds, meaningfully. 'You're going to be brilliant at running a stage school.'

'It's only on weekends,' I say, but Penny's compliment fills me with a warm glow. I am so excited to get started. I know Dad would be proud of me running my own business, even if it's just Saturdays, for now. True to form, Katie pulled some strings and persuaded someone at AA to offer me the perfect space, at a low rent. It also helped that in Connor's headline story about Tom's arrest and crimes, he made sure to mention the new stage school about to open, the first one in the area. I've already been receiving requests from parents to sign their children up. Mum has been getting involved too, with a surprising flair for business, helping sort the licences I need and the furniture, whilst Didi has helped with the business accounts.

413

Once the sun has started to lower in the sky and Penny can no longer stifle her yawns, she and Liam decide it is time to go home. We say our goodbyes and they head towards their car, arm in arm.

'How long do you reckon wedded bliss lasts?' Connor asks, as we watch them go.

'I don't know. Until the baby's born?'

'Until she watches the wedding video and sees him pissing on that tree, I bet.'

I laugh.

'You failed to mention that in your piece on the wedding.'

At the mention of his writing, Connor takes my hand. I am getting used to it now: I don't pull away.

'There's something I need to talk to you about.' He hesitates. 'I've been offered a job. In London.'

My heart sinks, even though I have been expecting this. Connor has always had bigger dreams than one small town could offer.

'Congratulations,' I say, trying to sound genuinely happy for him. My smile feels a bit frozen, however.

'I haven't accepted it, yet.'

'You have to accept it, Connor. It's what you've always wanted.'

He looks directly at me.

'There are other things I want, too. Things that are here.'

My breath catches, but I try to keep my voice steady.

'Connor, you can't stay here for me.'

'I know,' he cuts me off gently. 'But it's more than that. Keith's retiring next year and he's asked me to take over the paper.'

I raise my eyebrows.

'Wow. What did you tell him?'

'That I would think about it.'

'And what *do* you think?'

'I'm tempted. More tempted than I thought I would be.'

I look at him and see the honesty in his expression. Perhaps, like me, he's no longer the same person who was desperate to escape this town. Perhaps we've both found reasons to stay.

Connor grips my hand tightly and I grip it back. I am not sure how I am going to let go, if that is what he decides. But I won't think about it, just yet. And, after all, I have got through far worse.

We watch the sun as it sinks lower in the sky, casting a golden hue across the expanse of water; water that saved my life from Tom a few weeks ago. Silhouetted against the sky, right along the other end of the beach, the Ferris wheel slowly turns, its neon lights beginning to twinkle against the fading sunlight. It is a timeless scene, the fairground on the pier: the old with the new, the day with the night.

It is only once the sky has turned a deep, dusky blue, that I realise, for the first time, how pretty the lights of the fair are.

Acknowledgements

I would first like to thank every single person who has read this book: time is precious and I am truly grateful.

I would like to thank my soon-to-be-husband Si for his support, patience and confidence in me over the past year or so. It has been an incredibly difficult eighteen months for us both and yet you continue to be the foundation for us when I can't.

To my literary agent Rosie Pierce, who has always cheered my writing and plays such an active, hands-on role in my books. On top of that, your kind and supportive nature as I have navigated this book in particular has been invaluable. Thank you.

To my editor, Phoebe Morgan, who is an incredibly talented editor and author, which shows in the editorial process. Your calm, steady approach to everything, as well as being an all-round lovely person to work with, is such a pleasure. A big thank you, also, to Jake Carr and George Biggs, for all you've done on *The Funfair*, and to Lewis Csizmazia and the design team for the beautiful cover.

I can't conceive of an acknowledgement that doesn't thank the very talented Sarah Moss: this time, in particular, for your astonishing patience as I consistently sent lengthy voice notes about my storylines and characters which you have always responded to in depth. And to the incredible

Acknowledgements

Kath Shaw, who never fails to sacrifice her own time to read and edit drafts, or to advise on aspects of our books. You are both so special and so selfless.

A big thanks to all the local businesses in my lovely town of Hitchin who have supported me and other local authors: in particular, Next Page Books, Hermitage Road Cafe, and Hitchin Library. You are all part of what makes Hitchin such a vibrant community of readers and writers alike.

To my friends and family who have all offered unwavering support. You have been fantastic and I am so lucky to have such great people in my life.

If you enjoyed *The Funfair*, read on for the first chapter of *The Beach Hut* . . .

Prologue

That day
10.30pm
Matilda

The bonfire coughed, illuminating the row of brightly coloured beach huts behind us. The flames cast shadows on the hut fronts, like dark figures moving across the patios. Perhaps the figures were watching us.

Perhaps they were watching me.

This was a mistake. I shouldn't have come.

Through the darkness, the waves whispered from the shore. Caitlin was dancing near the fire, vodka sloshing around the bottle in her hand. Tom cheered loudly, but Dev's eyes were fixed unblinkingly on Caitlin as she lifted her arms above her head, sun-bleached hair falling across her face. Next to me, Kip leant over and passed another beer to Sophie. She took it, reluctantly. The boy beside Sophie slid a hand up her thigh: a flash of panic crossed her face.

Later, they would tell the police it had been the perfect summer. That there had been no warning signs, no hint of a storm on the horizon.

If only we had noticed the shadows that crept up the beach towards us.

If only we had known it would all go so horribly wrong.

Chapter One

Now

Sophie

Starlings swoop in the evening sky as Harry heaves my bag onto the faded wooden deck and peers up at me, his thin white hair caught in the salty breeze.

'Been a long time since I've seen you down here, Sophie.'

Twenty years, to be exact, but I don't say this. My eyes are gritty with tiredness and my neck aches: all I want to do right now is reach for the bottle of middle-shelf Malbec I bought earlier and blur the edges of my life.

Out of the corner of my eye, the row of beach huts stand shoulder to shoulder, flashes of familiarity here and there, even after all this time: the hollow clack of wooden wind chimes from the Parkers' patio, the black fishing buckets outside old Harry's. Tom's hut, painted a soft cream, next door to . . . I tear my eyes away, my stomach giving a painful lurch.

Harry hasn't moved.

'Holiday, is it?'

'It's being sold. There's stuff to clear, that sort of thing.'

The long look he gives me says he doesn't buy this excuse.

'Seems a shame. Nice hut, this.'

'It's never used anymore. Better someone else enjoy it.' My tone is hard, clipped. I am already longing for the anonymity of London: no one ever asks questions voluntarily. The fresh, briny air is making my head swim with tiredness.

'Real shame,' he repeats, with a click of his tongue. 'Hardly any of the original owners left anymore, just these City people who come down here demanding better phone signal.' He shoves his hands into his jacket pockets and squints at the shoreline, past the gently rising sand dunes, towards the bottom of the headland.

'Never been quite the same after what happened to that girl.'

I know where he is looking and I turn away, not wanting to see it reflected in his watery eyes. I don't need to be reminded of how her body was found, lifeless on the sharp rocks. Somewhere, up on the headland, there is a plaque dedicated to her. Matilda.

Harry probably thinks I am cold, not gazing mournfully out at the waves alongside him. As if he knew her. The breeze billows inside the hood of my waterproof, flapping against my ears as I stand, waiting.

At last, the old man pulls his gaze away from the shore and gives a sigh.

'I've got fish to see to. You look after yourself.' He walks away, back towards his hut.

Finally alone, I sit down on the deck and look out at the beach where I spent all my summers as a child. Despite my mood, it is a beautiful evening. Navy-pink clouds hang low over the slumbering waves and the tide is out, leaving a swath of glistening wet sand and clumps of seaweed in its wake. The beach is long, divided at intervals by lines of tumbling grey and white rocks, an obstacle course for daring children.

For most people, arriving at a wooden chalet on a quiet beach like this would be a balm, a peaceful break. It was once that for me, a long time ago. Now I don't know what it is. A wave of sadness breaks over me. *Stop it. Pull yourself together.* Getting to my feet, I rummage around in my handbag for the hut keys. They are still looped through the smooth piece of wood Dad attached them to. After unlocking the stiff doors, I step inside.

She's back.

I watch closely as Harry sets her bags down in front of the blue hut. No husband, no kids. Just her.

Sophie Douglas. She looks different, but I would have recognised her anywhere. I don't forget details. Not about her. Not about that summer. The wild brown hair she had as a teenager has disappeared; replaced with a sleek bob. Very London. Her expensive leather brogues are out of place on the sandy deck. I hear she's a real success now.

The white wine I was sipping on my own deck – so crisp a moment ago – now tastes like acid. Looking down, I am surprised to see I am pinching the skin of my right forearm. There are two small marks there now, like a snakebite.

My gaze turns towards the huts on the left, dotted along the curve of the sandbank. Most of the families who owned huts during that summer have gone. Those who remain seem to have moved on. Forgotten. Tossed into the sea, the memories sinking to the darkest depths, where the light doesn't touch.

My pulse quickens.

I have not forgotten.

Sophie Douglas will not have forgotten.